Danger: *Curves Ahead*

Lenore McGahy

February 2015

Danger: *Curves Ahead*

ISBN: 978-0-9861994-0-0
Printed in the United States of America

Contents

*For my daughters, Sabrina and Julie,
and every girl out there.
Curves or no curves, you are*
BE-YOU-TIFUL!

and

*To my husband, Sean, who always believes in
me,
no matter what.*

It's here...

I swear, this mirror has to be warped. Do I seriously look like this to the rest of the world? Ugh. I can't stand it. If I just lose like, 10 pounds, I would probably be somewhat hot. Like Jasmine. She's such a bitch, but she is sooo gorgeous. Life isn't fair. How can she be so mean to everyone and still get any guy she wants? Because she looks like she does? I hate her.

ding dong
Brynlee!! Can you get the door please?! My hands are soapy!
        Yeah, mom! I got it!

Oh my God, I bet that's my outfit for the competition. It's about time! Everyone else got theirs earlier this week! This shit better look good. The last thing I need is to look like a fat ass in front of all those people.

Can you sign please, Miss?
        Sure, right here?
Yup, that'll do it. Thank you, young lady. Have a good night.
        Thank you, you too.

Yup, it's from Dance Extreme International. Great. Ok, God, if you're listening, pleeeeaaase let me look good in this outfit.
Oh my god, are you kidding me?! A bra and white pants!? I don't have the boobs for this top! And white pants, seriously?! Freaking kill me. My ass is going to look huge, not to mention my gut hanging over. Why is Ms. Val trying to ruin my life? Where the hell is my phone? I need to vidchat Natalya.

Hi Brynlee! Whatcha doin'?
        Nat!! I look so damn stupid in this outfit for the dance
        competition. I swear, I'm gonna cry. How am I supposed to
        go out in public like this?
Calm down, Brynlee. Hold the phone so I can see the outfit. I'm sure you look great in it.

Natalya, I feel like a damn beluga whale. Ms. Val is trying to ruin me.

Oh my God, Brynlee, that is so freaking cute on you! Why are you so upset? You look great.

Are you on crack? Nat, you and I both know white pants make my ass look like the size of China. And a bra? Really?! I'm not auditioning for some porn magazine! It's a hip hop competition, for crying out loud! And I have to go to class in this tonight!

Why?

It's dress rehearsal.

Well, good, then you won't be the only one. But, you'll be the hottest one, that's for sure.

I love you Nat, but I definitely won't be the hottest one. Have you seen Jenna, the 13 year old? Her boobs are HUGE!! She will definitely be the hottest one there. But that's ok. I don't need to be the hottest one, but I sure as hell don't want to be the nasty one. And right now, that's what I am.

Brynlee, stop. Listen to me. I'm around models and supermodels all the time. And you look hot compared to most of those models. They have nothing to them. I mean, look at me, no boobs, no ass, just a tall and lanky twig. You have what guys like. You have curves, you have a nice ass, and you're beautiful. And that outfit looks hot as hell on you.

I love you, Natalya. And you are definitely not a twig. You are drop-dead gorgeous!! You're a model, for crying out loud! They don't make ugly girls models.

Brynlee! Dinner's ready!

Ok, mom, I'll be right down!

Ugh, Natalya, I gotta go. I'll vidchat you again after practice.

Ok, and listen, you really do look great. Kill'em at practice.

Ha, funny joke. But thanks. See ya.

Great. Dinner. I don't want to eat anything. I feel fat enough in this, I don't need the extra bloat. Thank god we have stairs in this house. Every little bit of exercise helps.

Ok Brynlee, hurry and eat dinner. We have to go.

What's for dinner, mom?

Grilled Chicken Caesar salad. Ooh, your competition stuff came!!
It's adorable! You need a little more in the upper region for that bra-
top, though. Well, you've got plenty on the lower region... Maybe
you'll even out this year. You are only 15, after all.

Yeah.

*Wow, Mom, do you have to be such a bitch? I KNOW I have small
boobs and a big ass. I don't need my own mother to constantly
remind me. Ok, B, don't cry. She'll pick on you for that too. Breathe.
BREATHE. Ok, just eat dinner so you don't pass out again at
practice. And, ignore the mother. The competition is tomorrow night
and then you have a two-week break soon after. You can hit the gym
with Natalya-Blu every day. Goals. Remember the goals. Just.
Don't. Cry.*

Honey, don't take too many croutons. You can't afford them.
Besides, I put them in the salad for your father. He loves croutons.
We can pick dinner up for him after practice. Just leave him a little
salad to hold him over. And croutons.

Mom, seriously, I took three croutons. Three. Would you
back off please?

Well, I just don't want you don't put on too much weight. It gets a lot
harder to lose as you get older, trust me.

And God forbid you have a fat daughter.

Brynlee, I didn't say that. I just don't want you to struggle. Life is
much easier when you're beautiful. My idiot first husband taught me
that.

Yes, Mother, I know.

*Why? Why do I always have to hear about the idiot first husband?
He's not my father. You're not married to him anymore. Let it go
already. Good God! I am so tired of her constantly living in the past
and dragging me into it. Just because he was an asshole doesn't
mean I should suffer for it. Jeez.*

Hurry, Bryn. We're going to be late.

I'm hurrying! And I don't care if we're late.

What's the attitude?

I don't have an attitude.

Ok, whatever. Just finish up so we can go.

I'm done. I'll be right back, I need to get my bag. I'll meet you in the car.

Ok, what did I do with my bag? Oh, under the bed. I forgot, I stuffed it under there when I "cleaned up". Must've done a pretty good job, too, because "Hitler" didn't get on my case for that. That's a first.

Bye Dad! See ya later!

Have fun tonight! And, hey, break a leg. I'm really looking forward to the competition tomorrow night! I think Uncle Dave and Aunt Holly may come to watch, too.

Oh, that's cool. I haven't seen them in a few weeks. I love Aunt Holly.

beep beep

Your mother's honking. You better go before she has a fit.

Haha, ok, Dad, love you. And, there's a little salad to hold you over until we get home.

Okay great, thank you. Love you too, sweetie.

Brynlee, what took you so long?

I was getting my bag and I said bye to dad.

You need to move a little faster. Honestly, Bryn, I don't know what I'm going to do with you.

Mom, why do I need to hurry? We have plenty of time to get there, and I'm already dressed in this ridiculous attire. Seriously, why the heck would Ms. Val order this kind of stuff?

I don't know, honey. Not everyone can wear that kind of costume. You look ok, but it doesn't do much for you. You don't have the chest. And white pants, after Labor Day even, don't really look good on you. Maybe if you lost a few pounds…

Mother, I already know I look like shit.

Watch your mouth, missy!

Well, stop telling me I look like crap. I already know.

You don't look like crap. You are just a bit bottom heavy, that's all. You need to watch what you eat, and for crying out loud, move a little faster!

And you need to just shut up. Jeez! Don't do it, Brynlee. Don't cry. Go to your happy place... Beach, hot guys, flip flops.... No tears. No. Tears.

Are you crying?
>No.
What are you crying for?
>I'm not crying. I sniffed.
You're way too sensitive.
>Whatever.

And you're way too critical. Just leave me alone. Mad, not sad. New motto. Be mad, no crying. And pray she shuts the hell up. God, why does this car ride feel like the longest ride ever?! Oh, maybe because it IS the longest ride ever.

Finally! That silence was deafening. But I actually didn't mind. At least she didn't rag on me the whole time like she usually does. How did I get so lucky to be her kid? Why couldn't I just be born a boy? Maybe she wouldn't be such a bitch to me. Oh my God, just pick any parking spot, please, so I can get the hell out of this car!

Now remember, Brynlee, dance your little heart out in there. Tomorrow night is the competition, and we want to win, win, win!
>I know, Mother.
I'll be in there in a few minutes. I just need to make a phone call.

Of course, a phone call. What else is new?

The upload...

Good evening, ladies! Welcome back! I hope you're all rested up from practice Tuesday night. We've got a lot to do before tomorrow night's competition, so let's not dilly-dally. Lookin' good, girls.

Hey Brynlee! The outfit looks great on you! I hope mine looks that good. I haven't even tried it on yet.
　　　　Hey Peri! Thanks.

Ok, why on earth does Peri "hope" hers looks good? She looks good in everything. She's gorgeous. I'd give anything to look like her. Life is so unfair, I swear.
Oh God, there's Jenna, little miss hot-toddler. How the hell does a 13 year old look like that? And of course all the guys want to date her. Next year when she's a freshman, good God... I'll never get a date with her around. Oh shit, there's my mother. I guess her stupid phone call is done. She really pisses me off. Ok, I am not going to look at her tonight.

Hi Brynlee. Are you ok? You're so quiet tonight.
　　　　Yeah, Lacey, I'm good. Thanks.
You sure? You haven't said anything since you came in. If you need to talk, text me after practice.
　　　　Thanks, Lace. I'll be ok.
Ok, cool. Let's get out there before Ms. Val starts barking at us. You know how she gets.
　　　　Yeah.

Brynlee! Fix your bra thing. Brynlee...
　　　　Mother, it's fine.
Fix it. It's...
　　　　Mother. Stop!

Ugh!! Just leave me alone. Mad, not sad... Mad. Not. Sad...

Ladies! Three minutes! Let's hurry it up so we can start stretches!

Ok, is there anyone else in the locker room? No? Ok, Jenna, would you lead us in stretches please? Then I want you all to get into position for our first number, Brynlee and Lacey, I want you up front. Carly, you are behind them. This is our new formation for this number, so I hope you were all paying attention to all positions Tuesday. This is for tomorrow night. Ok, hit the music Jhonae, on three. One... two....

Ok, B, you've got this. Don't let the mother distract you... you need to keep your head in the game here, and focus. Remember why you're here. One, two, three....

What the heck? Why is everyone clapping? Ummm... Why was I the only one dancing? Oh my God, I'm so embarrassed right now. Locker room....

Brynlee, that was amazing!!
> Oh my gosh, Bryn! I didn't know you could dance like that!!

Brynlee, Wow!!
> Way to go, girl!

Brynlee, can I speak with you for...

I need to get out of here...
...Ok, let me just sit here for a minute. I don't know what just happened but I am not going back out there. Forget that. I'm so confu... What the hell, why is my phone blowing up in my locker? "Damn, girl! Great job!" "Holy crap, you're amazing!" "that was hottt!" What are these people texting me about?! I don't even know all these people, how did they get my number? What the f...

I don't know what's wrong, but we need you back out here! Let's go!
Yes, Ms. Val. I'll be right there!

Oh my God, if she only knew what I have to live with. Let her try to live with my mother for a while, with all of her nitpicking and jabs every single day. But wait, what the heck are all of these texts about? This phone won't shut up! Ok, whatever, let me just put the phone back in my locker and get out there before I am penalized with fifty pushups. I sure as hell don't need that right now. I've had enough embarrassment for one night, I don't need to be scolded too.

Alright, ladies, let's get started… again. This time I want to see everyone dance with the same intensity and passion that we all just watched Brynlee demonstrate! You ladies dance like that tomorrow night and we've got this competition, easy! Jhonae, again on three, ready? One, two….

YES, ladies!!! Yes! THAT's it! That is what real, committed dancers look like! That was the best I've seen in months! Beautiful, ladies. Beautiful. Okay, let's move onto the next two numbers. Make them look like the last one, and we'll be out of here early tonight! Okay, Jhonae, play it! One, two…..
Excellent! Quickly, right into the last number, and one, two, THREE!
Clap clap clap
Ladies, that was unbelievable!! I am so very proud of all of you this semester. You've done a great job, put in a lot of hard work, and tonight you've shown me, Jhonae, each other, but most importantly YOURSELVES, that when you set your heart on something and really want it, you can do anything you want. With that kind of passion, you'll take the world by storm! By the way, I hope everyone likes the outfits for tomorrow night. You all look great in them.
As a matter of fact, Ms. Val, I hate the outfit. And no, we don't ALL look great in them.
I want you all at the venue one hour before the regularly scheduled arrival time, okay ladies? One. Hour. Be ready to get final makeup done. Jhonae has some special touches planned for that.   Go home, rest up, eat well throughout the day, and a little something light to eat, LIGHT, just before you leave your house. I don't want anyone complaining they're going to throw up right before we go on. You've all done fantastic tonight.   You should be proud of yourselves.
Clap clap clap
Okay, brynlee, can I speak with you a moment in my office, please?
          Sure, Ms. Val.

Oh God, I wonder what this is about. I'm sure it has something to do with my running out of practice before. Seriously, I just want to get my stuff and go home.

Yes, Ms. Val?

> Brynlee, you did amazing tonight. I am very proud of you. Not only did you show us all the passion for hip hop you've had bottled up deep, but your performance tonight really seemed to inspire everyone else. The rehearsal was outstanding, everyone looked great, and you really shined out there. I don't know why you felt the need to run out of practice, but the way you danced right before that was brilliant! I'd like you to consider working with me semi-privately. I'll also be asking Lacey to join us. I think the two of you have really got what it takes to make it in this business, if that's what you want. Lacey doesn't seem to have as much passion as I've seen come out of you, but I think the two of you work very well together. You sync. That's important. And when you dance together, her passion ignites a bit.

I don't know, Ms. Val.

> I'll speak with your mother about it, of course, but I wanted to put it out there to you first. You're special, Brynlee. You have an amazing talent that I would hate to see wasted. I've seen it for quite some time now. But tonight really solidified my decision to work with you on the side.

Thank you, Ms. Val.

> It would mean a lot more than just semi-local competitions with the academy.

What do you mean?

> Well, without going into details and getting way ahead of ourselves, I have a friend in California that is in the music industry who is always looking for fresh talent. It could lead to something bigger than you may be thinking for yourself. But, of course, that all depends on you, and Lacey, and your commitment.

Oh wow.

> Let me ask you this, first. Do you two get along well enough to become partners? You'd be spending a lot of time together.

Well… I mean, I guess so.

> How about this… Think about it. Let's get thru the competition tomorrow night, take the weekend to relax and recover from the victory, and think about it. I won't talk to Lacey about it until I have an answer from you. And please, if you or your mother have any questions about it in the meantime, call me.

Please, don't mention this to my mother just yet. I'd like to make this decision on my own, without her badgering me about it.

> Oh, sure, hon. I'll wait for your decision before speaking to her about it. Actually, if you decide you're in and this is something you'd like to pursue a bit further, I'd like to have your dad here too. I think it's important to have both parents here. This is a huge decision, and could lead to big things that may change lifestyle, eventually.

Well, now I'm intrigued.

> Well, let's remember not to get ahead of ourselves. It'll take a lot of hard work, sweat, and even some tears, I'm sure. But if you continue to dance the way you did tonight, and show the world that Brynlee's got it, you really can go far. Sweetie, I believe in you. You just have to believe in yourself. Don't let your negative thoughts get in your way.

Thanks, Ms. Val.

> Your mom is peeking in here. Looks like she's ready to go. Rest up, hon, you've got a competition to win!

Thanks. Goodnight, Ms. Val.

> Goodnight.

Brynlee, are you ready? Your father is probably hungry, since I didn't leave him anything but "rabbit food" to eat. We'll stop by the pizza place and pick up a meatball hero for him.

> Yeah, Mom, I'm ready.

As soon as we get home throw that outfit in the laundry so I can wash it for tomorrow. It's all sweaty, and kinda stinks to high heaven.

> Wow, thanks a lot.

Well, it does. Sweat mixed with new clothes chemicals is not a pleasant aroma.

> Whatever.

You girls looked good tonight.

Thanks.

You looked a little spacey, though. Are you feeling okay?

I feel fine, mother.

Ok well, maybe you'll be better tomorrow night.

Better tomorrow night? Were you not watching us in there? Ms. Val said we did the best we've ever done!

Actually, I stepped outside just after the music came on. I had to take a phone call.

Of course you did.

What's that supposed to mean?

Nothing. Just forget it.

Brynlee, I don't know what's gotten into you lately, but I don't like it.

I know. You never do.

That's enough, young lady. When we get home, you can go right to your room. I don't want to hear another bit of sass come out of that mouth.

Fine.

Nothing I do is ever good enough for you. And whenever I do things that I think you'd be proud of, you miss it because you "had to take a call". Who the hell are you talking to, anyway? Not me, that's for sure. All you ever do is bitch at me and tell me I'm not good enough. Well, YOU'RE not good enough. What kind of mother puts her own kid down constantly, and misses every proud moment because she had to "take a call"? I don't know how I ended up with you for a mother. At least Dad loves me. I don't think you're even capable of loving. You're such a bitch. God, are we almost freaking home? I just want to get out of this damn car, hug my daddy, and go snuggle up in my bed, away from the mother. Oh my God, I forgot we had to stop at the pizza place. I'm waiting in the car.

Here, here's twenty bucks. Go in and get dad's dinner. It's under my name.

Ugh. Can't you just go in? I look disgusting.

You look fine, now just go.

Oh my god! I look fine? Did hell just freeze over? She spoke nice words to me! But I still look like crap and don't want to go in here.

Hi, I'm picking up an order for Heidi.

Brynlee! Hey!

       Oh, hey Victoria.

Wow, Brynlee, I didn't know you could dance like that!

       What do you mean?

The video! Girl, that was fantastic!

       What video?! What are you talking about?

Oh my God, you don't know?

       Know what!? Please tell me what the hell is going on, because weird shit has been happening all night since I got to the academy.

Oh!! Well, Carly's brother Blake uploaded a video of you at the academy tonight. It was awesome! You guys were all dancing, and then one girl stops to watch you, and then next thing you know, the rest of them are semi-circled around you, and so are your instructors, and there you are, freaking killing it all by yourself! It was like you were in your own little world!

       Are you serious?

Yes! Dead serious!! You looked like a professional dancer showing the class how it's done. Girl, the video is going viral! And by the way, you look hot in that outfit! All the guys even think so.

       All the guys? What guys?

Bryn, everyone!

       Oh my God.

Yeah, Samantha seems a tad jealous.

       Oh great. She already hates me.

Don't worry about her.

       Easy for you to say. You're her best friend.

Ah, whatever. You can seriously dance, Bryn. And now everyone knows it.

Order for Heidi is ready!

Well, I'll see you at school tomorrow. Great job! And congrats! You're going to be an internet sensation!

       Great. See ya. And, Victoria, thanks.

You got it.

Oh. My. God. I think I'm going to die. Like, I can't even... no wonder my phone was blowing up in my locker! And Blake was there?! How did I miss that?! He's soooo hot, like oh my God. And he was watching ME! I seriously could just die right now. Kill me.

Change, please?

      Here.

What's wrong with you? Who was that you were talking to?

      Nothing's wrong. I'm fine.

Who was that girl?

      Victoria. She's one of the popular girls.

Was she being mean to you?

      No, mother. She's one of the nice ones.

One of the nice ones? How many popular girls are there?

      I don't know, a few.

Why aren't you popular?

      Mother. Please just leave me alone.

Talking to you is like talking to a wall.

Please, God, just get me home. I don't want to think right now. I just want my pillow to cry in.

Am I hearing things?

Hi Daddy, here's your dinner.

> Hi sweetie! How was practice?

It was okay.

> What's wrong? Did it not go well? You're home a little earlier than usual.

No, it was fine. I'm just tired. I'm going up to my room. Love you.

> Love you too, Bryn.

Brynlee, don't forget to put that costume in the washing machine.

> Mother, it's not a costume.

Just put it in the wash without an attitude, please.

Oh my GOD. LEAVE ME ALONE. I'll put it in the damn wash so you can get rid of my stench. Good God, get this stupid bra thing off of me. Uh. And these stupid white pants. I hate this outfit. Where are my sweatpants? What the heck? I thought I left them…

knock knock

Brynlee, let me have that cosss… outfit, and I'll just put it in the wash now. I see you straightened up your room a bit.

> Yeah. Here. Do you know where my grey sweatpants are?

Honey, how would I know where your sweatpants are?

> I don't know. I can't find them.

So wear something else. I don't know why you wear those hideous things anyway. They do nothing for you.

> I don't care. They're comfy and I want to wear them.

Well, I don't know where they are. Maybe you should take better care of your things and then you'd know where you put them.

Ugh, just get out. Okay, I need to find my sweatpants. Oh, here they are. How the heck did they get stuffed there? Ah, and my daddy's cozy shirt. That's better. I love this shirt, it's so soft. Lemme just plop on my bed and cry in peace now. What the freak happened tonight? Ok, I guess I should muster up the courage to watch this video. I can't believe Blake did that. Why? I don't understand. Ok, I don't even know what to look for it under. Oh, wait, Blake has his own video page. Ok... Oh my God, there it is. Do I dare? I'm scared. Screw it. Play.

Ok, we all look kinda cool in these outfits together. I look fat though. Why did Carly stop and look at me, though? Rewind. Play. Oh, she missed her step. And looked at me to catch up. That's when she stopped. Oh, now Jenna stopped to see... Oh my God, they're all stopping. And there I am, just dancing. How did I not notice they all stopped? Holy cow, I'm so embarrassed. My fat ass in that outfit, though.

you look amazing

Wait, what? Stop video. Who said that? Mom? Mom? Okay that was weird. Why would my mother say I look amazing, anyway? I'm delirious. Play video. Victoria was right, I do look like I'm in my own little world. I can't believe I am dancing like that. Oh my God. Wow. Ok, I need to vidchat Natalya. I wonder if she saw this yet.

Brynlee!! Oh my God, you looked AMAZING tonight!!

You saw it, I guess?

Who hasn't?!

Oh my God, Natalya, I, I seriously don't know what the hell happened tonight.

Well, I do. You were INCREDIBLE! You killed it on that dance floor! And apparently Blake thought so too!

I know, what the heck? I didn't even know he was there! How did I miss that?

He's so hot!

I know! I had no idea he was even home from college. He must've been there watching his sister. But why was he recording practice? Maybe Carly asked him to. Or their mom. I don't know. All I know is, my fat ass is on the internet for the whole entire world to see!

But Brynlee, you look fantastic, and you danced your ass off, and the video is going viral! I keep getting texts from everyone saying how great you look.

Yeah, I ran into the locker room when I realized I was the only one dancing and my phone was going crazy in my locker! I keep getting texts from people I don't even know! How are they even getting my number?

I have no idea. Do you have it posted somewhere, maybe? Photogram or something?

      I don't think so. I'll look later. I'm going to have to put my phone on silent though, because it seriously won't shut up.

So, what happened, anyway?

      I don't know. My mother and I were arguing. She's such a bitch and won't stop ragging on me, ever. So, as usual, she pissed me off. I don't know why, but tonight it just got to me even more than usual. I must be PMSing.

Well, you looked like you were really into the music. You were zoning. I mean, I've seen you dance, but I've never seen you zone like that. It was really crazy. I was kinda mesmerized watching you.

      That's funny, because I was kinda mesmerized by the beat. I don't know. It was weird. I had no idea everyone stopped. I had no idea they were all watching me. And you know me, I can always tell when someone is staring at me.

I know. You've got that weird sense.

      Yeah. But not tonight, apparently. It freaks me out a little. Okay, a lot.

But why, Brynlee? Maybe that's the place you need to be to dance the way you did. Maybe that zone is where you need to go to bring out the dancer in you that's deep inside. You really let loose tonight. It's like you didn't care what anyone thought, you just did you. The real you.

      I guess.

Maybe you should stop thinking so much about what other people think of you, and just do you. You're a phenomenal dancer, B.

she's right, you know

      Who said that???

Said what?

      "She's right, you know". Who said that?

Bryn, are you ok?

      I swear, I'm hearing things. Never mind.

So, from now on, stop caring what other people think, and be the you deep down.

      That's easier said than done, Natalya. Try living with my mother.

Listen, who cares what she says. I'm telling you, you're beautiful, and an amazing dancer. And that outfit looks awesome on you. I'm your best friend. I would not lie to you.

Thanks. I really appreciate it. But it's a lot easier said than done.

Well, I'll just keep reminding you.

Haha, okay.

So, now, Blake! I wonder what made him decide to upload that video of you.

Oh my God, I have no idea. But he did it pretty quick, because as soon as I got in the locker room, I was getting text after text. And then Ms. Val... OH MY GOD! I forgot to tell you!

Tell me what? There's more?

YES!! After rehearsal, Ms. Val wanted to see me in her office. She asked me if I wanted to do semi-privates with Lacey, because she knows someone in the industry who is always looking for new talent!

What?! Oh my God, that's awesome! And now that this video is getting so many views... This could be... Holy crap, Brynlee!!

Yeah! Tonight has been ridiculously crazy!

So? Are you going to do it?

I don't know. It's a huge commitment. Regular practice, plus semis. I'd have no time for anything or anyone else.

What did your mom say?

She doesn't know about it yet.

What? Why?

I asked Ms. Val not to say anything to her yet. I want to make my own decision without her nagging or bitching. She wants both of my parents to be there, anyway.

Oh my gosh, your dad is going to be psyched.

Well, we'll see. It's probably a lot more money.

Yeah, but you'd be sharing the cost with Lacey. Is she excited about it?

She doesn't know either. Ms. Val asked me first. I think it's up to me, and if I say yes, then she'll ask her.

Well, you two dance great together, and she's pretty cool.

Yeah, she is now.

Just remember, I'M your best friend first.

You know it!

Wow, that's so cool. What a crazy night you've had. And I'm sitting over here in my room like "I like chips".

Hahaha, Nat, you're crazy! I love you!

Love you too, B. Oh my god, we could end up at the Music Awards on TV together one day - You'll be dancing backup with some famous chick as she gets her Video of the Year award, and I'll be strutting the runway in the latest fashion on the arm of some hot singer as he's waiting to get his award for Top Male Artist!

Yeah! Then we can party together at the big after-party at the hottest hotel in Vegas!

Yes! Haha, our futures are looking so bright!

Where's muh shades?

Brynlee! We'd have all the hottest guys at our fingertips!

Oh my gosh, I know!! Movie stars, singers, dancers….

Really hot guys with money! And nice cars!

But then again, let's not forget about the paparazzi…

Oh, yeah, but that's ok. They'd be after them, not us.

True. Until we're the famous ones! You, Natalya the Supermodel, and me, like Sasha T.!

Well, if you're going to be the next Sasha T., you need to take singing lessons with those dance lessons!

Hey, I sing okay! Hahaha!

Yeah, ok Bryn, haha. Well, I should go study for my Chemistry test tomorrow.

Yeah, I should go, too. My head's starting to hurt from all the chaos tonight. I'll talk to ya later.

Ok cool. Text me if anything else crazy happens.

I doubt anything more could happen tonight. But I will. See ya.

See ya.

And then this...

*Imagine me and Natalya at the music awards together one day?
Damn, that would be crazy!.*

It could happen, you know.

*Huh? Ok I swear I'm hearing things. Maybe I should just go to sleep.
Or at least shut this light off and try. It's so early though. Maybe I'll
just lay here in the dark and try to get rid of this headache...*

*Gosh, my mind is racing! I can't sleep when I have such a big
decision to make. Do I want to do semis with Ms. Val and Lacey?
That'd be a lot of practice. Can I even handle that much practice
with school? I mean, if I want to get into a good dance school after
high school, it would probably be a good idea. And I'm sure my
parents would be good with it. Especially my mother. She'd be all
over that "keeping active" mess. And the extra practicing probably
would help me lose the ten pounds I've been wanting to lose. No, no,
not lose – because that would imply I want to find it again. Okay, the
ten pounds I want to get rid of. Man, then I would look great.*

You look great now.

*Ummmm, ok, now I'm really starting to freak out. God, please tell
me I'm not losing my mind.*

You're not losing your mind.

Who said that?!

     I did.

Oh my God, slightly freaking out. Do I turn on this light? Yes.

     Hi Brynlee.

AHH!!! WHO ARE YOU?!?! WHAT are you?!

     Ok calm down. Please put that book down. I'm not going
     to hurt you.

Who, what the hell are you?! Am I going crazy?!

     No, Brynlee, you are not going crazy.

I think I need medication.

     Listen, you are not going crazy. You do not need
     medication. And please don't squish me like a bug with

that book. I am not going to hurt you. I'm here to help.
Help?! What?! Oh my God. What the hell is going on right now?
Ok, put the book down and I'll explain.
Okay, but make one move and you're flat.
Okay, okay. Sheesh. My name is Nova. I'm your Teacup Dandy.
You're my what?! What the hell is a TeaCup Dandy?
We're like your personal guides.
We? You mean there are more of you?
Haha, yes. Millions.
Umm, okay? I'm definitely losing it. Lemme call Natalya...
Please, just listen. You aren't crazy. You're not losing your mind. I am real. You're talking to a real being. I am here to help you.
Help me with what?
With the way you see yourself. Just hush, and listen to me. I have been around you all your life. You just never knew it until now. It wasn't until you were ready for me that I chose to come show myself to you. I am here to show you the truth.
The truth about what?
The truth about you, Brynlee. You believe lies about yourself. I am here to help you see the truth.
Whoa. This is crazy.
I know it's a little hard to understand, and even tough to believe, but I promise you, this is really happening.
Can other people see you, and hear you?
No, well, yes, but no. Other Teacups can, but you are the only human that can hear and see me, specifically. The other Teacups have their girls that can only see and hear them.
Does every girl have their own?
Yes.
So wait, Natalya has her own, too?
Yes.
Why didn't she tell me?
I cannot tell you that.
Do you know her Teacup?
I do. She's very sweet. We're great friends. But let's get

back to you. Brynlee, you are too hard on yourself. You are beautiful. I am here to help you see that, and help you know it deep inside.

Oh my God, are you a shrink? Lol! No pun intended!

Haha, good one! I love your sense of humor. You've always kept me giggling. No, I'm not a "shrink", haha. But I am a messenger of the truth. You see, back in earlier centuries in Europe, a Dandy was someone who acted like something they were not. They wore top hats, like mine, to try to show the people around them that they were better than they actually were. They dressed that way to distinguish themselves from the lower class. It was a "how you dressed showed who you are" sort of thing, kind of like it is today. You see it every day in school. Girls are always trying to wear the hottest fashions to fit in. That's how it was back then, only Dandies were men. My top hat, and the rest of my attire represents you, and who you are trying to be, rather than who you actually are.

Wow. That's freakin' deep.

It is. And every Teacup wears attire that represents the girl they are here for, and who the girl is and is not. You see, most people in the world are trying to prove they are someone they aren't, all to fit into a world of people they don't know, whose opinions about them don't matter. Everyone has a story that the world doesn't know, because the girl hides the truth. We are here to help you see the truth.

And you're called Teacups because of your size?

Exactly. I can fit into your pocket, sit on your shoulder, chill out on your purse, whatever. You never knew I was there. But if I was people-size, you might get an inkling something was up. That'd make it a little more difficult to hide myself.

But now you don't have to hide.

No. Now I'm visible to you. Oh, and I can hear your thoughts. That's why you can hear me when you're thinking. Because I hear your thoughts, I speak to you and you hear me. I've kept quiet, mostly, until tonight.

Mostly?

> Yes. I sometimes sing to you, and talk to you while you're sleeping. It's so funny when you're having a sleepover with a friend, and I talk to you, and you answer me. They think you're talking in your sleep, which you are, but it's because you're talking back to me! Not because you're dreaming!

Oh my God, are you serious? That's hysterical.

> It is, really.

So when Natalya is talking in her sleep, is she talking to her Teacup?

> Yes, she is! Well, mostly. Sometimes you girls do actually talk in your sleep. But since we hear your thoughts, we know what you're dreaming. So, it's very entertaining for us sometimes.

Wow, that could be embarrassing.

> Nah, don't worry about it. I love you, and you have nothing to be embarrassed about. But don't worry. Her Teacup can't hear your thoughts, and I can't hear hers. We're limited. It would be too much for us, because then we'd want to help all of you.

Oh okay, good. So do Teacups all hang out together when we're around other people?

> Yes, and no. We exist for a purpose. When you're awake, we are on mission. When you're at a sleepover, and you're sleeping, yes, we hang out. But it's not like people do. We don't talk about people or each other, like in a gossip sense. We help each other to help you.

Who is your boss? Do you have a leader?

> Well, that's a huge question to answer, and in time, you'll know. Plus, I think we've gone over a lot of information already tonight.

So, can I tell people about you? Like Natalya?

> Hmmm. How do I say this? When one human is ready to know about another's, the one who's further along will have it be known. If you are not ready, you will not be able to speak of it.

Does something happen? Will something happen to me if I try?

> Yes, sort of. Nothing will happen "to you", but

something does "happen", so to speak. It's hard to explain. Just don't worry about telling anyone just yet. You'll know when it's your time.

Okay. One last question. Isn't this something that happens to little girls? I mean, I'm 15, for crying out loud.

Well, like I said, when it's appropriate for us to reveal ourselves, we do. It can happen when girls are 5, 15, or even 25 in special circumstances. I know it's strange that you, a teen, are talking to an "invisible friend".

You're not kidding.

But trust me, you are not the only teen girl out there, or even in your school, who knows about her Teacup. Some haven't met theirs yet. You just won't know who has and who hasn't, unless you are meant to know. As you are learning and understanding the truth about yourself more and more, you will know the others who know. You will be a different person to the world. You will be the you that you were meant to be. And you will do amazing and beautiful things to help the world be a better place. It is your destiny. But you have to want to. Just because I have revealed myself to you doesn't mean that you will change "just because". You have to want to change. And just because you decide to hear the truth, doesn't mean it'll be easy. It won't be. It's not meant to be easy. But that's why I'm here. And I will never leave you.

Umm, okay, wow. I mean, of course I want to change. I want to be the real me. I want to be who I am destined to be. I just don't know how.

That's okay. You leave the how up to me. I know what I'm doing.

Okay. Thanks, Nova.

Okay, so are you going to see who texted you?

Oh my gosh, I didn't even hear my phone.

Yeah, that's been happening a lot to you today. Haha.

Yeah, I know. Oh my GOD! It's BLAKE!!

Blake!

Oh, my God, Nova, what do I do?!

How about you start by texting him back? Teeheehee!

It's not funny, Nova!

Well, what did he say?

He said, "hey! It's Blake", with a smiley face!!

Okay, so say "Hi".

That's ridiculous. I can't just say " Hi".

Why not? Okay, say "Hey, what's up?"

Yeah, okay, that's good.

Brynlee, stop freaking out. He's just a boy.

A very HOT boy that I've had a crush on since I can remember!

Yes, I know. Remember? I know these things.

Oh. Yeah. Okay. "Hey Blake. What's up?"

"Hey, you were great tonight!"

He said I was great tonight. Nova? Nova, where'd you go? Ugh.
Okay Brynlee, don't freak out. Like Nova said, he's just a boy...

"Thanks"

"I hope you're not mad I uploaded that video"

"I'm actually just confused, but I'm not mad"

"Well, I was recording my sister so my other sister can see it,
because she can't go to the competition tomorrow night, and
apparently cameras aren't allowed"

"Oh, yeah, they're not"

"And then you just kept dancing, and you were really badass"

"Well, I wouldn't say that"

"Really, you were. I had to post it. You were too good not to!"

"Wow, I don't know what to say"

"You don't have to say anything. You really are great. I felt like
people other than just family of dancers needed to see it"

"Okay, thanks, I guess"

"Are you mad?"

"No. Not at all".

"Ok, cool. Well, I'll see ya tomorrow night"

"Ok, see ya"

Oh my God, oh my God, oh my God!!! Oh. My. God!!! I HAVE TO call Natalya!

NATALYA!! Holy CRAP!!
> Brynlee, what's wrong?!
Guess who just texted me!
> Who?
BLAKE!
> Are you serious?! What'd he say?
He said I was badass tonight and that he thought other people needed to see it and that's why he uploaded the video of me, and that he hoped I wasn't mad at him for it! Why in the world would I be mad at him? He's BLAKE!
> Oh my gosh, B! What else?!
That's about it. He said he'd see me tomorrow night. Holy crap, I could just die right now.
> Do you think he likes you?
Probably not.
> Why not?
Because, Natalya, I'm just Brynlee. He's probably got a ton of hot girls at college he's into. Why would he be into some little high school girl?
> You're about to be 16! That's only two years younger than him.
But I'm a sophomore. He's in college. That's like a senior dating a freshman! Not gonna happen.
> Seniors date freshmen all the time.
But he's in college. Cooollllllege.
> Okay, Bryn, whatever you say. I think he likes you.
Well, I can dream. Anyway, I just had to tell you that. I'll let you go study. I'm going to die and go to heaven now.
> Haha, ok. Text me if anything else happens.
Okay I will.

Holy. Cow. Seriously, can I just die and go to Heaven right now? Blake texted ME! He took time out of his life, his absolutely amazing and beautiful life to text me, Brynlee, the little girl who who's been crushing on him since I first saw him at the dance academy. Oh my gosh, that was so long ago. And five years later he is even better looking than I would've imagined. I'd give anything to be his girlfriend. Or wife! "Brynlee Carrington" sounds sooo good. Blake and Brynlee Carrington. Mr. and Mrs. Blake Carrington... Ugh! He would never date me anyway, so why am I even dreaming about it? He can have any girl in the world, he would never choose me. And I'm sure he's got tons of college girls falling all over him. And they're probably drop-dead gorgeous, with big boobs and long hair, and they're probably all tall and skinny... I can't compare to that. I'm short and fat, with...

Stop right there.

Nova! You scared me!

Oh, sorry about that. Brynlee, you are beautiful. Please stop speaking negatively about yourself.

But it's true.

No, it's not true. Your first step is to stop putting yourself down. Do not speak a bad word about yourself out loud.

Well, that's kinda hard to do.

Yes, it is hard to do, but it's not impossible.

It seems impossible to me.

Tell me, why is it that you feel so badly about yourself?

Because. I don't look the way I want to look.

How is it that you want to look?

I want to be tall and beautiful, not short and fat.

First of all, Brynlee, you are neither short, nor are you fat. How tall are you?

I think I'm 5'5".

Okay, you are average height for your age.

Oh great, I'm average.

Just because you are of average height doesn't mean that you are an average person.

Yeah, ok, whatever.

Why do you want to be taller?

I want to be taller so I look thinner.

Why do you want to look thinner?

I don't want to just look thinner. I want to BE thinner.

Why is that?

So I can be... good enough.

Oh, Brynlee, please don't cry. Why is it that you feel you aren't good enough? Good enough for what, or for who?

I don't know.

Yes, yes you do know. Please, tell me why you feel this way.
Ugh! I want to be good enough for... for my MOTHER!

Brynlee?! Did you call me?
No, Mother!
Okay, I thought you called me. Are you alright up there?
Yes, Mother. I'm fine.

Seriously, Nova! Why did you have to ask me that?
Thanks a lot.
Well, my dear, I had to ask you that so you can heal. You see, you won't begin to heal until you understand why you hurt to begin with. So tell me, why is it that you don't feel good enough for your mother?
I really don't want to talk about it. Please, just leave me alone.
Sure, that's fine. We can talk about it some other time. But I want you to know, you are good enough.
Okay fine. I'm good enough. Now, please, leave me alone.

Maybe one day I'll be good enough. If only I could be good enough for someone like Blake. Oh my God, I forgot, Nova can hear my thoughts! Nova, stop listening to me think.
I'm not listening. Just act like I'm not here.
Ugh! How am I supposed to act like she's not here?! I know she's here. And I know she knows what I'm thinking. This is freaking ridiculous. This can't actually be happening. Maybe I'm having some weird side effect from this headache. Maybe it's some kind of crazy migraine, like when people talk about auras and stuff, whatever that means. Maybe this is one of those. I don't know. Whatever. Maybe this is all a dream, and today didn't really happen. Yeah, that's the only explanation that could make sense. Well, I guess I'll just wait to wake up. This could take hours. It's still dark out. Can I change dream scenes now? Lemme change this scene to being at the coast in Cali, or somewhere in the tropics. With Blake. There we are, just the two of us, sitting in the sand, holding hands and listening to... the... wav......

Tonight's the night...

beep beep beep
*Oh my God! I really have to change this stupid alarm! I'm gonna
have a damn heart attack one of these days if I don't! Jeez! Oh my
gosh, tonight's the night! Now I need to just figure out how to get in
the zone like I was last night. LAST NIGHT! Wow, ok, did that all
really happen? Let me check my phone... Oh my God, it really
happened! Blake really did text me! And Nova...*
Nova? Are you there?
*Ok, maybe that part was just part of my dream. Whew! That was a
weird freaking dream, that's for sure. I'll have to tell Natalya-Blu
about that one later at school. I do not want to go to school today.
My stomach isn't feeling all that great. I wonder if the mother will let
me stay home today. I guess it doesn't hurt to go down and ask,
right?*

Hey Mom, I'm not feeling too good today. I'm just gonna stay home,
okay?

> No, young lady, it is not okay. You need to go to school.
> Besides, how would it look if you stayed home from school
> but then went to the competition tonight?

But I really don't feel good. My stomach doesn't feel right and my
head still hurts from last night.

> Are you getting your period? Maybe that's why. Is it that
> time of the month?

Ew, Mother, why do you have to talk about it?

> Brynlee, it's human nature. Why are you so embarrassed
> about it?

I'm not. I just don't feel like talking to my mother about it.

> You don't have a problem talking to your friends about your
> period, so it should be easier to talk about it with your own
> mother. I gave birth to you, for Heaven's sake.

Oh my God, never mind.

*Jeez, why is she so gross? Although, maybe I am getting my period.
That could be why I feel so bloated. I haven't checked the calendar*

*in months. I should probably start doing that again so I know when
to expect to be cranky. Okay, what's the password to my app...? Ha,
okay, good memory. Holy crap, I am due, like, tomorrow! Shit, I
better not get it today! I have the competition tonight! And I have to
wear those stupid freaking white pants!! I swear, it had to be a man
who designed white pants! Men are jealous they can't give birth, and
this is one of the ways they are trying to get back at us. White pants
make asses look fatter, and what self-respecting woman on earth
wants their ass to look any fatter? I mean, a big ass is one thing, but
a fat one? Um, no. Speaking of pants, what should I wear today?
Well, I know I need to wear dark stuff, just in case. Whatever. I'll
figure it out after I shower.
Ahhh, this hot water feels so good, especially on my head. I wish this
headache would go away. I guess I can thank my period for that,
which sucks because nothing I take will help. I just hope it doesn't
get worse. I'll just let the hot water beat on it and hope it goes away.*

knock knock knock
Brynlee, hurry up, please! You're going to be late.
     I'm almost done, mom.
You still need to eat breakfast.
     I'm not hungry. My stomach hurts too much.
You have to eat something, hon. Your body will go into starvation
mode if you don't eat.
     I know, I know. I'll be out in a minute.
Okay, just hurry please.

*Why? Why, every time I say I don't want to eat, do I have to get
lectured on starvation mode and getting fat? I'm not freaking
hungry. I will seriously throw up. I guess I'm done with this nice hot
shower. I need to beg Daddy to put one of those heat lamps in here
so it's not so cold getting out. Ooh, and a towel warmer, too! That
would be amazing. And if we want to get really fancy, floor tiles that
warm up at the flick of a switch. I need to find a rich man to marry. I
like the little luxuries in life. There's nothing wrong with that, right?
But first I need to lose some weight. I should probably decide if I'm
going to do semis with Ms. Val.
Whoa! Nice hair! Brush, where's my brush? Oh wheeerrrre is my
hairbrush? Anyway, if I train with Ms. Val, and she really does have
connections, it could be a great opportunity for me. And Daddy*

travels to Cali for work all the time, so that wouldn't be a big deal, I don't think. I guess it would depend on where in California I would have to go, and when. The biggest question, though, is IF. IF I even get a shot. Well, we. Lacey too. Wow, she doesn't even know yet. She's gonna be so excited! I want to be there when Ms. Val asks her. But first, I need to make a decision. Ooh, it's going to be a good hair day today! Thank God! Let's hope the face looks as good. Hmmm, cat eyes today, or no? Yup, I'm feeling catlike today.

So if I say yes, then that'll mean extra practice days, which means less time with my friends. But, Natalya's modeling schedule is picking up again for the new season, so I won't see her a whole lot, anyway. And since Lacey hasn't been so bitchy, we've been trying to hang out, so this would make that a lot easier. And, it would keep me out of a lot of school drama, because I'd be too busy dancing to know what's going on anyway, except for during school.

Hmmm, maybe I should've used brown instead of black eyeliner. Eh, whatever. It looks decent, so I'm good. I wish I didn't have to wear makeup. I wish I was naturally beautiful like Jasmine and Natalya and little miss hot-toddler **rolls eyes** *.*

Okay, I'm doing it. Now, let's just hope my parents let me.

Looks like it's a boot day, because I'm feeling pretty confident. It's crazy how girls pick outfits based on feelings and emotions. It's a cat-eyes, boots, scarf and red shirt kind of day. They say red is a power color, so, there ya go. I'm wearing my red shirt today. Plus, I think red is Luke's favorite color, and he's kinda hot. Besides, he's been flirty lately. I doubt he is interested in me that way, though. He likes his girls to be beautiful and skinny, of which I am neither. At least I have brown hair. That's all he seems to date, are brunettes. Why, I don't know. Guys are weird.

Bryn, are you almost done? You're going to be late!

      Here I come. Okay, I'm ready.

Well it took you… Wow, sweetie, you look nice today! What's going on?

I look nice?! Did she seriously just say I look NICE? Holy crap! Is the world ending?

      Thanks, Mom.

Really, though, is something big happening at school today?

No. I'm just having a good hair day and figured I'd roll with it.

Well, you really look pretty. Makeup and everything. Oh, by the way, I spoke with Aunt Holly last night, and she and Uncle Dave will be a little late, but they are coming. She said they'll most likely just miss the opening mumbo jumbo.

Oh, ok cool.

Yeah, I didn't think the complimenting would last too long. But hey, I'll take what I can get. Lord knows she doesn't hand out compliments all too often. Who am I kidding? She NEVER hands out compliments. I think she'd melt if it happened too often!

Ok, here's some fruit for you.

Mom, I'm not hungry. I told you, I don't feel good.

I know, hon, but you don't want to go into...

Into starvation mode, I know. I can't eat right now. Here, I'll take an apple, and if I think I can hold it down, I'll eat it during first period, okay?

Well, I guess that's better than nothing. Tell your father we're leaving, and let him know I'm coming right back. My meeting for this morning got cancelled.

What meeting?

A meeting I had scheduled. Don't worry about it. Just hurry so you're not late.

What meeting? She doesn't work. Who the heck is she meeting up with? Maybe it's who she's always on the phone with. I swear, if my mother is cheating on my dad, I'll kick her ass myself. She better not be! Oh God, B, let's not think about that. She's probably just getting facial injections done or a pedicure or something.

Bye Daddy! Have a good day today!

It's that time already, huh? Are you ready for tonight?

Yeah, I think so.

Good. I know I sure am! I can't wait to cheer my Babygirl on! And Uncle Dave and Aunt Holly will definitely be there.

I know, Mom told me. I'm so excited. They haven't seen me dance in a long time.

I know. They'll be blown away by how much you've
improved!
Well, let's hope so, anyway!
I'm sure of it, sweetie. You'll blow us all away! And you'll
bring home that first place trophy!
I love you, Daddy.
Love you too, Babygirl. Have a great day today.
Thanks Daddy.

Ok Mom, let's go. *Oh, she's on the phone. *Sigh*. Please hurry and
start the car, it's freezing in here. Thank you. I'm just going to crank
this heat a little bit. There, now it just has to hurry up and warm up.*
Sorry, hon. That cancelled meeting just got changed to later
today. So, I won't be able to pick you up today. Do you
think you can get a ride from a friend? Maybe Mrs. Sierzant
can bring you home when she picks up Natalya.
Yeah, probably. Who was that you were talking to?
Oh, that was someone I have a meeting with. If you want, I
can call Paulina and ask her if she wouldn't mind bringing
you home. That way Natalya doesn't have to text her during
school.
I'm sure it'll be fine, Mom. What kind of meeting do you have?
Meeting? Oh, it's... Oh, hold on. Your father's calling...,
"Hi Kyle...

*She's saved by the bell, again. How does that always happen? She
always seems to get out of answering my questions.*

... I love you, too, honey. Ok bye." Sorry sweetie. Ok, so
listen, your outfit... notice I didn't call it a costume... is
hanging in the laundry room. It's all pressed and ready.
Those straps were such a pain to iron, but it's all done.
Make sure you eat the salad in the fridge after school so you
aren't famished right before we leave for the competition.
Okay. Thanks for cleaning my outfit.
You do look very nice today. I see Natalya's style may be
starting to rub off on you a bit. You look a little more
ladylike.
Umm, thanks, I guess?
I'd love to see you dress a little more like her now and then.

She always looks so beautiful.

Mom, she's a model. Of course she looks beautiful. She IS beautiful.

Well, stick with her and you just might have a chance.

What's that supposed to mean?

What I mean is, she's well put together, and women who are well put together always get ahead in life, especially if they're in great shape, like she is, and her mother. Some women are just naturally blessed. The rest of us, not so much.

Wow, Mom, okay.

Here we go again. I thought she was done comparing me to my best friend. Guess not.

I don't mean it in a mean way, honey. It's just that, some girls are naturally gorgeous, and some have to use artificial enhancement, and work a little harder to be good enough.

Good enough for what, exactly, Mom?

Well, good enough for... a good husband...

Alrighty, I see where I get my screwed up thinking from.

...after I divorced that jerk I was married to, I realized I needed to do something to look better, and find a better man. Had I just taken care of myself, and worked out from the get-go, maybe Josh wouldn't have cheated on me. Maybe he wouldn't have beaten me if I was the kind of woman I should've been.

Beaten you? He beat my mother?

Mom, that's ridiculous! Why are we even talking about him anyway? You're not married to him anymore. Dad is a fabulous husband and father.

Yes, honey, he sure is a wonderful man. And I am lucky to have him. I just have to work hard to keep him.

Work hard to keep him? But he loves you. He loves us. Isn't love enough? Wow, Mom is really messed up. She's never really talked like that before. I had no idea that asshole beat her. Maybe that's why she's... I wanna cry so bad right now. Don't do it, B. Mad, not sad. Remember your motto.

I love you, Mom.
      I love you, too, Brynlee.

Holy crap. What is going on right now? She's holding my hand. She hasn't held my hand since I was a little girl, like, in kindergarten. How the heck am I supposed to wipe this damn tear off of my face without her knowing about it? And my stupid motto isn't working right now. She sniffed! Oh my God, is she crying right now too? Ok, don't look. She probably doesn't want me to know, just like I don't want her to know. Get your junk together, B. And she's squeezing harder. And another sniffle. Oh my God, I think I'm gonna lose it. Hold yourself together, don't let her know you know she's crying!

      Well, that conversation took a crazy turn, fast. Okayyyy…
      Alright, here we are. Have a good day at school today. I'll
      see you after my meeting.
Okay, have fun, whatever you're doing.

That was the most intense few minutes ever. My mom was crying, she told me she loves me twice, and she held my hand. I swear, I don't know what's going on lately, but it's getting crazy. Or, I have officially stepped into another realm. Speaking of realm, I have to tell Natalya that crazy dream I had about Nova, the little faerie, elfy thing.

Another day in prison...

There she is now! Perfect timing…

Hey Natalya! Good morning Mrs. Sierzant!

    Good morning, Brynlee.

Would you mind giving me a ride home after school today? Mom has a meeting somewhere that just got changed to this afternoon, and she didn't have time to call you. Dad's got conference calls all day and won't be available.

    Sure, honey, not a problem. I'll text your mom and let her know I'll bring you home. Have a good day girls! I love you Natalya!

Thank you!

    Bye mom, love you!

    …So? Any more texts from Blake?

No. But I didn't think there would be.

    Well, we can hope, can't we?

You can hope. I'll just forget it ever happened.

    Why? Blake texted you! Why would he text you if he didn't at least like you a little bit?

Because, Natalya, he's nice. He's just a nice guy who would never be interested in me.

    You're always so hard on yourself. Why can't you for once believe that you are actually good enough for a guy you like to like you back?

Did you get all your studying done?

    Brynlee, don't try to change the subject.

Seriously, Nat, I don't want to talk about it, okay? My mother and I just had the strangest conversation about this stuff, and I just don't want to talk about it.

    Strange? What do you mean?

It was really weird. She told me she loves me, twice! She was crying and held my hand… Too much crazy stuff has been happening lately, and I… I don't know. I can't handle it all.

    Why was she crying? Is she okay?

Yeah, she's fine. Just brought up the jerk she was married to again and... Never mind. I don't want to start crying again. She just told me something I never knew, and it kinda made me look at her a little differently. I'll have to tell you more about it later. I have to stay focused for tonight.

Oh my God, tonight! You're going to do great! Especially if you dance like you did in that video!

Let's hope I don't have to hear about that today. I'm really not in the mood.

Ha! Well, you should probably prepare for it. I bet those girls over there are watching it right now - Jasmine's pointing over here.

Oh great.

Well, brace yourself. Here she comes.

Hey Natalya!

Hey Jasmine.

Hey Brynlee! I just saw the video that guy Blake uploaded of you. Nice moves!

Thanks.

I have to say, you actually pulled off that outfit, too. That kind of thing doesn't usually look good on shorter girls, but it actually looked decent on you.

Umm, what's that supposed to mean?

Exactly what I said. Usually shorter girls look stocky in that kind of outfit, especially girls with shorter torsos, like the redhead next to you. But you didn't look stocky. It looked really good.

Umm, thanks, I guess.

So your competition's tonight? I might come watch to see if you can dance like that under pressure.

You can't. You need a ticket, and it's sold out.

Oh wow, so I guess this little dance thing is kinda a big deal, huh?

I guess.

Well, maybe next time.

Yeah. Maybe next time.

Well, good luck tonight, Brynlee. Or is it, break a leg?

It's whatever.

Natalya, as always, looking gorgeous. Why don't we plan to hang out sometime soon?

Yeah, sure. Text me sometime. My schedule's booking up

fast though.

Oh that's right, Spring season photo shoots. I'd love to tag along! I'm interested in the industry.

Yeah, ok. Sounds good.

See ya later, Nat. Later, Bryn.

Bye.

Ugh, why is she such a bitch? And are you seriously going to hang out with her?

She wasn't that bad today. And I don't know. I might. We've started talking a little bit in biology, and she actually isn't all that bad. I think it's just the way she says stuff and it comes out wrong, or maybe the tone of her voice.

Or maybe she's just a bitch.

Or that.

Seriously though, why does someone who is so gorgeous have to be so damn mean to everyone? Doesn't she realize how much prettier she'd be if she was just nice?

I honestly don't think she's as bad as you think. But even so, she doesn't have to be any prettier; she gets all the guys she wants.

Yeah, it sucks. I wonder why her and Samantha aren't friends.

Why do you wonder?

Well, because, they're both bitches. In the movies, all the mean girls hang out together.

I don't know, Bryn. Maybe I'll try to find out why they don't hang out anymore. They used to a long time ago, didn't they?

Yeah, in like 5th grade.

Weird. Well, let's get to class. I want to cram the last little bit of studying I can before this test.

You'll do fine, Nat. You're so smart. And you're always studying.

Well, just pray for me. I need to pass this test. I need to get 100% on it.

Why? You already have a perfect grade in that class.

Because I need to KEEP that perfect grade.

I'm sure you'll do great. Besides, it's ok if you don't get a perfect score. You're the smartest one in our graduating class.

I'd like to stay that way.

Yeah, okay, well, I'll catch up with you after 3rd. Good luck, and don't stress it.

       Ok, see ya then. Thanks.

She's been acting a little weird lately about her grades. I wonder if her mother is coming down on her about it. Why can't my mom worry about my grades instead of my weight? Well, I know she'll do fine on that test. I swear, she is always studying. I hope this new season doesn't stress her out too much.

Hey Brynlee!

       Oh, hey Kat!

Nice moves ya got there!

       Thanks.

Hey Bryn, did you get my text last night?

       Hi, Courtney, I might've, but my phone was kinda going
       crazy last night so I stopped checking it.

Oh, well, I was telling you that the video was awesome, and you looked amazing!

       Aww, thanks Court. I had no idea about any of it – the
       video, I mean. I didn't realize I was the only one dancing,
       either.

Yeah, I could tell. No worries, though. You totally kicked ass! If I don't see you at lunch, good luck tonight!

       Thank you.

Ok, I really don't know how to handle all this attention! I'm the invisible one. Girls like Samantha, Victoria, Jasmine, even Natalya; they're the ones who get all the attention. Oh my God, there's Luke! He's so hot.

Hi Brynlee!

       Is he talking to me? Um, Hi Luke.

So I saw that video last night.

       Yeah, I'm hearing a lot of people saw it.

I bet they did. It was great!

       Thanks.

So, listen, I was wondering if maybe you wanna hang out this weekend. Maybe tomorrow? I know your competition is tonight, so you're busy.

Sure, that'd be great. Do you have my number?
I actually don't have it. Here, put it in my phone.
Okay.

Oh my God, is this actually happening right now? Shit, what's my number?! Calm down, he's just a boy...

Great, thanks. I'll shoot you a quick text here so you have mine too.
There.
Got it.
Cool. So, maybe I'll catch up with you at lunch, but if not, I'll text you tomorrow and we can make plans.
Okay.
See ya later, cutie.
Bye, Luke.

He's hot. Even hotter than I thought. And he is interested in me. Hmmm, wonder why. Is it because of that video? Well, we'll see where this goes. I mean, well, whatever. Let me get to class.

Great job dancing, Brynlee!
Thanks, Marissa!

Okay, kinda liking this attention. Now, if my teachers would show me some love like this, that'd be great! Maybe I can get straight A's this semester like Natalya-Blu.

Good morning, Miss Sheffield.
Good morning, Mr. Thompson.
I wondered what all the buzz was this morning when students started arriving, and one was kind enough to show me. You're a great dancer, Brynlee. You've got fabulous potential – fabulous. Let's keep up the good work in here, and your future will surely be a bright one.
Thank you, Mr. Thompson.

Awww, he's the sweetest teacher. I don't know why people make fun of him all the time. I mean, he's gay. So what? This is the second decade of the new millennium, for crying out loud. Let's get over it. Gosh. He just made my day. What a gem.

Ok class, as you know, we are scheduled to have the last test next Tuesday before the final exam for this semester. Let's go over any questions you might…

*Ugh! I forgot about that test! Thank God he didn't schedule it for Monday. Everyone wants to enjoy their weekends, even him. And I've got a date. That's right. A date. With Luke, the hottie. This should be interesting. I wonder what we're going to do. *sigh* He'll probably want to catch a bite to eat somewhere. Okay, it'll be okay. We all need to eat. Food is necessary to live. Speaking of food, can it be lunchtime now? I don't really feel like sitting in class. I'm not feeling that great. I've got cramps, which sucks, because I have to wear white pants tonight! I need to remember to bring extra tampons and pads. I should just wear stuff anyway, just in case, because that could really have the potential to suck, big time. Oh my God, could you imagine? I have to talk to Ms. Val about not ordering white pants for us anymore. Surely that just slipped her mind. I mean, we've got middle-schoolers who probably haven't even gotten their periods yet. I can't even think of how embarrassing and traumatic it could be for one of them to get it while they're dancing in white pants, unprepared! Damn, do I have any ibuprofen? I really need to clean out this purse. There's entirely too much junk in here that i…*

Miss Sheffield, can you please stop rummaging through your purse and pay attention. The clanging of all your equipment is very distracting.
        Sorry, Mr. Thompson.

Lord, please let me find some ibuprofen, and please get me to lunch soon! Oh great, now I have to pee. Hurry up, bell!

Finally! Lunchtime!

Man, I thought lunchtime would never get here! This feels like the longest day ever and I have to pee so bad right now. I'm so glad I found some ibuprofen before, because those cramps were getting out of control. Let me throw these books in my locker and go to the bathroom before I meet up with Natalya. Ugh! I hate this locker! This stupid door is always sticking. I feel like a doofis when I try to open this thing, with my head all jerky and stuff. I must look super sexy opening it up every period! Yup, that's right. Sexy B, opening her locker!

Brynlee! Hey! Where are you and Natalya sitting at lunch?

> Oh, hey Jasmine. Um, I guess where we usually sit – near the back door to the atrium. Why?

Well, I was talking to Natalya during 2nd period, and I thought I might join you guys. If that's okay with you.

> Ummm, I guess.

I mean, I don't have to if you don't want me to.

> Well, I'm just a little confused. You hate my guts, but you want to sit with me and my friends, who you also don't like, at lunch?

Wow, Brynlee. I don't hate you. I never did. And I have nothing against your friends either.

> Well, you could've fooled me.

Umm, I'm sorry if I gave you the wrong impression. But, I mean, I guess I'll just sit with my usual crowd then. Never mind.

What the hell? That was weird. Why, all of a sudden, is she trying to hang out with Natalya? Whatever. I can't stand her. All of a sudden she's being "nice"? She's so fake. But then again, aren't most cheerleaders? Ew. Oh great, I think I just got my period. I hate using these bathrooms. They're so nasty. Seriously, this bathroom is so skeevy, it makes my skin crawl. And, of course, I did get it. Why? Why today, of all days? Well, let's look at the bright side... At least now I can stop bloating and maybe I'll lose a few pounds. Maybe even before tonight! Then I won't feel like my gut is hanging out over my pants like a muffin top! Holy crap! Who the heck is spraying all that perfume? Smells pretty, but damn! I'm going to choke to death!

Oh, that figures. It's Samantha.

Hey Brynlee, I saw your video.
> Oh, that's cool.

Yeah. Looks good, I guess. I mean, I've seen better, but it was alright.
> Thanks.

So, a lot of the guys have been talking about it and your little outfit.
> Whatever, I don't really care.

Well, you should. They have a lot to say about you.
> So?

Well, some of it's not so nice.
> Yeah? And?

Well, I just thought you'd like to know that some of them don't think you should be wearing that little costume. Some of us agree that maybe you need to cover up a bit. Those kinds of outfits are for skinny girls. Bigger girls, like you, shouldn't be wearing that stuff. No offense.
> Well, you know what, Samantha? I don't really give a shit what you think. Your opinion is irrelevant. No offense.

Listen, I'm just trying to help you out so you don't make a fool of yourself.
> Well, not to worry, hon. I won't make a fool of myself. I'll be just fine. Oh, and a little tip for you – you should probably not be such a bitch. It does nothing for you. Some of your little guy friends said that as well. Maybe you should check who your friends are, and WHY they're your friends.

What's that supposed to mean?
> You're a big girl, Sammy. You figure it out. Later.

Get me out of this bathroom. Oh my God, I hate her. First Jasmine and then Samantha. Who's next?

Hey Brynlee, did you see Samantha in there?
> Yes, Victoria, the bitch is in the bathroom.

Wow, what's wrong? What happened?

Ugh! She was just telling me how all the guys think I shouldn't be wearing the outfit I have to wear for the competition because I'm not skinny enough.

What?! They did not say that at all! Quite the opposite, actually! I told you last night at the pizza place she's a little jealous. All the guys I heard say anything about you said nothing but good things, Brynlee, I swear.

Well, whatever. I told her off, so she's probably even more bitchy now.

Haha, did you really?

Yeah. I did. I'm really tired of her crap.

Oh my God, Bryn! Good for you!

Yeah, the really quiet redheaded girl just got an earful! I think she was really uncomfortable. I feel bad, but it had to be said. I'm so done with her crap.

To be honest, a lot of us are. We've been pulling away from her ever so slightly. That could be adding to it. Sorry you had to deal with her. And I'm sorry she lied to you. I hope you didn't believe any of it.

Honestly, I started to. But then I remembered who I was talking to.

Good. Well, wish me luck. I'm going to have to deal with the aftermath.

Sorry, Vic.

Haha, no worries. I've got this. See ya.

See ya.

Wow, her friends are pulling away from her? Well, I don't blame them. A person can only take so much crap. And Victoria is really sweet. I guess some of the other cheerleaders are probably pretty nice, if she's hanging out with them and they're all leaving the "precious Samantha". Oh good, there's Natalya.

Natalya! Wait up!

Hey! Did you see Jasmine? She said she wanted to sit with us at lunch.

Yeah, I saw her. She won't be sitting with us today.

Why not? What happened?

Well, I basically asked her what the heck? Like, why does she want to sit with us all of a sudden when she hates us?

What? Bryn, why would you do that?

Why not?

> I told you, she's not that bad, and she doesn't hate us. I'm
> going to go find her.

Fine. I'll meet you at the table.

Okay this is ridiculous, but whatever. If Natalya wants to hang out with her, I'll suck it up and let her sit with us. There must be some good in her if Nat wants to be friends with her. Oh my God, the ibuprofen is wearing off. I'm going to have to take more. I guess I should get a water bottle so it doesn't stick to my throat again. That always sucks, getting medicine stuck in the throat. Especially if it's chalky, ew! Gross. Why are water bottles so expensive? I mean really. $1.50 for water? This is a school, gosh. Isn't stuff supposed to be cheaper at school?

Ok I found her. She'll be here in a minute. Please, do you think you can try to be nice to her?

> I guess so. I still don't understand why you want to be
> friends with her, but, if that's what you want, then I'll be
> nice.

Thank you. She's really not bad. You just have to get to know her a little bit.

> I guess I'll try – for you.

Thank you, best friend. I love you.

> I love you too. Ugh, here she comes. I mean, oh look! Here
> she comes!

Haha, you're a trip...... Hey Jasmine!

> Hey ladies.

Have a seat.

> Thanks Natalya. Listen, Brynlee, I'm sorry about before.
> And I really meant what I said. I don't hate you. I never did.

It's okay. I'm sorry too. I didn't mean be so bitchy before. I was just confused, that's all. I really did think you hated us.

> I know I come off like a real bitch sometimes, with my tone
> and snarky attitude. I'm working on that. I mean, I'm a
> cheerleader. I'm supposed to lead with cheer, not sass,
> right?

Haha, yeah.

> But really though. Natalya and I have been talking lately in
> class, and Nat, you're really sweet.

Thank you.

> And Brynlee, if you're what Natalya says you are, then
> you're just as sweet. And to be honest, I need some nice
> friends in my life.

Why? What's going on with your cheer gang?

> Oh, nothing really. They're fine. It's just that, I don't know.
> We seem to want different things in life. Most of them want
> to just party and hook up, and really, I'm looking to study
> so I can get into a good college as soon as I graduate high
> school. I don't have time to screw up with too much
> partying and junk. Plus, I want a serious, long-term
> relationship, not just casual sex with random guys.

What do you want to study?

> Well, I'd like to get into the marketing field, but I'd like to
> focus on scouting for just the right talent myself. I want to
> work for a big ad agency and be in charge of the whole
> shebang, but also handpick the talent. Like, if I was a scout
> right now, I would totally pick you for something after
> seeing that video last night!

Really?

> Yeah, absolutely! And you too, Natalya, because you are
> absolutely drop dead gorgeous.

That's really sweet, Jasmine.

> I'm serious though. But, yeah, I've got goals, and they
> aren't their goals. We're still friends, of course, and we
> always will be, I'm sure. Just, well, we're evolving,
> differently.

Wow, that's crazy. You guys have been friends for years! Like, since
middle school cheer!

> Yeah, I know. Oh well, no biggie. So yeah, I'm sorry if my
> attitude made me appear to be a bitch. I never meant to be.
> Lord knows I do not want to be classified in the same
> category as Samantha Britt.

Oh my God!! I had a run-in with her in the bathroom just before I
saw you Nat!

> What? What happened?

Oh my God, okay well, I got my period. Great timing, right?
Anyway, I was taking care of stuff when someone started spraying
all this perfume. When I saw her I was like "oh my God". Anyway,
she was talking all this crap saying how all the guys who saw the

video were saying I shouldn't wear my hip hop outfit because I'm not skinny enough.

What?! No way!

Yeah! And then I told her off and told her she should lose her attitude and check her friends because guys only want her for one thing.

Did you seriously say that? Oh my God, I wish I was in there!

Oh my God, Jasmine, you would've died laughing. I didn't say exactly those words, but I implied them. To be honest, I'm not really sure she understood. She's not the brightest bulb in the box.

Wow, B, I'm so proud of you!

So am I!

Aww, thanks, guys. It felt good to finally stick up for myself. After that, I ran into Victoria in the hall. She was looking for her. I told her what Samantha said and she was like "that's a lie". And she also told me she and her friends are starting to pull away from her a little bit because they're tired of her crap.

Holy crap! Really? That's crazy.

I know! But that's what she said, so we'll see. Samantha will probably be extra bitchy for a while.

Wow, poor Samantha!

Jasmine, are you serious?

Hahaha, no! I'm kidding! She needs to be knocked down a few pegs. Believe me, I know. I'm coming down a few myself.

Aww, well, we all need to be humbled here and there. I'm really sorry I judged you, Jasmine.

I'm sorry too, to both of you. I'm just glad I finally met… Um, came to my senses.

Well, we're glad too.

Thanks for letting me chill with you guys for a bit. I'm going to go sit with the gang before they get sad and miss me. *Wink* See ya later, and thanks again.

No problem. See ya!

See ya in 7th!

See, Brynlee? I told you.

Okay, okay. I'm sorry I didn't trust your judgment.

I told you, she's not that bad.

Well, she used to be. Something's changed. She's different.
Maybe so, but whatever. She's cool, and I think we could all be good friends. So, wow! I can't believe you told Samantha off! That's awesome.

        Yeah, but the really quiet girl with the red hair, I don't know her name, she was in there and I think I made her feel uncomfortable. I feel bad.

Oh, I think her name is Emily.

        Yeah, I think you're right. I'm going to apologize to her when I see her.

Isn't that her over there?

        Oh yeah, it is. I'll be right back.

No way, I'm going with you. If she talks, I want to hear it.

        Okay, let's go.

        Hi, Emily?

Yeah?

        Hi, I'm Brynlee, and this is my bestie, Natalya.

Yeah, I know who you guys are. You're the gorgeous model, and you're the amazing dancer.

        Awww, you're so sweet. Thank you. Listen, I want to apologize for what happened in the bathroom before.

Why? You didn't do anything to me.

        I know, but I was bitching out Samantha, and I realized it probably made you feel pretty uncomfortable.

Are you kidding? That was great! I was just telling my friends all about it.

        Oh. Okay.

Yeah, finally someone stuck up to that... that bitch! She started crying after you left, you know.

        What? Are you serious?

Completely. And then she yelled at me because I was looking at her with a smile on my face.

        Oh no, I am so sorry!

Nope. Don't be. I told her off too.

        No way!! But you're so quiet!

Only when I don't have anything to say. But I had stuff to say to her. She's been mean to me way too long.

        Good for you, Emily!

Thanks for setting the scene for it. It was great! You were great! And now, I feel great. Victoria walked in while I was telling her off, and she started to giggle. Then she smiled at me and nodded as I walked out.

> That's awesome! Well, I'm glad it worked out and you didn't feel awkward.

Not at all. Thanks for checking though. I really appreciate it. Oh, and good luck tonight. You're gonna do fantastic! Especially if you dance like you did in that video!

> Aww, thanks Emily. Well, we should get back to our table. See ya. Bye guys!

Bye!

Holy crap, Brynlee, did you hear that?

> Yeah, I did. I wonder how fast that's going to get around. Oh look, the rest of us are at the table finally! I wonder where they were.

Hey girls, where have ya been?

> WE have been chatting with Miss Victoria Newman in the hallway about a certain two somebodies telling Samantha off in the bathroom! Nat, were you there too?

No, I missed the whole thing, but we just got the lowdown from the quiet girl, Emily, on her half of the story.

> Crazy, right? Victoria said she walked in after talking to Brynlee and there's the quiet girl reaming Samantha out. I can't believe it! I didn't know she even speaks.

I know, right? We didn't either. But Bryn wanted to apologize for making her feel awkward in there and she told us all about it! And she wasn't shy about it, either, right B?

> Yeah, I mean, she must just be a girl of few words usually, because she was telling us all about it. What did Victoria have to say, Jessica?

Just how first you told her off, and then she walked in on Emily telling her off, but Samantha was already crying, and, yeah. I'm so proud of you, Brynlee!

> Yeah, I'm proud of you, too.

Me too!

> Thanks, guys. It felt really good. And to know there was a witness, and she did it too, and that Samantha's own best friend witnessed it from the quiet girl… Like, that's stuff

people would never believe, you know? I kinda feel bad now, though.

What?! Don't feel bad. She deserved it.

I don't know. I don't want to stoop to her level, and I kinda feel like I just did.

No way, Brynlee. You could never be like her.

Yeah, you have a good heart.

Aww, thanks, you guys. I appreciate that.

You bet! Well, we need to go grab lunch. We'll catch up with you two later.

Bye girls!

See you girls later!

Hahaha, I love it!

Okay, let's not get too happy about this, Nat. I mean, we can be happy about it, but let's not make a huge deal over it.

Yeah, I guess you're right. Then we're as bad as she is, and we don't want to turn into her.

True. Very true. So yeah, in the meantime, guess who asked me for my number and who wants to hang out tomorrow!

Hmmm, let me guess... Luke!

How'd you guess?

Well, because Dylan asked me for my number, and wanted to know if I wanted to hang out, and told me that Luke was asking you out for tomorrow and we should all hang out together!

What?! No way! That's great! Do you still like Dylan?

Actually, I do. I have just been so busy studying and all, that I kind of forgot about him. Is that mean?

No! Why would that be mean? You're focusing on your studies.

Ok good.

Did he say what we're all going to do?

Not really. He mentioned something about getting something to eat...

Of course he did.

...and, wait, what's that supposed to mean?

Well, I'm just trying to lose weight and we're going to get and eat crap all night.

For goodness sake, Bryn, you are gorgeous. Please stop

thinking you need to lose weight.

Sorry. I can't help it.

Okay, well, help it. We can pick the place to go. We can go to the pizza place with the salad bar, if you want. That way, you and I can eat healthy, and they can pig out like guys do.

Okay, sounds good. I'm excited.

Me too. We need to get out and have fun after this crazy week.

Nat, you are not kidding! What a completely bizarre week it's been. After tonight's competition, I just want to let loose and have fun!

Right there with ya! ***Ding ding ding*** Really? The bell already? Okay, I guess I'll see you after school. Meet at the post?

Okay. Oh hey, how was your test?

It was fine. I think I aced it.

Well, I know you did.

Thanks. See ya.

Crazy, crazy day. Holy crap. Now to just get thru tonight and I can breathe a little. Thankfully, that ibuprofen kicked in quick. I hope it lasts a little longer this time. Maybe I should take two next time, like the bottle says. Nah, I don't want to pump my body with chemicals. I need to stay healthy. I've got gigs to get in Cali. I have to stay on top of my game. That reminds me, I guess I'll tell Ms. Val that I'm in tonight. She'll be so excited. I just hope we win the competition. Okay, day, hurry up. I've got things to do, a competition to win, and a date tomorrow! This should be a fun weekend!

Prison release...

Somebody kill me! This stupid class is so boring! I hate art history. How the heck did I even get stuck in this stupid elective? And how many more days do we have to listen to Ms. Collins talk about the boring renaissance period? The art was so... old. Like, it's not pretty at all. It's so drab and boring and churchy. I mean, it's cool that Leonardo DaVinci painted the Last Supper and the Mona Lisa, but still. Mona Lisa wasn't even cute. Why people think it's such a beautiful painting is beyond me. There are much better paintings out there of way more beautiful women. I don't get it. And what's with the Last Supper? I mean, it looks like chaos at the table, like they're all arguing over buns and Jesus is just there like "Chill. Eat.". Pretty funny. I wonder what it was like living back then. I wonder if there were popular hot guys, or if only the royals were popular and considered hot because they were royal and stuff. Ew, could you imagine wearing those clothes? And no phones. How would I text Natalya and... Luke? Haha, chisel it into a rock and chuck it at them! Hahaha!

Miss Sheffield, would you like to share with the rest of us what you find so amusing about this slide?

No thanks. I'm good.

I expect you will keep the giggling silenced from now on.

Yes, Ms. Collins. Sorry.

Ugh, she's cranky. I can't believe Luke asked me out! Hmmm, I wonder if we'll end up dating. Nah, probably not. I doubt he's actually into me like that. He probably just wants to hang out because of all the attention I'm getting from the video. Oh my God, sooo many people have said stuff about that to me today. Like, I almost feel a little snobbish the way I keep saying "thanks", like I expect them to tell me how great I was. I mean, it was pretty crazy, and I guess I looked pretty good. But I need to be better. Especially tonight. Let's just hope we can all keep together and no one forgets the routine. Carly, especially. She looked like she forgot in the video, so let's hope she's got it. I'm sure she does. She's usually the first

one to pick stuff up. Well, besides Jenna Hot-Toddler. Seriously, that girl. She's so damn gorgeous and only in 8th grade! And her boobs are ginormous! How does that even happen? Little Miss Perfect. I wonder what it's like to be her, all beautiful and hot and stuff, and only in middle school. Like, what's she gonna look like in 5 years when she goes to college? She'll probably be a model for some babe calendar or something. And she'll probably date all the hottest guys and get anything she wants just because of her looks. Some people have it so easy. Mom's right. If you look good, you can have the best in life, no problem. Guys, money, big house, nice cars, perfect kids…
That's not true, Brynlee.
Yes it is.

Miss Sheffield, did you have a question?
        Umm, no, sorry.
Okay, well, speak up if you do.
        Sorry.

What the hell?
Brynlee, don't believe those things you're telling yourself. They're lies.
        Nova?

Miss Sheffield, do I need to ask you to leave my classroom?
        No, Ms. Collins. I'm sorry. I thought there was a bug on me.

Remember, I can hear your thoughts. Just think to me.
        Nova! What are you doing here? Wait, you're real? I
        thought I was just dreaming last night.
No, I'm very real, and what I'm hearing is you telling yourself lies.
        What lies? What are you talking about?
You don't have to look a certain way to get the "good things in life".
        Well, it sure does seem that way to me. Look around,
        Nova. All the beautiful girls have boyfriends, hot
        boyfriends. They live in big houses, wear nice clothes…
If you haven't noticed, you, too, wear nice clothes, and live in a very nice house.
        Well, I mean, you know what I mean.

Yes, actually, I do know what you mean. And, Brynlee, it's a lie. Sure, there are many beautiful people in the world who have wonderful lives, but they didn't achieve those lives just because of the way they look. Yes, there are some that do, like actresses and other entertainers, but what you aren't thinking about is it also takes talent, hard work, commitment and motivation. Look at Natalya. She's a model. But did it come easy to her?

Yeah, it did. Her mom set her up. And she's naturally beautiful and thin... and tall.

Really? Is that what you really believe and know in your heart? Think about all those conversations you two have had about how hard it is on her body to put in so many hours in the studio, under the hot lights for photo shoots and on the runway. Remember how she cried about her skin having to be covered up because she was breaking out from all the makeup, and all the rejections she had to deal with because she didn't have "the right look".

Oh, yeah.

And what about all the time away from family events and friends' parties because she was working?

Ok, Nova, ok. I get it.

And do you think her mom became so popular just because of her looks? She had a really rough life growing up. She took any jobs she could to make ends meet while she was pursuing her acting career.

I know.

Okay, so, please stop telling yourself that you have to look a certain way to "have it all". That's just not true.

Ugh, I guess.

Listen, I don't know if you're really realizing what's in the works right now.

What do you mean?

Well, you've been dancing for quite some time now. You've put in a lot of hard work, sweat, tears, and even pain.

Yeah, and?

And Ms. Val has just asked you to study privately with her and Lacey because she believes you have what it takes to get far in the dance industry.

Yeah, she did, didn't she?

Yes, she did. And she also told you she has connections. That's how it works. Hard work, dedication, and sometimes knowing the right people. Now, we don't know where this will all lead, but you've got an excellent opportunity to reach your dreams. Now tell me, is this all happening because of the way you look?

No, definitely not.

Well, I can guarantee you, someone out there will think so. Someone one day will look at you and say the same thing – that you got where you did because of your looks.

I'm sure they wouldn't say that.

Why not? You said it about Natalya, and you KNEW her story.

Wow, now I feel bad.

Don't feel badly. It's what you've been taught to think. Many, many girls are taught the same lies, whether it's because that's what their moms have been taught, or the men in their lives tell them or show them with their actions. It's a very vicious cycle.

I guess it is. I never thought of it like that.

Oh, my dear, I have so much work to do to enlighten you. And if you still want to reach your full potential, if you are still willing to become all that you are meant to be, we're going to have to start with one tip.

I am! What tip?

Haha, don't say my name out loud when I appear! People will begin to think you're crazy.

Hahaha, ok, Nova. But do you think you can maybe be a little more subtle in the way you appear?

I'll try. Just remember I'm always with you. I will not leave you. You can just think my name and most of the time I'll answer.

Most of the time? Why not all of the time?

Well, because, some things you'll just have to figure out. But I'm always here to guide you. Like now, the bell is about to ring.

Oh thank God! I really don't like this class.

I've noticed.

C'mon, bell, ring already! **Ding ding ding** *Oh thank God!*

Miss Sheffield, may I speak with you a moment?

Sure, Ms. Collins.

Oh Lord, here we go.

Miss Sheffield, you weren't quite yourself today in class. Is everything alright?

   Yes, Ms. Collins. I'm fine.

Well, I realize that you have a big competition this evening, in which I'm sure you'll do quite well, having seen the video all the students have been raving about.

   Really? They have?

Indeed, they have. I must admit, I'm rather impressed with your abilities. It's quite beautiful to watch, actually, and I'm not really into that style of dance, so believe me when I tell you, you're quite good. Excellent, rather.

   Wow, thank you.

You're very welcome, my dear. However, let's not let your passions completely steamroll your education. You still must graduate to get into any good university. That is your plan for the future, I assume?

   Yes, I'd like to study dance and movement.

Well then, I assure you, if you stay on top of your studies, any university would be lucky to have you. I understand this isn't the most exciting elective for most, however, it does count toward your GPA. Perhaps I can attempt to add a little zest to the class. I'd much rather my students want to be here and actually learn about art history than fail. It does reflect on my teaching, you know. And frankly, I'd like to continue to teach. I enjoy your generation so much.

   Oh, okay, Miss Collins, that'd be great. Maybe if we could
   do cool projects instead of just listening to boring lectures.
   Oh my gosh! I'm so sorry.

Oh Dear, don't worry. I know listening to lectures can be very.... boring. I will take your suggestion into consideration. I think I'll spend the weekend researching ways to liven it up a bit in here to penetrate your generation. Thank you, Brynlee. And break a leg tonight!

   Thank you Miss Collins. And good luck researching. I'm
   sure you'll find something.

I will, indeed.

Well that was unexpected! She's kinda nice. I'm so glad she's going to try to make it fun. I mean, we still have half the year to go! Damn,

I need to hurry. Natalya's probably at the post already. I hope her mom's not here yet!

Hey Brynlee, good luck tonight!
       Yeah, Bryn, good luck!
Thanks, Maddie! Thanks Jess!
       Hey, maybe we can all hang out tomorrow night!
Well, I kinda have a date, and so does Natalya.
       What? With who? Do tell!
With Luke, and Dylan. It's kind of a double date. But I can't talk now, I have to meet Natalya and her mom for a ride home. Text Natalya – she'll fill you in! Bye girls!
       See ya Bryn!

Oh my gosh, is that Mrs. Sierzant pulling up already? No, whew! Okay, there's Natalya-Blu.

Hey!
       Oh hey Bryn, there you are! What in the world took you so long?
Oh my God, Ms. Collins wanted to see me after class because I was a little "disruptive" today.
       What? Are you serious? What'd you do?
Okay, so I was giggling to myself, but it must've been pretty loud, and then I said No…
       Giggling? About what?
Oh, I was imagining texting back in Jesus' time, and I thought about text-chiseling a rock and throwing it at you!
       Oh my God! You are crazy!
Haha, I know! And then…
       Hey, there's my mom! I can't wait to tell her about Dylan and Luke!
Oh yeah, Jess and Maddie will probably text you later. I ran into them on the way out here and told them about our date thing because they wanted to hang out tomorrow.
       Oh okay. I can't wait to tell them too!
Yeah, they seemed excited to know what happened.

Hi Mother!
       Hi Mrs Sierzant!

Hi girls! How was your day today?

> It was great! Oh my gosh, mom! Brynlee told Samantha off today in the bathroom!

Really? What happened, Brynlee?

> Well, she was putting me down about the way I look in my competition outfit, so I let her have it.

Well, good for you, sweetheart! Don't let anyone speak to you that way. You're a beautiful girl and that outfit looks fabulous on you! It fits your body so nicely, shows off your wonderful curves. You look fabulously feminine in it.

> Wow, thanks, Mrs. Sierzant.

Darling, please, we're so close. Would you please call me Paulina?

> Oh, I don't...

Or how about mom? Can she call you mom, Mom? Haha!

> Of course she can! Either one is fine with me. But please, no more with the "Mrs." business. It makes me feel so old. And I'm not old. My mother in law, she's the old one. You can call her "Mrs." or even Ma'am. That'll really set her off! Hahaha!

Mother!

> Oh, Natalya, I'm joking. So tell me, girls, what do you have planned for the weekend, besides your competition, of course?

Well, Brynlee and I have dates tomorrow night!

> Mmmm! Sounds tasty! Who with?

Well, Luke asked Bryn out, and his friend Dylan asked me out, and said we should double date.

> Oh that sounds fun, girls! Tell me, are these boys good looking?

Oh my gosh, Mrs.... I mean, Mom! Yes!! Very cute!

> Well, I can't wait to meet these boys.

Yeah, they're great.

> Wonderful! Well, here we are, darling. Please tell your mother I will call her tomorrow morning. I want to hear all about the competition.

Okay, I'll tell her. Thank you for the ride! Nat, I'll text you in a bit.

> Oh, and Brynlee, break a leg out there! And shake that adorable little body of yours like you mean it!

Haha, I will, Mrs... Mom.

> See ya later, Bryn! Don't forget to text me!

I won't forget!

She's so sweet. I love her. I feel funny calling her "mom" though. But it'd be even weirder calling her Paulina. I can't do that. She's too elegant and sophisticated for me call her "Paulina". I feel like it'd be disrespectful if I did. I mean, if she was a little trashy or something...

What on earth is that supposed to mean?

    Nova, I thought you were going to be more subtle!

Tell me, please, what that was supposed to mean!

    I don't know. She's too proper, I guess.

No, what do you mean by "trashy"? Are you trying to say that if she was less proper she'd deserve less respect?

        No, that's not what I meant. I mean, I guess if she wasn't
        so put together and dressed so nice, and so beautiful..

There's another lie you've been taught.

        What?

The way a person dresses does not make them any more or less worthy of respect. That's what the Dandies thought back in the day. That was their thinking. It's all a farce. A lie. Everyone deserves respect, but it's their character that determines the level of respect. Everyone deserves to be treated with dignity, even if it's the most basic level of dignity. Their appearance, their possessions, their personal style does not determine those levels. You were firsthand witness to that today in the bathroom, with Samantha.

        What? I don't get it.

She dresses very nicely, all the time. She carries herself in proper form and stature...

        My language, Nova.

Sorry. She comes off as proper and somewhat sophisticated to those who don't know her. But her character is deeply flawed and broken. Therefore, your level of respect for her is very low.

        Actually, it's non-existent. She's a bitch.

Well, okay, you haven't any respect for her. Do you see?

        Yeah, I guess I do.

Okay, good. Then we're making progress.

        But I still can't bring myself to call Mrs. Sierzant
        "Paulina". I even have a hard time calling her "mom". I

already have a mom. And as messed up as she might be, I love her. I feel like I'm betraying her if I call someone else "mom", even if we are really close.

Well, why not speak to her about it?

I don't know. I don't want to offend her, or hurt her feelings. Or worse, make her feel old!

I'm sure she will understand. Maybe you'll come to an agreement on what to call her that you both feel comfortable with.

I guess so. I'll talk to her tomorrow, when Natalya and I are getting ready for our double.

Well, until then, you've got a competition to get ready for.

I know! I'm nervous.

Why are you nervous? You're going to do great.

I don't know. I just am. And it's weird coming home and no one else is here. This is a big day for me. I need mental and emotional support. When's my mother's meeting going to end? What kind of meeting is she at, anyway? And does Daddy even know? God, I hate being out of the loop! Why won't someone just tell me what the heck is going on in this family?!

Sorry, you'll have to get those answers from your parents. I can't help you, there.

Well, why not? I thought you are supposed to tell me the truth.

I am, and I do.

Fine. Whatever.

Sorry. Now go up and get ready to win win win!

Yes, okay. Thanks Nova.

It's almost time!

Alright, I guess I'll just have to mentally prepare myself for this. I can do this. It'll be great. It's what I've been training for. But this is a big one. It's okay. Alright, so mom said she hung my outfit in the laundry room. I should probably start to do my hair and makeup, but Ms. Val said Jhonae has something special planned. So, hmmm, I wonder if I should do my makeup as usual, or not? I mean, she didn't say not to. Jhonae can just do the usual final touches and whatever else she has planned. I wonder what it is. Well, whatever it is, I hope it's cool. Jhonae has amazing make-up talent. I don't know why she doesn't do that professionally. I mean, she could work in Hollywood, with the stars, or in New York City! Why does she want to stay here, in Sherwood, Oregon? I mean, it's great here. I love it. But, she belongs in a place where she can use her talent and make a crapload of money! Maybe it's because her girlfriend is originally from here. They can stay near her family and their friends. I wonder what her girlfriend is like. Why hasn't she brought her to the dance academy? She hardly ever talks about her. Maybe she'll be at the competition tonight. That'd be cool, because we're all dying to meet her. But anyway, ok, so... How shall I do my makeup today? I should text Lacey and ask her what she's doing, since we're both up front. It'd probably look better if we aren't ridiculously different.

"Hey Lacey! How are you doing your makeup for tonight?

Okay, hopefully she'll text me right back so I can just get ready now. Maybe I should go eat the food mom left for me. I really hope it's not just lettuce. I'm kind of tired of eating like a rabbit, even though I'm not that hungry right now. I know as soon as we pull out of the driveway I'll be starving if I don't eat now. Okay, let's see here, what did mom leave in here for me besides lettuce? Oh thank God! There's stuff in this salad! Oh hell yes! Shrimp! Oh my God, I love shrimp. I'll have to remember to hug mom later for this! Oh, wait. There's another salad here too... with nothing but lettuce. Ugh! Hmmm, should I text mom too? God, I just wish she was home right now instead of at some stupid meeting! Whatever. I'll text her too.

"Mom, which salad is mine?"

She probably won't even answer me. Okay, well, maybe I'll just start eating the good salad, and then if she answers I can tell her I already started...

"Hi honey. I'm in a meeting, but it's the salad with the shrimp in it."
Oh thank God!
"K thx mom"

This salad looks so freaking good right now. I'll eat some now, and then I'll go get ready and finish this later. It's so crazy how when I have PMS I can eat a farm, but as soon as I get my period, it's like, nah, I'll just eat an almond. Haha, what kind of crazy shit is that, anyway? Why do we girls have to deal with this crap, and guys just, wham bam thank you ma'am? Life's just not fair. This salad is freaking Heaven, holy crap! Ooh, is that Lacey texting me back? Yes...

"I think purple n black. That wld look good w/ the outfit"
"Okay, cool. I'll do the same"
"Good, we'll match"
"Yeah, since we're up front"
"Exactly"

Good choice, Lace. I love purple, and I think it'll go really nice with the white pants and this shimmery black bra thing. Hey, is that Daddy? Cool, Daddy's home! I didn't think he'd be back until much later. I guess his meetings got cut short today. I'm glad he's home early. He always gets me motivated right before competitions. Aww, he looks like he had a good day today. He should try this salad!

Hi Daddy!
       Hi Sweetpea!
You're home earlier than I thought you'd be! How was your day?
       It was pretty good. I rearranged my schedule so I could be
       home early today.
Well, I'm glad! I like when you're home early. Dad, you have to try this salad Mom made! It's so good!

Oh, thank you, hon, but I actually had a late lunch with some colleagues, so I'm not hungry right now.

C'mon, you have to at least have a bite.

Okay, give me a bite…. Mmm, that is good. Your mother must've been watching the Complete Eats Channel today. Speaking of your mother, where is she?

She's at some meeting.

Oh that's right! It got rescheduled.

Daddy, what kind of meeting is she at, anyway?

Oh, it's just a… Uh, hold on… "Hello, this is Kyle"

OH COME ON! Are you kidding me?! I'm never going to find out where my mother is! Forget it! I don't care anymore, Jeez! I swear, this is totally ridiculous. Whatever.

Sorry, Brynlee. That was a new client confirming for Monday.

A new client? That's exciting! How old is she? Is she beautiful?

Yes, she's a very pretty girl. I guess she's about your age.

That's cool. I wish I was pretty enough to be in the magazine.

Honey, you are beautiful! But Mom and I didn't want you to live that lifestyle. That's why we never had you model for it.

Oh wow. Don't I get a vote?

Well, no. Not really.

Why not?

Because, Bryn, your mom and I decided that we don't want you to be put through the rigor of a model's life. And they are always under such scrutiny about their looks and weight. We didn't want that for you.

Seriously? Do you not realize I am already under that kind of scrutiny?

No you're not.

Dad, seriously? Do you not hear how Mom rags on me all the time?

Your mother doesn't rag on you about the way you look.

Yes, she does! All the time! Don't you hear her when she tells me I'm fat, and how I need to lose weight?

No, I've never heard her tell you that.

Daddy, you should listen more. She tells me all the time.

Oh, Babygirl, I'm sorry. If it helps, I don't think you're fat at all. I think you're perfect just the way you are.

Thanks Daddy. I love you.

I love you, too, Princess. Please don't cry. I think you need Daddy hugs.

Yes I do!

Sweetpea, you really are perfect. And I promise, I'll listen more to how your mother speaks to you. Okay?

Okay, Daddy. Thank you. You're the best.

I have to be. I have the best daughter. Now, don't you have a competition to get ready for?

Yeah.

Well, finish up that salad and go get ready. I think Uncle Dave and Aunt Holly will be able to meet us here, and then we can all go together.

Okay, that'd be great.

I love my daddy. He's the best, but seriously, how has he not heard Mom rag on me? I mean, she does it all the damn time. All the time. I don't know. Maybe he really doesn't hear it. Men don't listen like women do. Unless they're gay, like Mr. Thompson. He's a great listener. I wonder why that is? Why are gay men better listeners than straight men? Are they more in touch with their feminine side, if that even is a thing? And is it all of them, or just some? He's a great teacher, but he'd be a really awesome counselor or psychologist. Why doesn't Daddy hear what goes on? Well, whatever. Men. Ya can't live with 'em, pass the donuts. Oh, wait a minute, what am I saying? Pass the carrot sticks and hummus! Donuts are fattening, and you know what they say – "a moment on the lips, a lifetime on the hips". Lord knows I don't need any more of ANYTHING on these hips! I already look larger than life in this outfit I have to wear tonight. I really need to beg Ms. Val to order stuff that cover us a little. Ugh that reminds me, I need mom to pick up more cover-up. My skin is horrible this month.

"Mom can u plz pick up cover-up on ur way home? Thx."

Hopefully she'll get that before she's home. So, I guess I should hold off on doing my makeup for a little while. Maybe I'll just lay down and relax. This bed is so comfy. I should probably set my alarm, just in case I fall asleep. I am so tired. I hate that. Why do I have to be tired every time I get my period? Is it not enough I have to deal with having my period, do I also have to have cramps that make me want to kill a kitten AND be so tired I could sleep until Prince Charming comes around? All this after a week of emotional schizophrenia and wanting to eat the entire state of Montana! Oh! And let's not forget being, feeling and looking like a sumo wrestler! Heck, even sumo wrestlers look better than I do! At least they don't break out with volcanoes on their face! Hahaha, that'd be a crazy painting! Me as a sumo wrestler in a hip hop outfit, with volcanoes erupting on my face, and a HUGE plate of meat and desserts and fried everything in front of me!

Wow, Brynlee, you've got quite the imagination, don't you?

      Hi Nova. Haha, yeah, I guess so.

It's a little exaggerated, wouldn't you say?

      Yeah, but right now, it's how I feel. And it'd probably be pretty funny if someone did paint it.

Well, I guess it could be an interpretation of the exaggeration of your menstrual feelings.

      Um, yeah, okay. Whatever.

Surely you don't feel that way about yourself.

      Well, no, not that bad, but close.

How close?

      Well, I mean, I feel really fat. Really fat like a sumo wrestler.

Really? Is that a true representation of your actual feelings about yourself? Honestly?

      I don't know. Sometimes, I guess.

Let's do an exercise.

      Nova, I was trying to rest before I get ready.

Well, actually, you were imagining silly pictures with volcano faces.

      Ugh. Okay.

Now, without looking at yourself, stand up in front of your mirror and close your eyes for me, and keep them closed.

      For how long?

I'll let you know. Now, with your eyes still closed, I want you to repeat after me. I am beautiful.

      What? No. This is stupid.

Please, just do it. You said you want to grow. So please.... I am beautiful.

Sigh I am beautiful.
Okay, now say it louder. I am beautiful.
I. Am. Beautiful.
My appearance does not reflect my worth.
My appearance does not reflect my worth.
My character is beautiful, therefore, I am beautiful.
Seriously, Nova, this is dumb.
Say it.
Ugh! My character is beautiful, therefore, I am beautiful.
Say it again.
My character is beautiful, therefore, I am beautiful.
Now, I want you to open your eyes.
Are we almost done? I'd like to chill.
Almost. While you have your eyes open, I want you to get
closer to the mirror.
How close?
Close enough that you can see the specks in your eyes.
I have specks in my eyes?
Yes, you do, actually. They're quite lovely.
Hmm. I never noticed.
Okay, now look into your eyes. Check them out for a minute so
you're not distracted by them, since you didn't know about your
specks.
Haha, okay, now what?
Now look into your eyes, repeat after me... I am beautiful.
C'mon, Nova.
Brynlee... I am beautiful. Say it.
I am beautiful.
Say it slower and louder this time.
Sigh I am.... Beautiful.
I am beautiful no matter what size I am.
I am beautiful no matter what size I am.
My appearance does not reflect my worth.
My appearance does not reflect my worth.
My appearance does not reflect my true beauty.
My appearance does not...
Why are you crying?
Because! This is stupid. I don't want to do this anymore.
Please. Please just finish this.

Ugh, fine. My appearance does not reflect my true beauty.

I am beautiful inside, therefore, I am beautiful.

I am beauti...

Look into your eyes, please.

I am beautiful inside, therefore I am beautiful.

Wonderful! You did fabulous!

Can I lay down now?

Sure. Go ahead. How did that feel?

I told you. It was stupid.

Tell me more.

There's nothing to tell. It was just stupid.

Why were you crying?

I don't know.

Really, why were you crying?

Because. You were making me say stuff I don't believe.

That's precisely why I wanted you to say it.

Why? I don't get it. That's so mean.

It's not mean. We're going to do this often. You've been brainwashed to believe stuff that simply isn't true. So now we're going to undo that.

But it is true. Look around. Guys only want girls that are perfect.

Tell me, what is this definition of "perfect"?

You know, skinny, beautiful, big boobs...

Do you honestly believe that's all boys are looking for in a girl?

I mean, yeah. Otherwise, why would they date people like Samantha?

There are lots of reasons why boys would date someone like her. Some of them aren't nice reasons, however.

But still, she gets dates.

Need I remind you that you have a date tomorrow night?

I remember. But he is probably only doing it for those same reasons, because I am not skinny or beautiful, like Samantha.

No, you're not like Samantha. You're not mean to people. You don't judge people based on what they wear or who their mom is, or where the family lives. And no, your body isn't shaped exactly like her, either. But no one's is. And she's not the perfect specimen of the human female form.

Huh?

She's not human perfection. There is no human perfection. No one is perfect, not in size, not in shape, because there is no actual perfect human that humans are supposed to look like. You're all different. Haven't you noticed?

Yes, I've noticed. But, I mean, I'm not the ideal.

Not whose ideal?

Anyone's.

That's ridiculous. Not all men have the same ideal.

Yes they do.

Brynlee, let me ask you this. Are you attracted to Natalya's ex-boyfriend, Seth?

Ew, no.

Okay, and is Natalya still attracted to him?

Haha, yeah, I think she'll always be. She still says he's perfect.

But you don't think so?

God no. He's too lanky. And I don't really care for red hair on guys unless you can see their eyebrows. I know, it's silly, but I like dark eyebrows.

Well, then what makes you think all boys like the same type of girl?

I don't know, they just do.

That's absurd. You're being stubborn.

I am not being stubborn! Look around, Nova. You'll see.

Okay, listen. I know for a fact that boys are not all looking for the same thing. I mean, yes, they all do look for some of the same things, but we aren't talking about THAT right now. I do know that they are not all looking for the same looks in a girl, nor are they all only looking for looks; some actually care about personality, and character.

Yeah, right! At my age? No.

Yes. Trust me. Not all boys, or men for that matter, are shallow. Many, if not most, have been raised with values. Like your dad, for instance.

My dad?

Yes. He didn't marry your mother just because she's beautiful.

Sometimes I wonder why he did marry her. She's a

bitch.

Well, why not go downstairs and ask him?

I'm not going to ask my father why he married my
mother.

Why not? It's a legitimate question. Go ahead, ask him.

Ugh, fine. I'll ask him.

*He's gonna think I'm off my rocker. Why would a daughter randomly
ask her dad why he married her mother? This is crazy.*

Hey Daddy, can I ask you something?

Sure, sweetie, what is it?

Um, okay, why did you marry Mom? Like, what was it about her that
you knew you wanted to spend the rest of your life with her?

Well, a lot of things, really.

Like what? Why did you even like her to begin with? Was it the way
she looked?

Well, your mother is very beautiful, but that wasn't why I
liked her. That was a bonus. There was something about her
I couldn't pinpoint, but I knew I wanted to get to know her
better.

That's it?

Haha, no, no. When I first met your mother, there was a
twinkle in her eye when she looked at me. It was something
I never saw in anyone else's eyes before. It was like I could
see her soul. And then we got to know each other a little,
and I realized that she had a really good heart. She was a
very kind lady, she cared deeply about her friends, and even
some people she didn't know.

Are you serious, or are you just messing with me?

Why would I joke about that? Of course I'm serious. Your
mom is a beautiful woman inside with a generous and
caring heart. That's why I love her.

Not because she's pretty?

Her beauty isn't why I love her, but I do love her beauty. I
think your mother is the most beautiful woman in the entire
history of the world. And you, my princess, are the most
beautiful young lady in the history of the world.

I love you, Daddy.

I love you too, Sweetpea. What's with the questions?

Oh nothing. Just wondering, is all. I'm going to get ready now.

Okay, Sweetpea.

Wow! That just made my heart melt! Daddy is so sweet! I wonder if mom knows how lucky she is. I'm sure she does. She'd be crazy if she didn't. But why is it that the woman he told me about and the mom I know sound like two different people?

Well? What'd he say?

Okay, okay, you were right. But that doesn't count. My daddy is the exception to the rule. He's special.

He is special. But there are others like him, you know. And there's one out there for you, too, and he dreams about you.

You're crazy! No guy out there dreams about me! "Yes, hello, I'm Brynlee, your dream girl!" You kill me, Nova. You're just too funny.

You'll see. One day, you'll see.

Okay, whatever. I need to get ready, now that my relaxation time is over.

Just remember what we said. You are beautiful.

Yeah, yeah. Oh, good! Mom's home. I hope she got my cover-up.

Mom, did you get my…

Yes, dear. Hello to you too!

Oh, sorry. I'm just trying to get ready and I really need that cover-up.

Well, you are breaking out quite a bit. I hope this is the right color.

It is. Thanks, mom.

You're welcome.

How was your meeting?

It was fine. Go get ready, before we're late. Hi honey, you're home early.

Yes, I rearranged my schedule so I could get home early.

How was your meeting?

Oh, it was fine. Bryn, did you eat the salad?

Oh my God, Mom, that salad was sooo good!

Yes, Heidi, it was really good.

You ate Bryn's salad?

No, no. She insisted I try a bite. It was great.

Well, thank you honey. I saw it on the Complete Eats
Channel…. What? Why are you two laughing?
Hahaha, Dad said that's probably where you got the recipe!
Oh, well, yes, I did. And I bet you're both glad, too!
We sure are, mom!
Absolutely, honey. Best salad ever.
Bryn, go get ready. Your father and I have to talk about something,
anyway.
What?
Mind your business. Go get ready.
Ugh, fine.

*I hate when they do that. Why can't you just tell me? Why does
everything have to be a stupid secret? Well, at least she got my
cover-up for me. Now I can put my makeup on. It has to look really
good, since Blake is going to be there. I mean, I know I don't have a
chance with him, but I can at least look my best, right? Imagine if he
came up to me after the show and told me how beautiful I look and
how fantastic I did, and congratulated me on our win with a huge
hug? That'd be great. But it will never happen. It's only just a
dream, and that's all it ever will be. But, what's life without dreams,
right? Some come true, and some live forever in the dream world,
never to be realized. How sad. I wonder how many unrealized
dreams are out there floating around, wishing people would chase
after them. And when the person who dreamt them dies, do the
dreams just hit the ground, flat, or do they keep floating, waiting for
someone else to take notice and chase after it? Were they originated
by a person, or do they exist on their own? I picture them to look like
thought bubbles, but with wings like butterflies or dragonflies, or
even faerie wings. And they just float around until a dreamer
attaches themselves to it. And sometimes if it's a big dream, like
becoming president or something, they glow or sparkle, depending
on the size. I wonder if my dream of being a famous dancer glows or
sparkles. I mean, I'm chasing the dream, so surely it must, especially
since it's pretty big. And when the dream comes true, what happens
to it? Does it disintegrate? Does it burst open like fireworks? Or
does it become part of the dreamer's soul? Maybe I'll write a book
about that one day. That'd make a pretty cool book, I think. Hmmm,
maybe I'll start writing this weekend, and not wait. Was that just a
new dream being born? Does it sparkle or shimmer? Awww, dreams*

are so cute! Speaking of sparkle, I should add some to this eye shadow. Damn, my eyes look good! I'm getting better and better at this makeup stuff. Where's my phone? I need to take an eye selfie. Darn it, I blinked. There, that's better. Oh hey, nice eyeball! Oh wow, Nova's right, I do have specks. They're kinda cool. I never really noticed how pretty my eyes are. It's probably just because of all the makeup, though. I can almost see into my soul. Oh, never mind. That's just a reflection of my phone. Okay, enough nonsense. I need to do this hair and get dressed. It's almost time to go, and Jhonae has to put her finishing touches on me, whatever that may be. I hope what I already did doesn't interfere with whatever she's going to do, because my eyes look good right now.

knock knock
Come in!

Hi Brynlee.

Oh my God, Aunt Holly!

Hi sweetie! Wow! You look GREAT! Your makeup looks fabulous! Did you do it or your mom?

I just got done putting it on.

Well, sweetie, it looks fabulous. I'll have to have you come do my makeup when Uncle Dave takes me out on the town next time!

Oh my gosh, I would love to! I'm so glad you're here! I thought you were going to be late.

Well, we were, but we both somehow managed to get off of work on time today, and here we are! We wanted to ride with you guys to the competition. It's so much more fun to go in a bigger group, you know?

Haha, yeah. Well, I'm glad you're here. Will you help me do something with this hair?

Absolutely! What shall we do with it?

I don't know. I was thinking of maybe keeping most of it down, and just pinning the bangs, but maybe curl it some so it's big.

Okay, well, why don't you go ahead and get your outfit on, I'm dying to see it on you, anyway, and then we'll do your hair. That way it won't get messed up while you're getting dressed.

Okay, be right back.

Okay, Aunt Holly is always honest about everything. Sometimes she's brutally honest, but at least I'll get a good and clear opinion from someone I can totally trust. And she never puts me down like Mom does. It's so crazy they are sisters. How does that even happen? Okay, here goes nothing...

Okay, I'm ready.

    Holy cow, Bryn! That looks fantastic on you! My, how you are growing into a young woman so quickly! Okay, stop growing. I'm going to put a brick on your head so you at least slow down and not grow up so fast.

Aww, Aunt Holly, I love you.

    I love you too, Sweetie. I remember when you were my sweet little Brynie-boo, and now you're this beautiful young lady, who really doesn't look so young, if you know what I mean.

Does this look okay on me? I feel so fat and squishy.

    Oh my heaven, you look stunning, Bryn! You're neither fat nor squishy, I assure you!

Well, I feel like it. Plus, I got my period, so I'm bloated and stuff.

    Oh no! And of course you would have to wear white pants!

I know! What the heck? Oh, I should probably make sure I'm fully protected. Be right back.

    Yes, definitely use extra protection with those pants! You don't need a mishap or anything.

Aww, I love her. She's the best aunt, I swear. Oh my God, I really hope this will be enough to make sure I don't bleed through. I would just die. I should bring extra and change right before we go on. That's what I'll do. I wonder if any of the other girls have their period right now. This totally and completely sucks. Ugh, okay, now time for hair.

    Listen, doll, you look too good to be going out in public like this. How about we change the outfit and cover you up a little bit? We don't want any perverted little boys looking at my little princess with google eyes.

Oh don't worry, Aunt Hol, boys don't look at me like that.

    Are you kidding?! I'm sure that's not true at all!

It is. They like the skinny, beautiful girls.

Brynlee, sweetie, I guess you haven't noticed, but you are skinny and beautiful!

Thanks Aunt Holly, but not really.

Listen, have I ever lied to you, ever?

No.

Then why would I start now? You know me – I'm Ms. Brutally Honest. Isn't that what your parents call me?

Haha, yeah, they do. And you are.

Well, then take my word for it. Okay, actually, you're right. You aren't skinny. You're thin and fit. Look at the muscles on you!

Skinny, thin, what's the difference?

Well, hon, the word skinny can have a bad connotation, just like when people call other people fat. Haven't you ever heard anyone say "you're so skinny, go eat a cheeseburger"? Like they're boney.

Yeah, I have, actually. A lot.

Well, see what I mean? It's not nice at all. But, it could go either way. Like, "Wow, you're so skinny, I wish I was that skinny". You know? So, I say thin when referring to it in the positive way. And you, my dear, are thin and muscular. I'd love to have those abs! But I don't exercise, so…

But you look great! You're so beautiful. You don't need to exercise.

Oh, but I do! I'm getting older, and I want everything to continue to work properly. I don't want to be some middle-aged lady who can't get up off of the floor! I want to be healthy well into my dinosaur age.

Hahaha! That's hysterical!

You know, and here I go with the brutally honest thing, here – your boobs have gotten much bigger. I don't know if this top is big enough for you. You went from being a little kid who had lil boobies to BAM! Boobs! Are they going to bounce out while you're dancing? I mean, I'm sitting here doing your hair, and I look down and there they are, all big and stuff.

No, they won't bounce out. They're not as big as you think. Wait till you see Jenna. Now her boobs are huge! And she's only in middle school!

How does that happen? I wasn't blessed with boobs until I just about graduated high school, and neither was your mom! At least you got them a little sooner than we did.

Yeah, I don't know. You'll know exactly who she is, though. She's the girl with the boobs.

Okay, I'll keep an eye out.

Oh you'll know immediately.

Haha, I bet! There, how's the hair?

Oh my gosh, Aunt Holly! It looks great! Thank you so much!

You're welcome, hon. Oh there's the hugs I've been missing! It's been too long!

Yeah, three months is way too long.

It sure is. It's crazy how much you've grown in that time. Or maybe I'm just noticing because of this crazy cute outfit! Gracious, it looks so good on you. I would do without the white pants, though, and use any other color. I mean, who wears white pants after Labor Day, for crying out loud!

Right? I was going to remind Ms. Val about that for next time.

Good idea. I'll second it! Now, let's get downstairs. Uncle Dave is dying for a hug.

Okay. Thanks Aunt Holly. You're my fave.

I love you Brynie-boo. Sorry, but you'll always be my lil Brynie-boo.

That's okay. Just not in front of the hot guys.

Are you kidding? ESPECIALLY in front of the hot guys! Hahaha!

Yeah, not funny.

Yes, it actually is.

No, it actually isn't.

Oh, we'll see, the next time a hot guy comes around.

Well, that'll be never, soooo....

Oh stop it!

Hi, Uncle Dave!

Brynlee! Holy cow! Someone get this girl a robe!

Oh, Uncle Dave, you're crazy.

Crazy about my lil Brynie-boo! Give me a hug! I'm jonesin'.

Jonesin'?

Yeah, that's old guy talk for "having withdrawals". Oh yeah, there it is, best hug ever!

Hasn't she gotten so grown up, David?

Yeah, honey, a little too grown up! Kyle, you allow her to leave the house like this?

Well, Dave, I've got no choice. It's the required attire for the evening. And no, I don't like it one bit.

Well, that makes two of us, man! Brynlee, when did you get so grown up?

Apparently in the last three months, according to Aunt Holly.

Yup, that's definitely when it must've happened. You know, as your uncle, it's my responsibility to beat up all the boys who try to date you.

Please don't do that. I already don't get dates.

That's not what I heard, Sweetie.

Why, Mom, what did you hear?

Well, Paulina told me that you and Natalya-Blu have a double date planned for tomorrow.

Yeah, we do. She wasn't going to call you until tomorrow…

Who with? And why didn't you tell me?

Because, Mother, you haven't been home yet today, and this just happened at school this morning. And besides, it's no big deal.

What do you mean, no big deal? My niece has a date and it's no big deal? I beg to differ. And when I find out who this boy is, I'm kicking his ass!

No, Uncle Dave. I need to get married one day.

Sure, okay, yeah, one day. Not today. Not for at least ten years.

I'll be in my mid-20's by then! I don't want to be an old hag when I get married!

Yeah, Dave, I don't want to be an older hag mother of the bride, either!

Thanks, Mom. We finally see eye to eye on something.

It's nice, isn't it?

Yes! My wife and daughter finally agree!

I still want to beat the kid up.

Oh David.

Well gang, we should get going. Heidi, let's take your car. Mine is full of paperwork.

That's fine honey. I'm telling you, Holly, when Bryn starts driving, her car will look just like Kyle's!

If I remember correctly, Sis, you weren't the neatest person when we were her age.

No, I guess not. But I grew out of it. Kyle never did, did you honey?

No, no I didn't. And that's why we're taking your car.

Well then, okay. Everyone pile in. Brynlee, hon, you sit up front so your pants don't get wrinkled.

Okay. Looks like it's me and you, Daddy. We have shotgun.

Yes. And just think, this time next year you will be driving us to your competition!

In my own car?

No, probably not. It'll be too messy, according to your mother!

Haha, yeah, it probably will be. Like Daddy, like daughter.

I wouldn't have it any other way, Pumpkin!

Me either, Daddy.

Awww, I love my daddy. I love my family. How did I get so lucky? This is what it's all about, right here. Family. And I've got the best.

Oh my gosh, we're here!

Well, Pumpkin, here we are. Are you nervous?
>Nah, not really.

Holy shit, yes I am. I totally just lied.
Well good. You're going to do great.
>Thanks Daddy.

Yes, Brynlee honey, remember, just focus.
>Yeah, Brynie-boo, you'll do fantastic. We're so excited to see you dance. Just keep your stuff in, okay?

Haha, sure, Aunt Holly, I will.
>And I'll be watching out for boys.

Oh, David, stop.
>What? I swore to protect my niece.

He did, Holly. I have witnesses.
>Kyle! Okay, Brynlee, I'll walk in with you. You three go on in. Here are the tickets. Get good seats, please.

Love you Brynie!
>Love you guys!

Okay, Bryn, you look nervous. Are you nervous?
>Only a little.

Well, you look great. Your makeup looks fabulous. That's twice in one day. Have you been practicing?
>Yeah, a little.

Well, you're getting good at it.
>Thanks, Mom.

And let me see your pants, turn around.
>Why? Mom, stop.

I want to make sure they aren't too wrinkled from sitting in the car.
>Mom, they're fine. What was I supposed to do, stand?

Well, no, but maybe you should've changed here instead.
>I'll be fine.

Yeah, they're not bad. It's okay. Okay there's Jhonae. What is she doing to Lacey?
>Oh my God, yay! Body paint and glitter!

Oh boy, I hope that doesn't stain the white pants.

It's okay, Mom.

Wow, that looks fantastic! Okay, go. I'll go catch up with Daddy, Holly and Dave. Love you, Brynlee. Break a leg out there!

Thanks Mom.

I am so freaking excited! Body paint! And Jhonae is a pro! How cool is this!

Hi Jhonae! The body paint looks so freaking amazing!

Oh, thank you doll. Spin, Lacey. Okay Brynlee, go find Ms. Val and check in, and then come back. I'll paint you after I finish up Lacey's body art.

Sure thing. Hey Lace! You ready?

Yup, sure am! You?

Brynlee, go! Lacey, spin.

Okay, okay... Be right back.

Damn, Lacey looks hot! I can't wait to see the whole company all painted up and in dress. Where the heck is Ms. Val? Oh, there she is.

Hi Ms. Val! I'm here.

Okay, great, Brynlee. Now, go find Jhonae to get painted up.

I found her already. She's just finishing Lacey up.

Okay, fabulous.

Oh, Ms. Val? I need to talk to you after the competition.

Sure thing, doll. Let's get through this with a win, first.

You bet.

Alrighty, back to Jhonae and Lacey. I can't wait to tell Ms. Val that I want to do the semi-privates. If we don't win, it'll be good news for her. If we do win, she'll be over the top excited. Wait, what am I talking about? Of course we're going to win! How could I even think like that? Okay, time to get in the zone.

I'm back.

Okay, great. One more swirl and I... am... done. Okay, Miss Lacey. Go stand under the dryer for a few so the paint can set.

Where's that?

Oh, I'm sorry. Right over there. That's my girlfriend
Candice holding the dryer.

Oh my gosh! Finally we get to meet your girlfriend! Bryn! Weren't
we just talking about wanting to meet her?

Yeah, we were. Jhonae, why haven't you ever brought her
to class?

Oh, she works weird hours, and takes classes online. She's usually
studying or listening to lectures when I come to class.

Oh, we thought you didn't want us to meet her.

Well, we do like to keep our private life private, but since tonight is
such a big deal, she wanted to come and cheer you girls on, and help
out some.

She's adorable!

I know, right?

I love her hair! It's so funky and cute. What is she studying?

Spin a little to the right. She is studying to be a holistic nutrition
practitioner. She's already a nurse, so she wants to expand her
horizons so she's able to help people naturally. She's very down to
earth and organic.

That's so cool. You date a tree-hugger!

Yeah, I guess I do.

I guess it's true what they say – opposites attract.

Yeah, I guess in this instance, it is.

So are you two gonna get married?

Girl, you ask a lot of questions. I just told you I like to keep my
private life private. But when I do actually get married, I'll be sure to
text you and let you know about it. How's that?

K. Don't forget. Maybe Lacey and I can dance at your
wedding!

Haha, sure. So, I guess you're planning on partnering up with Lacey?
Is that what I hear?

Well, I haven't talked to Ms. Val yet, and Lacey doesn't
know anything about it.

Well, I know Ms. Val is hoping you do. She sees a lot of potential in
you, girl. Lacey too. You stick with her and keep dancing the way
you do, and she'll take you far, I can promise you that.

What if Lacey can't or won't do it, though?

Well, you know her better than I do. What do you think she'll do?

See, that's the thing. We don't really know each other that
well. We only just starting talking some this past semester.

Why is that?

> We go to different schools, number one, and two, she was kinda mean, so we just danced and that's it. No communication, really.

Oh that's right! She goes to private school. I forgot.

> Yeah. Northern Collegiate High School. The rich kids' school.

Oh, is that what you call it?

> Yeah, I hear it's over 20 grand a year to go there. It's like the best Arts school on the West Coast.

Well, you know, just because kids go there doesn't necessarily mean their family is rich. There are a bunch of ways to go to private school. Scholarship, tuition assistance, payment plans, inheritance, some parents get a second mortgage on their homes. Spin.

> Yeah, I guess so. But trust me. Her family is rich. They don't act like it though. They're not all stuck up and snobby.

Well, that's good. I like humble people. And anyway, I've seen plenty of people lose it all in the blink of an eye. A few of my parents' friends lost everything back in the early 2000's, after 9/11.

> Oh really? We're starting to learn about that time. I was just a baby then.

Yeah, I was pretty young, myself. Okay, girl, you are all done. Now go on over to Candice and she'll dry this up. And don't ask her so many questions. Okay?

> Okay. Thanks Jhonae.

Damn, I look HOT! Look at this body paint! Oh good, more of the girls are starting to show up. They're going to love this!

Hi, Candice? I'm Brynlee. Jhonae sent me over to go under the dryer.

> Oh hi, Brynlee. I've heard a lot about you. It's nice to meet you.

You have? Uh-oh, I hope it wasn't bad stuff you heard.

> Oh no, hon, Jhonae loves you! She tells me all the time what an amazing dancer you are. Now I finally get to see for myself. Is this dryer too hot?

No, it's fine, thank you. Aww, she really said that?

> Oh, yeah! She talks about you, Lacey, and Carly a lot. The other girls, too, but mostly you three.

Oh, wow. Cool.

Yes. She was telling me how Ms. Val has high hopes for you. I'm excited to see you up on that stage tonight! And damn, you look great!

I know, Jhonae did such an awesome job with this body paint!
She really did. It shows off your killer curves!

Killer? Haha, I wouldn't say "killer".

Oh, I would! I'd give anything to have your little body, and I'm what, like ten years older than you? What are you, fifteen, sixteen?

I'm fifteen, but my birthday is coming up. I can't wait.

Oooh, sweet sixteen! I remember my sweet sixteen. Do you have special plans? Having a big party or going on a special date?

No, no special plans. I want to keep it low-key. My family might just go out to dinner, and I'll bring my best friend, Natalya-Blu.

Well, that's great! Natalya-Blu? That's an interesting name.

Yeah, she's from Poland. Her mom is a famous European actress, and they moved here when she got a part in a movie. I forget which one, though. And she also wanted to pursue Natalya's modeling career. She's gorgeous.

Wow! You're best friend is a model, her mom is a famous actress, and you're going to be a world famous dancer. Sweet!

I guess we'll see about that last part. So, Jhonae says you're studying holistic stuff. That's pretty interesting.

Yeah, it is. There's so much to learn. But I love it. And I love helping people get healthy the natural way.

Yeah, people take way too many drugs these days – prescribed and illegal.

They sure do. Okay, hon, you're all set. It was nice to meet you. You'll do great.

Thank you. It's nice to meet you, too.

She's so nice! I wish I had a big sister like her. That would've been so cool.

Brynlee, let's see your body paint. Nice! We almost match.

Oh my gosh, Lacey, we look so freaking hot right now.

I know! Hold on, we need a picture of this. Gotta post it online. Let's go over to that mirror.

I love this mirror. It's so huge! I need one of these in my room.

I know, right? Me too! I just have one of those ugly mirrors attached to the back of my door.

Oh, me too! It's all bent and warped and stuff. It makes me look odd-shaped.

Haha, right? Okay, smile.

Lace, you have to send me that. We look great!

Sure thing. There, it's sent.

Thanks. So, are you ready for this?

As I'll ever be, I guess. How about you?

Yeah, I think I'm ready. My Aunt Holly and Uncle Dave are here, so I want to really impress them. Oh, and Candice, too!

Oh my gosh, she's so sweet! She was saying how Jhonae talks about us all the time!

I know! She told me the same thing!

I wasn't sure how she'd be, though.

What do you mean?

I mean, she's a lesbian.

So?

I don't know. I guess I don't know too many lesbians, sooo... I don't know. Jhonae is the only one I know.

Do you not have gay people at your school?

I'm sure we do. I mean, it is an Art-focused school. To be sure there are gays there. They just aren't out, I guess. It's such a snooty school, and all the parents are so, I don't know, so snooty, like. God forbid one of them has a gay kid. You know?

Yeah, I guess. I mean, they're no different than us. They're just attracted to the same sex, that's all.

Yeah, I guess you're right. I'm sorry. Please don't hate me for that. I feel like I live in such a bubble. I hate it. I wanna switch schools so bad. But, at least the dance academy is normal.

Normal? You don't think it's a bubble of its own?

No, I mean, all the girls are from public school, with normal lives.

Well, I mean, I wouldn't exactly call public normal.

Typical, maybe, but not normal. Is there even such a thing as normal anymore?

I guess not. All I know is, my school isn't normal, and it's definitely not typical. It sucks.

I'm sorry, Lace. Maybe you can transfer.
I doubt it. But whatever. Let's focus on winning tonight.

Yes. Let's. Oh wow, look at those outfits! Those are hot!
Yeah they are! I like ours, too.

I don't. I mean, I do, but, seriously, I have my period, and these pants are white. And my boobs aren't big enough for this bra thing. But, then again, my Aunt Holly made a good point – if my boobs were any bigger, they might bounce out while we're dancing!

Oh my God! Could you imagine? How the heck is Jenna gonna keep hers in?

I don't know. Maybe she'll tape.

Yeah, maybe. Oh, look. There she is. Yup, looks like she taped. I feel like she did that once before because one of the outfits was really low-cut.

Probably. Hey Jenna! You need to go over to Jhonae and get painted.

Thanks, Brynlee. Wow, you two look so good!

So do you.

Thanks. My boobs are squished, though.

Yeah, we don't have that problem.

Be glad. I feel like I can't breathe. Hey, is that Jhonae's girlfriend? She's pretty.

Yeah, that's Candice. You'll get to meet her when you go have your paint dried. Hurry, so we can see what Jhonae paints on you.

Okay.

Seriously? Did she just tell us to be glad we have little boobs?

Yup. I mean, I guess it would be uncomfortable to have tape restricting your breathing. But still, I'd rather that, than look like a boy!

Well, I don't have that "problem" either. And my mother constantly reminds me that I need to lose weight. It's so annoying.

Really?

Yeah. Like, the other night before rehearsal, she was really blasting me bad, and that's why I was so upset. I guess I was trying so hard to zone her out that I didn't realize the rest of you stopped dancing.

Oh! Is that what happened? I was wondering, but you looked really upset, so I didn't want to make it worse. Oh, and then I saw the video!

Oh. The video.

Yeah, it was awesome! I can't believe Blake uploaded it!

I know.

Well, we all need to dance like that again, tonight. We do that and we will definitely win! Speaking of Blake, there's Carly. I wonder if he's here.

He said he was going to be here.

You talked to him?!

Yeah, he texted me to make sure I wasn't mad at him for uploading the video.

Oh my God, you're so lucky!

Nah, it wasn't like that at all.

Yeah, but he actually texted you. He is so hot.

I know! But he's in college, and you and I are just lowly little sophomores in high school. And he's probably got girlfriends galore, you know?

Yeah. But still, we can dream, can't we? And besides, in three years, it won't matter, because we'll be in college too, and he'll be looking at us then, for sure! Once you graduate high school, age doesn't matter as much, I don't think. Do you?

I sure hope not. You're so positive, Lacey. I like that about you.

Well, this is the new me. I was never like this, not at all.

Yeah, you were kinda mean.

I'm sorry. I've done a lot of growing recently, with the help of a little friend.

Oh really? Who?

Ummm, her name... is Lryic.

Cool name.

Yeah, she's definitely cool. And unique.

Unique? How so?

Well, she... ummm... She wears this cute little hat....

Ladies! Five minutes and we meet in Room B! Five minutes, ladies!

Alright! Are you ready, Brynlee?

Yes! You?

Absolutely! We've got this! This is our night! Let's go.

        Wait, I need to run to the bathroom real quick. Gotta make sure I'm well protected.

Okay, I'll come with you and check my makeup.

        Oh, it looks great, by the way. Nice color choice! You were right, it does look good with this outfit.

Right? I thought long and hard about it, and after looking online for cool makeup, I thought purple would be best.

        Well, good choice! I love it. Okay, I'll be right out.

Okay, I didn't realize she hates her school so much. That sucks. I wonder why her parents won't let her transfer to public. I can't imagine going to a school where everyone is so stuck up. It'd be like a school full of Samanthas! Ew. I'd vomit.

        Can you tell I have a pad on?

Turn around… nope. You're good.

        Okay, good

How's my hair?

        Looks great! Your makeup looks so good with your gorgeous red hair! How about me?

You are lookin' good, Brynlee!

        Thanks! We both look great!

Okay let's go. Room B?

        Yup. Holy cow, it's almost time!

I know!

Hello, ladies! Everyone looks fantastic! Brynlee, Lacey, great hair and makeup! I love that you two coordinated your looks. Jhonae did a great job painting everyone! I think we're just waiting on Peri. She's under the dryer right now. And ladies, let's all be sure to thank Ms. Candice for helping out tonight…

Alright, B, this is it. This little dream bubble is about to do whatever it does when a dream is caught. Are you ready, little dream bubble? Or should I say, bubbles? There's a bunch of them right here in this room, floating around with their pretty little wings, all about to be captured! Wow! Look at Peri! Really, how is one girl so freaking beautiful?

Damn, Peri! Look at you! You look freaking incredible!!

Aww, thanks, Brynlee, so do you! Your eyes look
gorgeous! Did you do your own makeup?
Yeah, I wanted to match Lacey. Look at hers, too.
Oh damn! God, you two look great!

Ladies, please, let's pay attention. I know we're all excited about
this, but we must remain focused. Like I was saying, we need to…

*Yes, focus. Oh my God, Blake is probably out there right now. Okay,
so what? He's just a boy. Just focus on the dream, B. Remember,
sass during the routine, big smile at the end. Give it your all. No
matter what, I will be proud of myself and everyone here. We've
trained hard for tonight, we blew Ms. Val away at rehearsal, and
apparently, I went viral, and still going. We've got this.*
Brylee, you're going to do great!
Thanks, Nova! I hope so! I always get nervous right
before we compete.
Well, don't worry about it. You are such a talented dancer, and
you have all worked hard for this competition. Just focus, and
get into your zone.
Yeah, the zone.
Oh, by the way, you girls all look fabulous!
Thanks, Nova. We do, don't we?
You do.

…and you girls will be just fine. I am proud of each and every one of
you. Just get out there and dance your hearts out. Okay, ladies, let's
get out there. We're up third.

Here we go...

Alrighty, here we go!

Brynlee, hold on. Are you good?
>Yes, Ms. Val.

Are you in whatever zone you were in the other night?
>Yes, I am.

Good. By the way, there's someone I'd like you to meet after the competition.
>Oh really? Who?

Oh, a friend of mine from out of town. He's very excited to meet you. He apparently saw a video that Carly's brother uploaded and wanted to see my star student for himself.
>Oh, okay. Man, everyone has seen that video! I need to talk to you after the competition is over, anyway.

Sure, is everything okay?
>Yup. Everything's fine.

Great. Now get out there and kill 'em!

I wonder who this guy is. Wait a minute. How'd he get a ticket? I thought it was sold out! Dang it! Natalya could've come if I knew there were still tickets available! Well, maybe the dance instructors get tickets too, for their family and friends. Who knows? Natalya's probably hanging out with the girls, anyway. Maybe she can come to the next one.

How is this first company, Lace?
>They're pretty good. The two girls in the back are making a lot of mistakes, though, and they just started.

Oh wow, that sucks.
>Yeah, but that's good for us. I can't find my parents out there. I see yours, though. Is that your aunt and uncle to the right?

Yup, sure is. Your parents must be on the other side.
>Yeah, must be. Your mom and aunt look like twins.

They do, don't they? They're not, though. My mom is older by a few years.

Well, they're both so pretty. You look just like them.
Aww, thanks. Aunt Holly is really cool. I'll introduce you to her after.

Okay, cool. Oh my God, did you see that? That blond girl totally screwed up. Aww, I feel bad. It looks like she's about to cry!

Oh man, that sucks so bad. Look at the judges. That one dude looks disappointed.

He really does. Holy crap, Bryn, I think I know that lady judge on the end! She looks like a sub at my school!
Ummm, is she nice?

No! She's a bitch! Well, then again, all the subs are. I swear I think they hate every one of us. I can't really blame them though.

Okay, well, maybe she's different outside of school. And if not, I hope she doesn't recognize you!

No shit, me too! Maybe all this makeup and hair will keep me incognito.

Let's hope so! Well, you know what? We're dancers at a dance competition. Surely she will be professional enough not to take her hatred for your school out on us.

Well, that's what I'm banking on. That, and that she doesn't recognize me. I wasn't the nicest person the past few years.

Ugh! Think positive, Lace. Let's forget about her and just focus on this routine.

Yes, let's. Okay, second company is up. Oh, those are the cool outfits! Wow, that looks awesome with them all out there like that. I bet we look that good.

Nah, we look better!
Definitely.

Hey guys, did you see that last company? There were like three girls who totally screwed up.

Yeah, we saw. What do you think, Peri, we've got this, or no?

Oh definitely! I mean, look at us!
Haha, yeah! Look. At. Us!

Damn, these girls are good! They're all in perfect synch. Holy shit! Did you just see that?!

Yeah, we saw. That was awesome. That's okay. We can still take this.

That girl in the orange top just screwed up!

What? I didn't see it, did you Peri?

No, I didn't. Are you sure, Lacey?

Yes! Totally sure. Look at Ms. Val. She's got that face on like someone just screwed up. See?

You're right!

Okay, I can't take it. I'm going back over there.

Okay, Peri, listen, just like at rehearsal.

Got it.

Oh my God, Bryn, do you think she'll be okay? She seems really nervous.

Yeah, she'll be fine. These girls are good.

They are. But watch that girl in the orange. She keeps making tiny mistakes, but I think the judges are catching them. See? There was another one.

I saw it! Okay, deep breath.

Okay ladies, we're up next. Remember to focus and breathe. Get out there and dance just like at rehearsal, and we'll come out on top, no doubt. No matter what, it's your attitude that counts the most. Win or lose, attitude is everything. Okay? And Jhonae and I are so proud of you girls. Now, get out there and make the rest of the world proud of you, too! Focus and breathe. Focus. And breathe. Go!

Holy crap, holy crap! Okay, breathe, Brynlee. Breathe. In through the nose, out through the mouth. Okay, here we go.
We've got this, ladies!
There's Lacey's parents. I wonder if she sees them. Wow, these judges look intense. That's okay. I'll look intense right back. Gotta have sass. Holy shit, I wanna puke!
Brynlee, breathe! You're going to hyperventilate!

I told you, Nova, I get really nervous!

You're going to do great! Just breathe. Get in the zone.

Ladies and gentlemen, our third competitors are from the Southwest side of...

Okay, this is it. Dream bubbles captured. One, two, three...

... Down down up, and three and four...
... Punch punch! HA! Nailed that move! ...
... YES!! ...
... Step step punch, pull cross slice...
... BAM! Hell yeah!! ...
... Step it back, step it back, down down up...
... And two and three and ... Mm-mm POW! ...
... And 180, bronco, clap, bronco, clap and BAM! Ow, shit! That hurt my wrist.
...And three and four and... stomp!
OH MY GOD!! Holy crap, I think we just nailed it!! Hahaha!! Look at the judges! They're all smiling! Damn, these people are going crazy!! Woohoooo!!

LADIES!!! YES!! That was AMAZING!! You girls totally nailed it!!

Oh my God, Lacey, we NAILED IT!
  Holy shit!

Lacey, Brynlee!! Those Broncos were FANTASTIC! And Jenna, excellent facial expressions and everything! Really, you all were fantastic! We're so proud of you! Jhonae?
  Yeah, girls, you KILLED IT out there!! Man, I knew it! I
  knew you'd nail it. Excellent! Oh my God, SO proud!! So
  proud!
Okay, let's head back into Room B and get some water, and we can come back out and watch the rest. Peri, walk with me... Honey you were amazing! I told you there was nothing to be...

Brynlee, we did it! Oh my God, girls! We did it!
  Yeah we did! I knew it! Did you see those judges? Even the
  one you think is a sub! She was smiling and everything!!
I know! How freaking cool was that?!
  Hey, did you see your parents?
No, I didn't. Did you?
  Yeah, they were sitting right up front, all the way to the left.
  They were beaming with pride!
Really, they were? Awww! I was so busy focusing and trying not to look at the judges while we were dancing that I didn't notice they were sitting there, right up front!

Yeah, I tried not to look at the judges, but I couldn't help it.
Hey Carly, great job out there!

Thanks, Brynlee, you guys too!

Thanks! Okay, sooo… now we wait. Damn, I can't believe it! We freakin' nailed that shit!

It feels so good to be over, though. I was nervous about those judges. Especially Miss Grump-ass! Hahaha! Watch, it's not even her.

That'd be hysterical. Oh Jeez, this water is like Heaven right now.

It sure is! Hey, look at Brooke. Why is she crying?

I don't know. I hope she's okay.

Me too. Hey, Lyndsay, why is Brooke crying? Is she okay?

Oh, I don't know. Let me go ask Taryn. Maybe she knows…

I hope she didn't hurt herself out there.

Yeah, me too. But we would've known, because Ms. Val would've said something right away.

Okay, Taryn thinks she's just breaking down after all the stress. No worries. She sometimes does that after a big test at school, too. Especially when she's PMSing.

Oh, okay, thanks.

Yup, no problem.

Wow, she's that stressed out, huh? Why have I never noticed that before?

I don't know. I haven't either. Weird. I'm glad I don't do that. My makeup would be a train wreck!

Okay, girls, we can head back out there now.

Jhonae, is Brooke okay?

Yeah, she's fine. Let's go watch the rest of the competition.

Brynlee, Lacey! Guess what I just heard!

What? What did you hear?

I just overheard Ms. Val tell Brooke she's gonna miss her.

What? Is she leaving?

I don't know. That's all I heard.

Where is she now?

I think she's fixing her face. Her mascara started to smudge a little.

Damn, okay, thanks, Carly.

We can't lose Brooke. She's too good. And we don't have that many seniors.

Yeah, I know. I hope she's not going anywhere. She did look upset, though. Not just stressed out, you know?

Yeah, I know. Damn! Lacey! Did you see what that girl just did?!

No, I missed it.

Okay watch these guys. They're really good.

Oh shit! That girl just fell! She's not getting up. What the heck?

It looks like she sprained her ankle on that landing. Damn, they're pulling her off. Here she comes, look out.

Holy crap, did you see how swollen it is already?

Yeah, that totally sucks. I guess she won't be dancing for a while.

Nope, guess not.

How many companies are left?

I don't know, like eight, maybe?

Oh my God! I wanna win and go see my aunt and uncle already! I'm dying to know what they thought! I need to sit down and just chill out for a bit. I can't watch anymore.

Okay, I'll let you know if anyone looks as good as we did.

Okay, thanks.

This chair looks good. Let me just sit here for a few. Oh my God, we were awesome! My wrist is a little sore from doing those broncos, but that's okay. I could go get some ice, I guess.

Jhonae, I'll be right back. I'm going to get some ice for my wrist.

Are you okay? Is it from the broncos?

I'm fine. Yeah, I think so. It's just a little sore, that's all.

Okay sure. You want me to go with?

Nah, I'm good.

Okay, well Ms. Val is still back there, so…

Okay thanks.

Oh damn, there's that girl with the ankle.

Hey, are you okay? That looks like it hurts pretty bad.

Yeah, it hurts like a bitch, but I'm fine, thanks.

Well, if it helps, you guys were killing it out there!

Oh, thanks. I hope I didn't just screw us.

I doubt it. I hope you feel better.

Thanks.

Shit, that ankle was huge! I wonder if she broke it! Here come the medics. Ooh, and that must be her mom and dad. The mom looks worried. I would be too. I don't think she'll be dancing any too soon. I wonder how Brooke's doing. Maybe she's still back here. Nope. But Ms. Val is.

Hey Ms. Val.

> Hi hon, what're you doing back here?

I came to get some ice for my wrist.

> Are you okay?

Yeah, it's just sore. But there's a girl from one of the companies that just went on that may have busted her ankle.

> Oh my!

Yeah, I stopped to see if she was okay on my way back here, and that thing was swollen pretty bad.

> Oh, wow. Do they need help?

No, the medics just got back here.

> Okay, the ice pack is in the cooler.

Okay, thank you. Hey, is Brooke okay? We noticed she was crying after our routine.

> Yes, she's fine. Although, tonight was her last performance with us. She didn't want everyone to know until after tonight, but her family is moving.

Far?

> Yes, to the East Coast. They're moving to New Jersey. But please, tell no one yet. She wants me to tell everyone after the competition.

Okay, sure. Wow, New Jersey? Why?

> Her dad's company just promoted him and he has to transfer to the East. He'll be in charge of the Northeast region for his company. I'm not sure what the company does, though. Oh, you wanted to talk to me? We have a few minutes before Brooke gets back. She went to redo her makeup.

Oh, yes, I thought about privates, and I'd like to go ahead and do it. I think Lacey and I will be great together.

> Oh my gosh, Brynlee, that's fantastic news! Oh, whoops!
> Did I just crack your back with that hug?

Haha, yeah, and it felt good!

> Oh, haha, good. Oh, I'm so thrilled right now. Now, we just

have to tell your parents and present the offer to Lacey and her family as well. But, we'll wait. I'll request both of your parents to be at the next class to do so. Okay? Let's just win this competition tonight.

Okay, sounds good.

Oh, Brynlee, yay!

She's so excited! Awesome! Now let's hope my mom and dad are just as excited! And Lacey and her family too. Oh, man, they're boarding her ankle up! That doesn't look good.

Hey, feel better!

It's broken. I won't be dancing for a while.

Damn! I'm sorry.

Thanks.

That totally sucks. Wow, that company coming off the stage looks excited. Let me ask Lacey what I missed.

Hey, what'd I miss?

Well, they just nailed their routine too.

Oh really? How good were they?

Really good. But I still think we were better.

Let's hope so. Oh hey, you know that girl they pulled off? She broke her ankle.

No way!

Yup.

Damn, that sucks. How do you know?

I saw her on the way to get ice, and I stopped to see how she was. Then on the way back I stopped again because the medics had her ankle boarded up. She said it was broken.

Damn.

Yeah. She was pretty cool, under the circumstances.

That's good.

How many more are left?

I think just two.

Ugh! Okay. The suspense is killing me.

Oh, I know, right?

I'm going to go sit with this ice.

Okay. Is it still sore?

Well, right now it's freezing, but yeah.

I'm sorry.

Thanks.

Good God, two companies left. I think this is worse than the suspense leading up to actually competing! It would be so awesome if we win this. We have to. Our routine was flawless! There's no way Ms. Val would've been so excited if we screwed up even a little bit. Her face would've shown it. But she was smiling and excited, and her arms weren't crossed like they are when she's in thought on how to fix something we mess up or don't get right. Man, this icepack is cold. Let me take it off for a few minutes. Ew, look at my stomach. I should sit up straight, maybe then it won't look like I have rolls. Nope, that didn't work. I still have gut hanging over these pants. Maybe I'll just stand. I feel so heavy, like I have concrete on my shoulders. What the heck? I really need to lose weight. This sucks. I mean, look at Peri. She's so skinny, and gorgeous. I want an ass like hers. Oh my God, it's like her and Taryn have the same exact body. That's so crazy. How does that even happen? Man, I'd give anything to look like them. God, I need to lose like 15 pounds. How am I supposed to get through Christmas break and not gain an ounce? Maybe I'll talk to mom about skipping Holiday dinner this year and just having, I don't know, salad. Like the salad with shrimp she made today. That was so good! The problem is the stupid cookies everyone bakes. Well, I'm not going to eat any. Nope. I'm not. Okay, is that the last company? Lacey, is that it?

> Yeah, they were the last ones.

Oh my Gosh, okay, time to freak out.

> > I know! I'm so… I don't know! Not nervous, but excited, but, ugh! I don't know how to explain it.

I know! Me too!

Alright, ladies, this is it! The moment we've been waiting for! The judges are tallying up the scores, so we should know any minute now. Remember, no matter what, we're so proud of you. Ooh, it looks like they're almost ready to announce. Fingers crossed…

Brynlee! What if…

> > What?

What if we don't win?

> > It'll be okay, Lacey. Because we ARE going to win!

Oh my God! Thank GOD! We didn't get third! Wasn't that the

company the girl with the broken ankle is from?
> Yeah. How did they get third? Well, good for them. She'll be happy.

Okay, okay, shhhh! Here's second!
> Holy shit! Okay, we're still in the running!! Man, those girls were good, too. Shit, if we don't win, then that means the third place team was better than us. There's no way!

Okay ladies! This is it!! The moment of truth…

"And now, the company that has won first place in 27th Annual West Coast Dance Competition goes to…"

OH MY GOD!! WE WON!!!!
> OH MY GOD LACEY!!

Let's go ladies!! Get out there!!

I can't believe it! We just got first place!! I'm so freaking excited right now! Oh my God! I knew it, I knew we could do it!! Oh my God, I'm crying right now. There goes my makeup!

"Congratulations, ladies! You put on a great performance, and a job well done! And congratulations to all the participants in this year's dance competition! We look forward to seeing you all…"

Oh my gosh! Hi Daddy! Hi Mom! Aww, Aunt Holly is crying! Oh crap, there's Blake! He looks sooo good right now! Ahhh! Okay, let's get off this stage and celebrate, already!

Congratulations, Brynlee! You deserve it!
> Thank you, Ms. Val!

Fabulous performance, Brynlee! You girls were ah-mazing!
> Aww, thank you Jhonae! And thank you for the great body paint!

You got it, girl. It was my pleasure. Now, let me find Candice…

Lyndsay, Taryn, we did it!!
> Oh my God, I know! I'm so excited! And girl, you nailed it,

like, no lie.
No, WE nailed it!

Yeah we did! Hey, we're gonna catch up to Brooke. Good job out there.

You too!

Oh wow, I almost forgot! Brooke's moving! I wonder if she's going to tell us in the room or at practice next week. Lyndsay and Taryn don't even know. That sucks. Aw crap, I left the ice pack on the chair. I should get it.
Oh, sorry, excuse me. Sorry.
Oh good, it's still here. I need to take some ibuprofen.

Hey, congratulations! You girls did a great job. You totally deserve the win.

Thank you! Congrats on getting second. Tough competition this year.

Yeah. See ya!

They were our biggest competition, I think. Well, from what I saw, anyway. They were really good. I don't understand how that one company got third. I mean, they were good, but that girl totally screwed up, and then broke her ankle! But I mean, there were other girls making mistakes as well, so, I don't know. There were definitely others who did better, I thought. Well, whatever. We got first place, and that's all I care about. I wonder who Ms. Val wanted me to meet.

Okay, ladies, fabulous performance tonight! Congratulations! We knew you could do it. Our competition was tough, and there were some really good companies tonight. But! Your hard work really paid off. I'm sure I speak for Jhonae, as well, when I say how very, very proud we are of each and every one of you. You all had a part in winning tonight. You each displayed remarkable talent out there. But don't let this win go to your heads! We have another competition in a few months, and I don't want anyone to get cocky and think we will win automatically. The next competition is a lot bigger, and our competitors will be a lot stronger. We've got a lot to do these next few months. Also, I have an announcement to make. Tonight was our last competition with Brooke. Her family, unfortunately for us, is moving across the country to New Jersey, and tonight was her last night with us. So, if you all would, please sign the card we have over by Jhonae and Candice, and give her one last hug. I'm sure many of you will keep in touch on social media and through texting, as will I, so we'll have to be sure to keep each other updated on what's going on. Brooke, you've been an amazing student. You are an extremely talented dancer, and I have no doubt in my mind that whatever dance company you join in Jersey, you will certainly bring excellence to their team. Selfishly, I do not want you to go, but I know you will grow, and hopefully we'll meet up and compete at Nationals in the Fall. We love you, hon. Good luck to you in all that you do. And congratulations on your graduation in June! Would you like to say a few words?

> Sure. I just want to thank you guys for being such a great group to dance with. I love you all, and I hope this isn't the last time we see each other. I do have the opportunity to graduate this month, so I think I'm going to. I really don't want to be the new girl half-way into my senior year. It sucks I'll miss prom, but hey, if I'm lucky, one of the guys from school here will ask me and I can fly home for it. Then I'll be sure to come visit. Thanks for making my last night dancing here so special. I love you guys. We did it!!

Oh, thank you Brooke! Ugh, I'm tearing up now. Okay, ladies, congratulations!

Oh boy, we're all crying now! Thanks a lot, Brooke! Haha, aww, I'm going to miss her. She's so sweet. I need to sign this card. Okay hmmm... "Brooke, thank you for being such a great friend and dance partner. I'm going to miss you in class and seeing you in the halls at school. Good luck in whatever you choose to do. We have to keep in touch. Keep dancing! Love ya! –Brynlee". I hate writing these things. I never know what to say. And of course I write a mini paragraph and everyone else will probably just write "good luck in NJ". Well, except for Lyndsay. She's her best friend. I wonder if she already knew but didn't say anything to anyone – including Taryn. Surely she told her best friends.

Aww, Brooke! I can't believe you're moving!
> I know. I still can't believe it.
So you think you'll graduate this month?
> Yeah, I'm thinking about it. I mean, I have all my classes

done that I need, and I really don't want to be the new girl with only a few months left. It's hard to make friends in high school as it is, let alone be totally new to the school, or the state, for that matter! I would've liked to be able to stay and finish school here, but my parents want me with them.

Really? I mean, can't you stay with family?

I could. My uncle and his new wife live in the same town, but my parents said they're newlyweds and don't need to become temporary parents to a teenager.

Ugh, that sucks.

I know.

What about grandparents?

They're here too… Well, they travel a lot. They're hardly ever home. I don't know. I'll keep begging them to let me stay with my uncle. His wife loves me and already offered without me asking or anything.

When do you leave?

We're supposed to leave the day before Christmas break, so I only have a few weeks to convince them before the next semester starts.

Oh, so why not come to dance until you leave?

Well, I don't want to mess up anything with positions.

Oh, yeah. Well I hope you can convince them to let you stay. It won't be the same without you here.

Thanks, Brynlee. That means a lot. Listen, keep striving. You're such a talented dancer. You're the best one in the class, if you ask me.

Oh, thanks, but…

No, really. I mean it. The other girls all look up to you. Even Taryn, Lyndsay and Peri. You might be young, but you've got what it takes. Don't ever stop, okay?

You either!

I really hope her parents let her stay. Hmm, who's that guy talking to Ms. Val? I wonder if that's who she wants me to meet. He's kinda cute, for an old guy.

Hey Lace, who's that guy?

I'm not really sure.

He's kinda cute, though.

Yeah, for an old guy!

Haha, that's what I was thinking!

He's got kind of a, hmmm, I don't know, a Johnny Cliff look to him.

Oh my gosh, he really does! Imagine if they were related?

That'd be crazy!

Bye Lacey, bye Brynlee!

See ya later, Peri! Hey, text me and maybe us three can hang out over break.

Yeah, that'd be great! Bryn, I'll see you at school Monday.

Yup, you got it! Oh, hey, great job tonight!

Yeah, you guys, too! Thanks. See ya.

Hey Brynlee.

Oh! Um, hi Blake. *Holy cow! Blake is talking to me right now! Ok, keep cool. Don't wanna look stupid or anything.*

You girls were great up there! Even better than the rehearsal I uploaded.

Oh, well thank you.

What happened to your wrist?

Oh, it's just sore. Probably from doing those broncos.

Damn, that sucks. They were awesome, though!

Oh my God, I can't believe I'm talking to him! And he said we were great! Can I just go ahead and die now? Thank you.

Well, congratulations on your win. Umm, I'll text you sometime. Later.

Okay, see ya.

Oh my God, Brynlee!! Blake hottie-pants came over just to talk to you!

I could absolutely die right now. Am I red? I feel like my face is on fire.

Yeah, you're a little red, not bad though. But did you hear what he said? He's going to text you sometime! I think he likes you!

No way. Don't be ridiculous.

I'm serious, Brynlee. He came over here to talk to you, not us, you!

And he snuck up behind us! I feel like all the blood rushed to my feet when I realized who it was! And of course, now my face is all red. I hope he couldn't tell I was freaking out. Nah, I doubt it. I couldn't even tell. You played it really cool. You did good. You HAVE TO text me as soon as he texts you, okay?

Don't worry. He won't text me.

Bryn! He just smiled at you! Did you see that?

Oh my God, he must know we're talking about him. Okay, stop looking over there!

Smile back!

No! That's creepy!

It's not creepy! It's flirting! Just flirt with the guy.

I can't! I feel stupid.

Girl, I am going to slap you. Just smile back. He keeps staring at you.

He does not. Stop it. *But wait, is he? He's sooo cute!*

Look at him.

Ugh! Thanks a lot! Now he saw me look at him.

That's because he was already staring at you! Jeez!

Okay, whatever. This is silly. Where the heck are our parents?

I don't know. Mine are probably outside shmoozing with the "rich and wealthies".

Rich and wealthies? There's a difference?

Yeah, you know… The people who act like they have money and the people who actually do have money.

Oh. Alrighty then. Well, I don't know what's taking my parents so long. My mother is probably on the phone talking to God knows who about God knows what. Hey, I think Ms. Val wants us.

Can I breathe yet?

Yeah, looks like she's waving us to come over.
> Let's go.

Brynlee, Lacey, I'd like for you both to meet my friend Alex.
> Hi. I'm Brynlee.

And I'm Lacey.
> Well it's a pleasure to meet you both. Very impressive
> moves you both have. Ms. Val told me how great you girls
> are, so I had to come and see for myself. I must say, I am
> quite impressed.

Thank you.
> Yes, thank you.

You had some tough competition tonight, but to be honest, you blew
them away, hands down.
> Yes, I told Alex he wouldn't be disappointed when he came
> to see you perform. I've been trying to get him to come to
> class and see you all, but the timing was just never right.
> He's a very busy man.

Oh? What do you do?
> I'm in the entertainment industry in L.A.

Oh wow! That's so cool.
> Yeah, you must meet a lot of famous people, huh?

I do, actually. But I also like to work with up and coming talent.
That's my favorite. Famous people can sometimes be a little…
pompous. I'm not a huge fan of pompous.
> Yeah, us either.

Well, ladies, it was great to finally meet you both. And
congratulations on an amazing win. You deserve it. Val, I have to get
going. I'll call you and we'll set up a time to discuss…
> Yes, sounds great. Thank you Alex. Safe trip back. Ladies,
> are your parents here? I need to speak with them both. Ah,
> but first, Lacey, can I talk with you a moment?

Sure Ms. Val.
> Brynlee, if you'll excuse us, I'd like to speak with Lacey
> about you know what.

Oh yeah, of course!

Well that guy was nice. Oh shit! I bet that was Ms. Val's friend that she told me about! Oh my God, if it was him... then we just basically auditioned for him! Ha! And we WON! Okay, B, don't get crazy. God, where the heck is my family? Almost everyone else is gone! Blake's still here though. Umm, and he is looking at me right now. Oh shit, he's coming over here!

Hey!
        Hi again.
I didn't think I'd get the chance to talk to you without other people around.
        Oh, well, here I am. Alone.
Well, here I am, not leaving you alone.
        Haha, that's okay.
So yeah, you were really great out there. And you look really... hot!
        Holy shit! Someone pinch me. He just said I look hot!
        Thank you.
Were you nervous? Carly was so nervous on the way here, I thought she was going to throw up in the car!
        Oh no, really?
Yeah. It was pretty funny.
        Aww, she didn't seem too nervous.
Well, she was.
        I think I was more nervous waiting for them to announce the
        winner than I was before we started dancing.
Yeah, I could see how that could be nerve-racking. I knew you guys were going to win. You were the best ones out there. I mean, there were a few others that were good, but you were great. Especially you, Brynlee. I really like watching you dance. You get so into it, like you're in another world. There's something about it that's so cool to watch.
        Really?
Yeah. Well, looks like we're finally leaving, thank God, because I'm starving.
        Oh, well, I hope you get food soon! *Okay, that was a stupid
        thing to say. Duh.*
Yeah, thanks. So, I'll text you.
        Okay cool.

Did that really just happen? Did he really just say he likes to watch me dance? I wonder if he'll actually text me or if... Oh thank God, my parents are finally here! Oh look, Lacey's parents are with them. Oh, Lacey! I wonder what she said!

Sweetie, congratulations! You were great!

      Yes! Congratulations, Brynlee! We are so proud of you! And Aunt Holly and Uncle Dave were blown away by your performance!

Thanks. Where are they?

      Oh they're waiting outside for us. They're chatting with some guy. You know Uncle Dave, he talks to anything that breathes!

Haha, yeah, I know!

      Sorry we took so long. We were talking to the Graysons.

Yeah, Lacey and I were wondering where you all were.

      Sorry, sweetie, Mr. Grayson and I were talking business.

Why, Daddy? I didn't know he's in the same field as you.

      He's not. We were just bouncing ideas off of each other about general business stuff. He's pretty cool. We may play golf next weekend.

Daddy, do you even play golf?

      No, hon, he doesn't. And neither does Mr. Grayson. But they think it'd be fun to go embarrass themselves out there with all the wanna-be professionals.

Oh, Mr. Grayson's trying to impress people?

      I hardly think either one of us will be doing any impressing. And if we do, it'll be with our comedic antics.

Honey, just be sure you and Bill don't accidentally throw the club and hit someone in the head!

      Yeah, Daddy, or knock someone out with the golf ball!

Ha ha ha, you two are quite the comedians, aren't you? Let's go say goodbye to Valerie.

Valerie! Congratulations. That was fantastic!

      Thank you, Kyle, Heidi. So, I was just telling Bill and Kelly that there's something I'd like to speak with you all about. If we could, I'd like to set up a meeting for this...

Brynlee! C'mere!

Well?

Why didn't you tell me? Oh my God! Is she serious?

Yes! What'd you say?

I said "of course I would!" But, I mean, my parents have to okay it first.

Yeah, mine too. Oh, Lace, I'm so excited! I'm glad you said yes.

I know! Me too! We're gonna be great together.

Did she tell you about her friend?

No, what friend?

Oh! Well… damn, looks like we're getting ready to leave. Ya know what, I'll just text you about it.

You can't leave me in suspense like this, Brynlee!

I promise, I'll text you after I get home from dinner.

Okay do NOT forget!

Oh, I won't. Trust me.

Okay, Bryn, let's go find your fans and get some dinner.

Please! I am so hungry, I could eat a cow.

Easy now, hon. You have to watch your figure.

Mother, please. I'm hungry.

Yes, but you don't want to binge while you're so hungry. It's not healthy, and you don't need to put on any more weight.

What are you talking about, Heidi? She hasn't gained any weight.

Kyle, she needs to be careful. She has a tendency to be a little bottom heavy.

That's ridiculous. Leave the girl alone. She's a growing teenager. She needs to eat.

Kyle, just hush and stay out of this.

See Daddy? I told you.

Sorry, Sweetpea.

It's okay.

What are you two whispering about?

Nothing, Mother.

Well, let's walk a little faster. They're going to lock us in here.

Good God, Mother, there are still plenty of people in here that they won't lock us in.

Oh look! There's Holly.

Aunt Holly!

Brynie-boo! You did AMAZING! Congratulations!

Oh, thanks Aunt Holly!

Sweetie, I never, in a million years, thought I would ever see you dance like, like a professional that we see in music videos! I mean, I knew you were good, but we never expected to see that you've come so far! Wow! I am still in awe. Dave too!

Where is Uncle Dave?

Oh, he's talking to some guy he met earlier. I don't know who he is. He doesn't have a daughter here or anything, but he is kinda cute.

Wait, does he have dark hair, and kinda look like Johnny Cliff?

Yeah, now that you mention it, he does resemble Johnny a little.

I met him! His name is Alex, and he's one of Ms. Val's friends from Los Angeles, and he's in the entertainment industry! He said he was really impressed with us!

Oh wow! That's great!

Oh, is that who Ms. Val wanted your father and I to meet?

What?! She wanted you guys to meet him, too?

Yes, but I guess we took a little too long.

Ugh!

What's wrong, hon?

Oh, nothing, Mother.

It's okay, Brynie-boo. Next time. Until then, let's eat. I'm starving! And I know you must be also. You girls sure did work up an appetite up there!

Yeah, I'm starving and exhausted. I think the stress made me more tired than the actual dancing and stuff.

I can't even imagine. Gosh, we're so proud of you.

Thanks, Aunt Hol. Oh, good, there's Uncle Dave!

Brynie-boo! That was incredible!

Thanks Uncle Dave.

Okay, we're all here, so let's go get some dinner. Kyle, do you mind driving? I'm starting to get a bit of a headache. I think the combination of the lights and the loud music did it.

Yeah, sure, honey.

Do you need some headache meds, Mom? I have some here. I guess I should take some, too.

Sure, thanks honey. Why do you need headache meds? Do you have cramps?

No, Mother. My wrist is sore.

Oh, sweetie, are you okay?

      Yeah, I'll be fine, Daddy. It's probably from doing those broncos.

What's a bronco?

      Oh, it's when I jumped down on both hands and jumped back up, you know, like a bull.

Oh, okay. Sorry, I don't know dance talk that well.

      I know, Daddy. It's okay. It's not like you have models doing it for photo-shoots or the marketing team when you're doing layouts in the conference room.

Yeah, I guess you're right, Sweetpea.

      Okay, what do you guys think about going to Cafe…

I have to text Natalya and let her know we won!

"Hey Nat! We won!!!!!!!!"

Oh my God, and I have to tell her about Blake!

"And Blake!!!"

"Natalyaaaaa!!!!!"

I wonder what she's doing tonight. I really wish she could've been there to see us win. Oh my freaking word, why do my parents have to argue about dinner? Café Bellissimo is fine. Why does my mother not like that place?

Mom, what's wrong with Café Bellissimo?

      I'm just so tired of Italian. Why don't we try that vegetarian restaurant?

I'm with Heidi, let's try the vegetarian place. I heard that was really good!

      Ooh no! Can we go to the Kabuki Grill? They have sushi!

Well, luckily, I was thinking ahead and made reservations at the grill, because somehow I knew that Brynlee would want sushi, and Dave would want filet mignon.

      Good thinking, Kyle! Thanks for looking out for a brother.

You got it, man. Sorry, ladies. You'll have to do the veg thing some other time.

      That's okay. Maybe we can go there for New Year's Eve lunch.

That sounds wonderful, Heidi. Just us girls. Brynlee, you too, okay?

      Sure. I like vegetarian food. It's really good.

Y'know, I thought about going vegetarian before. Maybe I should try it again. I hate the way they are so mean to the cows and pigs. They are so cute. I feel like you can look into their souls if you look at a cow's eyes long enough. They're such sweet animals, with their big ol' moos. Ew, that reminds me. We are supposed to be dissecting a frog in biology soon. I'm not sure I can do it.

"Yay!! You won! Omg, how was it? And what happened with Blake?!"
"It was great! We performed perfectly!" "Blake talked to me TWICE. He said he'd txt me!"
"Omg, r u serious?!"
*"Yeah. Lacey said he was staying at me!" "*staring. Ugh! Stupid autocorrect!"*
"See?! I told u he likes u!"
"Idk. It was weird tho"
"When is he gonna txt u?"
"Idk. But he said it twice!"
"Bryn, what if he asks u out?!"
"Don't get crazy. I'm sure he doesn't want to date me"
"We'll see" "what r u doing now?"
*"We're going to Kabuki Grill. Thnk God, im so hungey!" "*hungry! what r u doing?"*
"Nothing really. Just studying"
"k. I'll vidchat u when I get home. I have so much to tell u"
"K sounds good. Enjoy your dinner"
"Thx"
Oh, man, I feel like I can finally breathe! The last couple days have been nuts and so stressful. And now I can relax and just think about Blake. And Luke! I almost forgot about our double date with Luke and Dylan tomorrow night! Oh brother, I have nothing to wear. I wonder if Aunt Holly would wanna go shopping tomorrow to help me find something to wear...

Hey Aunt Hol, are you busy tomorrow?

       No, I don't think so, honey. Dave, are we busy tomorrow?
       We don't have anything planned, do we?

No babe, we're all clear, nothing on my schedule.
       Why, what's up?

Well, I was wondering if you'd want to go shopping with me to find something to wear for my double date tomorrow night. I don't have anything good to wear that I haven't already worn a million times.

Sure, I think that'd be fun. Where do you want to go?

I guess we could go to The Towne Centre, if that's okay.

Sure, sounds great. But, you have to let me pick out an outfit for you.

Sure, okay. I like your style so I guess I'm safe.

Well, it won't be my style, but you have to be open to anything, okay? Deal?

Ummm… Okay. Deal. *Oh Lord, what did I just agree to? Is she going to dress me like a freak? Or worse, like a freaking princess? Surely she wouldn't. I mean, it's Aunt Holly. She's cool enough not to torment me.*

Good, I'll pick you up around 10?

10? I'm a growing teenager, I need rest. How about 2?

No, no, no. Way too late. We're women. We need at least a few hours. How about 10:30?

Oh boy, okay. Mom, will you be sure to wake me up at 9 so I can get ready?

Sure, but I don't want any sass outta you about it. You asked me, remember?

I promise. No sass. Thanks Mom. Thanks Aunt Holly. Dad, are we almost there? I'm so hungry!

Yes, Sweetpea, we're just about there.

Thank goodness! I can't wait to have some sushi! And maybe a cheeseburger.

Easy there, Brynlee. You don't want to overdo it. You need to watch your figure.

Heidi, let the child eat. She's hungry. And she hardly needs to watch her figure.

All I was saying, dear, is that she needs to be careful. She doesn't need to put on extra weight, and then struggle to take it off later.

Still, she's fine. My little Sweetpea is perfect. And she's worked up an appetite, so let her eat, for crying out loud.

Ha! Twice in one night! See? He just needed to pay attention to what she says to me. I doubt I'll get the cheeseburger, but still, if I want one, why not, right? Besides, if I do actually become a vegetarian, I want to enjoy the last bit of meat I'm ever going to have. Man, this place is packed! Good thing daddy made a reservation! Otherwise, we'd never eat!

Alright, family, let's go! I hope our table is ready. I can taste the sushi already!

I'm going to explode!

My pillow! I love my pillow. I love my bed. It's so cozy! And I am so full I feel like I'm going to vomit. Although, it could be from all the water I drank, too. I must've peed 50 times tonight. I think I should go get some ice for my wrist. It's still sore. That's weird, because I took ibuprofen and everything. Did I come down on it too hard? Or maybe I landed wrong. I don't know. It looks a little weird. Maybe I should have mom and dad look at it. Eh, I'll wait until tomorrow and see how it feels. If it still hurts I'll have them take me to the doctor, but after I'm done shopping for my date. I really hope Aunt Holly picks out something decent for me to wear. I love shopping with her. She has the cutest style. It's different. I like that she doesn't dress like everyone else does. I mean, all the girls at school dress exactly alike. Well, except for the boho girls, and the hipsters. I guess I fall into a category in between those two. Where the heck is the ice pack? God, mom's got so much stuff in this freezer. Ah, finally found it. Sheesh! I'll just keep this on for like ten minutes, and then off for ten. I think that's how it goes. I should probably get a towel or something this time. Maybe then I'll be able to keep it on longer than three seconds. Maybe that's why it still hurts. I probably didn't ice it properly before. Oh well. Oh, I should vidchat Natalya. I have so much to tell her.

Hey!

      Congratulations, Brynlee! You must be ecstatic!

Oh my gosh, I can't believe we won! I mean, I can, but I can't. Y'know?

      Haha, I know what you mean. How good does it feel?

It feels fantastic! Tonight was just so surreal. I have so much to tell you, but I'm exhausted, so I'll talk quick to get you up to speed.

      Okay, go.

Okay. We nailed our routine. Some girl broke her ankle doing some crazy flip, but they came in third. Then, we found out Brooke is moving…

      Brooke? Brooke Dalton?

Yeah! Can you believe it? She's moving all the way to New Jersey!

Holy crap! Cross country?
Yeah! Crazy. But anyway, then Blake snuck up behind me and Lacey and was talking to us for a minute and said he'd text me sometime. Ms. Val introduced us to a friend of hers who is in the entertainment industry, but I'm not sure exactly what he does. He said we were great and then he left. I told Ms. Val that I'd do the semi-privates, she was psyched, and then while she was asking Lacey, Blake came over to talk to me again! Told me he likes watching me dance, said, again, that he'd text me, and then he left. Our parents came in, Ms. Val told them and Lacey's parents that she'd like to set up a meeting to talk to them about something. We left, had dinner, and now I'm home.

Shit, Bryn, that's crazy! What a night, huh?
You're not kidding! I'm so exhausted from all the stress and excitement, and this bed feels so good to lay in right now.

Well, you look exhausted. What's up with the ice?
Oh, I hurt my wrist somehow. I think I maybe landed too hard during the broncos.

Oh damn! Is it swollen?
I don't know, maybe a little. Hard to tell because I'm icing it right now. I'll have to see what it looks like in the morning. If it still hurts then I'll tell mom to take me to the doctor after I go shopping with Aunt Holly.

Ooh, you're going shopping?
Yeah, do you want to come with us? I'm sure Aunt Holly won't mind.

Oh, thanks, but I have to study.
But didn't you study tonight?

I did, but I need to study more tomorrow. You go and have fun. Are you looking for anything specific?
Yeah, I'm looking for an outfit for our date tomorrow night.

Oh, nice! I'm not sure what I'm going to wear. Do you have any idea what you're looking for?
Not a clue. Actually I made a deal with Aunt Holly that I would let her pick something out for me if she would go with me.

Cool, she has a great style. It's cute and sassy, with flair.
Is that what you call it? See, that's why you're a model for fashion magazines and I dance.

You're crazy. You have a cute style too, Bryn.
If you say so.

You do. It's a cross between hipster and hippie bohemian.
Funny, that's what I thought before!

Yeah. I like it. I like how you're not afraid to be yourself.

And you do you pretty damn good.

Thanks BFF!

Anytime BFF!

Alright, well, I should go. And you can get back to studying, even though you don't need to, Miss Smartypants.

Yeah, yeah, whatever. Vidchat me after you're done shopping so I can see what you're gonna wear. Maybe I can throw something together that'll coordinate with what you're wearing.

Okay, I will. Night.

Goodnight, winner!

"Winner". Gosh, that sounds so good. And my medal is so pretty.

"Hi Brynlee"

Holy crap! Holy crap! Holy crap! Blake just texted me!
So answer him!

Nova! Holy crap!

Yes, you've said that three times already. Remember, he's just a boy. And you've talked to him twice already today, in person. Remember?

I know! But I didn't expect him to actually text me! This is crazy shit. Why the heck is he texting me?

Well, you aren't going to find out anything if you don't answer him.

Ahhhh!! I'm so nervous!

What are you nervous about? You have already talked to him!

I know, I know. Okay. Can I do this on my own, please?

Sure. I'll just sit right over here.

"Hi Blake"
"How was dinner? Did you guys go out?"
"Yeah, we went to Kabuki Grill. You?"
"We went to Filet"
"Is that the seafood place?"
"Yeah. Do you like seafood?"

"I love seafood!"
"Well, maybe we should go sometime"

Holy shit, Nova! Did he just ask me out on a maybe-date?
       Yes, that's what it sounded like to me.
Oh my God, what do I say?
       I can't answer that for you.

"Sure, that'd be great"
"Well, I'll be back in town next weekend. You wanna go then?"

Nova! Oh my God! Did I just die? Did you see pigs fly past my window? Did hell just freeze over?
       Answer him before he thinks you're not interested!

"Sure, that sounds like fun"
"Cool. I'll text you during the week and we can figure out the details"
"Okay, sure"
"Congrats again :) "
"Thank you :) "

Okay, I need to screenshot this and send it to Natalya. She's gonna freak out.
       Don't forget, she's studying.
I know, but she has to see this. There, it's sent. I can't believe it. What just happened? Nova, pinch me, please.
       Why is it so hard for you to believe that Blake might actually like you?
I don't know. Why would he?
       Why wouldn't he?
Because, Nova, I'm a sophomore in high school. I'm not tall and skinny and beautiful. I don't dress like the other girls. I'm just – me.
       Did you ever stop to think that maybe he doesn't want to date someone who's just like everyone else? Maybe he likes the fact that you're unique. You're not afraid to be who you are, you don't follow the crowd to try to fit in. Not everyone likes that, you know. It's comical to me and the other dandies that for a generation who so

badly doesn't want to be average, girls who always try so hard to be better than everyone else, are all the same. They dress the same, talk the same, everyone's hair is the same. You all even want to have the same shape. Please explain that to me. Tell me what the thought process is behind the madness.

I never looked at it like that. I don't know, I guess we all want to be popular, we want people to like us. We don't want to be left out or made fun of, or bullied. We want the guys to like us. We want to get dates and have boyfriends.

But, do you want all that and at the same time lose your sense of self? Do you really want to look and dress and act like everyone else? Wouldn't that get boring? If all the boys were like that, you know, the same, how would you feel?

Yeah, I guess you're right. I guess it would get pretty boring.

What would anyone have to say about you that would be unique and special about you? "Oh, Brynlee, yeah, she's the one with the light colored Hamptonite jeans. The one with the long straight hair. The one who's size 6. You still don't know which one she is? Oh, that's because they all look the same." That just sounds so ridiculous.

Yeah, okay, it does sound a little ridiculous.

Of course, I'm not knocking light Hamptonite jeans or long straight hair, or even being a size 6 if that is who someone truly is. But if that's not the real person deep down inside, if you don't absolutely love the Hamptonite style or long, straight hair, and if you're naturally a size 12, then yes, why buy it, have it and strive for it?

Well, I don't really care about dressing like everyone else. But I do wish I was skinny like the other girls.

Why, Brynlee? You're so beautiful. Beauty comes in all shapes, sizes and colors. Embrace who you are. Embrace how you were created. You are not defined by one quality or characteristic, like the scar on your knee or your long brown hair – those things don't make you who you are; your shape and size don't make you who you are. You are what's in your heart and your mind, you are the soul your body encompasses. As we age, our bodies will deteriorate, but our souls continue to develop and flourish. Okay, it looks like right now is the perfect time to have our daily session.

Oh God, no.

Yes. Get up. Stand in front of the mirror.

Ugh!

"No effing way!!!!!!"

Ha! Saved by the text!

We're not finished. I will not let you out of this.

Okay, okay.

"Right?!?!"

"Go ahead, say it"

"Say what?"

"That I was right and u were wrong"

"Well, let's not get crazy, Natalya. Let's see if it actually happens first"

"Why would he ask if he didn't intend to take u out?"

"I don't know"

"Okay then"

"Ttyt"

I really don't understand how you can all be so positive about Blake.

Okay, Brynlee, let me ask you this. If this was happening with Natalya instead of you, what would you be telling her?

That he likes her.

Then why would you say that about her, but not believe it about yourself?

Ugh! Stop, okay? Just stop. I am not Natalya. Natalya is tall and skinny and beautiful. She is a model, for crying out loud! I am not her.

Does Blake know Natalya?

Yeah, of course he does. Why?

Then why isn't he texting her asking her out?

Can we just get this over with, please?

116

Sure. Stand in front of the mirror. Look into your eyes. Repeat after me: I am beautiful.

I am beautiful.

I am beautiful no matter what size I am.

I am beautiful no matter what size I am.

My appearance does not reflect my worth.

My appearance does not reflect my worth.

My appearance does not reflect my true beauty.

My appearance does not reflect my true beauty.

I am beautiful on the inside, therefore I am beautiful on the outside.

I am beautiful on the inside, therefore I am beautiful on the outside.

I am beautiful.

I am beautiful.

There, how was that?

Fine.

How did it feel today?

Fine.

I see that you are a little irritated, but that's okay. We are making progress. You didn't cry this time.

That's because I'm pissed off.

Why, because I am right?

Whatever, Nova. I'm going to sleep. I'm exhausted.

Goodnight, beautiful Brynlee.

Goodnight.

I wish I could believe those words. I wish I could believe that I'm beautiful, that I'm good enough. I just want to be good enough.

Am I still dreaming?

"Good morning"

Oh my God, who is texting me so early? It's only 8 o'clock! Who the heck is even up this early on a... Blake?! "Good morning" Holy shit! Ummm...

"Good morning"
"Did I wake you up"
"Lol, yeah. But I have to get up anyway"
"Oh, sorry"
"It's ok. Not a problem"
"I couldn't really sleep last night"
"Apparently, lol. How come?"
"Well, I was thinking about you up on stage"
No freaking way! Is he serious? Am I still sleeping? This is a dream, right? "You were?"
"Yeah"
"Cool... I think"
"Yeah. It is"
"Sorry I kept you up! What were you thinking about?"
"Just how amazing you were up there"
"Thank you. :) "
"You seem different"
"Different? How?"
"Idk. More confident"
"Confident?"
"Yeah. It was cool to watch."
"Thanks"
"I can see it in your eyes too"
"You can?"
"You have beautiful eyes"
"Aww, that's sweet"
"I guess that's mostly what I was thinking about"
"My eyes kept you awake?"
"Corny, I know"

"No it's not. It's sweet"

"So, are you dating anyone?"

"No. Going on a double tonight, but not legit dating anyone"

"Oh cool"

"I mean, not really"

"Lol, no, I mean I don't wanna text you if you have a bf"

"Oh, no, you're good. No bf here. How about you? Got a gf?"

"Nah"

"Really? I would've thought you had a bunch of girls in college?"

"No, they all party too much. I'm not into that type"

"What type are you into?" *Did I really just ask him that right now? What the heck was I thinking?!*

"I like laid-back, confident girls who know what they want and go after it"

"That's cool. No one at your school like that?"

"None I'm interested in"

"I'm sorry"

"Don't be. I've got my eye on someone"

"Well that's good"

"Yeah. We'll see how it goes though"

"Well, I'm sure you won't have a problem getting her"

"Why do you say that"

Why did I say that? How do I answer this without looking like a groveling idiot or a love-sick teeny-bopper? "You're a good-looking guy, you're not an asshole, you have goals…"

"Glad to know I'm not an asshole! Lol!"

"Lol"

"So, you think I'm good-looking, huh?"

Oh my God! SO freaking hot! "Actually, I do. I have for a long time" *Ugh! Why did I just send that?!*

"Good to know" "I think you're pretty cute" "very, actually"
AHHHHHHHH!!! *HOLY SHIT!!!*

Brynlee? Are you okay?!

       Yeah, Daddy! Sorry! I thought I saw a spider on my bed!

Oh, okay. Did you get it?

       Yeah, I got it!

I got it, alright! Holy crap, okay… "Wow, thank you"

"You seem surprised"

"I guess I just never thought you'd think I was cute"
"Why not?"
Okay, B, sound confident. He likes confident girls. Be very careful how you answer this one. "Because I'm just a sophomore"
"That doesn't bother me" "You're still cute. And a really great dancer"
"Aww, thank you"
"Well, I should get in the shower. Family day today"
"Yeah, have to get ready to go shopping"
"Sounds fun"
"Yeah"
"Well, I'll text you later, if that's ok"
"Totally ok"
" :) "
" :) "

He thinks I'm cute?! And confident?! And he's not dating anyone! And neither am I! I seriously can't believe that Blake Carrington texted ME because he was up all night thinking about ME! Little sophomore ME! Why, I don't know, but WHO CARES! He is SO HOT, and he's nice, and he thinks I'm cute, and... annnnnd I have a date tonight with Luke! Ugh, do I even want to go now? Yes, I have to go. Natalya-Blu will kill me if I don't go. She likes Dylan and if I blow this for her she'll never speak to me again. Besides, Luke is so cute. How do I go from having zero guys in my life to all of a sudden having two? I mean, I don't actually HAVE anyone, but, well, ugh. Blake didn't seem to be bothered that I'm going on a date, so that's good. Wow, what if I had to choose between Blake and Luke? Who would I choose? They're both so cute. I'd never see Blake, since he's in college. Oh, but I've liked him forever! And his family is so sweet. I don't know anything about Luke's family at all, and I don't really know him, either, except he dated Samantha. Ew. Makes me wonder why he asked me out on this date to begin with. Is it because of the video? He's never shown any interest in me before. He's been gaga over stupid Samantha since 7th grade! Well, he's either a popularity chaser or he thinks he can get something out of me. He can forget that! I am not a slut, and I don't intend to be a slut. This girl is not that desperate for attention from some stupid boy. Wow, was my mom like that with her ex? Did she stay with him because she was desperate? Why would she have been? My mom was so beautiful *back then. I mean, she still is, but, I mean... What was it about that asshole that she was so needy for him? I will not be like that. I will not marry an asshole. Heck, I won't even date one. I really hope Blake doesn't turn out to be one. Is that why he's single? Is that why none of the college girls are with him? Or are they really party girls and he really isn't interested in that? Surely there are girls there that don't party all the time. He did say he wasn't interested in any of them, but why? Are they not pretty enough? Are they too fat? Why on earth is he texting me?* I swear this all just seems like a dream, and I haven't really woken up yet. Let me look at my phone one more time and see if it really happened. Yes! It really happened!*

Knock knock
Brynlee, are you on the phone?
> No.
Oh, who are you talking to in here?
> Oh, just myself.
You're up pretty early.
> Someone texted me and it woke me up.
Oh, okay. Do you want breakfast?
> No thanks. I'm going to jump in the shower and get ready before Aunt Holly gets here. I'll eat before we leave.
Well, you've got plenty of time since you're up an entire hour before you wanted me to wake you. There's fresh fruit I just cut up, and if you want there's cereal or I can make you some scrambled or hard-boiled eggs.
> Okay, thanks mom. I'll probably just have some fruit and almonds.
Okay, but not too many almonds. They're high in fat.
> I know.

I have to do some reading up on this "fat" stuff. All this information is so confusing. Some say you need fat, some say fat is bad for you. Carbs, no carbs, gluten, no gluten. What the hell is gluten, anyway? And why are we hearing about it all of a sudden? Did Grams and Gramps ever hear of gluten when they were growing up? Is it something that affects how big your butt gets? Gluteus Maximus, gluten... I don't know. But I'm definitely researching this stuff, and vegetarianism. I think there are a few vegetarians at my school. I should talk to them about it. Hmm, I think Sophia a vegetarian. I'll ask Natalya.

"Morning! Hey, is Sophia a vegetarian?"

What time is it? Oh, whoops! It's only 8:25. I bet I just woke her up.

"I have no idea. Why are you asking me this at 8:25 on Saturday morning?"
"Sorry. Blake texted me at 8 and I've been up ever since."
"Blake texted u again?!"
"He did!"
"Damn, Bryn! He must really like you!"
 "He said he couldn't sleep last night bc he was thinking about me!"
"OMG!! Are you serious?!"
"Totally!" "He asked if it was ok if he texts me later!"
"I hope u said yes!"
"Duh! Of course I did!"
"Wow! So cool!"
"Well, sorry I woke you up. I'm gonna jump in the shower"
"Ok text me later"
"Ok"

Whoops! It's okay. She still loves me. Well, I guess I should get in the shower and get ready to go. Such a good day already, and it's not even 9am! I love when that happens! Let's hope the rest of the day is just as good.

She's so wise...

Okay, Aunt Holly, I'm ready.
     Good, let's get this party started!
Let's do it! Bye Mom!
     You two have fun!
So Brynie, where shall we start?
     I guess The Towne Centre is a good place to start, what do
     you think?
Sounds good to me!
     Can I ask you a question, Aunt Holly?
Sure, what's up?
     Well, I've been thinking about becoming a vegetarian. What
     do you think?
Oh, really? What made you think about this?
     I don't know, really. I guess because I want to lose weight.
Sweetie, you don't need to lose any weight. You look great just the
way you are.
     Well, Mom thinks I need to lose a few pounds, and I kind of
     agree with her.
From what I can see, Brynie, if you lose any weight, it'll be muscle.
You definitely don't want to lose muscle. And you don't have any fat
to lose.
     Well, you haven't seen me naked.
No, I haven't. But I have seen you in a bathing suit and in those
skimpy outfits for dance, and you are all muscle.
     I just hate the way my legs jiggle when I walk, and when I
     sit, I have fat rolls.
Fat rolls? Let me see.
     See?
Honey, that's skin.
     It is not.
Yeah, it is.
     Whatever.
Ok, listen, if you're serious, you should do some research first. There
are plenty of unhealthy and overweight vegetarians and vegans out
there. Just because it's labelled vegetarian or vegan doesn't mean it's

healthy for you.

Are you sure?

Absolutely. There are cookies out there that are considered vegan, but they are still fattening because of all the sugar and preservatives in them. Maybe what you should consider, instead, is a healthy diet, and I don't mean diet like restrictive, starve yourself diet like people talk about. I mean a dietary lifestyle.

Oh? Like what kind of diet?

Well, first let me ask you this, is losing weight the only reason you want to become a vegetarian?

Umm, I don't know. I mean, I don't really like the fact that those cute little cows are hurt so we can eat, but it doesn't bother me enough to not eat steak, you know what I mean?

Yeah, I do. I feel the same way. There are people who feel very strongly about it, and those are people who are ethical vegans. And that's okay, too. It's a matter of personal beliefs and opinions, and sometimes religion.

Oh, okay.

Also, there are many types of vegetarians.

There are?

Yes. There are lacto-vegetarians, who don't eat animal products except for dairy, like milk, cheese, butter, ice cream. Then there are ovo-vegetarians, who eat eggs, but no meat, then there are lacto-ovo vegetarians who eat eggs and dairy, but no meat.

Oh wow, I didn't know that.

There are also pescatarians who eat fish, but no other animal products, except maybe eggs, or dairy, or both, but no chicken or beef or anything. But a lot of people don't consider that a true vegetarian. Then you've got flexitarians, who eat meat products occasionally, but not all the time.

How do you know all this stuff?

Well, I have a good friend, Liz, who is a vegan, and we talk about it a lot. I'm considering changing my diet as well.

You are? What kind of change are you thinking?

Well, after talking to Liz, and doing some of my own research, I want to transition into an almost whole foods plant-based diet.

What is that?

Well, it's when you eat no processed foods, you eat lots of fruits and veggies, beans, and whole grains like quinoa and brown rice.

What about pasta and tortillas?

Sure, you can eat those too. I want to learn how to make my own from scratch. But that's why I say ALMOST whole foods plant-based. There are some things I love that I don't want to give up completely, like salmon and cheesecake. You know how much I love cheesecake!

Oh, I know! But it's so good, how could you not love it? Exactly! I don't want to put a label on myself, so basically, I'm going to eat as healthy as possible, without being obsessed or obnoxious about it. So, I'm cutting out all the packaged foods that I possibly can, I gave up red meat already...

What's wrong with red meat?

Well, some say it's bad for you, some say it's fine. There are a lot of farmers who feed their cows, and other animals, an unnatural diet, so meat is a lot different than it used to be. So unless we buy meat from a farmer who lets his cows roam free in the fields and eat what cows naturally eat, I don't buy it for Uncle Dave. The same thing with fish. Unless it's "wild caught", I don't buy it.

Oh. Wow, that's a lot of stuff to know.

I'll talk to your mom and see if it's okay if you watch a few documentaries with me about the food we eat, and if it's okay that I help you do research. Then you can make your own decisions. But only if it's okay with her. It's a huge undertaking to change your lifestyle from all you've ever known your whole life. That's why there are so many girls your age who are vitamin deficient and unhealthy. They jump into a lifestyle without knowing all there is to know. You're still growing and developing. You need proper nutrition, and without it you can get very sick. But, then again, humans are getting very sick from eating the way we do, not knowing that the food we eat is making us that way because of GMO's and sugar and chemicals and stuff.

What are GMO's?

GMO's are genetically modified organisms. They are genetically engineered food, artificially manipulated. Many studies have proven GMO's are bad for our health, and many countries around the world have banned them. Some still say they're okay, but I think there's still too much controversy. But, that's a lot to get into. We can learn about that later, okay? First let's learn about what type of diet you want to follow. The main thing is to focus on being healthy, not skinny. Okay? There are a lot of women who are skinny and not healthy, and there are a lot of women who are not skinny, but are super healthy. If you are healthy, your body will function properly, heal itself faster and easier, and your skin and hair will be radiantly beautiful. Eating a proper healthy diet for your body will keep your body the size it's meant to be. Of course, exercise in necessary too, but you get plenty of that with all the dancing you do.

      Thanks Aunt Holly. I don't think I could ever talk to my mom about this stuff. She's usually too busy, and she rags on me all the time, anyway.

What do you mean?

      She puts me down a lot, telling me I need to watch my weight, and I just can't talk to her like I can talk to you.

I noticed she said something about your weight last night. Sweetie, your mom loves you so much. She had a hard few years before your dad came along. She's afraid you'll end up like her.

      I know, but it hurts when she talks to me like that, and when she compares me to my best friend and stuff.

I'm sure it does. Have you tried telling her that?

      No. We just fight and argue.

Well, maybe you should try.

      I don't know. We'll see.

In the meantime, I'll talk to her about this healthy lifestyle change, okay? It's something we can all do together. But, you may have to learn a lot more than you think.

      Like what?

Like how to cook. Not everyone agrees with healthy living. And if my sister is one of those people, you're going to have to take responsibility for yourself in that area, with your parents' permission, of course.

      Well, I'm sure Daddy will be fine with it.

Probably. But I don't think he'll want to give up that filet mignon!

      Haha, no, probably not! He and Uncle Dave love their filet!
      Especially if it's surf and turf!

Yeah! Seafood and steak, their ultimate feast!

      Don't forget the baked potato smothered in all that stuff!

Exactly. Yeah, it may take us a while to get everyone on board with us.

      If we ever do! Hey, let's go in here and see what they have.

Yeah, sure. Well, at least we have each other.

      Thanks, Aunt Hol.

I'm glad you feel comfortable enough coming to me about things.

You know you can talk to me about anything, right?

     Yes, I know. Thank you.

Even boys, and sex and all that. What do you think of this cute dress?

     Ugh, don't worry about that. I'm lucky I can even get a date! Nah, too girly.

Sweetie, don't rush it. Boys bring so much drama to our lives.

     Oh, I know. But guess what!

What?

     This really hot guy, Blake, whose sister is in my dance class, texted me this morning because he couldn't stop thinking about me last night!

Oh really? What about this?

     Ooh, that's cute! And, yeah, I thought I was dreaming!

What's his deal?

     Well, his sister is Carly. He's a freshman in college.

A freshman, huh? Don't tell Uncle Dave about him! He'll want to beat his ass!

     Haha, I know! He's really nice, and sooooo cute!

Well, just because he's cute doesn't mean…

     Doesn't mean he's not an asshole, I know. But he's not. Not so far, anyway. He never seemed to be. I've liked him for a while now, but I didn't think he'd be interested in me because I'm like three years younger than him. He's 18, but he has a late birthday, so he just turned 18.

Well, that's not horrible, I guess. You are almost 16, so that's not so bad. How about that shirt with these pants?

     Yeah. I was worried he wouldn't want to date a sophomore in high school. But then again, we're not dating, so…. That might look cute together, with a cool pair of boots!

Well, just take it slow. No need to rush things. Yes, definitely boots.

     Yeah. Exactly. Besides, I need to focus on dance. I've got goals.

I like to hear that! Young women need goals and dreams to shoot for.

     Yeah, I don't want to end up stuck in life with no direction, no career, working at some stupid job I hate for the rest of my life.

That, my dear, is some very intelligent thinking. My niece is a very wise girl!

Well, I just see kids who graduated high school and they didn't go to college, and that's okay, except they get these jobs that suck, they hardly make any money, some of them are drunks or whacked out on drugs half the time, and they have zero direction or motivation to do anything in life. I feel bad for them, because there's so much out there. I want to see the world, experience all that life has to offer, meet amazing people and do amazing things! I don't want to get to be an old lady and look back on my life and wish I did things differently, or wish I could've given my kids better.

That's pretty deep for a fifteen year old.

Well, I look at my mom, and I don't want to be like her. She's always talking about her ex and what a jerk he was, and I think she regrets that part of her life.

He was a real jerk. But he's gone now, and she's much better off. And she has you!

Yeah, but after all this time, she still talks about him. Did you know he used to beat her?

Yes, I know. That was a very hard time for a lot of us, not just her. Of course, she had it the worst, but it's extremely difficult to watch someone you love go through it and not be able to do anything about it.

Why couldn't you do anything?

Well, she didn't want us to. She didn't want to leave, until the beatings started to happen. Abuse, whether it's emotionally, physically, or even mentally, is sometimes hard for people to leave, because they think it's their fault, and if they could change "that one thing" or "those few things" about themselves, the abuse will stop. Sometimes, the victim even thinks they can change the abuser. Unfortunately, none of that stuff is correct. An abuser has issues that they need to address with professional help, otherwise, it won't stop. The emotional and mental abuse and manipulation is worse, in my opinion.

Why?

Because that stuff stays with you. If the victim being physically abused leaves for good, the abuser doesn't hurt them physically anymore. Although, it still takes a toll on them mentally and emotionally. Mental and emotional abuse, and manipulation are more psychologically damaging. It really changes the way the victim thinks about themselves. And, it happens constantly. Of course, I'm not a professional, so I don't know for sure, but that's what I've witnessed. But your mom is safe now, with a wonderful husband and a beautiful daughter. She couldn't have gotten a better family if she tried.

We are great, aren't we?

You really are! The best! Why don't you try this stuff on, real quick?

Okay. Be right back.

Wow, I actually look cute in this! Sweet! Now if I can just find a nice pair of brown boots, that'll look hot. I have to look good for this date tonight.

How does this look together?

Oh Brynlee, that looks great! Do you like it?

I do.

Well, let's get it, and if we see something you like better, we can return it.

I thought you were going to pick out my outfit for tonight and I had no say?

I changed my mind. It's more fun with both of us picking stuff out together. Besides, I can do that for Christmas.

True. Okay, let's get it. Thank you.

You're welcome. That really looks adorable.

Yeah, now I just have to find the right boots and accessories.

We have plenty of time to do that.

Okay, I'll get dressed. Be right out.

Aunt Holly is so cute. I can't believe we're both thinking about vegetarianism! That's so crazy! Well, I'm glad, because with all that information, I'm going to need her help. I highly doubt Mom is going to be all into it, though. Whatever. Then I'll just learn how to cook, that's all. Lemme hurry so we can keep shopping.

Alright, here you go. Let's go find you some boots and accessories to go with this.

Thank you. There's a shop with really nice shoes and boots down there.

Cool, let's go. So, tell me about this boy you have a date with tonight.

      Well, to be honest, I don't know him all that well. Believe it or not, after all these years of going to school together, we've never been in any of the same classes except PE, and we didn't talk much.

Really? Crazy.

      Yeah. He seems pretty cool, I guess. He used to date Samantha, the biggest bitch in school, but they aren't together anymore.

The biggest bitch, huh?

      Yeah. I don't know how anyone could tolerate her enough to date her for so long, but he did, amazingly enough.

Well, love does strange things to people, or at least, what they think is love, anyway. Sometimes it's good, and sometimes it's not.

      Yeah, I can imagine.

So is this boy, what's his name again?

      Luke.

Is he into sports and stuff? Or is he a gamer?

      He's on the football team at school and he plays soccer. He's nice, but I don't know if it's fake or not, yet. His best friend, Dylan, likes Natalya. His grades are decent, and he's been on the honor roll most of the time. Other than that, I don't know.

Well, at least you know that much, right?

      Right.

What are you guys going to do tonight? Anything fun?

      I have no idea what we're doing. I haven't talk to anyone about it yet.

Oh, well, there's supposed to be this really good movie that just came out last night about a girl who…

      Oh, you mean the new one with Alicia Madden?

Yes! That's the one!

      Yeah, I don't think the guys are going to want to go see a chick-flick.

Haha, true.

      I think we're just going to let them decide. We don't really care what we do, as long as we do something and not just sit home all night.

Yes, I know that feeling. What do you think of these boots?

      I'm not really a fan of that color brown. Looks a little like mushy dog crap.

Ew, okay, what about these?

Yes! Those are hot!

Okay, let's get your size. So, this Dylan kid likes Natalya, huh?

Yeah, seems like it.

Does she like him too?

Yeah, a lot. She's liked him for a while.

Well that's good, they finally get to hang out.

Yeah, I don't really know why they never got together before this. I heard a while back that he likes her. And he hasn't dated anyone in a while, so I don't know. He's pretty cool, though. He's on the football team, too.

Ooh, Bryn, those look nice! What do you think?

Oh my God, I LOVE these!

Okay, perfect! Let's get 'em.

But Aunt Holly, they are so expensive!

So?

So, I don't want you to spend that kind of money.

Why not?

Because. That's a lot of money for a pair of boots.

Listen, until I have kids of my own, I will spend whatever I want on my favorite niece. And after I have kids, you can babysit for free sometimes, how's that?

Deal! Thank you sooo much!

Anytime, sweetie. Now, we still have to accessorize your new ensemble, and then we can get some lunch. What are you in the mood for?

Oh, I don't know. What's a good choice for our new dietary lifestyle?

Well, we can have sushi, we can go to that salad place, or we can go to that vegetarian restaurant we wanted to go to last night.

Shouldn't we wait for Mom to come with us?

Yeah, I suppose we should. And you just had sushi last night, so do you want to try the salad place, or we can go to the Farmer's Market Café. I hear that place is good, and all their food is organic and comes straight from the local farms. I think they even have a vegan menu.

Oooh, yeah, let's try that place!

Okay cool. I'll call and make a reservation.

*This will be cool. I get to try out a new restaurant for my first
lifestyle change with someone who knows what they're doing. I hope
the menu has good choices. I really don't want to eat something like
liver or whatever. That crap is so gross. Ugh, when grams made liver
for Thanksgiving that one year, I thought I was going to puke all
over the table! Ooh, look at that cute necklace! It's so bohemian!
Oh shit, never mind. It's $110! Ooh, I like this one better. Please
don't be expensive... Yes! It's only thirty-five bucks! I can buy it so
Aunt Holly doesn't have to spend any more money. She's spent
enough on me today, and we are still going to lunch!*

Okay, reservation's set for 12:30. We still have plenty of time before
then to find stuff.
   Cool. Hey, what do you think of this necklace?
That is too cute. I love the colors. It'll look so pretty on top of that
white shirt you just got. It'll stand out nicely.
   Or, do you like this one?
That's pretty, too. I don't know, it's a tough decision. They're both
so cute and would look great. I tell you what, let's just get them both.
   Oh, no, I'm buying this time.
No ma'am. Today is my treat. Don't try to argue, either.
   But, Aunt Holly...
Nope. My treat. That's final. That'll just be one more free
babysitting night I get! There's a method to my madness, you see.
It's like I'm pre-paying for babysitting services while I have the
money!
   Ugh! You better have kids soon. I'll be leaving for college
   in two and a half years, you know.
Oh, I know. You're growing up way too fast for my happiness. But
then again, shopping is way more fun than playing with dollies.
   What? I never played with dollies!
And thank God for that!
   Okay let's get out of here before I find more stuff I have to
   decide between.
Okay. There's a shop upstairs I want to check out. It's a little fancier
than the last store, but I really think you'll like it. They just opened.
   What kind of stuff do they have?
They have dresses, pants, and all that. You'll see.

   This place is nice! But I think they're going to be really

expensive. Are you sure about this?

Yes, let's look around. Bryn! Look at this dress! It would look amazing on you! You have to try it on.

Wow, that is drop-dead gorgeous! How much is it?

Would you please stop worrying about how much stuff costs and just try it on?

Ugh, okay. It's seriously so pretty.

Let's see what else there is. Wow, this store is so you!

I know! I'm so excited! Oh my God!

Okay, this would look cute on both of us. We should try it on and maybe we can twin.

Aww, yeah! Let's do it.

Welcome, ladies. Can I bring these to a dressing room for you both?

Sure. Thank you.

No problem. Are you still looking around? We have another room in the back with more formal attire.

Thank you, we're still looking.

Oh, you've picked some great things here. This dress is gorgeous, and I think it'll look fabulous on both of you. We also have it in deep purple. Would you like me to get your sizes in that color as well?

Sure. Thank you.

No problem. I'll have these waiting for you in the dressing room.

Thank you.

Aunt Holly, the deep purple would look so pretty with your hair color.

Yeah, you're right. Maybe we can sorta-twin. I'll get the purple and you get the red.

Well, hopefully it'll look as good on as it does on the hanger.

Let's hope so. I really like it.

I know, me too.

Do you see anything else you like?

I see a lot of stuff I like, but that dress!

Yeah, I agree. Let's go try them on.

Okay. Let's do it.

Well? How does it look?

I don't know, I don't have it zipped yet.

Wow, I love it. Hurry and come out so I can see it on you,

Brynie.

Here I come.

Oh wow! That's HOT! We have to get you that!

Aunt Hol, you look gorgeous! You have to get it!

You think so?

Oh my God, yes! Uncle Dave won't know what to do with himself when he sees you in that! I love the purple on you, too!

Okay Brynlee, you get the red one, I'll get this purple.

My new boots will look so cute with this! Don't you think?

Oh heck yes! Why don't you try them on with it real quick?

Good idea! God, these boots are so comfortable, and so cute with this dress!

Let's see… Oh yeah, for sure, you have to get it. And I think this is the outfit for tonight.

Yes, I think so, too. But I'll have to wear leggings, so I don't freeze my ass off.

Good idea, especially since you don't know what you're doing tonight, yet.

So, we can return the first outfit then. I love this dress!

No, why return it? You need all of this stuff. They look too good on you to return them.

Are you sure?

Positive. Now, let's pay for this, and wander around a bit before we go get some lunch.

Thank you so much, Aunt Holly. You really didn't have to get me all this stuff.

Sweetie, I told you, I want to. Now, not another word about it.

She's too good to me.

Okay, like, seriously?

There are so many good choices on this menu, I don't know what to pick!

Well, what looks really good to you, besides everything?

I want to try something different, like totally off the wall, so I think I'll pick from the vegan menu. I'm thinking about maybe this vegan moussaka, or maybe quinoa confetti salad. What about you?

Oh, Bryn, you may have to help me decide. I'm looking at a few things, but I think my top two are the reuben from the vegan menu or the seared scallops.

The reuben sounds really good. What do they make it with?

Looks like it's made with tofu and vegan cheese. I've never had vegan cheese before.

Well, let's both be adventurous and try something new. I say you should get the reuben.

Okay, I'll do that, and I think you should try the moussaka. Have you ever had regular moussaka before?

No, I don't think I ever even heard of it.

Do you like eggplant?

Yeah, I think so. I mean, I like eggplant parmesan.

Oh okay, then I think you'll probably like this. And if not, we'll just order dessert. Oh my, they have cheesecake!

They do?

Yes, on the vegan menu. You know I have to try it, no matter what. Oh, I see they have it on the regular menu as well. Ugh, decisions...

Well, maybe you should try the vegan kind, and that way, if you like it, you can have that on your new diet.

That's true. Was that your phone or mine?

I think it's mine. Yup. Oh, it's Luke!

"Good morning Brynlee"

"Haha, it's afternoon!"

"Oh, lol, my bad" "we still on for tonight?"

"Yup, sure are. Ideas for tonight?"

"Dinner and then whatever we all decide sound good?"

"Sounds good to me"

"How'd you do, last night? Did you win?"

"We did!"

"I knew you would! Congrats!"

"Thank you"

"I wish I could've been there"

"Maybe next time"

"Pick you up at 6?"

"Sure, I'll be at Natalya's"

"Okay cool. See you tonight cutie"

" :) "

" :) "

Aww, he called me "cutie" again.

      Cutie? Be careful with that one.

Why?

      Could end up to be a player.

Yeah, he could. But I'm not worried about it. He won't get far with this girl.

      I like to hear that. My niece has values and standards. Good for you, sweetie. Just be sure to let him know your boundaries.

Oh, he knows. The whole school knows. I have a rep for being a prude.

      Haha, you do? That's not so common these days.

Yeah, I know. I mean, I'd be offended if I wasn't so proud of it.

      Good for you!

Yeah, you really don't hear of anyone being a prude anymore. Nowadays, everyone is having sex, or doing stuff, even in middle school.

      Middle school?!

Yup. There's a freshman who had a baby last month.

      Are you serious?

Totally. She was dating some guy from another school who dumped her as soon as he found out she was pregnant.

      What a jerk! Is she keeping the baby?

As far as I know, she is. I hope she does, anyway. I know I would.

      Well, it's a hard thing, especially when she's so young. But if her parents are supportive, she'll be okay.

I hope so. She's really nice. Quiet, but nice. I heard a rumor she's coming back to school in a couple of weeks.

>That must be so tough, being a young mom like that and having to still finish high school. She barely got started!

I know. It's crazy. But yeah, I'm the prude at school. I don't even know how that got started. It's not like I've been on all these dates that there have been chances for me to do anything anyway.

>Well, you know how high school can be. Someone needs to start something with someone just so they make themselves feel better.

Yeah, I don't understand why that is. Can't people just mind their own business? Jeez.

>Well, I think it all starts with having low self-esteem. If someone has low or no self-esteem, they feel the need to tear other people down so they look better. But, in actuality, they look like bullies, or bitches, or whatever.

Like Samantha! I wonder if that's why she's the way she is. But she's gorgeous, so I don't know how she would have low self-esteem.

>It has nothing to do with looks, hon. It has everything to do with the way we are spoken to, treated, what we experience, stuff like that.

Hmmm. Interesting.

>Yeah, I pity people like that. There are plenty of people in the world who feel badly about themselves, but don't put others down. They, at least, don't try to make others feel bad too.

Hmm, like me.

>Brynlee, please don't feel badly about yourself. You are beautiful, inside and out. You are smart, an amazing dancer, you have a family who loves you, friends who support you...

I know. I know. Oh good, our food is here!

>Wow, that was quick. This Reuben looks delicious! So does your moussaka!

Oh my gosh, it all looks so good! I hope I can finish this.

>Well, if not, leftovers! Besides, we have to save room for dessert.

Definitely! I'd like to dive into that cheesecake like it's the Caribbean Sea!

>I'm right there with ya!

Oh my, this moussaka is to die for! It's sooo good! I can definitely eat this whole thing!

How's your Reuben, Aunt Holly?
      It's outstanding! Your moussaka? Do you like it?
I love it. It is so good. Oh. My. GOD!
      It's that good, huh?
No I mean, yes, it is, but that's not what… You're not going to believe who just walked in!
      Who?
BLAKE! And his entire family.
      Really? Is it that guy with the blue shirt on?
Yes!
      Oh, Brynlee, he IS cute! He's the one who couldn't stop thinking about you?
Yes! He's so hot. Oh my God, I think he saw me. He did! Did you see that smile? And he waves so cute! I can't even…
      Yeah, Bryn, he's very cute. And guess what, he's coming over here.
Are you serious?
      Dead serious.
Holy crap. Okay. I hope I don't have food in my teeth. Do I have food in my teeth?
      Nope. All good.

Hey Brynlee!
      That smile, oh my God! Hi Blake!
Sorry to interrupt. I had to come say hi. Is that okay?
      Sure. Oh, this is my Aunt Holly. Aunt Holly, this is Blake.
Nice to meet you Blake.
      Nice to meet you, as well.
Hey, would you two please excuse me? I'm going to the ladies room.
      Sure.
Wow, so, what are you doing here?
      Oh my aunt and I were shopping and decided to come here for lunch. How about you? Family luncheon?
Yeah. My mom wanted to come. She likes this place a lot. She says they have really good steak.

Well, that's good. I'm trying food off of the vegan menu today. Dare to be different.

Well, whatever it is, it looks good. Is it okay if I sit until your aunt comes back?

Of course.

It's crazy that we ran into each other here. I'm really glad we did, though. I get to look I to those eyes again.

Oh crap, my face is getting hot I must look so stupid right now.

You're blushing. Hasn't anyone ever told you that you have beautiful eyes before?

Well, no, no one besides my... No, actually. You're the first. *Whoops! Almost slipped about Nova!*

Then, apparently, they're not looking. So, you've got a date tonight, huh?

Yeah.

You don't sound too excited about it.

I don't know. I'm excited to get out of the house and hang out. The date part though, I don't know.

Not your type?

No, not really.

What is your type? What kind of guy do you like?

Umm, I don't know really. Nice, tall...

What about me? Am I your type?

Is that a trick question?

No. I'm serious.

Well, yeah, I guess you could be. We don't know each other that well, so, I don't know.

Okay, listen, I'm gonna cut to the chase. Besides, I'm too old to play games, even though plenty of guys my age play games. I'm not into that crap. I like you, Brynlee, and I would really love the chance to get to know you better. But, given the fact that you're still in high school, and I'm in college...

Shit. Here it comes. We can never date.

... and I don't come home a whole lot right now because I'm a freshman and they discourage that, I think we should take it real slow. IF you're down for that, of course. If you're even into me like that.

Oh! Umm...

I was going to wait until Christmas break to tell you this, but since you're going on a date tonight, I don't want to miss my chance.

I don't know what to say.

So, I guess I need to know, are you into me like that?

Well, yeah, actually. I have been for a while now.

Well good. So, then can I assume we're still on for that seafood date next weekend? It'll be the last time I'm home until Christmas, and I'd really like to see you.

Sure. *Oh. My. GOD!! I have a date with Blake next weekend!*

Excellent. Well, here comes your aunt. I'll text you later on, okay?

Okay. Looking forward to it. *Did I seriously just say that? I'm such a doofis.*

Me too. Can I get a hug?

Sure. *He smells soooo good. Holy God! No, please don't let go...*

Bye, Brynlee. Bye, Aunt Holly. It was nice to meet you.

Bye Blake. Nice meeting you, as well.

I think I'm going to pass out.

Did I give you two enough time to chat without making you feel uncomfortable?

Aunt Holly! I think I'm gonna cry right now!

Why? What happened? Was he mean to you? I'll kick his ass!

No! No! He wasn't mean at all! He asked me out on a date for next weekend!

Are you serious? That's great! Wait, what'd you say?

I said yes! I'm so confused, though. Why would someone like Blake want to go out on a date with me?

What do you mean, why would he? That's easy, you're a great girl!

But he's in college. College!

Look, Brynie, as you get older, age doesn't matter so much. Maybe he doesn't care about that irrelevant stuff. Maybe he sees the awesome person you are and wants to be in your life.

Well, okay, forget wearing the red dress tonight. I'm saving that for Blake. It's definitely my favorite and I want to look really cute for him. At this point, tonight's date is for Natalya and Dylan.

Well, you don't have to discount Luke's potential just yet. You may find you like him better, and that you two click more.

I could, but I doubt it. I don't know. I have a feeling he's going to be the typical high school jock who is just trying to get with as many girls as he can, and since I'm the "class prude", I feel like he wants to try to "break me in". Like it'll be points for him. And I'm not going there.

Well, I think if that's how you feel in your gut, then go with your gut.

True.

So with that, I want you to be on guard tonight. Take extra care to protect yourself from anything and everything. Okay?

Like how?

Well, first of all, do not leave your drink unattended. If you go out to eat and you girls get up to use the bathroom, order a new drink when you get back. The date rape drug is getting more common in younger kids. It's not just with college and older people that it happens. If you have a bottled drink, like soda or whatever, take it with you.

Okay, what else?

Well, you're outfit is good. It's not easily removable. The harder your clothes are to get off, the better off you are.

Good.

And absolutely do not drink or do drugs. You have to stay alert, and be in control of your thoughts and actions at all times. Okay?

Yes. Thank you. I'll be sure to fill Natalya in on that stuff, too. It'll be good for her to know anyway, since she's a model, and that industry is scary.

You're not kidding. It's really scary out there for the women in that industry, for sure! And beautiful young girls like yourselves have to be extra careful. Wow, I'm getting full. Here's the struggle, do I finish this and not have any room for cheesecake, do I finish this and stuff myself with cheesecake, or do I take the rest home and have the cheesecake?

Well, I say take the rest home, have cheesecake. And I think I'll join you in that decision. And now we have leftovers for tomorrow!

Good choice. No need to overindulge. That would defeat the whole "eating healthy" thing. So, what should we do after lunch? We can continue to shop, or we can head back home. Up to you.

I guess we can head back home. I think enough money's been spent today, and we scored big with the cute stuff we got. Thank you so much, again, Aunt Holly. I really appreciate it. And I love my new stuff.

I know you do, and you're very welcome. I needed a day like today.
I've been missing my Brynie-boo.

Yeah, I needed some Aunt Holly time.

If you see our waitress, wave her over here so we can order dessert. I
can't wait to try it!

Me either! It sounds so yummy.

Just so you know, Blake keeps looking over here at you.

He does?

He does. I think he really likes you, hon.

Are you sure he's not just looking past me at some other
girl?

Well, considering the only people behind us are old bald men, I'm
definitely sure he's looking at you.

Wow. It's like a dream come true. I'm still having a hard
time believing it.

Well, believe it.

*How does one simply believe something that's unbelievable? I guess
time will be the only thing that'll help that happen. Things like this
just don't happen to girls like me. I'm just Brynlee.*

You should listen to your aunt, Brynlee. You're amazing, just
like she said.

Nova, hey! Yay! I'm getting better at thinking to you
when you pop in!

Yes, you are getting better. Now, get better at believing you are
good enough to be liked by your dream boy, okay?

I'm working on it.

We still have a lot of work to do.

Okay, well, let's not work on it here. Aunt Holly is going
to think I'm spacing out.

Okay. We'll talk later.

*Blake Carrington, you are one very beautiful man. And for some
strange reason, you like me. Aww, he smiled at me! I can't wait to
hang out with him next weekend. It's going to be the longest week of
my life!*

Okay, Hon, are you ready to go?

Yup. Let's not forget our lunch for tomorrow. I hope Daddy
doesn't eat my leftovers, but I wouldn't blame him if he
does!

Yeah, Uncle Dave better not touch my food. Actually, all I have to do is write "tofu" or "vegan" on it and he won't go near it. Haha, yup, that's what I'll do.

> Well, why don't you let him try it? Maybe he'll like it and want to hop on board with us.

You know, that's not a bad idea. Good thinking! Hey, looks like Blake is headed this way.

> He really is?

Yup. Turn around.

Hey, I just wanted to come say goodbye.

> That's so sweet. Thank you.

Bryn, I'm going to run to the ladies room one more time before we leave. Blake, again, nice to meet you.

> You too. So, did you enjoy your lunch?

I really did! How about you?

> Yeah, it was really good. But it was better because I got to look at you the whole time. Wow, that sounded a little creeperish, didn't it?

Well, if I didn't know you, yeah.

> Haha, sorry. I just never realized how pretty you are. Your smile made me smile. My dad thought I was high!

Are you serious?

> Yeah, he said "son, why do you keep smiling for no reason? Are you high?"

What'd you say?

> Well, Carly told him I was staring at you.

She did?

> Yeah. She was right. I couldn't help myself. You're beautiful. Your smile is beautiful.

Great, I'm blushing again. Aww, thank you.

> So, um, have fun on your date tonight. But not too much fun, okay?

Oh, don't worry. I won't.

> I wish it was me you were going out with tonight.

I mean, I can text you where we'll be, if you feel like coincidentally showing up.

> I'd love to, but nah, I shouldn't. Do you think that would be messed up of me to do?

I don't think so. Besides, I might need a bail out.

Well, if you feel like you need to be bailed out, then absolutely. I'll be your knight in shining armor, and I'll come save you from the evil dragon.

You'd really save me?

If it means hanging out with you, even if just for ten minutes, then yeah, I would.

Okay, Prince Charming, we'll see. *Prince Charming? Really? That was so corny.*

Fare thee well, my most beauteous Princess. Until then, I bid thee adieu. I await your signal of distress.

Aye, I await thee and thy trusty steed. Fare thee well, my Prince.

Bye, beautiful.

I wonder if he'd come if I texted him. But, that'd be wrong, wouldn't it? I mean, no one has to know. As far as they know, it's completely a coincidence. Maybe I should see how it goes with Luke. Ugh, but I don't think it's going to come to anything. We're not each other's type. He's hot, but damn, so is Blake. Maybe I should go get Aunt Holly. She's probably just chillin' in the ladies room trying to give us enough time.

Hey, Aunt Hol, I'm ready when you are.

Okay good. There's only so much you can do to waste time in here. You know?

Yeah, without looking like you're doing some crazy business!

Well, this is awkward...

How am I supposed to be excited about this date with Luke after all that happened with Blake? I don't know how I'm going to do this. I hope I don't ruin it for Natalya and Dylan. Oh, I should call her.

Hello?

      Hey! Whatcha doing?

Just getting ready. How was shopping?

      It was great!

Hey, can you vidchat me instead? That way I can finish doing my makeup and you can show me the stuff you got.

      Sure.

Thanks.

Hey. So show me what you got!

      Okay, but let me show you what I'm wearing tonight first.

Yeah, cool.

      Here it is. What do you think?

Wow! Great pants!

      I know, right? And this shirt is so comfortable!

I love it!

      Yes. I thought I'd wear this necklace with it. It's nice and colorful against the white shirt.

Yes! Nice. I love it.

      Dude, check out these boots! They cost a crapload of money, though, holy shit!

Damn, those are nice! I could use a pair like those.

      You should totally get them! We can match! Wait a minute, I picked something my model best friend likes and would wear? I guess you're rubbing off on me!

Haha, I guess so! They're so you, though! So maybe you're the one rubbing off on me!

      Maybe. Fashionista turned boho-hippie.

Hey, I have to stay current and look good in everything. If my feet were smaller, I'd just borrow them.

      Well, if your feet were smaller, you'd fall over. You're too tall for my foot size.

Haha, true! Okay, let's see what else you got.

Oh, you mean the outfit I'm wearing on my date with Blake next weekend?

Yeah. Wait, what?!

Yup.

Holy shit, what happened?! Tell me everything!

Well, you know he texted me this morning. Then when we were at lunch, his family walked in. He came over to our table, Aunt Holly conveniently had to pee, he told me he likes me, stared at me the whole time, asked me to go out for dinner next weekend, and said we should take things slow because he's away at college and hardly ever home. He called me beautiful, and that was it in a nutshell.

Brynlee! I told you! Did I not tell you? I told you!

You did. You were right.

And…

And I was wrong.

That's right. And don't you forget it.

Anyway, have you talked to Dylan at all?

Yeah, did you talk to Luke?

I did. He said we'll get dinner and then decide together what to do after.

Yeah, that's what Dylan said, too. Any ideas?

No. You?

Not really. I want to do something fun, though. Maybe the trampoline place or bowling, or maybe the arcade?

Yeah, that sounds fun. Or we could do laser tag or go ice skating.

Yeah, that's fun too.

Well, we'll mention those options later at dinner.

Yes, cool.

So what time should I come over? Luke said they are going to pick us up at 6.

Come over whenever you want.

Okay, I'll be over in a little bit.

Okay. See you then. Just walk in.

Okay. Bye.

Bye.

Who was texting me while I was on the phone?
"Hello, Princess"
"Just wanted to say I'm glad I saw you today"
"Your eyes send me into another realm"
Aww, he's so cute!
"I'm glad I saw you, too, Prince Charming" "rescue me later"
"At your word, I am there"
" :) "
" ;) "

*uh-oh. Winky face. Well, maybe he doesn't mean it like that. God, I
hope not. My little corny Prince Charming comment turned into
something cute. I'm glad, because otherwise I'd feel like an idiot.
Haha, the village idiot! So, I have a few hours. What should I do?*
I think you should stand in front of the mirror.

Nova, I do not need to stand in front of the mirror.
Yes, you do.
Ugh!
Come on. Get over there.
Okay, fine.
Repeat after...
No, I got this. I can do it.
Excellent! Go for it.
I am beautiful. My appearance doesn't determine my
worth. I am beautiful on the inside, therefore I am
beautiful on the outside. I am beautiful. There, how's
that?
Perfect! I'm so proud of you!
Thanks.
How did it feel today?
Actually, it didn't feel as awkward as it did the first
couple of times. And I didn't want to cry this time.
Probably because I'm still on a Blake high.
Could be. Or, it could be you're a quick study, and it's sinking in
quicker than I thought it would.
Maybe. I don't know.
Well, I want you to say it at least once a day. Now that I know
you can do it without me saying it first, I'll just be your
reminder.
Okay.
Good. Well, get ready for your date.

I'm just going to do my makeup. I'll do the rest at
Natalya's. Hey, Nova...

Yes?

Thank you.

For what?

For helping me to see myself differently. It might take a
little longer than we both hope, but thank you.

You're welcome. And you seem to be catching on pretty
quickly, if I do say so myself. I'd like to talk more about what
you and Aunt Holly talked about today. But we can do that
tonight or tomorrow okay?

About what?

Well, everything, really. We'll talk later. Until then, have fun,
and don't stress.

I'm not stressed.

No, but you're about to. Don't. It'll all work out the way it's
supposed to. And I'm here if you need me.

I know you are. Thank you. You've been a huge help.

Fabulous! Then I'm doing my job.

Speaking of job, you never told me who your boss is.

You'll know, in time.

How will I know?

You'll just know. Don't worry.

*I love how she just knows that I'll know, but she won't tell me. Okay.
No big deal. I guess I should get my stuff together and get over to
Natalya's house. I really dig this outfit. These pants are so cool.
And my studded belt will look awesome with this! Okay, lemme just
find my satchel, shove this stuff in there, and see if maybe Daddy will
drive me over. I'll tell him he can have the leftover moussaka if he
gets hungry. It's not steak, but that stuff is so good! I'd love to eat
there again, and maybe try the Reuben, or something totally new. Oh
good, here's my satchel. Now I just have to grab my makeup, and
there, I'm ready. Now, to find Daddy. I think he's out in the garage.*

Hey Mom, have you seen Daddy?

He was in the garage, but he may have gone next door to
talk to Mr. Clemmons.

Okay, I'll check.

Daddy? *Nope, not in the garage. Maybe they're outside talking...*
Oh, there you are! Hey Daddy, will you bring me to Natalya's please?

> Hi, Sweetpea, sure. I just have to run in and wash my hands and grab my keys.

Okay. Thank you.

> Sure, no problem, honey. I'll be right out.

Okay.

I wonder what he was out here tinkering with. It's cute that he tries to do handy stuff. He's not really a handy kind of guy. He's an office professional. They usually play golf and hang out at swanky taverns, not usually building or tinkering with stuff. Maybe he's trying to learn something new, since golf isn't his thing. Ooh, hey, maybe I can get him to try and build me a window seat! I'd love to have one of those. Then I could sit there and watch the rain and listen to the thunder as I try to track every raindrop that hits my window. I can sit there and dream about my wedding day and the guy I'm going to marry, and the cute little house and white picket fence we'll live in, with our cute little kids and spunky little dog.

Okay, I'm ready. You didn't say goodbye to your mother.

> Oh, whoops! I'll text her. "Bye mom. Love you"

So, this kid you're going on a date with. He better respect my daughter.

> Don't worry, Daddy. I'll make sure of it, or I'll put him in his place.

That's my girl.

> Whatcha doing in the garage?

Oh, I was just cleaning it up a bit.

> Daddy, do you think you can try to build me a window seat for my room? I need a place to daydream besides staring at the boring ceiling from my bed. It's so blah, and blah daydreaming spots make for blah daydreams.

We'll see, Sweetpea. I'll talk to mom and see what she thinks. But I don't think it'll be a problem.

> Can you even build a window seat?

Sure, I can build one. You don't think I can build a windowseat?

> Well, you're not that handy. You're more of a hang-out kinda guy.

So what, I can't hang out and build stuff?

That's not what I meant, Daddy. You know what I mean.
I know. I'm just messing with ya. But yes, I can build a bench. If it makes you feel better, I'll have Uncle Dave come help me. How's that?

Um, can he build anything?
He used to be in construction.

I didn't know that. Why isn't he anymore?
He got tired of working out in the elements. It's not much fun working outside during the rainy season.

Well, at least it's not like Seattle.
This is true. So listen, Brynlee, this boy Luke. If he tries to have sex with you…

Daddy! Why would you say that?
Come on, honey. I'm a guy. I know what guys want. And he's still young and probably doesn't have total control of his desires just yet.

Yup, we've just reached a new level of awkward. Oh my gosh, Daddy…

Now, Bryn, honey, listen to me. You be sure to set your boundaries now, and make sure he knows what they are in advance, before it gets to a point where it's too late.

I know, Daddy. You don't have to worry.
Oh, but Sweetpea, I do. You're my daughter. I love you very much. It's my job to protect you, and if I can't be there, it's my job to make sure you can protect yourself. Far too many girls these days allow boys to have what they want, believing all the bullshit they tell them, and then find themselves psychologically messed up, pregnant, and sometimes even dead. Sex is not something to be taken lightly or to happen casually. My hope is that you wait until you're married, but I know that probably isn't realistic. But, what is realistic is that you wait for the right young man to come along, when you're much older than 15, you two date a long while, and then you can make a decision from there.

Daddy, you don't have to worry. I'm not looking to have sex with anyone right now. And Aunt Holly already filled me in on not leaving my drink unattended and all that. And I know how to swing a mean left hook they wouldn't expect, and a good kick to the family jewels will send even the strongest man to the ground where I can finish him off and run. I'm good, Daddy. All this dancing gave me some crazy strength.

Now that's my baby girl! Maybe we should sign you up for a self-defense course, just for added benefit.

Okay, sure! That sounds like fun, actually. Can Natalya come too?

Absolutely. Two beautiful girls like you need to know how to protect yourselves from jerks.

Yeah, and she's not as muscular as I am.

No, she's not. So she should definitely take a course in self-defense. I'll look up classes when I get back to the house. I'm sorry I didn't think of this sooner. It's like just yesterday you were my little tiny princess with the long banana curls and ribbons in her hair, watching Little Bunny and Clarence the Magical Mutt, and now you're dating and... well, I'm having a hard time with it. Just know that I love you so very much, Sweetpea. I'm your biggest fan, and you can always come to me about anything.

Well, now that we have the most awkward conversation behind us, I'll be sure to do that, Daddy. And I love you, too. You're the best daddy ever!

Good. Now, go have fun, but not too much fun. Tell Andrej I'll give him a call later. I'll talk to him about the self-defense class for you two.

Okay, thanks Daddy. Oh, by the way, there's leftover moussaka in the fridge from lunch today when we were shopping. You should eat it. It is really good!

Thank you, Sweetpea. I might just do that. I love you.

I'll text you or mom later.

Sounds good.

Well, that went better than it could have, I suppose. Awkward, yes, but not to the point where I wanted to cry or anything. I wonder if Natalya's dad ever talked to her about that. I'm excited about self-defense classes, though! I hope Nat will want to do it. Otherwise, maybe Lacey will.

Hi Mr. Sierzant!

Hello Brynlee. How are you today?

I'm great! My dad said he'll give you a call later. He wants to talk to you about something.

Oh, okay, wonderful. Natalya is in the kitchen with her mother.

Thank you.

Oh, hello Brynlee!
> Hi Mrs., I mean, Mom. Um, before I forget, can I talk to you about something?

Sure, honey, what is it?
> Well, I don't want to have this come out wrong, but I feel funny calling you "mom". I don't know why. You're like my second mom, but calling you "second mom" sounds stupid.

So, just call me Paulina, honey.
> Well, you see, I feel funny calling you that too. Like it's disrespectful. And you're such a respectable lady, that I can't bring myself to call you by your first name.

Oh Brynlee, you don't have to feel that way with me. I don't mind at all, but if you feel uncomfortable, then let's find something we are both happy with. How about "Mum"? Would that be okay?
> "Mum". Yeah, I think that'll be okay. I can even say it with a British accent, haha. 'Ello, Mum!

Haha, that's great, Brynlee, dahling!
> Haha! It is, isn't it?

Okay, we have a lot to do, so let's go get ready.
> Yeah, okay, Natalya, let's. Thanks, Mum!

Anytime, dahling!

So? Have you heard from Blake anymore today?
> Actually, he texted while we were vidchatting before.

Really?
> Haha, yeah! Have you talked to Dylan anymore?

A little. He texted me before and asked what color shirt I was wearing. He said wants to match, for some reason. Is that weird?
> Aww, I think it's cute.

Well, if you say so. I think it's weird. But whatever. Maybe he's just one of those "cutesy couple" kind of guys.
> Football player Dylan? Maybe. Maybe he's the sensitive type.

Well, he's cute, that's for sure. I really hope he smells nice. That really gets me, when a guy smells good.
> Yeah, I know!

Okay, so this is what I'm thinking of wearing. What do you think?

It's really pretty, but I don't know.

Why not?

> Well, I was talking to Aunt Holly before, and she was telling me we should wear stuff that's difficult to remove, just in case they try something.

Do you really think they're gonna try anything?

> You just never know, Nat. And to be honest, I don't want to make it any easier for them.

I don't know, they don't seem like that type. But then again, does any guy?

> No, not usually. I mean, there are some creepy looking guys out there, but none we go to school with. I'd just rather we be on the safe side. Oh, and she also said not to leave our drinks unattended. So, if while we're out to eat, if we get up to go to the bathroom, we should order a totally different drink when we get back to the table. Or if we have a bottle of soda, we should take it with us.

Why? Do you think they'd slip us roofies?

> No, but you just never know. Someone else could. And they could beat Luke and Dylan's asses and take advantage of us. Better to be safe than sorry. Oh, by the way, how would you feel about taking self-defense classes?

I don't know, I mean, my modeling schedule is booking up. I'd have to see if I can fit it in.

> Okay, because my dad is signing me up and he'll sign you up too. He's calling your dad later to talk about it.

I think it's a great idea, and it could be fun. I just hope I can. Maybe Jasmine can come with us?

> Yeah, maybe. I was thinking Lacey, maybe, too.

Yeah, all four of us. That'd be a fun class.

> Okay, let's ask them too. But first, check your schedule.

Okay.

> So besides talking about self-defense classes, my dad and I had quite the awkward conversation about sex on the way over here.

Oh my God, really?

> Yeah, he just basically said he wants me to wait until I get married, and that Luke better be respectful, and all that. I told him not to worry. That's when the self-defense conversation began.

Oh, wow! Could you just die when that happened?

Yeah, at first. But then it was no big deal. I know he loves me and he's just protecting me.

Your dad is so cool.

Both of our dads are.

You're right. Okay so help me find something to wear.

Hmm, let's see. What about these jeans and a brown belt, and maybe, hmmm, this shirt with it?

Um, yeah, that's cute. And those jeans are comfortable, so, yeah. Boots?

Yes, boots. These look good on you.

Yeah, but they have a heel, and I don't want to tower over him.

You won't. He's pretty tall. Isn't he like 6'1"?

I think so. But I'm 5'9", so if I wear those we'll be almost even.

Oh, alright. How about these, then?

I really don't like those. They remind me of Peter Pan.

What? That's funny, okay… Gosh, you have so many pairs of boots! I wish we wore the same size.

Yeah, me too. Then I could wear your new boots!

Yeah, but not tonight, and definitely not next weekend.

Oh yeah, the date with Blake! I love when I'm right.

I know. You never let me forget.

That's just so you'll listen to me next time, silly.

Yeah, yeah, whatever. Okay, these are the boots to wear tonight.

Alright, those are good. A little equestrian, a little medieval. That'll look good.

What are you doing with your hair?

Nothing special. What about you?

Nope, me either. Can I tell you a secret?

Duh! Of course!

After what happened with Blake, I'm not as excited about hanging with Luke as I was.

Well, that's understandable. I wouldn't be either.

You wouldn't?

No. Blake is way beyond Luke and Dylan!

I mean, I'm not going to not give him a chance, but I'd much rather date Blake. I just have a weird feeling Luke is just trying to see how far he can get with me, since I'm the "prude". I feel like there are bets going around.

What?! That's crazy.

Is it really, though?

No, I guess not. Do you think it's the same with Dylan and me?

No. I think Dylan really likes you. I think he has for a while.

Why do you get that feeling, about Luke, I mean?

I don't know. He hasn't texted me, really. Blake has been all over that since the video situation, and I don't know.

Well, we'll make sure to stick together all night, okay?

Okay. Thanks, Natalya.

Why are you thanking me? We're best friends. Sisters! We have to stick together.

You're damn right we do! It's nice to know we have each other's back, no matter what.

Yes, we do.

I guess we should get dressed, and then chill out for a while?

Yeah, we've got a while before they come pick us up. Where are we going to eat? Do you know?

No clue. Oh, I forgot to tell your mom, I tried vegan moussaka today. It was so good!

Oh, really? What made you try that?

Well, me and Aunt Holly are starting a new dietary lifestyle.

You're gonna be a vegan?

No, not exactly. We're going to be mostly whole foods plant-based, but I'll still eat seafood, because you know I can't live without sushi!

Oh, so you're pescatarian!

Um, I guess. We're not going to label ourselves. We just both want to be healthier and she's apparently done a lot of research.

Well, you know, if you need help or whatever, you can talk to me and my mom. She's got some great recipes.

I will, thanks. How come you aren't vegan like your mom?

I don't know. I just really like meat, I guess. I don't eat a lot of it, though, since mom is an ethical vegan and won't cook it, but I eat some when I can.

Is she mad that you're not?

No, not at all. Oh, Brynlee, that looks so cute on you! Let me hurry.

Yeah, hurry. Then we can take selfies and go chill out.

Yes, and get some snacks. I'm hungry from all of this food talk.
Me too!

Well, here goes...

Okay, it's 5:30. They'll be here soon. I guess I'll just try to make the best of this for Natalya, if nothing else. I am pretty hungry, so there's something to look forward to. Aww, Natalya looks nervous. Are you nervous, Natalya?

No, why?

Because, you're rubbing your hands together like crazy. You're going to rub them raw!

Am I? I hadn't noticed. Hmm, oh well. Alright, I'm a little nervous. I just don't want Dylan to turn out to be a jerk.

I'm sure he won't be. If anyone will be a jerk, it'll be Luke.

Well, I hope that's not the case either.

Yeah, me too. Oh, I think he just texted me. *"My dear Princess, I await your call. I stand ready should you need me"*. Nope, wasn't him. *"My Prince, I shall cry out to thee. Lol!"*

Oh, okay. They should be here soon. What are you smiling about, over there?

Oh nothing.

Who texted you? Oh my Gosh, was it Blake?

Yeah. *I guess it was obvious? Great, now I'm blushing again.*

You're blushing! And you can't stop smiling! What did he say?

Okay, it's crazy. Don't be mad, okay?

About what?!

He told me today he'd come bail me out if I needed it.

You'd leave me there?!

No! He would come hang out if Luke is an ass.

Oh okay, good! I would be so mad if you left me alone with them!

I would never! We stick together! I'd bring you and Dylan with us and leave Luke alone!

Wow, you really don't think it's going to work out with you two, do you?

I really don't.

Well, do you want to just cancel?

No way! We're going on this date.

157

Are you sure? I don't want you to feel uncomfortable or have to deal with an ass. But maybe we shouldn't be quick to judge him just because he dated a bitch.

I know. I feel bad because I already have him branded as a jerk, meanwhile, he could end up to be really nice. So I have to find out what he's really like.

Okay. Dylan just texted and said they'll be here in a few minutes. They're dropping his little brother off around the corner for a birthday party.

Cool. Well, are you ready?

I guess as ready as I'm going to be. Let's go wait outside. I don't really want my dad to fire fifty questions at them.

Okay. Let's go.

Bye Mom, bye Dad!

Bye Mum! Bye Mr. Sierzant!

Do we not get to meet these young gentlemen who are taking our beauties out for the evening?

No, Dad, next time, okay?

I guess so. Next time for sure. But I'm standing on the porch with my shotgun when they get here.

Daddy!

Haha! Do it, Mr. Sierzant! You know my dad and Uncle Dave would be right here with you if they were here right now!

Andrej! What in the world?!

I'm just sending a message, my love. A very strong message.

I hardly think standing on the porch with a shotgun is necessary. I'll be right back. I'm getting my butcher knife!

Alright, honey. If you must.

Oh my God, Natalya, I LOVE your parents!! I swear you guys are like, the best parents, Mr. Sierzant!

Please, Brynlee, if you're going to call my wife "Mum", I insist you call me "Poppa" or "Da'da", but it must have the emphasis on the last da. I refuse to be the old one in this family. You've insisted on being proper far too long, my dear.

Okay, Da'da it is. Mum, your butcher knife fits you splendidly!

Thank you, dahling. I love your accent.

Why, thank you.

Come on, guys. Do you really have to stand here looking like psychopaths?

Oh, please, Natalya. You know we're going to do the same thing to our kids when they're about to go on a date.

True.

Embrace it. Be proud of the insanity. It's so rare these days.

Okay, Mother. Where's the noose and the bat?

Haha, there's my psychotic little girl!

Oh look, here they are. Okay, love you both!

Bye girls. Have fun, and be careful!

We will!

Yup, they're crazy. That's why I love them. And that's why we're all friends. Life is perfect with friends like this.

Hey ladies! How's it going?

Good, you?

Pretty good. So, uh, Natalya, why are your parents on the porch with weapons?

Oh, to send a strong message to you two.

Oh, well, message received.

Good. You just scored a point by opening our doors, by the way.

Oh, well, thank God. And, you look really pretty tonight.

Thank you, Dylan.

Yeah, Brynlee, you look great. Those boots are hot.

Thanks, Luke.

Yeah, no problem. So, where do you guys want to go to eat?

It doesn't really matter. Anywhere except fast food.

C'mon, why would we bring you to a fast food place? We do have some class, you know.

I didn't mean it like that.

I know, I'm just messing with ya. But really, what do you feel like? Italian? Chinese? Burgers?

It really doesn't matter to me. What about you, Natalya?

I guess anywhere we can get a good salad.

Oh no, are you one of those girls, too?

What do you mean?

You only eat salad?

No, I mean a GOOD salad, like with chicken and veggies and stuff.

And fries. I have to have fries.

      Oh, okay. Good. I mean, I know you're a model and all, but I was hoping you like to eat food.

Yes, Dylan, I like food.

      Okay cool.

So, what do you think about just going somewhere like that pub with the bulldog playing bagpipes statue?

      Scotty MacFarland's? Yeah, sure, that sounds good to me. How about you, Bryn?

Yup, sounds good.

      Alright, cool.

Let me get the door for you ladies.

      Thanks, Luke.

Thank you.

      You're welcome.

Dude, I hope we get a good table. Last time I was here with my stepdad we ended up next to the bathrooms. We constantly heard flushing and hand dryers.

      Well, Dylan, let's ask for a table near the windows, then.

Okay. That way if the girls are really boring, we can people watch.

      Wow, Dylan!

I'm kidding! God!

      Dude, that's messed up.

Okay, listen, I say stupid shit when I'm nervous.

      You're nervous? Why?

Natalya, have you seen yourself? You're gorgeous.

      So? I'm just a regular girl.

No, no, you're definitely not regular. Neither of you are.

      Aww, that's sweet, Dylan. Nat, you may have nabbed yourself a good one. But, time will tell. It depends how much stupid comes out of his mouth.

Hahaha! Dude, I got the one with sass! Perfect!

      Is that a good thing?

Yeah, it is. Luke likes a girl with sass.

      Oh? Is that why you dated Samantha for so long?

Ugh, no. She's just a bitch. Let's not talk about her.

      Yeah, that's a sore subject. He can't stand her.

Not over her yet?

      Oh, definitely way over her. I was over her before it was

over! Anyway, I like your sass.

Yeah, I do have nice sass.

Yes, yes you do. Table for 4 please, near the window, if you can. Okay, let's go. After you, cutie.

Thanks.

I dig your outfit. It's different. I like how you're not like the rest of the girls. You have your own style. It's cool. And, yeah, those boots are definitely hot.

Yeah, I thought so too.

Here let me take your jackets.

Thank you.

Thanks.

So, you two are some very accomplished young women. Model, dancer… What's it like being so… Professional?

No, Luke, I wouldn't say I'm a professional. Maybe Natalya is, but I'm definitely not. Not yet, anyway.

Well, you're both famous, that's for sure! That video is going viral, still!

Are you serious?

Holy crap, Bryn! People are sharing it on Timeline!

Yeah, whatever.

I'm dead serious. So, what's it like to be so good at what you girls do?

I don't know, I mean, it's a lot of hard work.

Modeling is hard work?

Yes, Dylan, it is.

Oh, I had no idea. I mean, I seriously thought you just stand there and look pretty.

Wow.

Sorry, I'm not a model, so I don't know what's involved. To be honest, you're the only model I know. Well, besides all the Photogram-famous wannabes out there! Haha!

You mean, like Samantha and Keri?

Please, don't bring her up. Seriously, I'm trying to have a good night, here. And that should be really easy, because we're in good company.

Aww, thanks.

So, do both of you get a lot of fan mail?

Dylan, I'm not famous.

Neither am I.

Well, I'm surprised, because you're both gorgeous and great at what you do.

Thank you.

He's right. You are both gorgeous.

What? Why are you looking at me like that, Luke?

I just noticed how cool your eyes are. They have these cool specks in them. How do you not stare at yourself all day?

Ha, that's a pickup line if I ever heard one!

No it's not. I'm serious. Your eyes are beautiful. You are beautiful.

Okay, I'm just going to put it out there. I don't mean to sound bitchy, but why exactly did you ask me out? I mean, you never gave me the time of day, and all of a sudden...

All of a sudden I was single and finally not getting shit from that bitch. I figured enough time had passed that she wouldn't mess with you about anything. But, oh, I hear you told her off yesterday!

Yeah, she did! Tell him what happened!

No, I'd rather not. So, why did you ask me out?

Well, you're different. Your style, your attitude, the way you treat people. You're not like every other girl out there... Except for Natalya. She's different too. Oh, I guess those two are in their own little world.

Yeah, I guess so. Go on.

I mean, the first thing that caught my attention was how gorgeous you are. But then I started to really notice you and how you are. You're not just some pretty face. There are plenty of good looking people in the world, but most people are assholes, either stabbing their friends in the back, or putting people down, or bullying, or whatever. I can't stand those people.

Then why the hell did you date the biggest bitch on the planet?

You really want to know?

Yeah, I really do.

Don't hate me.

Well, I can't promise that.

True. Okay, I'll tell you. Because I wanted to get laid. And since I'm on the football team, I knew she'd give it up. Bad, huh?

Yeah, I'd say that's pretty bad. I mean, I wouldn't wish even her to be used like that.

Well, it went both ways, trust me.

I'm sure it did. But it doesn't make it right.

I know. You hate me, don't you? You think I'm an asshole.

No, I don't hate you. I'm not going to judge you or your reasons. But I will tell you this – I'm not having sex with you. You can call me a prude all you want to.

What makes you think I want to have sex with you? I mean, yeah, you're hot, and I'm a guy, but I didn't ask you out just to try to have sex with you. I'm not that horrible. And why would I call you a prude?

Doesn't everybody?

No. That was Samantha who started that. No one believes a word she says.

Well apparently plenty of people believe it, but I really don't care. I'm not a whore and I don't intend to be.

And that's another thing I like about you. You are strong. You know who you are, and you're not willing to sacrifice that about yourself.

Well, good. I'm glad we got that out of the way then.

Look, you may not want to ever see me again after what I just told you, but I swear I'm not the stereotypical asshole people think football players are. My dad made sure to teach me how ladies should be treated. I screwed up once and paid for it bad for a long time. I am not doing that again, trust me.

We'll see how tonight goes.

Hey, are you ready to order?

Yeah, I am. Are you?

Yeah. Hey, you two lovebirds, are you ready to order? They didn't hear me.

Natalya!

Yeah?

Are you two ready to order?

I am, are you Dylan?

I am.

Okay good.

I really don't know what to make of him. I can't tell if he's a jerk or not, yet. We'll see. At least those two are hitting it off. They're so involved in their own conversation, they don't even know we exist. That's cute. I should take a picture of them. They'll never notice.

Hey, I'm going to go wash my hands. I touched something greasy on the way in and it's kinda gross. Nat, can you watch my…purse?

Oh! Yeah, sure.

I'll order for you, what are you having?

Oh, thanks, Luke. I'm going to have the Guacamole burger.

No salad?

Nah, I'm in the mood for a turkey burger.

Thank God! A girl that likes to eat!

Yes, I like to eat. I'll be right back.

Maybe he's not so bad. He is really cute. He's got such a nice smile. Aww, and the way he looked when he said "don't hate me". It was like he was so sad he had to tell me. He was so vulnerable at that point. I hope I wasn't a huge bitch to him. But at least he knows I won't tolerate that crap. And oh my God, he smells so good! And he has such pretty eyes. I love green eyes on guys. Okay, Brynlee, easy there. Let's not start falling for him so easily. What about Blake?

Yes, what about Blake?

Nova!

Don't worry about Blake. You're not dating. You just started talking to him.

I know, but I really like him a lot. But I kinda like Luke, well, so far.

Don't stress out. You're young and single. Just have fun.

Okay.

And by the way, you look beautiful. Luke's right.

Thank you, Nova.

Hallelujah! She didn't argue with me!

Okay I have to get back out there.

Okay go.

She's right. I'm not dating anyone. I'm just going to have fun, and see what happens.

I'm back.

Oh good. After you.

Thank you.

The waitress came. I ordered your guacamole burger with fries, and Natalya ordered you a water with lemon. Is that good?

Perfect. Thank you. So, tell me about Luke. What are you all about? You seem to know so much about me, and I don't know anything about you.

Well, I like sports, obviously. I listen to all types of music, but alternative stuff is my favorite. I want to go to college and major in Sports Training and Sport Psychology, possibly minor in Business with an emphasis in Marketing. I have an older brother who is married and has two kids, my parents are still married, and we are Catholic, but don't go to church. Oh, and there's this girl who has caught my attention, who I really want to get know a lot better.

Oh really? She must be pretty special to capture the attention of such an ambitious guy like yourself.

Oh, she's really special. Unlike anyone I've ever met. And her eyes make me want to write a song.

Write a song, huh? Why don't you?

I just might.

Holy God, he's making me melt. I can't wait to hear it.

Tell me about the competition last night. That's so awesome you guys won! Congratulations.

Thank you. It was crazy. We had some tough competition, but our routine was flawless. We nailed every single move.

Was it the same routine I saw on the video?

Yeah, same one.

Some of that stuff you do is sick! You'll have to teach me how to do that crazy jump to the floor into a half a handstand thing.

Oh, that's a bronco. Sure, I'll show you, but I have to wait a week or so. I hurt my wrist doing it and I want it to heal up before I do them again.

Oh, man, are you okay?

Yeah, it's just a little sore. No big deal. I just have to let it rest, that's all. I hardly notice it now. It was really sore last night though. I thought I may have fractured it, but I guess not.

Well, actually, you could've gotten a small hairline fracture. Maybe it doesn't hurt because it's already healing up. Just try not to overuse it. Maybe you should wrap it for a few days so you don't forget it's hurt and you do something to it.

That's a good idea.

We can get wrap after we leave here, if you want. I'll wrap it for you.

That's okay. I have an ace bandage at home.

No really, I'd like to do that for you.

You really don't have to.

I insist.

Okay. I won't argue.

Good. Oh, I ordered an appetizer for us. Do you like hummus?

I love hummus!

Oh good. They have really good hummus here, I'm told. It comes with olives, veggies, and all that stuff.

I didn't picture you as someone who would like hummus and veggies.

Why, because I'm a guy?

Yeah, and a football player. I pictures you more as a meat and potatoes and beer kind of guy.

Well, I do like meat and potatoes, but I don't drink.

You don't?

Why do you seem surprised?

I don't know. I thought I was the only one who doesn't drink. It seems like everyone drinks these days. Every party I hear about there's at least three girls getting falling down drunk, and guys too.

Not this guy. Actually, Dylan doesn't drink, either.

Interesting. What about weed? Do you smoke?

Hell no. I'd get kicked off the football team.

But football season is over.

Doesn't matter. Once you're on the team, you're part of the team all year long. I'd get stripped of my jacket, my class ring, I'd lose my letter, and I'd have no chance of making the team next year. I have to play my senior year! It's my last chance to play football.

What about college?

Nah, not good enough. Plus, I want to focus on my degree. What about you? Do you smoke?

No. I prefer to be in total control of my body and my mind.

Me too! Wow, we have something huge in common. It's nice to know I'll never have to carry you home, all puking on me and my car.

I'm guessing that happened before?

Yeah. A lot. There's no bigger turnoff than a sloppy, slutty, puking, drunk girl.

Wow, that really sucks. I'm sorry that happened to you.

Me too. But, hey, you live and learn. I sure as hell learned what kind of girl I don't want to date again!

So what are you looking for?

You really want to know?

I do.

You. I'm looking to date a girl like you. Brynlee, you're amazing. And I don't even know all about you yet. But everything you tell me about yourself, you just keep confirming the fact that you must might be my dream girl.

Oh stop. I'm hardly anyone's dream girl.

Oh, but you are. You're gorgeous, you're sweet, you're confident in who you are, you've got sass, you're straight up, not a drunk or a whore, you have your own sense of style, you're not afraid to eat food, and you don't try to fake argue when I compliment you, except when I tell you you're my dream girl, so that shows me you're humble, and you're definitely not full of yourself or think you're better than everyone else. That, my friend, is dream girl status.

Umm, I don't really know what to say.

You don't have to say anything. Just soak in the compliment and get ready to eat some hummus.

Haha, okay. But, thank you.

Thank YOU. It's refreshing to know someone like you.
Okay, open up, try this.

Haha, ah!

Well? Is it good?

Chew fast. Don't talk with your mouth full. I love how I'm the guinea pig!

Oh no, that's not how I meant for it to go. There, I'll have some too. Man, this is good.

It really is. Thanks for ordering it.

So, what's your favorite food?

Sushi and seafood. How about you?

Steak, seafood, pizza and hibachi. I've never tried sushi, though.

Oh, you'll have to try it sometime. We can go to my favorite place one day, if you want.

Yeah, that'd be great. Are you sure the raw fish is safe?
Yeah, they use sushi grade fish. I've never gotten sick, and I eat
sushi a lot.

Okay, then it's a date. I will try sushi for the first time with
my dream girl. But, if I get sick, you'll have to take care of
me.
You won't get sick. But if you do, then I promise, I'll take care of
you.

That'd be great. Oh good, here comes our dinner. Hey dude,
dinner's here. Dylan! Yup, LaLa land, these two.

Dream girl, dream boy...

He is such a gentleman. Insisting he pay for dinner, holding the door for me... I think I pegged him all wrong. But, not going to let my guard down. Anyone can pretend to be something they're not. Look at those two back there. They've been in their own little world since we sat down at the restaurant. I wonder what we're going to do now.

Hey, lovebirds! What do you guys wanna do? What do you want to do, Brynlee?

> Haha, they aren't answering. Too into their own little world. What do you have in mind?

Well, not the movies. We can't really hang out there. We could go bowling, ice skating, we could go back to my house and hang out. My parents are there, but they said if we want to we can. I've got a pool table, air hockey, video games, or we can watch a movie there or whatever.

> That sounds like fun. Your parents are home, for sure?

Yeah. They're chillin' with some friends, but they don't care if we hang out. They like it, actually, so they can make sure no one's drinking and stuff.

> Oh, okay, that sounds fun. Let's do that. You guys okay with that back there? Okay good.

Haha, nice. Okay, cool. I'm going to warn you, though, my parents are crazy. It's like they never outgrew their teen years.

> Perfect!

I get to meet his parents! Oh my God, I'm going to meet his parents! Do I look presentable enough to meet parents? What if they don't like me? What if they like the bitch and they're bitter about the breakup? What if I'm not pretty enough for their son? Why didn't I think of these things before I agreed to go there? Ugh!

Brynlee, calm down. You'll be fine. You are absolutely worth meeting, and they're going to love you.

> Seriously, though. I am not prepared to meet his parents! What if they hate me?

Honestly, why would they hate you? There's nothing about you to hate. You're a delightful young lady, Brynlee, and look at how excited Luke is for you to meet them.

Well, I don't really have much of a choice now, do I?
No, you don't. And you'll be fine. Just breathe.

Are you okay? Why so quiet?
Well, I just realized I'm going to meet your parents.
Oh! No big deal. They're cool, really.
What if they don't like me? I mean, I'm not exactly in your friend crowd.
Oh, actually they're looking forward to meeting you.
They are?
Yeah. I told them all about you. Well, what I knew at the time, anyway. I showed them the video of you dancing too. They both think you're beautiful. They said I am upgrading on many levels.
They did not! Stop!
I swear! You wait. They'll probably tell you the same thing!
Do I look okay to meet your mom, though? I dressed for a date, not to meet parents.
Are you kidding? She's going to love you.
Did you really show them the video?
I did. They were blown away. They wanted to know why I wasn't going to your competition last night. I had already told my brother I'd babysit, though, or I would've tried to find a ticket.
You babysit?
You sound surprised.
I don't even babysit!
Well, my nephews are awesome, so I hang out with them whenever I can. I would've texted you last night to see how you did, but I was with them all night, so that's why I didn't text until this afternoon. That's when I got home. I had to stop and pick up things for my mom for tonight on my way home.
Sounds like you're really tight with your family.
Yeah, we are.
How old are your nephews?
They're four and two. They're so cool. I can't wait to have kids like them.
Really?
I mean, I don't want kids while I'm too young or anything. I definitely want to graduate college first. But I don't want to wait

until I'm thirty, either.

Interesting.

What about you? Do you want kids?

Oh yeah, absolutely. But I want to finish college, too.

What about your dancing career? Are you going to try to make it in the big business?

I don't know what's going to happen. My dance instructor introduced me to her friend who I think is looking for talent. He's in California in the entertainment industry. So, I don't know.

Does that mean you might move there one day?

Not really sure. My dad commutes to the same area for work all the time, so I may just commute if anything happens, but that's a big if. Besides, it wouldn't be until after I graduate, anyway. I'm not leaving high school to chase some lofty dance dream in the land of fakes and phonies.

Yeah, I hear ya. Well, I think it's great you want to go to college instead of heading to the land of broken dreams. Not that you couldn't catch your dreams. You totally could. But you can do it while going to college. You could study there.

I could, just not sure I want to. I don't know. Wow, this is your house? Nice!

Thanks. It's pretty cool, but since my brother left, it's too big. They keep talking of downsizing, but we never do. Okay, are you ready?

Yup, I guess I'm ready.

Wait, let me get your door.

Hey, you two, we're here.

Thanks, dude. Your parents are home? Cool!

He's damn near perfect. I can't believe it. And he calls me his dream girl? How about he's my dream boy. I can't believe I didn't want to go on this date! He's holding my hand! My freaking stomach has butterflies right now! Aaaand I'm blushing. Perfect. Now I'm going to look like a tomato.

Natalya, is my face seriously red?

No, it's not. Just a little pink.

Oh my God! She speaks!

Haha, sorry. We've been a little…involved.

Yeah, I can tell. It's okay. Luke, I'm nervous.

Don't be. Trust me. Okay, here we go.

Hey Mom, Dad, Billy, Lori, this is Brynlee, and this is Natalya. You all know Dylan already, of course.

Hello ladies. It's so nice to meet you.

Yes, hi, welcome. Boys, you've got yourselves some very beautiful ladies here. I hope you remember your manners.

Yeah, Dad. We're good.

Brynlee, you are much more beautiful in person. I must say, you dance marvelously! Luke told us you had a dance competition last night. How did you do?

We came in first place, thank you for asking.

Wow, congratulations! It's not really a surprise, though. You're great. Lori, I have to show you the video of Brynlee dancing. You will not believe it. It's like something you'd see in a music video. Incredible.

Oh, thank you. You're too kind.

Well, I'm looking forward to seeing it.

Natalya, Dylan mentioned you're a model?

I am. I do fashion modeling.

Well, I can see why. You're stunning. Both of you are absolutely stunning.

Okay, well we're going down to the game room, Mom. You can learn all about them later, okay?

Absolutely. So very nice to meet you both.

Thank you, Mrs. DeSilva. It's nice to meet you all as well.

Luke, your parents are really nice.

Thanks, they're pretty cool. They toned it down some. Otherwise, my mother would've went on and on about how beautiful you are, and how incredible you dance. It's all true, but you probably would've felt uncomfortable at that point. When she's passionate about her opinions, the whole world knows it.

Aww, that's sweet, though. Wow, nice game room! I love the décor!

Thank you. Me and my dad came up with the idea, Mom made it happen. She's an interior designer.

Well, she's wonderful.

You're wonderful.

Haha... *Okay, he's incredible, and I really want to kiss him right now.*

You are. Oh my God, I want to kiss you so bad right now.
Holy shit, he wants to kiss me too! Why don't you?

I don't want you to think that that's all I'm after, so, I'll wait.

Um, okay?

I'm gonna prove to you that I'm not a jerk.

I don't think you're a jerk.

Okay, this is really difficult, so uh, let's play air hockey. What do you think?

Yeah, sure. I love air hockey! *Damn. I wish he would've just kissed me first.*

Sweet! Haha, I guess those two are just going to play pool and be in LaLa Land all night.

Looks that way, doesn't it?

I have to beat him at this game. And then if he doesn't kiss me, I'm going for it. We've had to watch those two gazing into each other's eyes and making out all night, and we barely held hands. I have to say, though, it is pretty cool to watch him try to prove himself. Maybe I'll let him squirm a while. Ugh! But I want to kiss him so bad! We'll see... SCORE! Haha, Point!

YES! My point!

Aw, come on, I gave you that one.

Oh please! I'm gonna kick your ass in this game.

Oh, you think so, huh?

No, I know so.

So you've got a competitive side to ya, too. I like it!

HAHA! I score again!

Oh come on! You cheated!

How the heck did I cheat? I don't cheat!

Yes you did! You swooshed your hair behind your shoulder! You distracted me!

What?! You're crazy!

HA! That's one for me!

You just got lucky. You better savor that point, because it's the only point you're gonna get! SCORE! You wanna quit yet?

I'm no quitter. I always go after and get what I want.

Well, you can forget about winning, because... SCORE AGAIN!
Ha! 4 to 1. Three more and I am champ.

173

Look at how freaking hot he is! Oh my GOD! I can't get over that smile. He's so much cuter than I thought he was. Maybe it's because I used to think he might be a jerk? I don't know. But he's definitely not a jerk... So far. His parents are so sweet. I doubt they'd raise a son who's an ass. Is he seriously the perfect guy? GOD I just want to kiss him right now. I have to hurry up and win this game.

Okay, listen…
>What?

My point! That is all.
>Alright, that's it.

What's wrong, Luke? Feeling bad about being beat by a girl? BAM!! 6 to 1. Game point, baby!
>Oh, you…. You're in for it now!

Oh really? What am I in for? Because it looks to me like POINT! Oh yeah, oh yeah! I won, you didn't. Winner, winner, winner….
>Hahaha, good game. God, you are so cute when you win!

Yes, that's right, I won! And it was cute.
>I like your little victory dance. How about a victory hug?

Definitely! *Okay, melting. Melting fast. Okay, I can't take it, I have to kiss him right now……*

>Wow! Um, okay, I was NOT expecting that!

Oh, I'm sorry. I guess I shouldn't have done that. *Oh no, he didn't like it.*
>Oh no, no, I'm glad you did! Damn, that was nice! Um, okay, I'm going to run upstairs and get us some drinks before I kiss you right back and I don't stop. I'll be right back.

Okay, that was amazing! He is such a great kisser. Holy cow! But did he really like it, or was it so horrible he had to run upstairs to get away from me? Ugh! I hope he isn't disgusted. Oh my God, what if he is? This will be so awkward. Please, God, please don't let him be disgusted. Please let him like me. Please tell me I didn't just ruin my chance with him. Please let me still be his dream girl…

Hey, sorry I took so long.
>You didn't. That was quick.

Okay good, because I couldn't wait to get back down here. I got an ace bandage to wrap your wrist.

Oh, you really don't have to…

I want to. Let me have your hand. So um, that kiss.

I'm sorry.

No! Don't be sorry! That was, like, the best kiss I ever got! The bad thing is, though, it left me wanting more.

Why is that a bad thing?

Brynlee, I really like you, a lot. And after what I told you, I don't want you to think I'm just trying to have sex with you. I swear it's not like that. I mean, of course, I'd love to have sex with you, haha, but I won't. I don't want you to think I'm that kind of guy. I really like you.

I like you, too, Luke. And I don't think you're that kind of guy. I mean, I get it. She was putting out and you took it. It happens, I guess.

Believe me, Brynlee. I'm not the same kid I was a year ago. Dad and I, we talk a lot, and he's helped me to realize the things I really want and what's really important to me.

That's great. He sounds like an awesome dad.

He is. He's helped me realize that I'm not looking to bang every girl that comes along, and that I don't have to be like all the other guys. He taught me about respect, and to be honest ,and if that's how he scored such a great life with my mom, then that's what I am gonna do. I want a life like they have.

Luke, that's so mature for a…

For a guy like me?

No, for a kid our age. Thank you for wrapping.

You're welcome. And, yeah, I know. It's kinda funny, I stopped having sex with Samantha a long time ago after Dad and I talked about it, and then I realized that sex was all we had. It sucked and I've been miserable for a long time. And the sex wasn't even that great, probably because I had zero feelings for her. That's when I figured out that I want a girl I click with, who's fun and nice and likes me for me, not because I'm on the football team. I swear, one shitty relationship and you grow up pretty quick.

Wow, Luke. I'm sorry it sucked so bad. I hate that she was such a bitch to you.

And then, you. You walked by me one day, weeks ago, and there was just something about you that I couldn't put my finger on. I couldn't stop thinking about you, and I don't know if you noticed, but I would be near your locker every morning just so I could see you. I was really nervous to ask you out.

Seriously?

Yeah. But I swear, I'm not a creeper!

And here I thought you were only asking me out tonight because of that video.

What? Where would you get that idea?

I don't know. I guess I couldn't imagine that "Luke, the hot football player" would ever be interested in me, especially after dating Samantha for so long.

Oh my God, are you kidding? She is nothing compared to you.

Well, I don't know about that.

Have you taken a real good look at yourself? Holy shit, Bryn, you're gorgeous! And, oh my God, those eyes! They're like, ugh! They're making me want to kiss you so bad!

Well? What are you waiting for?

I think I'm in love.....

Whew, okay, I think we should stop doing that. I have to, uh, calm down a bit.

Yeah, that's probably a good idea. Maybe we should keep talking some.

Yeah, that's good. We should do that. Okay, so here's a question, how are we ever going to hang out alone? It's taking some serious, SERIOUS self-control to not just be all over you right now.

Yeah, umm, I really don't know, and same.

Let's make a pact. We will not do anything more than kiss.

For how long? I mean, it can't be open ended like that, because then it won't work. We'll end up breaking the pact.

Yeah, true. But then again, if we put a date on it, then it's like, giving us permission to do stuff the next day.

Oh, I see what you're saying. Yeah, umm, I don't know. I mean, I always thought I'd wait a long, long time, like maybe even marriage. Is that stupid?

No, that's not stupid. Why would you think it would be?

I don't know. I guess because it doesn't happen these days.

Well, hey, if you want to wait until you're married, then you should.

That's the thing. I don't know if I want to wait. I mean, really, who the heck would want to date me if they have to wait that long?

I would.

   Oh, come on, Luke.

No, really. I would. I told you, that shit with the bitch really opened my eyes to things. In a way, I'm glad it did. What guy our age has that kind of insight into life, and love? I found out the hard way what love isn't. And, aren't we all just looking for love? Well, okay, maybe not guys in high school. But then again, I don't know. I just know that I'm looking for love. All that other stuff is bullshit. It sucks. Feeling empty sucks.

   Well, then, you might just be my dream boy. Unless, of
   course, you're bullshitting me just to get me into bed with
   you.

I swear to God, I'm not! I'll get my dad down here and you can ask him yourself!

   No, that's okay. I believe you.

Well, you know what? I want you to really believe me and not wonder. Hey Dad! Can you come down here real quick?

   Luke! Did you really just call him down here? Oh my God.

Hey Dylan, chill out! Dylan! Oh well, I tried to warn him.

   Why?

What's up, Son?

   Hey Dad, um, what are your thoughts on that, over there?

Hahaha, Luke, holy crap, they're gonna kill you!

   I know, but watch…

Dylan! Son, what are you doing?

   Oh, hey Mr. DeSilva.

Son, don't you think you should respect this beautiful young lady and not slobber on her all night?

   Yes, sir.

Luke, I trust you are sticking to your values and remembering what it is you really want?

   Yeah, Dad, I am.

Brynlee, is he being a gentleman?

   Yes, he is definitely being a gentleman.

Okay, good. Remember, Son, you told me you are looking for true love. What Dylan's doing, over there, is not how to find it.

   I know, Dad. It's all good.

Self-control, boys. You'll marry a good woman if you can control yourself now.

Thanks, Dad. Haha, see? Now you can rest assured I am not just telling you stuff to get you into bed.

Holy shit, that was hilarious!

Dude!! What the hell? Why didn't you tell me your dad was coming?

Dude, I tried. Maybe you two can stay up here and breathe a little.

Oh my Gosh, I'm so embarrassed. Brynlee! You could've said something.

Natalya, Luke tried! You two just happened to be smothering each other and didn't hear him, jeez!

Oh! I'm still so embarrassed.

Maybe you guys should go back to playing pool and getting to know each other more. Dude, I mean, respect the lady, hahaha!

Shut up, man! It's not like we're just all over each other, God!

Oh my gosh, Luke, your dad is awesome. Haha, I love how he called Dylan out! That was great!

Yeah, it was pretty funny. I set him up good, didn't I?

You really did.

You're a really cool girl, you know that?

Thanks. You're pretty cool, yourself.

So, what does this all mean? Where do we go from here?

I don't know. What do you think?

I think I want you to be my girlfriend. No, I know I want you to be my girlfriend.

Oh?

Do you think you could date a guy like me?

Absolutely.

Really? I might just be the happiest guy on Earth right now.

And I might just be the happiest girl on Earth right now. *Oh my God!!! I'm dating Luke!! Could tonight be any more perfect?! Awww! He kissed my cheek!!*

I kept it safe - cheek kiss.

You are so sweet.

Yeah, I try. So, are we setting our date as our wedding night?

You sure you want to date me knowing you may have to wait until our wedding night?

Of course! God, I'm not that shallow!

Oh, no, I didn't mean…

I'm kidding! Yes, I want to date you. Yes I will wait as
long as I have to, even if it means never with us because
you break up with me.

Why would I break up with you?

I don't know, you go away to college and break up with me
for some hot guy?

Wow, I'm not that shallow!

Touché!

How about this, let's be realistic. Let's set my 17th birthday as the
date.

Is our wedding night not realistic?

I don't know if you remember, but I kissed you first. I want to wait,
but I'm not really sure I will always want to wait.

Okay, your 17th birthday. Then we can reevaluate. But just
know that because you want to, I'm going to do everything
in my power to make sure we wait until our wedding night.
And we should probably try to make sure they wait until at
least tomorrow!

That's too funny! Hey! No sex in the corner!

Shut up, Brynlee! We're not having sex!

Hahaha! Love you, best friend!

God, Brynlee, you are so beautiful and funny and... Let's
watch a movie!

Okay! *How the hell are we going to wait until we get married? We
can do it. We can totally wait. I mean, look at how good we're doing.
It's funny how we are joking around about getting married. We just
started dating, not even ten minutes ago.* We can't ever be alone,
can we?

No, I'm thinking probably not. But when we are, self-
control. Okay?

Okay.

*I wonder if my parents would be mad if I got married when I'm
eighteen. And if his parents would be okay him marrying at
nineteen? Wow! He's my boyfriend! I have a boyfriend who just so
happens to be the hottest guy at school. And his arm is around me,
and he smells so good. He's so sweet, and knows what he wants in
life. And his kisses are amazing! Like, damn!*

What's got you smiling like that?

Was I smiling?

Yeah. You really get into your thoughts, huh?

Yeah, I guess so.

Well? What is it that makes my beautiful girlfriend smile like that?

You.

Best night ever!

Brynlee, I want you to know that this has really been the best night I've had in a really long time. You are so amazing, and I can't believe that I get to call you my girlfriend. Oh, and my parents love you, by the way.

They do?

Yeah, after they went back upstairs after they interrupted our movie to "bring us snacks", you know, to hang out with us, my mom texted me and said how lovely you are, and all that. She doesn't call too many people lovely.

Are you sure she wasn't being sarcastic?

Oh, I'm sure. That's her word of approval. If she didn't like you I would've gotten a "she's nice, dear".

Oh really?

Yeah. I've gotten a lot of those texts before.

Oh, have you?

Yeah. Not just about girls, though. About friends in general.

Well, I'm honored. And thank you for such a great night. I'm glad we got to know each other.

Yeah, me too. So, now that you're my girlfriend, you should probably wear my ring. It's a thing with football players. If you date one, you have to wear his ring, and I want you to wear mine.

Aww, Luke, I don't really know what to say. I'd love to wear your ring!

Good! I even have a chain for you to wear it on. It was my Dad's chain that my mom wore his ring on.

Oh my Gosh, really?

Yeah, here, let me put it on you. There. Damn, that looks good on you. I think we need to take a picture.

Okay.

Nice!

Can you send it to me?

Yup, it's on the way, and I just posted it online. So, we can probably expect a crapload of texts in a few minutes.

Oh good, I got it. Aww, we look so cute together!

We do, don't we? And... there goes my phone. And so it begins.

Oh, haha mine too.
Okay, let me walk you in.
   Be prepared, you may have to meet my parents now.
I'm cool with that. But first, a goodnight kiss…

God, I love kissing you.
   Does tonight really have to end?
I wish it didn't, but I don't want your parents to hate me, so I should walk you in now.
   Okay, let's go.

Hi Daddy. What are you doing in the kitchen so late?
   I was a little hungry, so I decided to make a snack.
Daddy, this is Luke. Luke, this is my dad.
   Hello Mr. Sheffield, it's nice to meet you.
Luke, nice strong handshake. Good to meet you. So, did you two have a good night? Where's Natalya? Is she staying the night tonight?
   We had a great night, and no, she had to go home. She said
   she has to study tomorrow.
I see you're wearing a football ring. I assume that would be yours, Luke?
   Yes sir, and if it's okay, I'd like to ask your permission to
   date your daughter.
Well, son, I appreciate your asking. Are you going to respect my daughter? She is a young lady of strong character, and she deserves to be respected.
   Yes, sir. Absolutely. My father taught me that respecting a
   woman is most important.
Your father's a good man. In that case, you have my permission to date Brynlee.
   Thank you, sir.
Well, I'm going to head upstairs now that my princess is home safe and sound. Luke, it was good to meet you. I expect I'll be seeing more of you around here.
   Yes sir. It was nice to meet you, too, sir. Goodnight.
Goodnight. And goodnight to you, Sweetpea. Lock up, okay? I love you.
   Love you, too, Daddy.
I like your Dad. He's a strong guy.

Oh my gosh! Did he squeeze your hand too tight? I'm so
sorry!

No, I don't mean that, I mean, he commands respect. I like that. He
and my dad would get along great.

Oh good! I thought he hurt your hand. He did that to a guy
once, and he was only here to study! We weren't dating or
anything. I was so embarrassed. Wait a minute, I just
realized something. Your mom and dad have been together
since high school? You said she wore his ring.

Yeah, they've been together for a long time! I think mom was a
freshman and dad was a sophomore or something. Or maybe they
were a year older than that, I don't know. All I know is, they've been
together forever.

That's so cute! I want to be able to say that one day.

Well, maybe this is our chance. Maybe we'll carry on the tradition.
My grandparents on both sides started dating at a young age too, but
of course, things were a lot different back in their day.

Well, I think it's so beautiful that they can say they were
high school sweethearts.

Maybe we'll say the same thing. If they can do it, we can do it.

This is true.

Well, I should get going.

Okay. Thank you so much for dinner and everything. I
really had a great time.

Me too. Are you busy tomorrow?

No, I don't think so.

If not, I'd love to hang out again, maybe grab some lunch? I don't
even care if we do absolutely nothing. I just want to be with you
doing whatever.

That'd be great. I'd like that a lot.

Well, I'll text you, then. We can make a plan.

Okay.

So, um, goodnight, Brynlee.

Goodnight. Thanks, again.

You bet. By the way, I'd kiss you again, but I don't want your dad to
walk in, so...

Aww, you're so sweet. *Another cheek kiss! That is
adorable!!* Goodnight. Drive safe.

I will, cutie.

Okay, I think I've just died and gone to Heaven. Can he get any sweeter? And he's so respectful. I can't believe he asked Daddy permission to date me! He totally scored huge bonus points with that! Who even does that anymore? Whose dad would ever teach them to do that these days? Probably no one. I bet Dylan wouldn't do that. It's crazy that they are best friends and are so different. I guess Mr. Sierzant holding a shotgun didn't really phase him one bit. But then again, Natalya looked like she was just fine with making out all night. They have liked each other for a while, though, so I guess it was just all built up. Oh, my bed is so comfy right now. And my pillow is the perfect amount of fluff to just lay here and think about Luke and everything that happened tonight.

So, I see you've gotten yourself a boyfriend. And he's a cutie, isn't he?

> Hi Nova. He is absolutely adorable. How did I get so lucky?

And why do you think that you're the lucky one? Didn't you hear what he was telling you tonight? How he said his last relationship had him feeling empty, and how miserable he was?

> Yes, I heard, but he's such a great guy, and I don't know.

You're a great girl, Brynlee, and I think you're both lucky.

> I guess. I just feel like I have a lot of work to do to be good enough for him. He comes from a great family. His parents are so nice, and he's so polite, and did you hear him ask Daddy permission to date me? Come on! He's a modern day gentleman, and I'm just Brynlee.

You are so much more than "just Brynlee". Even Luke told you all the things he likes about you; weren't you listening?

> I was. I just have a hard time believing it.

Okay, I think it's time for the talk.

> What talk?

You are having a hard time believing these things because your mom has raised you to believe that you have to be and look a certain way to attract the right kind of man. Unfortunately, it's because that's what her ex had her believe. Your mom was never like that. She was a very confident girl who didn't care what other people had to say. And then her ex came along. There was something about him that she was attracted to, but it wasn't a good something. He was bad from the start. He flirted with everyone all the time, he'd tell her he loved her, but then say he was in love with his ex-girlfriend, but not break up with your mom. He'd compare her to his ex all the time. He cheated on her multiple times, with multiple women, but she never left because he always lied to her and said it would never happen again, all the while intending to keep doing it. It started with manipulation, then he tried to control her.

How?

Well, he'd tell her not to eat certain things because she was starting to gain weight. He'd keep telling her about all the little imperfections, which, in reality weren't imperfections at all. They were her body's characteristics. No one is perfect, we talked about that the other day. But he had her believing that she should be. He would constantly gawk at other girls in front of her, so badly sometimes that she cried right there. After they got married, the mental and emotional abuse got worse. Then he started beating her because she didn't look like his ex. It only happened a few times before your mother got up enough courage to leave him. She was scared, at first, that he'd come after her, but he never did. By then it was too late; your mom had many psychological issues because of that relationship.

How do you know all this?

I've been your tea cup since you were born. I heard her tell your dad the story.

He didn't know before they got married?

He knew some, but he didn't know the whole story. One day she just broke down and told him the entire thing, from beginning to end.

Wow. I had no idea.

Unfortunately, your mom still deals with those issues, and they come out in her parenting. She knows you're good enough, but there's that voice of her ex that she hears in the back of her mind, and she gets scared. She just doesn't want the same thing to happen to you.

I don't understand, why didn't she ever get help?

I can't answer that. My point is, Brynlee, you don't have to be anything but you, ever.

I was so wrong about Luke.

185

Well, it's good to be on guard. Some guys are like Jekyll and Hyde. Luke is a great guy. He likes you exactly the way you are. You don't have to try to be anything for him.

>I don't know. I still feel like I should try to lose a few pounds.

You are perfect exactly the way you are and don't need to lose weight at all. But you should know that as you get older, you may get a little curvier since your body isn't done developing yet. Just don't mistake those curves for extra weight.

>Oh my God! No!

There's nothing wrong with being curvy. But curves can be dangerous, especially when you look the way you do.

>What do you mean, dangerous?

Well, women with curves can attract the wrong kind of attention, so you'll have to be careful and always be on guard for men who are only after one thing. Remember all the things your Aunt told you.

>Ugh! What if Luke doesn't like curves? Samantha isn't curvy, she's like a Victoria's Secret model.

He likes you for you, not just your looks. He doesn't like her, remember?

>Oh, Nova, I really hope so. I like him a lot. He's everything I've ever dreamed of. He really is my dream boy.

Well, he seems to be crazy about you.

>Tonight was seriously the best night ever. And we're hanging out again tomorrow. I can't wait to see him again.

I love to see you so happy.

>Me too.

So, I guess Blake is out of the picture?

>Holy crap, I forgot about Blake!

What are you going to do?

>I have to tell him I'm dating Luke.

If he doesn't already know.

>How would he know?

Luke uploaded that picture of the two of you. It might get back to him.

>I guess I should text him, huh?

Yes, you probably should.

> *Oh God, okay. Oh crap, I forgot about all these texts from before. Ugh, I don't feel like replying right now.*

"Hey Blake"

I hope he answers soon. I want this to be just like ripping off a bandage – painful at first but then all better.

"Hello, beautiful" "how was your date? I guess you didn't need to be rescued"
"Actually, I went really well"
"Oh. That doesn't sound good for me"
"Well…"
"I guess you guys hit it off?"
"Yeah, we did"
"Damn. I guess I was too late"
"I'm sorry"
"It's ok. Maybe if things don't work out…"
"Thanks for understanding"
"Well, it is what it is" "I'm happy for you"
"Thank you" "I'm really sorry Blake"
"It's ok. I just wish I didn't miss my chance" "I guess I'll catch ya later"
"Okay"
"Text me sometime. We're still friends, right?"
"Of course! I will. You too"
"You bet. Goodnight, beautiful"
"Goodnight"

Okay, that sucked.

> *I'm sure it did. I'm sorry, Brynlee.*

Thank you. It figures, I have liked him for years! I finally get a date with him for next weekend and I get a boyfriend! Really? I mean, come on.

> *Well, it's probably for the best.*

Yeah, I guess you're right. It would've been hard anyway, since we'd hardly ever see each other while he's at college and I'm still here. And it's not like I'm graduating any too soon. I still have two and a half years to go. At least with Luke, I can see him every day at school, every weekend, and he's not graduating for another year and a half. And when he goes to college, I'll only have one year left here.

Exactly.

Who in the world is texting me at this hour? Aww, it's Luke!

"Hey cutie. I want to let you know I'm home, and I miss you already"

"I miss you already, too"

"Can't wait until tomorrow. I want to learn more about you"

"You do? Like what?"

"Everything. I want to know everything there is to know about you"

"Well, there's not much else"

"I bet there's a lot to know"   "What are ya doing right this minute?"

"Just laying in bed, thinking about you"   "What are you doing?"

"Same. What are you thinking about?"

"I'm glad I was wrong about you. And how your smile makes me melt"

"I'm glad you were wrong about me too. I'm glad I was right about you"

"Oh were you?"

"Yup. Spot on"   "I thought you'd be perfect, and you are"

"Hardly"

"Perfect for me"

"Ditto"   "Thanks so much for tonight"

"You already thanked me. No need for thanks. It was my pleasure"

"Goodnight Luke"

"Goodnight cutie"

Time for our mirror exercise.

Oh, Nova, I'm too tired.

Come on, you have to do it every day.

Can I just lay here and do it? This bed is so comfy and I'm all warm and cozy.

I suppose we can do it here. Close your eyes and picture yourself in front of you. What do you see?

I see me and Luke on his couch in the game room, and he has his arm around me, and we're both smiling.

Okay, good. Look at your face. I want you to say "I am beautiful the way I am". Keep repeating it to yourself.

I am beautiful the way I am. I am beautiful the way I am. I am beautiful the... way I... am. I am... beautiful...

Such a beautiful day...

That was such a weird dream. Why in the world would I dream about bobsledding?

Good morning!
>Morning, Nova.

You're up early.
>I had the weirdest dream and I guess it woke me up.

What was it about?
>Bobsledding. I was bobsledding.

Well, that's different.
>I know!

Tell me about it. What happened?
>Well, I was with Natalya, and we were in Colorado for her winter photo-shoot, and these really hot guys asked us if we wanted to go bobsledding with them. At first we were on the beginner track, and then I saw a sign that said "Danger: Curves Ahead", and then all of a sudden the track got really curvy, and we were picking up speed. It was really bumpy, and Natalya was cracking up behind me. I remember thinking that if the turns got any worse we would flip out, but then the track got really straight. We were gaining speed fast, and there was what looked like a ski jump, and next thing I knew we were flying through the air. I saw a field of flowers below and in front of us, and then I woke up. Wait, why am I telling you? Don't you already know?

I do. I wanted to see if you could recall the dream.
>What in the world do you think it means?

Well, think about it a little bit.
>Okay? There were two hot guys. It was a beginner track. Then dangerous curves. It got really bumpy. Natalya was laughing. The track straightened out and then we were flying through the air over flowers. I don't see a point to it.

What did we talk about last night?

    We talked about my mom and why she is the way she is.

Yes, then what?

    We talked about how great Luke is.

And...

    And... then you told me that I'm not done developing, and curves can be dangerous! Oh! I get it now!

You do?

    It's early, but I get! The easy track represents the young me. Then I start to develop, and if I'm not careful, I can be taken advantage of! But then the track straightens out, which probably means I'll mentally develop and mature as well, figuring it all out, and once I do, I'll take off and be happy – the field of flowers!

Very good, Brynlee!

    But why was Natalya laughing?

I don't know. Maybe she was just enjoying the ride.

    Haha, like last night!

Exactly. Your dream doesn't necessarily just represent what you just told me, however. It could represent life in general. Life has its ups and downs, its easy paths and not so easy ones. It gets bumpy, it can be an adventure, but it sure is a beautiful ride.

    Okay, too much deepness for early Sunday morning.

    Wow, it's actually sunny out today.

It is, isn't it?

    I wonder what Luke and I are going to do today. I think I'll jump in the shower. I want to be ready when he texts me. Um, quick question. Did you change your outfit? You look different.

Why, yes, I did. I'm glad you noticed.

    I didn't know you had other clothes.

Well, as you begin to change, my clothes change.

    Huh?

You're beginning to see yourself differently. It happened a lot quicker than most, but with all that's happened in the last few days, all the positivity coming at you, your thoughts about yourself are changing. You're not so hard on yourself. Hadn't you noticed?

No, I didn't realize. But then again, I've been so
preoccupied with so much else.
Yes, you have. But you also haven't been bashing yourself
quite as much. Hence, my new clothes. And I must say, I do like
this outfit much better than the last one. It's less mainstream,
and more your style.
Wow, this is crazy. There's kind of a Nanny McDuffy
thing going on. That's trippy.
Oh, I love that woman! She's such a doll.
She's real?
Haha, no, I'm kidding! But I do love that movie.
Yes, me too. Okay, I'm jumping in the shower.

*That dream was crazy. But I get it. Curves on my body, curves in
life, if not handled properly, like in bobsledding, it could be
dangerous. Life is a beautiful ride, especially lately. So much has
happened in the last few days. I feel like I'm on Cloud 9, just
floating through the air. I wonder what we're going to do today. I
can't wait to see Luke again. What should I wear? I guess that
depends on what we're going to do. Maybe I'll text him and see what
he wants to do. No, I should let him text me first. I don't want to be
annoying and seem like this clingy girlfriend who won't leave him
alone. I definitely don't want to be one of those. This hot water feels
so good. My wrist is still a little sore. I wonder if I should wrap it
again. I guess I should, just to be on the safe side. Why in the world
do I smell bacon? It's making me hungry…*

*I really don't know what to wear today. Maybe I'll wear the cute
outfit I was saving for Blake. I think that'll be okay. The red looks
good with my hair color, and it really shows my style. He said he
likes that, so… Hmmm, should I straighten my hair today or leave it
wavy? I think I'll leave it wavy. If I want to know if he really likes
me for me, I might as well go all out and be the real me, no holds
barred, right? Better to find out sooner rather than later.*

I'm so proud of you!
Why?
Because you're going into today with confidence in who you
are. You're embracing you, and that, my dear, is very
impressive. You're a quick learner.

Thanks, Nova. I don't really want to waste time, you know? If he really likes me for me, then the huge dose of Brynlee he'll get today will determine that pretty quickly. And if he doesn't, well, I guess I'll find out.

Good girl. I think you'll be pleasantly surprised, though.

I sure do hope so. Trying to be like everyone else is so tiring, and it's not even fun.

Tell me about it. I didn't like my last outfit. This one is okay, but I can't wait to see what the next one will be like. The more you are the real you and you realize how great you are, the better I look!

So crazy, but so cool at the same time. Now I can't wait to see what your next outfit will be. I really want to believe I am what you say I am, and I'm working on it. I promise.

I know you are, and you're doing great. Like I said, it's happening much quicker than most. That outfit look fantastic, Brynlee!

Thank you. I'm going to go dry my hair and get makeup on, and then go and eat. That bacon smell has me starving! I wonder what the special occasion is.

I have no idea, but you're right. It does smell good.

Please, please let me have another good hair and makeup day!

Hair looks good! Makeup looks good! Now I can go eat.

You look beautiful! You did something different to your hair. What is it?

I parted it on the other side today.

Ah, yes! That's it. It looks so pretty.

Thank you. Does my makeup look okay?

It looks great.

Okay good. I'm going down to eat.

Okay. Enjoy your breakfast.

Good morning, Mom, good morning Daddy!

Good morning, Sweetpea! Well! Don't you look beautiful! What's the occasion?

Good morning, hon. You do look great! Yes, what is the occasion?

Oh, no occasion. Luke and I are hanging out today.

I see. Daddy told me he met him last night. He said he seems very respectable and nice.

Yup, he is.

He even asked for permission to date you?

He did.

I like this boy already. I'm sorry I didn't get to meet him last night.

Oh that's okay. You'll meet him today, hopefully.

Yes, Bryn, he is very respectful. I was impressed. But that doesn't mean he has free reign with my daughter. I'll be keeping a close watch on this young man.

It's okay, Daddy. You do what you have to do. Now, what's with the bacon? Where did it all go? I'm starving.

Oh, sorry, sweetie, I needed it for a recipe.

Ugh! And you didn't save me any?

Well, actually, I did.

You did? Thanks mom!

Yes, but you have to eat something else with it, maybe eggs, or some fruit?

I just want one piece. I'll have fruit with it, and some wheat toast.

Okay, hon.

Hey Mom, did Aunt Holly talk to you about our plan?

Do you mean about the diet?

Yes.

Yes, she did. I think it's a wonderful idea.

You do? I'm surprised.

Why are you surprised? I think learning how to be healthy is a great idea. And it'll help you to maybe lose a couple of pounds.

Mom, I don't think I need to lose any. I think I'm fine the way I am.

Well, you are, but a couple of pounds wouldn't hurt.

Heidi, Brynlee is beautiful. She doesn't need to lose weight.

Well, I just don't want her to end up with…

With what, mom? A jerk like your ex? I won't. Trust me.

No, I was going to say I don't want you to end up with a struggle later on. You're not done developing, and…

Mom, I know. I'll be fine. I like the way I look. I mean, look at me! I look hot today!

Easy, now. Maybe you should go put on sweatpants and a big baggy t-shirt. My little girl doesn't need to look hot, especially when she's going out with a boy all day.

Oh, Daddy. I love you.

I love you too, Sweetpea.

I love you, Mom, but I really wish you would stop being so negative about the way I look all the time. I do enough of that on my own.

I'm sorry, hon. I just worry about you, that's all.

I know you do, but I'll be fine. I promise. So you don't care if me and Aunt Holly research and possibly change our dietary lifestyle?

No, I think it's great. Maybe then you can teach me what you learn. But does this mean I'll have to learn new recipes?

Yeah, but I can learn, too. And I can even cook.

Whoa, whoa, why has no one asked the father if he is okay with this? Are you jumping on the vegetarian bandwagon?

No, Daddy, the healthy one.

Will we still have steak? I need to eat steak. I'm a man, and men eat steak.

I don't know, Daddy. Maybe, but maybe not as much.

Well, I don't think I'm okay with this.

Honey, let her learn. You'll be okay without steak. Besides, it might do you some good.

Are you saying I'm fat?

No, I'm saying you're getting old, and you need to watch your cholesterol.

I need protein. Men need protein.

Daddy, chill out. It'll be okay. Thanks, Mom.

I'm proud of you, Hon. You're growing up and learning to think for yourself.

Wow, thanks Mom.

Luke texted! "Good morning, cutie". Awww!

"Good morning, handsome!" *Okay, that was corny.*

"How are you this morning?"

"I'm great! How are you?"

"Great!" "So, my brother asked if I want to go to my nephew's basketball game today"

Oh, crap, does that mean we can't hang out?

"He said you can come. Would you want to?"

"Sure, that'll be fun"

"Awesome" "It's at noon. Can you be ready by 11?"
"I'm already dressed and ready for whatever"
"Hey, cool! Can I pick you up sooner, then?"
"Sure"

Hey Mom, Dad, is it okay if Luke picks me up soon? We're going to
his nephew's basketball game.
> Sure, hon, I don't see why not. I guess I should go make
> myself presentable so I can meet him.

Yes, Sweetpea, that's fine.
> Thank you!

"You can come anytime. My mom can't wait to meet you"
"Awesome! Ok, I'll be there in a little while. Just have to eat"
"Okay, cool"
"I'll text you when I'm on the way" "Bye cutie"
"Bye :) "

You're awfully smiley. You must really like this boy.
> I do, Daddy. He's really great. And his parents are so nice.

I'd like to meet his parents, if you two are going to be dating.
> We are dating, Daddy.

You know what I mean. Heidi, maybe we should have them over for
dinner next weekend.
> Sure, dear, that sounds like a great idea.

Wow, let's slow down a little. It's not like we're engaged! We just
started dating last night.
> I know, and it's a perfect time to meet his parents and see
> what kind of family he comes from.

Oh my God, okay. Just don't embarrass us, please. We're just kids.
> We won't embarrass you, hon. Promise.

*Seriously? Why do they have to meet them already? I mean, can't
they wait a few months? Like maybe February? That's a good three
months away. Well, whatever. They're gonna do what they're
gonna do. God, this bacon is so good. I haven't had this stuff in
forever! But, if I'm going to start eating healthier, I guess I should
get used to not eating it. Mom's using it in a recipe? What kind of
recipe? What's it for?*

Mom, is this new recipe for dinner tonight?
> No, it's for a potluck jewelry party I'm going to.

Apparently, there are going to be a ton of women there.
Oh really? Are you going to leave some here for me and Dad?
No, sorry. I made just enough to take with me.
I thought maybe you and I can grab something out to eat, if you'll be home, Sweetpea.
Oh, well, I don't know what Luke and I are going to do after the basketball game. I don't know how long he plans to hang out today.
Well, maybe he can come with us. I'd like to get to know this young man who's dating my daughter. You can tell a lot about a person from the way they eat.
Okay, we'll see.
Aww that's so cute. Daddy wants to get to know him better. How in the world can you tell how a person is by the way they eat? I'm not even going to open up that can. That's a whole other conversation I really don't feel like getting into. Oh, okay. I'll ask. I know he wants to tell me.
How can you tell about a person by the way they eat?
Well, it's the perfect place to see what kind of manners they have. Are their elbows on the table? Do they chew with their mouth closed or open? Do they speak with their mouth full, use a napkin, is there a napkin on their lap? What do they order if they're not paying, and if they are, do they say to order whatever you want, and do they cringe if you do? How do they treat the wait staff, with respect or do they talk down to them? Do they send food back for any little thing, and do they scrutinize the bill? How do they tip?
Okay, okay Daddy, I get it. Just remember, Luke is still a teenager. He might still be a little rough around the edges.
Well, he asked permission to date you. Something tells me he's a little more refined than your average high school football player, and that'll give me good insight as to what his family is like.
Oh Daddy.
He's right, Honey. Let him have this one.
Okay, I'll see if he wants to go out to dinner with us.
Great. You two pick where.
Okay.
Well, I'm going up to get ready before he comes. I don't want him thinking your mom's a hag.
You're not a hag, mom.
No, far from it, Honey. My wife is gorgeous.

Thank you, Kyle. I love you.
I love you, too, my love.
Aww, I want to be like that when I'm married.
Marry the right one, and you will be, hon. Trust me.

Oh, I trust you on that! You would know, that's for sure.

Another great day underway...

Bryn, I think Luke's here.

  Oh my gosh, okay. Mom, you're going to love him.

  Where'd Daddy go?

Oh, he's in the garage getting dinner out of the freezer for tomorrow.

  Oh, okay. I'll get the door.

Hey, cutie. Wow, you look… incredible! Holy cow, um, yeah, wow!

  I guess you like my outfit?

The outfit's great, but I'm talking about the girl in it. I suddenly feel unworthy.

  Aww, Luke, you're so sweet.

No, really. How did I get so lucky? God, you're beautiful!

  Okay, I really need to get this blushing thing under control.

  Thank you. You look great, yourself.

Thanks. So, do I get to meet your mom?

  Yeah, she's in the kitchen. Follow me.

I will follow you anywhere.

He'll follow me anywhere! I can't even stand how adorable his is!

Mom, this is Luke.

  Hello Luke, it's nice to meet you.

Hello, ma'am. It's my pleasure.

  Well, aren't you handsome! And tall!

Thank you, Mrs. Sheffield.

  So, Brynlee tells me you're going to your nephew's basketball game?

Yes, he's a little guy, and he loves when there are a lot of us cheering him on.

  Oh that sounds like fun. It's great you want to cheer him on. It's good for his self-esteem.

Yes, it is. He's gets a huge smile when he hears his name from the stands. I love it.

  Well, you sound like a very supportive uncle.

I am. I love my nephews.

  Oh, you have more than one?

Yes, my brother and his wife have two boys. They're great kids. I hope to have kids like them one day.

Not too soon, I hope!

No ma'am! I want to finish college and have my career set before kids come along.

What are you looking to do?

Well, right now I want to major in Sports Training and Sport Psychology, and I'd like to minor in Marketing.

Wow, a double major, and minor! That's a lot. Sounds like you're a very ambitious young man.

Well, I want to cover my bases, and be able to provide for my family one day.

Well, I think that's wonderful. I'm sure you'll do fine. You seem very mature for your age.

Yeah, I get that a lot lately. I guess I just realized at an early age what I want in life, and what's most important.

Well, Luke, that's more than a lot of adults I know! Very impressive.

Thank you.

Well, Mom, I guess we're going to go.

I don't know where your father went. He was just getting dinner out of the freezer.

Oh, that's okay. We'll go out through the garage and see if we see him. Love you. See you later.

It was nice to meet you, Mrs. Sheffield.

Luke, it was very nice to meet you, as well.

Your mom is really nice. I see where you get your looks from. She's really beautiful.

Thank you. Let's see if we can find my dad real quick.

Okay, cool. I don't want to be rude and leave without saying hi.

Daddy? Are you out here?

Yes, Sweetpea, I'm on the side of the house.

We're leaving, Daddy.

Hello, son, how are you this morning?

I'm great, thank you, Sir.

Have you met my wife? She was looking forward to meeting you.

I did. She's very nice.

I like to think so. Bryn, did you mention dinner?

No, go ahead.

Luke, if you don't already have plans for dinner, my wife is going out tonight to some jewelry thing, so I thought I'd take Brynlee out for dinner. We'd love to have you join us.

Wow, that'd be great. I'm sure it'll be fine. But, if it's okay, can I run it past my dad? My mom's going out tonight, too.

Hey! I wonder of our moms are going to the same place! That'd be cool, wouldn't it?

Sure, absolutely, make sure it's okay first. If your dad would like to join us, it's fine with me. I'd like to meet him.

Oh, okay, I'll mention it to him.

Sure. Brynie, you'll let me know?

Yup, sure will. Love you Daddy!

Love you too. Have fun! Bye, Luke. Take care of my baby girl.

I sure will, goodbye Mr. Sheffield. And thanks for the invitation.

You bet!

So, what do you think? Would you like me to go with you and your dad? I mean, if you want to spend time with him alone, I totally understand.

Are you kidding? Of course I want you to come! Dad said we pick where we go.

Okay, what about my dad? Do I ask him?

Sure, why not? My parents want to invite your parents over for dinner next weekend, so maybe it'll be less awkward for the two of us if our dads meet now.

True. We can mention it to him when we get to the game.

Where are we going now? It's still early.

I thought we could go down to the Greenway and hang out a while.

Okay, it's so pretty there.

I know, I love it there. I like to go and just chill and be in nature. I think a lot there. It's my little getaway.

You're lucky, you can just get in your car and drive there whenever you want to. I just asked my not-handy dad to build me a window seat. That would be my getaway.

Well, I can bring you there anytime you want me to. It can be our spot.

Umm, Luke, the light is green.

Oh, haha! My bad. I couldn't help but stare at you. You look so great. Your face is so radiant, like, it's glowing.

Radiant? I've never been told that before.

Really? It is. It's so mesmerizing. I could stare at you all day.

Well, for now, can you keep your eyes on the road? I'd like to live a long time.

Don't worry, I'm a good driver, and I'm here to protect you, not harm you. But if we sit at green lights, you'll have to let me know.

Haha, okay.

So, do you like being out in nature?

I love it! How could anyone live in the most beautiful state there is and not like to be out in nature?

I am so glad to hear that! Do you like skiing, snowboarding and hiking and stuff?

Definitely! You too?

Oh, hell yeah! I love anything that involves being outside and moving. But I didn't think you'd like to do stuff like skiing and snowboarding.

Why not?

Because you're a dancer. I figured you'd be afraid to hurt yourself and not be able to dance.

Nah, I mean, I can break my leg going down the stairs. I'm not going to miss out on life just because I'm afraid to get hurt. Besides, I love dancing, but it's not all there is to life.

That's a really great outlook. What else do you like?

I like basically any winter sport. I even had a dream I was bobsledding last night!

What? That's crazy.

Yeah, I thought so too. I like swimming, kayaking, wake boarding, rock climbing, biking, you name it.

What about sports? What kind of sports do you like?

I like everything except golf. I tried it, and I didn't like it. There's no thrill.

What's your favorite sport?

I guess I'd have to say football and hockey.

Well that's good to hear.

What's your favorite sport?

Well, to play, I'd say football. To watch, I like hockey and basketball, oh, and lacrosse.

I don't think I've ever watched lacrosse.

We'll have to watch it together, then.

   Okay.

Okay, stay right there. Let me get your door.

   I feel like a spoiled brat with him opening my door. Luke, you really don't have to open my door all the time. I feel like a spoiled brat.

I am a gentleman, and gentlemen open doors for their ladies. And anyway, then I can do this…

   Well, if you're going to kiss me like that every time you open my door for me, then you just go right ahead and keep doing it.

You see? There's a method to my madness. Besides, I've been wanting to do that since you opened your door, but I didn't think it'd be appropriate.

   You know, we're alone. We need to remember our boundaries.

Well, that's why we're in a public place. We can't be tempted. I mean, we could, but it's way more difficult out here in broad daylight with all these people out here running by us and walking their dogs and stuff.

   Good thinking. You're a smart guy, I like that. And I like you.

Good, because I like you, too. A lot. The more I find out about you, the harder I'm falling for you, Brynlee.

   I swear, this is all like a dream. It doesn't feel real.

What do you mean?

   I mean, here I am, just little ol' me, and I all of a sudden I have this amazing boyfriend who says he likes me for me, and, I don't know. It's just hard to believe, I guess.

Hard to believe that I would like you? Are you kidding? You're great! Everything about you is freakin' awesome! And then I find out, on top of all that, you like sports and nature and doing things. How much more perfect can you get?

   You're the perfect one! You hold and open my door for me, you're polite, respectful, and amazingly cute, you have goals, and you're family-oriented.

Well, I guess we're just perfect together.

   I guess so. It's like a fairytale. I never thought I'd live a fairytale.

Well, you deserve much better than a fairytale.

Is there better?

Well, in fairytales, there's always some evil witch or dragon or something.

I'm sure when we go to school tomorrow, the witches and the dragons will show themselves pretty quick, but I'm no daffodil. I'll slay those evil creatures without a thought!

Come on now, I need a chance to protect my girl.

How about we do it together?

Okay, deal. Actually, how about we just ignore them and let them squirm from watching how happy we are. Besides, I don't think there will be too many people who wouldn't want to see us together.

Why do you say that?

Most of the football team already knew I like you, and they all know we're dating. Their girlfriends know, and none of them have said anything negative. Most of them are happy for us.

Most of them?

Yeah, well, some don't really know you, so they haven't said anything one way or the other. And they all hated Samantha, so...

Well, that's good. I haven't talked to any of my friends yet. They all blew up my phone last night but I didn't feel like getting into the whole story, so they'll just have to wait.

Have you talked to Natalya today?

No, not yet. How about you, have you talked to Dylan?

No. He's probably still sleeping. He doesn't usually wake up until the afternoon.

Good God! I can't do that.

No, me either. So, now that your competition is over, now what? Do you have a break?

Not for a few weeks. That reminds me, my parents and I have a meeting with my dance instructor this week. We are going to discuss me studying privately with her and one other dancer.

Oh really? That sounds cool. Why privately?

Well, Ms. Val, my instructor, thinks I have potential and she wants to see how far I can go, so she wants me and my friend Lacey to study privately.

Is she the girl that was next to you in the video?

Yeah, oh yeah, I forgot about that.

So, that's her name? Lacey? I have to tell Ray. He was all gaga over her in that video. We should set them up. Where does she go to school?

       She goes to that really rich private school, Northern Collegiate Academy. It's supposed to be a really great Arts school.

Oh, that's cool. Ha, funny, his parents wanted to send him there but he wanted to stay in public so he could play football.

       Oh, I didn't know that.

Not too many people do. They like to stay humble. They're pretty cool. So, do you think she'd like Ray?

       Honestly, I don't know her all that well. We basically just dance together. It's only very recently we started to talk about hanging out.

Oh, maybe we can double date again.

       Haha, yeah, maybe. I'll talk to her about it next time I see her. Sounds like it could be fun.

Cool. So, do you want to take a walk down by the creek?

       Sure, let's go.

Are you warm enough?

       I am, thank you. It's so nice out today. It's nice to have a sunny day for once.

It is gorgeous out. A perfect day to be with the perfect girl. Tell me more about your private lessons. How often will they be? Can I go to watch?

       Well, I'm not really sure about the details. I'm sure you can come watch every once in a while, but we'll find more out at the meeting this week.

Are you excited about it?

       I am, really excited, actually.

I'm excited for you. I can't wait to see where dancing takes you. You're gonna go far, I just know it, and I want to be by your side the rest of the way, your biggest fan.

       I would love for you to be my biggest fan. And I will be your biggest fan.

I'd like that a lot. How's your wrist feeling today? Is it still sore or are you just being cautious?

       It was sore this morning when I first woke up, but it's not feeling too bad right now.

Good, I'm glad. You have to teach me how to do that bronco move.

       I will, don't worry. I promised and I'll keep my word.

Cool, I want to do one next season for my first touchdown. That'd be crazy, wouldn't it?

> It would be! You'll have a lot of gear on, though, won't you?

Yeah, but it's okay, I'll practice with it on. You know what? You should join the cheer squad and be my personal cheerleader!

> Um, yeah, probably not.

Why not? You'd be the best one out there! Hell, you could choreograph everything! Maybe our cheer squad would win something for once.

> Think about who's on the squad, Luke. I don't think that would such a good idea.

It was a thought. A hopeful, wishful thought. But I understand. I bet I could get the rest of the cheerleaders to make sure she doesn't try out again, especially if they know that you would try out. They would love to have a famous dancer as part of their little clique. They can't stand her, anyway. She treats them all like shit.

> I don't think so, Luke. Cheer is her passion, but it's not mine, and as much as I can't stand her, I wouldn't want to do anything to steal that from her. It wouldn't be right.

God, I love that about you. You have so much integrity, and you're so goodhearted no matter how people treat you. You're one of a kind, Brynlee Sheffield, and I have the privilege of being your boyfriend. Never in a million years did I think I'd ever find a girl like you, and now look at me! There is definitely a God and he's got my back, that's for sure.

> Yes, there is a God for sure! I don't know if I'd ever be this happy, otherwise.

I know what you mean. I never thought I'd be this happy. Life is so good right now. Let's just sit here for a little while and chill, and soak in all this nice weather and happiness.

> That's a great idea.

This is so nice just sitting here with him, enjoying the sunshine by this pretty creek. I love it here. It's so peaceful like there's nothing bad anywhere in the world. I wish we could just stay here like this forever, with his arm around me, holding hands. But the world awaits, and we have a basketball game to get to. Until then, I'm going to relax and savor this moment.

It just keeps getting better...

Well, I guess we should get going. I want to get there early enough to introduce you to Declan before he gets out on the court. When I told him I was bringing my girlfriend to watch him play, he got really excited.

> Aww, that's adorable. Well I can't wait to meet both of your nephews, and your brother and his wife, too.

Dawson is really shy, so he may not talk to you. Don't take it personally, though, okay?

> I won't. Maybe I'll be lucky and he'll warm up to me. I apparently have a way with boys in your family.

Haha, you sure do! He better not try to steal you away from me. I'll kick his ass!

> You're adorable. Is your brother and his wife as cool as your parents are? I think I'm more nervous to meet them than I was your parents. Young women can be so judgmental.

They're cool. And I think you and Stacey will get along great, especially since my mom already told her how lovely you are.

> Awww, she did?

She did. Mom likes you a lot. I told her we're getting married one day and she was like "well then, I guess I should start looking for my mother-of-the-groom gown, and a venue for the rehearsal dinner".

> She did not, stop joking around like that, silly!

I swear, she really did say that! And I can almost guarantee she'll bring it up at the game. She'll even get Stacey in on it.

> You're just trying to get me to not be so nervous. You're so cute.

Alright, don't believe me. Just don't be surprised when they start talking about it, that's all I'm saying.

> What's your brother like?

Kevin's cool. He's goofy and jokes around all the time, and he's probably the biggest ham there is. Oh, and he's a really good dad and husband.

> Well, he had a great role model, it seems.

I totally agree. My dad is the best role model there is for young men.

I couldn't have asked for a better dad.

> I know what you mean. My dad is the perfect dad for a little
> girl. I want my husband to be just like him for my
> daughters.

I'll keep that in mind.

> You should.

Your smile is so magnetic. I just can't look away.

> The road, buddy. Eyes on the road.

Okay, okay.

*Magnetic? My smile is magnetic. That has got to be one of the
nicest things I've ever heard. What romantic planet is this guy from?
I'm just going to sit here and watch him drive, because he is so cute!*

Here we are. Are you ready to meet the rest of the family?

> As ready as I'll ever be, I guess. Do you really think they'll
> like me?

I know they will. If my mom likes you, they'll like you, trust me.

> Okay, I'm sorry I'm so nervous. I just know how close you
> and your family are, and I don't want them to think I'm not
> good enough.

Are you kidding? You're too good for me! And you're eons better
than my last girlfriend!

> That's not really saying much, Luke. What are you, some
> kind of wise ass?

Haha, you know what I mean. Trust me, they're gonna like you. In
fact, I'm pretty certain they're going to love you. What's not to love?

> If you say so.

There they are, over to the left. Come on, let's go find Declan.

> These boys are so little and cute!

Here he comes! Hey Bud! How's it going?

> Good, Uncle Luke! Is this your girlfriend?

Yes, this is my girlfriend, Brynlee. Can you say hi to her?

> Hi. Uncle Luke was right, you're really pretty, like a
> princess.

Aren't you the sweetest? What a handsome young man. Are you
ready to win? I can't wait to see you play. Uncle Luke told me how
great you are out there.

> He did?

Yup, he did. He said you're so awesome! I'm excited to watch you play.

You are?

Yup, I sure am!

Uncle Luke, you didn't tell me princesses like basketball.

I didn't? Well, this one does. And she like football and hockey, too!

Do you like to play video games too?

Are you kidding? Who doesn't!

Uncle Luke, you should marry her.

I'm working on it, Bud. First we have to date a little while.

But, why? Why wait if you're in love?

We both have to finish school and go to college. Then we can get married. Okay?

Okay. I have to go play now. Coach Steve is waving me over. See ya.

Good luck out there!

Play hard, Bud!

I will, Uncle Luke!

Holy crap, he is so adorable! Did you hear him? We should get married because I like video games.

And let's not forget that we're in love.

Haha, yeah, he's such a sweet little boy!

Let's go introduce you to Dawson and the rest of the fam. Remember, he's really shy.

Okay.

Hey Mom, hey Dad!

Hello Son, hello Brynlee. It's so nice to see you again.

Yes, hello, you two. Brynlee, you look lovely.

Thank you, Mrs. DeSilva.

Brynlee, love, I'd like for you to meet my daughter-in-law Stacey, and my son Kevin. This is Brynlee.

Hi Brynlee.

Hi, it's so nice to meet you both.

Luke has not stopped talking about you for weeks. It's nice to finally meet you.

Dude, you're right, she's gorgeous! Looks like we know how to pick 'em, huh? DeSilva boys, making Dad proud!

Kevin, you're a nut.

Hey little guy! Can Uncle Luke get a hug? Aww, thanks buddy! Can you say hi to Brynlee?

Hi. I'm Brynlee. Is your name Dawson?

Wow, Bryn, he nodded at you! Kev, did you guys see that?

We did! That's it, now you have to marry her. He's never done that to someone he just met before!

I guess I better speed up that gown and venue shopping!

I wonder if Kevin's tux still fits. I'll have it dry cleaned this week.

See? I told you they'd bring it up! You guys are crazy. Dawson, do you think you can maybe shake her hand? We are gentlemen, you know, and gentlemen shakes hands.

Dude, Kevin!! Look!

Wow, what a strong handshake you have! I bet your daddy taught you how to shake hands like that! No? Was it Uncle Luke? It was?

Hahaha! I love you, little buddy!

Wow, Dawson, see if I let you drive my Ferrari when you get older!

Oh Kevin! Brynlee, I don't know how you did it, but there's something about you he really likes. He has never been so outgoing before! I think I could cry!

He's the sweetest little thing!

Brynlee, my grandson apparently adores you. Son, you've found yourself a fabulous young lady, that's for sure!

Thank you, that's so sweet.

Please, sit down and join us. They should be getting started soon. Luke, how was Declan with Brynlee?

Well, he called her a princess and said we should get married, basically.

Did he really? That's my boy! Why waste time, right? If you find a good one, wife her!

You're too funny, Dad.

I'm sorry, Brynlee, I hope we aren't embarrassing you.

No, not at all. I love how you all have fun together.

Oh we're not having fun, dear. We're one hundred percent serious.

Mom!

I'm sorry, it was too easy!

Brynlee, if you can put up with their antics, you're golden. Look at me, I survived.

Survived?! You're just as bad as we are, Stace!

I am not!

C'mon, Stacey! Remember what you did to the witch I dated?

Let's not bring that up here. The little one had nightmares for days after that!

> Oh no, what happened?

Whisper, please! Ears…

> Well, Stacey had to pee really bad, and everyone was doing stuff in the kitchen – we were getting ready for a huge Summer party. Anyway, she handed Dawson to Samantha and ran! He screamed his head off and she freaked out and got all pissed off at us for laughing so hard and not helping, and she got especially mad at Stacey. Samantha doesn't like kids, so that's what made us all laugh so hard. And Stacey totally did it on purpose. She could've just taken him with her like she usually does.

Oh no! The poor little guy!

> Yeah, so that's why it's a huge deal that he even nodded at you and shook your hand! He's already shy, but after that, he's been worse! Every time the witch came around him after that, he cried hysterically. Even Declan was glad when we broke up. He calls her "Ursula".

Ursula? Like from that mermaid show?

> Yup, exactly. He hates Ursula.

Can you blame him? She's mean!

> They both are!

Aww, he's so cute. Dawson, would you like to come sit on my lap? You can sit on this side, next to Uncle Luke.

> Mom! Look! He's going to Brynlee!

Someone get a picture of this!

> Hi. Are you comfy? Can you see your big brother from here? You can? Good.

Brynlee, wow! I am so shocked right now. I may need to take you with us to pre-school tomorrow!

> Why so shocked, Stacey? I mean, Brynlee is amazing. I guess the little guy can sense it.

I guess so!

> Luke, he's so cozy! I could snuggle him all day!

Whoa, whoa, what about me? I want to snuggle with you all day.

> Shhh! There are innocent little ears! Ooh, the game's about to start. Go Declan!!

Aww, sweetie, you just put the biggest smile on Declan's face!

Luke, it looks like your girlfriend is going to fit in just fine with our crazy family!

I know, mom. She's great, isn't she?

She most certainly is. Lovely, just lovely.

What do you think, little guy? Is she lovely like Grandma says? Yeah? I think so too. See that, Bryn? He smiled. He knows.

This little boy is adorable. I want to squeeze him so tight and take him home with me. I love this family. How in the world did they ever put up with Samantha? I can't even imagine her fitting in with them in the slightest. Does she even know how to take a joke? Does she ever smile? And how could she not love these adorable little boys?

Are you still comfy? Yes? Okay good. Let me know if you're not, okay? Luke, I love him. Can I take him home with me?

If you do, I'm moving in!

Okay, deal! He is the sweetest little boy, oh my goodness!

So you are definitely making me fall harder and harder for you. My family all thinks you're great, my nephews think you're great, my shy little nephew who hides behind his mommy even with family he knows, is sitting on your lap after just meeting you, on top of all the other stuff I love about you, God, I could fall in love with you way too fast.

Slow down with the perfect dream girl stuff, would ya?

You're just as great, Mr. Wonderful, so you should probably slow down with all the perfect dream boy stuff, too, you know! Girls fall in love a lot easier than boys do!

Would you two stop with all the mushy crap? Jeez! You make us want to vomit?!

Oh, Kevin, stop. If I recall correctly, you and Stacey were the same way when you started dating, and to be honest, your mother and I would make gag faces when you weren't looking.

Wow, Dad, thanks a lot.

Well, you two were quite corny and mushy, dear.

Aw, c'mon Ma, we weren't that bad!

Are you crazy? "Oh Stacey, you fill my world with rainbows and sunshine", or something like that, wasn't it Mom?

Yes, it was exactly like that!

Don't listen to them, Brynlee. Kevin and I weren't that bad.

Bah! Haha, okay. Whatever.

Oh hush, Luke. You were still in diapers, how would you remember?

Diapers?! You're on crack. I was definitely not in diapers. I was eight, maybe seven, but not in diapers. And we aren't half as bad as you two were.

I think it's precious. You two go ahead and be as mushy as you want to be. Brynlee is a lovely girl, and I don't blame you one bit wanting to be all lovey-dovey, Luke.

Thanks, Mom.

Dawson, let's cheer Declan on together, okay? Ready? One, two, three... Go Declan! Yay!

Brynlee, anytime you feel like playing with Dawson, feel free to come over. He really has taken to you quickly. Maybe you are exactly what he needs.

Um, Stace, she's exactly what I need.

Oh Luke, I'm sure you can put your big boy pants on and share your girlfriend with your nephew, can't you? Look at that wittle face!

Dawson, what do you think, should I share Brynlee with you?

Mhm.

I should? Okay, I will, but only because I love you, and because you're my favorite Dawson there ever was.

Awww! He's hugging me! How precious!

I have to get a picture of this! Honey, look at your shy little boy!

Incredible! Luke, I gotta hand it to ya, you have a good one. Don't let her go.

I really don't plan to.

That's good, because I don't plan on letting you go, either. I am so glad you asked me for my number.

And to think, I was so nervous I almost didn't! If it wasn't for Dylan, I don't think I would've gotten up the nerve.

How did he get you to do it?

He told me that he was going to ask Natalya to go out to dinner, and said that I needed to just grow a pair and talk to you, and get your number so we could double date.

Was I really that scary?

Scary? God no! Out of my league? Absolutely!

I am not out of your league. If anything, it's the other way around.

Yeah, I don't think so.

But I do. We shouldn't argue about this. There are little
ears. Ooh look! Declan is about to shoot! Yay Declan!
Yeah, buddy! Nice job!
Woo hoo!! That's my boy! Way to go Dec! That was
beautiful!
Yay! Your big brother just scored! Did you see? Clap hands…
Yay! Good job!

*This is awesome. I wish everyday could be this fun. Seriously,
though, can it? His brother and sister-in-law are hysterical. Oh my
gosh, and Declan calls Samantha "Ursula"! Little kids are so funny,
they just say what they feel and don't think twice about it! Aww, I
feel special, they actually like me! Even Dawson, the shy little guy!
He's got the cutest little face! How could anybody be around these
people and be so uptight and hateful like she is? I just don't get it.
But, hey, who care's about her, anyway? She's out of their lives and
now Luke has me. I'm so glad, because he and his family are so
wonderful.*

I love family day...

What a great game, little buddy! Did you hear us cheering you on?
> I heard her cheering, but I didn't hear you. I saw you, though.

You heard me cheering? I'm so glad. I tried to be really loud.
> You were. Uncle Luke wasn't.

I'll try and be louder next time, okay?
> Okay.

You played great! Great shot you had there, too! You got the only basket in the whole game, dude! Fist bump!
> Uncle Luke, can I get on your shoulders?

Sure, Bud. Ready? Hop on!
> Wow! Look at you up there! You're so tall!

Are you gonna marry Uncle Luke after college?
> I don't know, Declan. That's a long time from now, but maybe.

I want you to. You're pretty, and nice, and you cheer for me. Ursula never cheered for me. She never even came to my games. She was mean. Her heart is ugly, but your heart is beautiful. I think you should marry Uncle Luke. His heart is nice, too. And he says you're the most beautiful girl he's ever seen in the whole wide world.
> Haha, okay Bud, let's not tell all our secrets, okay?

But you didn't say it was a secret. You said you want to tell the whole world how much you like her. You did, you said that. Remember, Uncle Luke? Remember you said that?
> Yeah, Buddy, I remember.

That is so sweet, Declan. Thank you for telling me my heart is beautiful. You have a beautiful heart, too.
> No, boys are handsome. Girls are beautiful.

You're absolutely right! You have a handsome heart.
> Just like my Uncle Luke!

Exactly like your Uncle Luke!
> Well, Son, we have to get going. Your mother has a jewelry party to get to.

I bet it's the same one Brynlee's mom is going to! Mom, be sure to keep an eye out for a woman named Heidi. That's Brynlee's mom.

Oh, that would be wonderful if I met your mother there!
It would be. I'll text her and tell her to look for you.
        Perfect!
Hey Dad, you and I were invited to dinner with Brynlee and her dad.
What do you say, are you up for it?
        Sure, Son, I think that'd be great. I like to meet the dad of
        the girl who has my son's heart. He must be a fine
        gentleman.
Excellent! I'll text Daddy and let him know. Mrs. DeSilva, have
tons of fun at the jewelry party. It was so nice to see you again.
        It was lovely to see you also, Brynlee. I look forward to
        spending much more time together! Luke, honey, have a
        lovely day.
I will, Mom, you too.
        Okay, Dawson, Declan, time to give Grandma and Grandpa
        hugs and kisses. We have to go, too, because I am starving!
        I bet you are, too, huh?
Do we have to, Mommy? I want to play with Uncle Luke and his
girlfriend.
        Oh, sweetie, I think they want to spend some time doing big
        kid stuff. You'll see them soon.
Uncle Luke, you're not gonna get rid of her, are you? She's nice.
Way nicer than Ursula. She's like Snow White.
        That's adorable!
Don't worry, Bud, I'm not getting rid of her. I'm keeping her for a
long, long time.
        And then get married?
We'll see, Dec. I hope so.
        Me too. You have to marry Snow White!
Okay Declan, say goodbye. We have to go now.
        Thank you for coming to my game and cheering me on,
        Snow White.
You're welcome Declan. Thank you for letting me watch you play. I
had lots of fun.
        Hey Bud, her name is Brynlee. Do you think you can
        remember that?
I'll try. Bye Brynie.
        Bye Declan! Bye Stacey. It was very nice to meet you and
        your family.
Great to meet you! And thank you for letting my son open up like

that. This was huge! Right Kev? Huge!

Yeah, it really was. Thank you, Brynlee. You don't know how much this means to us – and Dawson.

It was my pleasure.

Bye guys. Have fun today.

Bye.

Okay, Dad, we'll catch up with you a little later.

Sounds good, Son. Love you. See you later Brynlee.

Bye Mr. DeSilva.

Luke! Your family is so great! I loved spending time with them here. And your nephews are adorable! They really love you, don't they?

Yeah, and the feeling is mutual. They're such cool little kids. I can't get enough of them.

I can see why!

So, what would you like to do now? Are you hungry? We can go grab some lunch if you want to.

Sure, what are you in the mood for?

I'm good for whatever. What are you in the mood for? Lady's choice.

I don't know, really. Do you like Mexican food?

I love Mexican food! Thank God, a girl that likes Mexican.

You'll quickly find out that I like just about anything. Thai, Japanese, Creole, you name it, and I will probably eat it.

A girl after my own heart!

Before I forget, let me text my parents and tell my mom to look for yours, and tell my dad that it'll be four of us for dinner. He's going to ask where we want to go, so what should I tell him?

Well we're having Mexican for lunch, so not that. What does your dad like to eat when he goes out?

Steak. Any kind of steak. Yours?

Same. Should we head into Portland or stay in Sherwood?

You wanna go into Portland? Maybe we can walk around a little, too.

Yeah, okay, sounds good. Maybe tell your dad to pick, since he probably knows more places than we do.

"Hey Daddy, there will be 4 of us for dinner. Luke's dad is coming too. We want to go into Portland. You pick the restaurant"

"Hey Mom, Luke's mom will be at the jewelry party. Look for her.
Her name is"…
What's your mom's name?
Shelly.
Thanks.
…"Shelly DeSilva. Light brown shoulder length hair, parted deep on
the side. About dad's height. Luke told her to look for you too"

 "Sure thing, Babygirl. Love you"
"Love you too Daddy"

I guess he'll let us know what time later on. This is so weird. Our
dads are meeting today, our moms might meet, and we just started
hanging out. Do you feel like you're in a whirlwind?
   Yeah, a little. I'm guessing you do too? Are you okay with
   all this? It's happening so fast.
As long as I'm with you, Luke, I'm okay with anything.
   Good, I was hoping you'd say that. It all just feels…
Right. It just feels right.
   Exactly!
Do you believe in soulmates?
   I never used to, but I think I'm starting to.
Yeah, me too. It's kind of crazy, because I never would've thought
that you and I would be together. You're a football player, I'm a
dancer, you hang out with jocks and cheerleaders, I hang out with
hipsters and bookworms… It's almost like, I don't know, like…
   Like we are meant to be together. Fate.
Yeah.
   Brynlee, you and I have way more in common than I ever
   would've thought. Much more in common than any other
   girl I know. Hell, more than most of my friends. We may
   seem like opposites to the rest of the world, but we're really
   not.
We're not, are we? It's like, we were at first, and opposites attracted,
but opposites attracted because we're not really so opposite.
   And to think I was almost too nervous to ask you out.
And to think, if you waited another week, it may not have happened.
   Why not?

I had a date for next weekend.

Oh really? With who?

Blake Carrington. He's a freshman in college.

Oh, I know who Blake is.

Why do you say it like that?

He's a player, but he's sly about it. He dates girls from different schools so none finds out about the others. He could write a book on how to cheat successfully. He's an asshole.

Oh, well, he seems nice enough.

Isn't he the one who uploaded the video of you?

Mhm, he is.

Yeah, he's definitely an asshole.

Well I'm glad I'm not going on that date, then.

Me too. See? It was totally fate that made this happen.

Yay for fate! Haha, I'd rather be with you any day.

Good, because I really can't imagine not being with you. It's only been less than 24 hours, but we fit so perfectly that it seems like we've known each other forever.

That's so sweet, Luke.

It's what you do to me. You make me all sappy and romantic, but I don't care. I have never been this happy. Man, I am gonna get so much crap from the guys.

Why? For dating me?

No, they're glad we're dating! For being a mushy sap master.

Hahaha! A mushy sap master? I have my very own mushy sap master!

All yours, Baby! Every mushy inch of me.

Now, now, some of those inches are off limits for a long time!

Maybe so, but they're still yours.

Bye-bye sap master, hello horn-dog!

Haha, you're crazy! I love your craziness. C'mere…

Damn, okay we should probably stop that. You're going to make it very difficult to…

Wait?

Yes.

I know. But I told you, I'm not touching you. I am a man of self-control.

But I'm not sure how much self-control I have.
I'll make sure we keep our boundaries. I'm the guy and I'll protect you.

And I'm the girl and I'll support you.
See? We already have this thing figured out. Let's just skip all the in-between stuff and get married. That should make my nephews very happy.

Sounds good, let's do it. I would need parental consent, though.
Me too. Almost eighteen, but not quite.

Speaking of parents, my mom texted back finally.

"Okay, I'll look for her"

Really? That's it? She's probably too busy planning another meeting.
What do you mean?

Oh, nothing. It's just, my mom and I are kind of going through a thing.
What kind of thing? Oh, never mind. You don't have to tell me. It's personal.

No, it's okay. Lately she's been on my case a lot, she is constantly on the phone, and she's been going to these meetings that I have no idea what they are about. And no one will tell me! Every time I'm about to get an answer out of someone, something happens and I'm left wondering.
What does she get on your case about? Just random stuff?

No, she gets on me about my weight.
What?! Why? You're perfect!

Ugh, it's a really long story. She used to be married to a total asshole who really messed her up, and because of it she's passing her mess off on me. I'm figuring out that she is the main reason why I have low self-esteem.
You? I don't see you having low self-esteem at all.

Well, I'm working on it, and I keep it to myself most of the time. I only open up to a couple of people.
And now me.

Ugh, and now you know. Great. I'm sorry.
Sorry for what? You have no reason to be sorry. And you have no reason to think badly about yourself. You are gorgeous, Brynlee.

Seriously, you're hot as hell. But more importantly, you're gorgeous on the inside. Trust me, I know. I've seen the exact opposite, and no matter what the girl looks like on the outside, if she's a bitch to the core, nothing makes her pretty. There are way too many girls like that out there, and definitely not nearly enough girls like you. I just so happened to fall into a bit of luck and got you to be my girlfriend!

Not luck, fate! And thank you. It really means a lot to me that you think that.

I don't think, I know. Please believe me. You are so beautiful.

Thank you, Luke.

So, what do you think the meetings are about?

I don't know. At first I thought she was cheating on my dad, but he knows about the meetings and is okay with them, so that's not it.

Maybe it's for work?

No, she doesn't work. Honestly, I've racked my brain trying to figure it out and I come up empty every time. The only thing I can think of is that she IS working and no one's telling me, but I don't really know why that would be a secret.

Or maybe she's going on interviews and doesn't want to say until she gets an offer somewhere.

Yeah, I guess that could be it, too. I hate being out of the loop like this. She's my mom, I should know what's going on.

I'm sorry. Well hey, if my mom hears anything about it, I'm sure I'll find out. I will definitely let you know if I do, okay?

Thank you. Please, don't take all this the wrong way. I love my mom. I really do. She just has issues, that's all.

Don't worry. I get it. We all have our issues, trust me. Now, I think you need a hug.

I do. Your hugs make the world perfect.

Only because I'm hugging you.

I feel safe when you hold me like this.

Good. Then I won't let go.

Please don't, ever.

I can't believe how easy he is to talk to. I just told him one of the biggest secrets about myself, and he wasn't just supportive, he gets it. He didn't talk to me like I'm crazy, or like my family is crazy. Not one second did I feel like he was judging me. Oh, Luke, are you really this perfect? Are you really this into me? God, please let it be so. I don't want him to let go of me. Never let go. I could stay like this for eternity.

A perfect weekend...

Luke, thank you for a perfect weekend.

    No, thank you. You're what made it perfect.

I can't believe how great our dads got along. I thought it would be awkward, but it was like they've known each other since high school!

    It really did. But then again, we have cool dads, so why wouldn't they get along, you know? I figured it would be awkward a little, too, but nope.

I wonder if our moms met at the jewelry party. And if they did, did they like each other? You know how women can be.

    Yeah, I know. But, I'm sure, if they met, they got along just fine.

I don't know. My mom, well, I don't know. Never mind.

    What? Tell me.

I wonder if my mom is with other people like she is with me. Does she say things to them that are offensive, and not mean it or know she's doing it?

    Your mom's a big girl. She knows how to make friends.

    Besides, she was great when I met her.

That's because you're a guy, and you're hot and nice and she wants me to find someone like you to marry.

    Well I guess she's in luck, because you did.

I just hope that if they did meet, they like each other.

    Stop worrying. Fate, remember?

I wish this weekend didn't have to end. I wish this night wouldn't end. It sucks that we don't have any classes together.

    It does suck. We'll have to get all the hugs we can get in the hallway until after school. Do you have dance tomorrow night?

No, not until Tuesday.

    Okay, well then we can hang out after school. I can bring you home. I can pick you up in the morning, too, if you want me to.

But that's out of your way.

    It's not too bad. Maybe five minutes. So can I pick you

up?

Sure, but only if you promise it's not too far out of your way.

Good, I'll text you when I leave my house.

Okay, I'll be outside waiting when you get here.

Um, no, you need to wait inside, and I will come to the door like a gentleman should.

Luke, you really don't have to...

Brynlee, I want to. Let me do this for you, please.

Alright.

Good, so I'll text you when I get home and we can figure out what time I should pick you up in the morning. But before I go, I have to kiss you. Is your dad going to pop in here all of a sudden?

No, he's in the shower. We're good.

Thank God, because I've been dying to do this for hours...

I hate to have to go after a kiss like that, but I guess I should.

Maybe just one more kiss…

Baby, you seriously make me so happy. I am one lucky guy.

Ugh, I wish you could stay.

So do I, cutie. Okay, I'll text you in like ten minutes, okay?

I'll be waiting.

He called me "Baby"! That is the cutest! Why does this night have to end? This was such a perfect weekend, oh my God. I don't think I've ever had a better three days in my entire life. And now I have a boyfriend, our dads get along great… That reminds me, where the heck is Mom? She must still be at the jewelry party. Must be a good one, because it's getting pretty late, and she's not home yet. She's usually home early from those things. Hmm. Well, whatever. I guess I could text her and let her know we're home. I hope she met Mrs. DeSilva. Then it won't be awkward next weekend if they come over for dinner. But if they did meet, will they want to get together again? Either way, Luke and I are hanging out, so I'm good with whatever. I do like hanging out with his family, a lot. Damn, I haven't talked to Natalya since last night, and even then we barely talked! I can't wait to tell her everything! I need to text her and see how it went with her and Dylan.

"Natalya!"

I wonder if they hung out at all today.

"Brynlee!"
"Whatcha doing?"
"Daydreaming. What are you doing?"
"What are you daydreaming about? Or should I say, who?"
"Oh, Bryn, you know me too well."
"Dylan?"
"Yeah <3 "
"What's going on with you two?"
"Well you see, my boyfriend and I hung out all day today!"
"Ahhhhh!!! Are you serious? Dylan asked you out?!"
"He did!" "How'd it go with you and Luke? Did you two hit it off?"
"Oh, you mean my boyfriend? Yeah, I'd say so!"
"Oh my God! Best friends are dating best friends!"
"Awww!"
"And you were worried he'd be a jerk"
"I was wrong. But apparently Blake is a big one"
"Blake? Why?"
"Luke knows him and said he's a player and a cheater"
"Holy crap! Really?"
"Yup. Glad that date didn't happen!"
"No kidding!"
"So you and Dylan stopped sucking face long enough for him to ask you out, huh?"
"Lol!" "What about you and Luke? Did he kiss you yet?"
"Um, yeah, and holy crap! <3 <3" "It's crazy tho, we have SO MUCH in common!"
"Awww, I'm so happy for you two!"
"I'm happy for you guys too!"
"We should all hang out again next weekend"
"That depends if you guys are going to be slobbering all over each other or not"
"I think we're passed that phase now. Our relationship has matured to some words too, lol"
"I hope you're kidding"
"Yes, I'm kidding! We went to the arcade today"

"That's cool" "Did you study today?"
"Not one bit" "Living on the edge"
"Uh oh, she's rebelling"
"Nah. Just living a little" "what did you two do today?"
"I met his brother's family. Our dads met when the four of us had dinner together"
"Really? Are they nice? Did the dads get along?"
"Very nice. His nephews are adorable! Dads got along too well"
"That's good tho, right?"
"Yeah, it is." "We'll have to catch up more tomorrow at lunch tho, okay? I'm beat"
"No prob. I'm beat too. Too much sucky-face, lol!
"LOL!"
"Nite!"
"Nite!"

They hit it off, didn't they? Natalya and I have always wanted to date two best friends, and now we are! That is so cute! School is going to be crazy tomorrow, that's for sure! Ha, I never replied to all those people last night. Oh well, I'm sure they know I was hanging out with Luke, so... He should be getting home soon. I think I'll get my pajamas on and cozy up in bed. Where the heck is mom? Let me see if dad's heard from her yet.

Hey Dad, have you heard from mom?
> Yes, Sweetpea, she called me a little while ago. She and a few ladies were going out for coffee.
Coffee? This late? Did she mention if she met Mrs. DeSilva?
> Actually, she did. She said she's a doll, and they were going for coffee with a few other ladies that were there.
A doll? So they got along good?
> I would imagine so, honey.
Oh thank God.
> So, you and Mr. DeSilva seemed to get along really well.
Yeah, he's cool. We're getting together for lunch this week to discuss business stuff.
> What do you think of Luke, Daddy?
Luke's a fine young man. His father raised him well. I approve of you dating him, but I am still keeping an eye on him. He's still a male, and I know what males want.

Oh Daddy, you don't need to worry about that. We talked about it, and we're going to wait a long time. Don't worry. He's a real gentleman and he wants to protect me.

We'll see. I'm still going to have a talk with him, man to man.

A talk?! What? No, you don't need to.

Well, I may not need to, but I'm going to. You're my little girl, and whether he thinks he's going to protect you or not, it's MY job. He may be a gentleman and all, but he's still a guy, and guys want sex.

Oh, Daddy. Ugh! You're so... You're such a dad!

Good, then I'm doing my job at least partially correct.

"Hey Babe!"

Yeah, you are. Thanks for taking us all out for dinner.

You're welcome, Sweetpea. You really like him, don't you?

I really do. More than I expected to.

Good. They seem like genuinely good people.

They do, don't they? I'm going back up. Love you.

I love you too, Brynlee.

"Hey handsome! Sorry, I was talking to my Daddy"

"That's okay. I'm home now, and I miss you"

"Ugh! I know, I miss you too!"

"This was the best weekend"

"It was definitely the best weekend ever!"

"I have no idea where my mom is"

"Dad said she went for coffee with my mom and a few others"

"They met? Sweet!"

"Apparently they got along great"

"See? Didn't I tell you they'd be fine?"

"You did"

"I understand your concern, tho. Women can be crazy. Especially when kids are involved"

"Oh, we're involved, alright! Lol!"

"I can still smell your perfume on my shirt"

"I'm sorry! Now you smell like a girl!"

"I am not sorry at all! I smell like MY girl!"

" <3 " "I'm going to sleep in your hoodie"

"Won't you be too hot?"

"Don't care. If I can't be in your arms, then I'll be in your hoodie"

"Thanks for letting me borrow it, btw"
"You can keep it. You look better in it than I do"
"I can? Oh my gosh, I love you! Thank you!"
"You're welcome, Baby"   "So, I'll pick you up at seven?"
"That's perfect. I'll be ready"
"Okay, goodnight beautiful"
"Goodnight Luke. <3 "
" <3 :) "

knock knock   Hi Bryn, how was your evening?

> Oh, hi Mom, when did you get home? I didn't hear you come in.

I just got home a few minutes ago.

> How was the jewelry party?

Oh, it was fun. It wasn't the typical home party this time.

> That's good. I don't know how you can go to those things all the time. They're so boring, and so expensive!

Well, sometimes they are, but it's really just a night out with some ladies. I met Luke's mom.

> Dad told me. How did that go?

It went fine. She's a very sweet lady, such a doll. She couldn't say enough good things about you. Apparently the entire family adores you, and are so happy that you two are dating. She was telling me about his last girlfriend. Wow, what a winner, huh?

> Yeah, she's a real winner alright.

I hear you broke her youngest grandson out of his shell?

> Oh my gosh, Mom, he is so adorable! He sat on my lap and everything! What a sweet little boy.

Well, Shelly tells me that he doesn't stop saying your name, and her oldest grandson keeps talking about when you and Luke get married! You must've really had made a great first impression!

> Um, I guess. They're just such nice people, Mom.

I'm sure if they're anything like Shelly, they are. We're going to grab coffee this week sometime, and we've already discussed dinner here next weekend. I think it will be fabulous getting to know their family. Shelly was telling me a little about Luke, and he really sounds like a nice boy.

> He is, Mom. I like him a lot.

I'm glad. You deserve to date a nice boy.

> Thanks, Mom.

Okay, so listen, do you think you can catch a ride home with Natalya again? I have a meeting that should be over by then, but I'm not sure I'll get to the school in time.

> Oh, Luke said he'll bring me home, and he's picking me up in the morning, too.

Well that worked out perfectly.

> Mom, what kind of meeting are you going to? And why is it such a big secret that I have to keep asking and never get an answer?

Oh, honey, it's not a secret. Have I not told you yet?

> No, you haven't. Every time I ask, either the stupid phone rings, or someone walks in, and no one ever tells me where you're going or who you're on the phone with!

Okay, well, I started seeing a counselor. Last week was the first time I saw her.

> A counselor? For what?

Aunt Holly convinced me that I need help to deal with my issues from my first marriage. I guess I just never got over the bitterness. She thought it'd be a good idea to see someone who will help me heal and move on with my life.

> Is it a shrink? Are you seeing a shrink?

No, she's a licensed counselor who helps women overcome whatever issues they need help with.

> Is that who you've been on the phone with all the time?
> Like when you missed rehearsal last week?

No. That would cost a fortune if I did phone counseling. It's Aunt Holly I've been on the phone with so much.

> Why didn't she tell me?

I guess she felt it's not her place.

> Oh. Well, that's good, I guess.

I had an extra-long session on Friday and another tomorrow. I have a lot of work I need to do to be mentally healthy again. She is also setting me up with a holistic health coach, who will help me with eating habits, relational stuff, and basically be my accountability partner. They are working together so I'm not left on my own between counseling sessions.

> That sounds like a lot.

It is. One thing that came out in my first session is the impact that my issues have had on you, and I am so very sorry, Brynlee.

> For what, mom?

I've been so afraid that you'd end up like I did with that jackass I first married, that I may have messed you up a bit. Honey, I love you and I did what I thought was the right thing by making you watch what you eat all the time.

It's okay, Mom. I know you love me.

Well, I'm working on those things, and I've already made progress! That's why I left you some bacon this morning!

Oh! I was wondering what was going on!

And I'm sorry about the comment about needing to lose a few pounds. You're beautiful, sweetie, just the way you are. I guess it took Luke's mom to open my eyes to that.

Why? What did she say?

She said how absolutely stunning you are, and she wishes she had a little body like yours when she was your age, and that Rob is going to have to keep reminding Luke about self-control and respecting a lady to make sure he doesn't do anything disrespectful. Apparently they've had long talks about what's important, and Luke really has his head on straight.

He does, that's for sure!

Well, he's still a boy, and at your age it can be difficult to control yourselves, so that's why Rob and Shelly intend to remind him daily. I think it would be a good idea to do the same here. You're almost sixteen, and your hormones are ricocheting all over the place, and Luke is a very handsome young man. I don't want you to do anything impulsive that could get the two of you in a situation you're not ready for.

Mom, don't worry. We already talked about it, set boundaries, and are waiting a long time.

Like, marriage?

Well, realistically we know that may not happen. We set my 17th birthday as our first boundary, and we're going to try to not be alone in places that might make it too easy.

Seventeen? That's too soon.

Mom, be realistic, please. And anyway, Luke said he's going to do whatever it takes to wait until we get married.

It's crazy to hear my little girl talk about getting married to a boy she just started dating. I guess it happens, though, and we should be prepared. But you do know the probability of that happening is low, right?

Well, I just want to take it day by day. I know we'll both go off to college and all that, but who knows, maybe we will stay together. As of right now I could stay with him forever. He's so great, Mom, but yes, I am only fifteen and still have two and a half years of high school. I'm realistic, but I'm also a teenage girl and live in a fantasy world. Only now I have my dream boy to share my fantasy world with.

You're one smart young lady, Brynlee, and so very beautiful. You marry that young man, if that's your dream. Please, though, wait until I'm old enough to be a mother-in-law!

Haha, I will, Mom. I've got a dance career to kick off, first. Which, by the way, he totally supports!

That's wonderful. It's great to have a man who fully supports you in your dreams. I finally have one I can be proud of.

I love you, Mom.

I love you too, Brynlee. I'll let you get to bed. It's late and you have school tomorrow.

Please, don't remind me. Let me go to sleep with happy thoughts.

Goodnight, my precious.

Goodnight Mom.

That was the best conversation with her, ever. I'm so glad she's getting help to get over the asshole. I don't know why she waited so long, but I sure am glad Aunt Holly talked her into it. I wonder what's been going on that she finally got through to her. Do I even want to know? Probably not. And that'll be why Daddy is okay with the meetings. Thank God it was nothing horrible, like an affair! I mean, she knows what it's like to be cheated on, I can't see her ever doing that to Daddy. She loves him so much. He's her knight in shining armor. And Luke is mine. How cool is it that his mom told Mommy all that stuff?

It's very cool, indeed!

Nova, did you hear all that? My mom is finally getting help!

I heard! I'm very happy for her, and you.

Me too. Maybe now she'll stop ragging on me so much.

Yes, I think that'll all stop completely, in due time.

And did you hear what she said Luke's mom said?!

I heard! That must make you feel great.

It really does. She called me stunning! Stunning, Nova!

That's more than beautiful, isn't it?

I would think so.

And his whole family likes me! Even the really shy one, who is just the sweetest little thing, I can't even!

He is quite adorable. He really took a liking to you very fast.

I did notice he kept looking at my shoulder. Nova, were you on my shoulder at the basketball game?

I was, indeed.

Do you think he saw you? Can't little kids see things?

No, I don't think he saw me. No one can see me except you and the other teacups.

Well, that's weird, then. Why would he look at my shoulder? Crazy. Well, whatever, he likes me, his family likes me, his uncle Luke likes me, and I couldn't be happier.

Brynlee, tell me how you feel about this, how it all makes you feel about yourself.

Well, I'm... elated! That's a good word to describe how I feel.

Tell me more.

I don't know, I feel accepted, approved, I don't know.

And why do you think that is?

Because they're so nice, and Luke is so great.

What is it that you like about him the most? What's your absolute favorite thing about him?

Hmm, the way he makes me feel. The way he treats me.

Okay, let me ask you this, do you think they, and he, make you feel this way, accepted, approved, etc., because of the way you look?

No, I guess not. I guess they like me for who I am.

And hasn't Luke said over and over that he likes who you are?

Well, he does tell me I'm beautiful too, but yeah, I see what you're saying. I'm sure his mom and dad didn't say "okay, son, she's pretty enough, you can date her".

No, I'm sure they didn't. I'm sure it was your personality and the way you were with their grandson, and how you got along great with them. You ARE good enough, Brynlee.

You're gonna make me cry again, Nova.

Good, because you need to feel inside what we all feel about you. You are an amazing and beautiful person on the inside. Luke knows it, and he's told you that. His family knows it. Your mom has even acknowledged it. You need to know it.

      I know I do. Ugh! It's a good thing I don't have to see anyone right now. I'm sure my mascara is all over my face now.

Yup, it is. And you're still beautiful.

      Thank you, Nova. You're the best teacup.

I really do try.

      Oh my God! Nova! Your clothes are changing!

They are, aren't they?

      Hey, nice outfit! I'd wear that in a heartbeat.

Indeed you would. It's very you. But! It's not the absolute total, deep down you just yet. We still have work to do, however, progress is happening at lightning speed, no doubt because of outside influences.

      Luke?

You got it. The entire DeSilva family, your parents, your aunt and uncle, and I think the fact that your mom is getting help helped a little, too.

      I feel different, that's for sure. Now I just have to get my head to catch up to the way I feel and I'll be good to go! And if someone like Luke, and his family, can like me for me, I guess I could learn to like myself as well.

I like what I'm hearing, Brynlee Sheffield. Okay, school tomorrow, so you must get ready for bed, but first...

      Haha, okay... I am beautiful...

Monday, Monday...

Hair and makeup look good, outfit is cute. Now I just need to grab a bite to eat because I'm starving, and I'll be totally ready when Luke gets here. I really wish it was summer already so we could just hang out every day. Well, he probably has a summer job, so that wouldn't happen, but maybe it could. Maybe we can get a job together. I'll have to ask him what he does when we're on summer break. This is actually the first Monday that I'm not dreading going to school. I can't imagine how many people are going to be coming up to me asking about me and Luke, and maybe even the competition.

"Good morning, beautiful! On my way"
"Good morning, handsome! I'm ready"

Good morning, Mom.

> Good morning, hon. Are you hungry? There are some banana bran muffins on the counter, or I can make you some eggs or something.

I think I'll grab a muffin, thanks. Luke's on his way, he'll be here soon.

> So, he's picking you up, huh? Is it out of the way for him?

He said it's not, but whatever. He insisted.

> That's really sweet. Is he a good driver?

Yes, a very good driver. He doesn't ever go more than three miles over the speed limit. I watched. He's very responsible, it seems.

> That's good to hear. I don't love the fact that some of your friends can drive, and you'll be driving too. I'm not ready for this. You're growing up way too fast, Brynlee. I'm having a hard time dealing with that, and the fact that I'm getting old.

Oh Mom, you're not getting old, you're just getting older. You're still young and beautiful.

> Thank you, hon. I needed to hear that today.

So you have your appointment today. Good luck, I guess? I don't know what to say for an appointment.

> Haha, thanks, Bryn. I don't need luck. Prayer maybe, but

not luck.
Why don't we go to church ever?

You know, I really don't know. Maybe we should start.
Luke's family is Catholic, but they don't go much. Maybe we can go to their church.

Maybe. We'll see.
Oh, Luke's here. Love you!

Have a good day, honey. I love you too.
Tell Dad, too!

I will.

Hey there, handsome!

Hello my beautiful girlfriend! Wow, you look great!
You're lookin' pretty good yourself, my sexy boyfriend.

Oh, you think I'm sexy, huh?
Yup. Damn straight.

Well, I have to be, because I have the sexiest girl there is.
Oh do you?

I do.
Well then, we're sexy together. Makes me feel bad for everyone else.

Are you ready, my sweet?
I guess I have to be. I'd rather spend the day with you somewhere on a beach in the tropics, watching dolphins and sipping some fancy drink with an umbrella, but I guess that'll have to wait until we're a little older.

I guess it will. We have forever, though, so, I'll wait. I'd be happy anywhere with you.
Ditto, babe. I do wish we didn't have to go to school, though.

After you, and don't touch that door.
You're so sweet.

Alrighty, here we go.

And here we go, off to another day of prison. At least I get to roll up with my boyfriend, hand in hand, happy as clams, facing the world together. Look at his face. God, he is so hot, I still can't believe he's my boyfriend. I can't wait to see reactions. This should be interesting, if nothing else....

I'm so happy I get to start today, and the week, off with you. Thank you for picking me up. I really appreciate it.

I couldn't wait to see you. Thank you for letting me pick
you up.
So, umm, are you going to kiss me before we go in?
Absolutely! … Damn, girl, these kisses of yours are the
best.
Only because I'm kissing you.
I'm one lucky guy! I guess we should go in now, huh?
Yeah I guess so.

Well, well, well, if it isn't America's most awkward couple.
Shut up, Samantha. Go away.
Oh come on, Luke, you know you don't really want that, do you?
Just ignore her, Luke. Let's go.
Aww, that's cute, Brynlee. You think he could just ignore me. Such a
shame for you that he can't do that so easily.
What are you talking about?
Brynlee, don't bother.
Don't bother? Why not, Lukey? Don't want her to know?
Know what?
She's talking out of her ass. Come on, let's find the gang.
I guess he doesn't want you to know that he hasn't quite gotten over
me yet.
In your dreams.
Actually, it's in my texts, but whatever. And no, Luke, I'm not
available to have sex tomorrow night. Sorry. But maybe Wednesday,
if you're lucky.
Seriously Samantha? You're going to stoop that low?
You really are desperate, aren't you?
Actually, Brynlee, he's the desperate one. I guess dating the
town prude isn't working out for him, so he knows who
loves him the right way.
Bryn, don't listen to her. She's full of shit.
Be careful, honey. He's not the guy you think he is. And
apparently, he's still not over me.
Okay, I'm going to class.
Bye Miss Don't-touch-me! Have a wonderful day!
Screw off, bitch.
Samantha, you really are a bitch, aren't you? Such a shame
I wasted so much time on you. The sex wasn't even worth
it. At least I found myself a girl I can be proud of. You?

You're nothing but a jealous whore, and that's all you'll ever be. Brynlee! Wait up!

Hey, you didn't believe her, I hope.
            No. I didn't.
I'm sorry you had to deal with that. I really thought enough time had passed that she wouldn't mess with you.
            Don't worry about me. I can handle that bitch.
Are you okay?
            I'm fine.
Brynlee wait. Look at me. I did not text her to have sex. As a matter of fact, I didn't text her at all.
            Okay.
You don't believe me.
            Look, I really need to get to class.
Brynlee, please. I'll show you my phone. Hell, I'll show you the bill when it comes. I did not text her, call her, nothing.
            I know you didn't.
So you believe me? I swear, I would never ever do that to you. I would never jeopardize a diamond for a pebble.
            Okay Luke. It's okay. I believe you. I'm just pissed, and it
            took everything in me not to knock her on her ass.
Okay good. Come here.
            Ugh! Why do you have to go and kiss me like that when
            I'm pissed off? Now my anger diminished and…
And you're back to being happy again?
            Stop! Don't smile at me like that! You're going to make
            me kiss you again. Dammit, Luke!

Damn, Baby, you kiss good even when you're pissed off. Jeez, I don't know how I went through life without you.
            You suffered. That's how.
You seriously don't even know! And apparently I still have to deal with her shit.
            No you don't. We need to just ignore her. She's irrelevant.
She's less than irrelevant. Now, let me walk you to class. We can catch up with the guys later.
            Actually, I have to go to the ladies room. I'll see you after
            first?
You're damn right, you will!

Ugh! I HATE THAT BITCH! The question is, was she lying or not? Of course I want to believe him, but she was so confident. I mean, he knows I have dance tomorrow night, so did he actually text her? Is that why he's so on board with waiting to have sex, because he's having it with her? I feel sick, like I could puke right now. I'll just hang out in this stall a minute or two. Oh my God, did that bitch just walk in here? Yes! I want to beat her ass right now. Who is she with? Oh, Victoria, great. I need to hear this... She did lie!! Are you freaking kidding me?! She had to see my reaction?! Aww, Victoria is sticking up for me. Oh shit! Oh my God! No way!

"Hey Babe, you're not going to believe this!"
"What?"
"I'm in a stall trying to calm down, and the bitch is in here with Victoria"
"Don't do anything crazy"
"She's just told Vic how she lied and she thinks she had me believing it and…"
"And?"
"Victoria is sticking up for me and is telling her off!" "Vic just said she's getting her kicked off the cheer squad…"
"Seriously?!"
"Yeah! She just called her a bitch and said they don't need to be friends anymore"
"Good!"
"Vic just walked out and now Samantha is crying and I'm stuck in this stall"
"Haha, what are you going to do?"
"I'm going to make her life miserable"
"Bryn, don't bother"
"Brb"

Hello, bitch.
        Brynlee! Where'd you come from?
I've been here all along. Now listen up, you little skank, leave me and Luke alone.
        Kinda hard when he still wants to have sex with me.
You're really an idiot, aren't you? I knew you were lying, and now I heard it straight from your whore mouth. Jealousy isn't becoming,

hon. Time to move on.

Please, you will never be what I was to him.

Oh really, Ursula?

How do you know about that?

His nephew told me. And the little one? Yeah, he sat on my lap and hugged me. And his mom thinks I'm lovely.

She called you lovely?

She did. Bet she never called you that, did she? But you know, I'm done wasting my breath on you, because you're irrelevant. Irrelevant to me, to Luke, and apparently now to Victoria and the rest of the girls. You dug your own grave, and damn, if you didn't just put yourself in it. I'd feel bad for you but you don't deserve that. Maybe this will open your eyes to see that you can't treat people like shit and think they'll actually put up with it forever. You mess with us, or anyone else again, and you'll have to answer to me, so I wouldn't attempt any more stupid moves. Got it?

Got it.

Clean up your face. You look pathetic.

Clap clap clap. You tell her, Brynlee!

Oh hey, Jasmine! I didn't know you were in here.

Oh my God, Jasmine, she just came at me and started…

Save it, Samantha. I heard every word you said to Victoria too. I guess I got my period on the right morning! You know what's funny? I got it all on video thru the door crack.

You did not.

Yup, all of it. I already sent it to Victoria, in case you tried to call her a liar. You're done in this school, sugar. Brynlee, you ready to get to class?

I am. Let's go. I'd like to introduce you to my boyfriend, Luke.

Please do!

Holy crap, Brynlee that was freaking awesome! First Friday, and now Monday. You're on a roll telling her off! And I got it all on video!

Did you seriously? I thought you were just saying that.

I totally did. Are you kidding? That's good stuff right there!

I kinda feel bad that I was so mean to her. But man, it felt good to get it out.

Oh come on, Brynlee, she deserved every bit of it. She's treated everyone, especially you, like crap for years, so it's about time someone put her in her place for good.

I guess. I just hate being so mean.

Please, you are one of the nicest people in this school. She pushed you to your limit. We all have limits, you know. You did what we all wish we could do. No one ever had the guts to stand up to her like you did, and you did it twice! I'm proud of you.

Thanks, Jasmine. I'm sorry we got off on the wrong foot.

Are you kidding? That was all my fault. Bygones, okay?

That'd be great.

So, lunch today? Same time, same place?

You bet. See you there.

Brynlee! Hey, Baby, what just happened?

I'm sorry I was so mean!

What are you talking about?

I just slammed Samantha in the bathroom and Jasmine was in there, but we didn't know, and she got the whole thing on video.

You slammed her, how? Like shoved her into the wall?

No, like told her off.

Oh! Don't apologize. Damn, I thought you slammed her physically.

Oh God, no. It would take an awful lot for me to do that.
But I wanted to.

I'm sure you did. So what happened?

Oh, I'm sure you'll see the video before first is over. Jasmine sent it to Victoria, and I'm sure it's going all around by now. I'm just sorry, that's all. You said I'm goodhearted no matter how people treat me, and then I went and tore her a new one.

Well, you slayed the dragon!

What?

The fairytale. You slayed the dragon in our fairytale.

I guess I did, didn't I?

Promise me, though, that you will let me protect you from now on.

I'd really like that. You're not disgusted with me?

How could you even think I'd be disgusted with you? Just because you did what everyone else wished they could do? You stuck up for yourself, Brynlee, and that's sexy as hell! That wasn't mean in any way. It was confidence and self-respect, and I could never be disgusted by that, or by you, ever.

Thank you, Luke.

Babe, you don't have to thank me, but you do have to hug me. I want to be the first to hug the girl who slayed the nasty dragon.

You don't have to ask me twice! I love having your strong arms around me. I told you, I feel safe here.

Hey, you two, you're going to be late to class if you don't get moving.

Natalya! Holy crap, you missed it! And Jasmine's joining us for lunch again.

Missed what? Tell me all about it! And, cool, okay.

Well, you'll probably hear it in first, I'm sure.

Yeah, don't worry, Natalya, I don't know the whole story yet either, but I bet we'll know within the next five minutes!

You didn't tell Luke?

Trust me, you will both see it for yourselves.

What are you talking about?

Never mind.

Okay, well, I don't want to be late, so I'll see you at lunch.

Let me walk you to class now, please?

Sure, I'd love that.

Well, now you can join the cheer squad! I hear there's a spot open.

You're too funny.

But I'm serious. I'm going to talk to Victoria about it later.

No, don't, really. That would be really mean if I took her spot.

Would you listen to yourself? You're still so nice, even after what she did. Let me just talk to her about it. You would want to do it, wouldn't you? They could use you for the rest of the basketball season. And there's competition, too.

I don't know. I'm not sure I'll have time, with dance and private lessons.

Well, let me talk to her, and you can think about it. Okay? You'd be perfect.

Ugh, okay, go ahead. But I'm not committing to or promising anything.

That's okay. Thank you. You're the best.

You're the best. Now, get to class before you're late.

Thanks for walking me.

The pleasure was all mine, Baby. I'll try to catch you in between classes, but if I can't, I'll meet you before lunch? Do you mind if I join you ladies?

Are you kidding? Of course you can join us! I wasn't sure you'd want to.

You bet, I do! A few of the guys might end up coming with me though, is that okay?

Of course.

Cool. Bye Babe.

Well, that was a stressful morning, and the first period bell didn't even ring yet! Oh Lord, people are staring and smiling. Here we go, another video starring me. Maybe I'll score a movie deal from all of this! Ugh!

Alone, at last!

Hey, Baby, are you ready to go?
> I am. Get me out of this place. I'm done with today, and just want to spend some time with you and have a great ending to this crazy day.

Hey Brynlee, Luke, wait up a second!

Oh Jeez, what does she want?
> I have no idea. This ought to be interesting.

Let's just see what she wants and take it with a grain of salt.
> Okay, but if she starts with us again, you're definitely gonna have to hold me back, Luke. I'm done with her. SO done.

Hey, listen, I'm sorry about this morning. Brynlee, I thought about what you said in the bathroom, and you're right. Jealousy isn't becoming. I know you probably don't believe a word I say, and I can't really blame you, but I want you to know I think you're a great dancer, and Luke is lucky to finally be with someone like you.
You're a great guy, Luke. You deserve to be happy.
> What are you trying to do, Samantha?

Nothing, Luke. I'm just sorry, that's all.
> Whatever. Let's go, Brynlee.

Samantha, I don't know if you're being honest right now or not, and truthfully, I don't care. For your sake, I hope you are, or you're going to be one miserable, old and lonely hag. Okay Luke, let's go.

Do you think she was serious?
> Don't know, don't care. All I care about is you, Babe, and us. She's irrelevant, so let's not put another ounce of energy into talking or thinking about her, okay cutie? Give me your face.

Haha, Luke, you slobbered on my cheek!
> I know! I wanted to make you giggle, put a smile on your face.

Aww, thank you. You put a smile on my face just being here. Just thinking about you makes me smile.

> Good, I'm glad. Baby you are the spark that gets my flame roaring…

Are you serenading me right now?

> I am! Do you like it?

I love it! I didn't know you can sing! Your voice is so dreamy!

> Dreamy?! What the heck, isn't that a word from, like, the 50's? Haha!

Yeah, but it's true! I could listen to you all day!

> Well, I mean, I don't want to make you go all gaga over me, you'll melt like butter.

Oh, is that so, Mr. Hotstuff?

> Haha, no, probably not.

Oh, I think you're probably right, I'd melt.

> Would you rather me sing, or do this?

I definitely loved that! The singing is good too, though. Tough choice, maybe you'll have to do both a few more times before I can make a real educated decision.

> I have no problem with that!

How about we take this somewhere else besides the school parking lot?

> Where to? My parents aren't home, so we shouldn't go there. How about your place, are your parents home?

No, Dad's working and Mom is at her appointment.

> Well, then that's out. Wait, what appointment?

Oh! Me and Mom talked last night. The meetings she has are with a counselor. She's finally getting help.

> That's awesome! I'm so glad for you.

Thank you. So, where should we go? Do you think we can handle being at home alone?

> I don't know if we should, Babe. I mean, one thing could lead to another…

Or, we could go make snacks, play video games, work out, whatever.

> How about I just take you out for something to eat, and we wait until one of our parents are home? Your mom will probably be the first one home, after her appointment.

As long as I'm with you, I'm good with whatever.

> Cool, what are you in the mood for?

Kissing!

Brynlee, you are so cute. But really, what are you in the mood to eat?

Um, I guess a salad, or something light. How about you?

I could go for a salad. There's a place in Portland that I hear is good. You want to try it?

Sure, let's go.

He sings! And he sings good! Jeez, he just gets more and more amazing. I just want to snuggle and chill. Maybe I can talk him into it.

Hey, are you sure we can't just go and chill at one of our houses? It's been one hell of a day, and I really just want to be alone with you, even if we sit across the room from each other.

I don't know, Bryn...

Please?

You're going to make it real tough, you know.

I'll put on my Daddy's ugliest shirt and a big ole pair of sweatpants if that helps.

It probably won't but I guess if you insist, we can go. But listen, we set boundaries. We need to keep those boundaries.

Of course. Gosh, you're acting like you're the one who wants to wait until the wedding night.

Haha, and you're the one acting like you don't. That's funny.

No, I do. I just know we can't go out to eat every time our parents aren't home. We'll end up broke and overweight from all the junk food!

True, okay, let's go. Whose house are we going to?

Let's go to your place. Or mine.

Haha, which is it going to be, cutie?

It's up to you. I don't care where we go, as long as we're together.

Okay, how about we go to my house? There's a ton of stuff we can do to keep busy there, and I think Mom left food.

Is my sweetie hungry? We can stop somewhere if you want to. I didn't know you were that hungry.

It's cool, Mom usually has something in the fridge, especially since they had friends over the other night. If not, we can always whip something up.

Alright, good. We can cook together, like we're newlyweds.

But we won't be doing newlywed stuff, remember?

I remember. We can still cook together, though. Or I can just cook for you.

You know how to cook?

No, not really. Just the basics, like pasta, eggs, English muffin pizzas, oh, and spring rolls!

Um, spring rolls aren't cooked!

You know what I mean, wise guy!

Alright, let's do it. Listen, I'm really sorry you had to deal with what's her face back there.

It's not your fault, but thanks. I really have no idea why she hates me so much. I never did anything to her.

It's not you, it's her. She is just really jealous of you. She has been for a long time.

Why, though? She's gorgeous, and she's a cheerleader, and I'm just...

You're just more gorgeous, and you're a great dancer, and you're nice. Anyway, she's not as good looking as you think she is. Makeup does wonders, trust me. Plus, her charcoal heart makes her even worse. You are naturally beautiful. You don't need makeup to look beautiful.

But you've never seen me without makeup.

Actually, I have. You've come to school without it, and trust me, I've noticed.

The only time I went to school without makeup was when I was sick and, oh my God! I looked like hell that day!

No you didn't. You looked so cute in your gray sweatpants and dance hoodie.

You remember what I was wearing? That was weeks ago.

Oh, I remember. I also remember thinking that you are more beautiful than any girl I've ever seen.

I can't believe you remember what I was wearing, and that you still asked me out after that.

Brynlee, I didn't think you'd ever date me.

That's crazy. I didn't think you'd ever want to date me, or give me the time of day.

Well, you were wrong. You're the best thing that's happened to me, ever, and that includes making the football team! You know how much I love playing football.

I know. You look so hot in that uniform, too.

I look even hotter out of it.

I bet you're right.

But you won't find out any too soon, so…

That's just wrong. But, um, ditto. So there.

Ugh, I know.

God, I bet he looks so damn good… No. I'm not even going to start thinking about that. That kind of thinking could be very dangerous. Ugh! I'm a fifteen, almost sixteen year old girl! I can't help but think those kinds of things! Distraction, I need a distraction. Oh, who am I kidding? He IS my distraction! Okay, Brynlee, you need to control yourself and your thoughts. Self-control is key. He's just so perfect, though! It's okay, I can do it. I can have self-control. I'm not some barbaric animal who acts on every impulsive desire. But look at him! No, don't look, it'll make it harder. Think about something else, like dance. Oh, I almost forgot, that meeting to tell the parents is tomorrow night before class. Will Ms. Val tell both sets of parents at the same time or separately? I hope together, so Lacey and I can freak out together. She's a doll. Oh crap, I never texted her, and was supposed to find out if she'd want to go on a double with us and Ray. I think they'd hit it off.

So Ray likes Lacey, huh?

Yeah, he does. That was random.

Oh, sorry, I was just thinking about dance and stuff to keep my mind out of the gutter, and I remembered you said he was gaga over her in the video.

Your mind was headed for the gutter?

Yeah, I had to stop looking at you, too. Self-control.

I'm glad to know I send your mind to the gutter. That'll come in handy one day.

Yeah, but I'm thinking it's probably going to be a lot sooner than my wedding night.

Nope, no, I am a man of honor, and I will not dishonor my princess. So you just keep on thinking about other things, and so will I. But yeah, why don't you text her and see if she'd be open to a half blind double date?

Half blind?

Well, you and I are already together, so half of us will be on a blind date, and half of us won't.

> Oh, haha, okay. I'll text her now. It'll help keep my
> thoughts fully clothed.

Good girl.

"Hey Lace! It's Brynlee"

> I don't know if she's out of school yet. Not sure what her
> bell schedule is. So, what did he like about her? She'll
> probably want to know.

Well, he thought she was, in his words, "as pretty as an angel", and loves her red hair. Then he got all perverted and started talking about her dancing like that for him.

> Oh.

Don't worry, he's not like that. He was just saying that crap because all the guys were around.

> Are you sure, because I don't want to set her up with some
> asshole who's going to screw her over for any girl that
> walks by.

No, he's seriously not like that. He's chill. When it's just us, he talks about wanting a long-term relationship. He's tired of the superficial crap. Now, if it was JD we're talking about, then yeah, he's the king of assholes. He's as bad as your boy Blake.

> Woah, Blake is NOT my boy. You are my boy, thank you
> very much.

You're darn right, I'm yours, and you're mine.

"Hey Brynlee! What's up?"
Hey, two things – one, would you be interested in double dating with me and my boyfriend this weekend, and two, do you know our parents' meeting with Ms. Val is at the same time or separate?"
"Boyfriend?! Do tell!" "And I think at the same time"
"Oh good, okay. I'll have to tell you all about it tomorrow night, or I'll text you later"
"Def text me l8r! I want 2 see a pic of him too. Don't 4get this time"
"Haha, okay, I'll text you tonight when I get home" "oh, so, double date?"
"What's the guy like?"
"Football player, cute, went gaga over you in the video"

"Oh Jeez, the video"
"Yeah"
"What's his name?
"Ray Carmichael"
"I'll look him up online and get back to you"
"Okay, check my followers, he's on there"
"Okay, I will"

Was that Lacey? What'd she say?
          She said she'll check him out and let me know.
Okay, cool. I'll let him know.
          No, wait until she says if she wants to or not, first. I don't
          want his feelings to get hurt if she says no.
True. He is a bit of a sensitive guy.
          Ray? Ray Carmichael is sensitive? Are we talking about
          the same Ray?
Yup, he sure is. He puts on a front, though.
          A pretty big one, apparently!
Yeah, but he's a good guy, I promise. I wouldn't try to set him up
with one of your friends if he wasn't.
          Okay, I guess I'll have to trust you on that one.
Yup, you have to just trust me.

"Brynlee! Holy crap."
It's Lacey, I wonder if she saw him already? "Holy crap what?"
"He's HOT"
Haha, she thinks he's hot!
Oh, cool. When we get home I'll text Ray.
"So, you wanna double date this weekend?"
"Hell yeah! Are you sure he was talking about me and not someone
else?"
"Lace, you're the only redhead in our company!"
"Oh, yeah, I guess so" "Damn, why didn't you tell me about him
sooner?"
"I just started dating his friend, Luke, this weekend"
"Oh! Okay. Friday, Saturday?"
          She wants to know, are we hanging out Friday or Saturday?
I'll let you know as soon I get in touch with Ray.
          Okay. "I'll find out and let you know"
"Omg I love you right now!"

"Love you too, Lace. I'll let you know in a little while"
"Ugh! Hurry!"
"Haha, ok"

> She's totally freaking out right now.

Is she, really? That's cool. It'll be good to see Ray with a nice girl. His last girlfriend was kinda bitchy, and man, was she whacked!

> Really, huh? What's with you guys dating all these bitches?

We're guys, we go where the easy girls are. Well, not anymore, not me anyway.

> Good!

Alright, let's go in and see what there is to eat. I don't know why, but I'm starving.

> Okay, but you have to text Ray right away, okay? Lacey's flipping out.

Okay, I'll text him right now.

> Thanks, Babe.

Anything for my girl!

> Want me to see what there is to eat for you?

Sure, if you want to, that'd be great. If there's nothing good in the fridge, check the pantry, over there by the back door.

> Okay

I'm so glad you're not afraid to eat in front of me.

> Why would I be?

I don't know. Some girls are weird like that. God only knows why.

> I think that's stupid. We all have to eat.

Yes! Thank you! Okay, Ray said Friday, so if they hit it off then we can hang out again Saturday all day.

> Okay, let me tell her.

He said to give her his number so she can text him.

> How about we give him her number. He's the guy. He should text her.

Yeah, okay. Text it to me and I'll forward it.

> Okay.

"Lace, how's Friday night? Oh, and I gave him your number so he can text you, ok?"
"Friday is PERFECT! Do you think he'll text me?"
"Yeah, he said to give you his number but we gave him yours to text you first"

"Oh my God, Bryn! I hope he does!"
"I'm sure he will"
"Holy shit! He just did!"
"That was quick"
"Ok, I'll text you later and let you know how it goes"
"Ok"

Ray moves quick, huh?
What, he texted her already? Damn!
Aww, she's so excited.
Yeah, he is too, apparently! He didn't waste any time, did he?
Good. I want her to be happy. This will be cool because now all six of us can hang out together!
Oh yeah, that's right! We should all do something really fun on Saturday night, like dinner and then maybe glow in the dark bowling?
That sounds fun. I haven't been glow in the dark bowling in a while.
Me either. I don't know why we don't go that much anymore. It's a lot of fun, and the bowling alley plays great music.
Yeah, they do.
Do you want to stay local?
Doesn't matter to me. Where does Lacey live? Does she live in Portland, or near here?
She lives here, she just commutes to school every day.
Damn, that's a half hour one way!
I know! Okay, let's stay local so we don't spend the whole night driving. Food's done.
Great! Let's eat!

Well, that's interesting...

Thanks for another great night, Luke.
> You're welcome, Baby.

God, you make it so hard to leave.
> Go, before it gets too late and your parents get pissed.
> They'll never let you bring me home this late again.

Are you kidding? They love you. They won't care as long as I'm with you.
> Well, we do have to get up for school in the morning. Text me when you get home.

I will. I'll pick you up the same time tomorrow morning?
> I can't wait!

Goodnight, Baby.
> Goodnight.

Hey Mom, love you, going to bed.
> Whoa, how was your day?

It was fine. Do you mind if we talk about it tomorrow? I have some homework to finish up and I'm beat. Oh, hi Daddy!
> Hi Sweetpea! Did you have a nice day?

Yeah, I guess. Love you, goodnight!
> Goodnight, hon. Oh, hey, is Luke picking you up again, or am I bringing you?

Luke's picking me up, and bringing me home.
> Okay, love you.

Thank God today got so much better than it was. I can't believe Samantha started crap with us. And what the heck was up with that apology? She surely wasn't serious, was she? People don't change in one school day, especially not when their name is Samantha Britt! Ugh, she pisses me off so bad, and I hate it because I turn into some totally different person because of her.

I think you handled it quite well, actually.
> Oh, thanks, Nova. I don't like what she makes me turn

into.

Well, you were quite angry, but under the circumstances, I think you were a lot better than what could've been. You said some things that were a little hurtful, but I think she's okay.

> Ugh! Did you hear her stupid fake apology after school?

I don't know, Brynlee, I'm not so sure it was fake.

> You can't be serious. How in the world would she change just like that in one school day?

A lot has happened to her the last few days, with everyone putting her in her place. I think you made the biggest impact on her, and maybe she really did take it to heart.

> Well, whatever. I can't stand her, and I don't believe a word she says.

I don't really blame you, to be honest. But I think you may want to reconsider your disbelief this one time.

> I'm not sure I can.

So, tomorrow night is the big night! The meeting with Ms. Val and both sets of parents!

> Oh my gosh, I know! I'm a little nervous.

Why?

> I hope they all say "yes".

Well, I guess we'll find out, won't we?

> Yeah. So Luke and I are double dating with Lacey and his friend Ray this Friday.

I heard! That's great! Lacey's nice.

> Yeah, she is. She never used to be, though.

I know. I remember. She's come a long way in a short period of time, too.

> Oh, you mean like me? Wait a minute! She has a tea cup, too!

She does?

> Nova, you know! She was telling me about how she had help from a special friend, Lyric. Do you know Lyric?

I can't say whether I do or I don't know Lyric.

> It was weird, because she was telling me about it and she was able to get her name out before we were interrupted!

Oh really?

Nova! You were there! Does this mean I can talk to her about you?

Well, if this Lyric friend is a teacup, then yes, you may be able to talk about me, but you may not. It depends on if you are ready, or if she's ready. If it's the right time, you'll know. You'll feel it.

Dude, this is too cool!

I am not a dude, thank you very much.

You know what I mean. Okay, I'm going to text her. We have to plan for Friday night, and I have to tell her about potential plans for Saturday. And I have to text Natalya. All of a sudden we don't talk much because we're with our men.

Try not to lose touch because of the boys, okay? Friendships are so important.

I know, but the good thing is, our men are best friends, so hanging out will be easy.

This is true. It'd be nice if all six of you could hang out all the time.

I know, it really would. I think Lacey and Natalya will get along pretty good. Now, if we can hook Jasmine up with another one of their friends, we'll be set.

Things really turned around with you two, huh?

They did. I like her. I told her I was sorry we got off on the wrong foot. She's actually really cool.

That's great, Brynlee. I'm proud of you, and of who you are becoming. It's nice to see people transform into who they really are. You're a strong, beautiful and intelligent young lady, and it seems by the way you handled Samantha, that your confidence is growing quickly.

I guess I am just now starting to realize that I am good enough and I deserve happiness. When that happiness was threatened, it pissed me off enough to fight for it and protect it. I couldn't have done that without your help in showing me my own worth. Thank you.

Oh, sweetie, don't cry. You're going to make me cry on this one!

Nova! Your tears glow!

Those are happy tears.

That is so freaking cool!

You think this is cool, wait until your wedding day! They'll glow
AND sparkle! Remember that, because sometimes other people
can see them.

No way! Really?

Yes, really. It's fun listening to them try to figure out what it is
that sparkles and glows!

I can't wait! I hope it's at my wedding to Luke!
I just might be, you never know.

Would you tell me if you did know?
Nope. I took an oath.

Ugh! Okay, I have to text Lacey.

"Hey! I know you said you'd text me but I couldn't wait. How'd it
go with Ray?"

"Great! He's such a nice guy!"

"Aww, I'm glad. Did you guys talk about Friday night?"

"A little. We mostly talked about ourselves and are getting to know
each other a little bit"

"That's great, Lace!"

"Thank you for getting us together. I can't wait to see him in person"

"I think you'll get along great"

"Me too" "Hey, how tall is he?"

"I don't know, maybe six foot?"

"Oh my God, r u serious?" "<3 <3 <3"

"Yeah, he and Luke are about the same height"

"Is he as hot in person as he is in the pics?"

"I'm sure you'll like him, trust me"

"Okay good" "Btw, I saw the pic of you and Luke together. So
cute!"

"Thanks. He's amazing"

"I hope Ray is equally as amazing"

"Don't worry, Luke says he's a great guy"

"He seems like it so far"

"So, can I ask you a question?"

"Sure"

"You started to tell me about how your friend, Lyric, helped you.
What's the deal with that?"

"Lyric? Yeah, um, we should just talk about that in person, ok?"

"Yeah, sure"

"Sorry, it's a long story"

"Oh, that's ok"

"I can fill you in more tomorrow when our parents are in the meeting"

"Ok, cool. The reason I ask is bc Luke's ex is a real bitch and she started crap today, but then did a 180 and apologized"

"Oh really? What happened?"

"That's a long story too. Tell you all about it tomorrow"

"Ok, good. Our stories will keep our minds off of the meeting"

"True. We'll need a distraction. I'm nervous"

"Me too" "I think it'll all work out in our favor tho"

"I hope so"

"I should go. I'm still texting Ray"

"Aww! Ok, nite!"

"Nite"

"Hey Babe! I'm home. Had to stop at Dylan's quick and give him money for gas to take Natalya home"

"Haha, are you serious?"

"Yeah, he's crazy"

"Aww they were hanging out?"

"Yeah. Those two…"

"Lip locked still?"

"Good God, yes. Are we that bad?"

"No. We actually talk and hang out"

"Ok good"

"I'll see you in the morning?"

"Definitely! Sleep tight, Beautiful"

"You too, handsome"

I love how he calls me beautiful. I'm starting to believe it. I am beautiful. I am beautiful. I am… seeing glowing tears! Nova!

I am so proud of you, Brynlee!

Nova, the ribbon on your hat just changed colors! Oh how wonderful!

What does that mean?

It means you're almost there! You are in the second to last phase!

What does the second to last phase mean?

It means you're really starting to believe it. This is a crucial time, because for you to enter into the last phase, you have to go through a situation that will really test your belief. That may not happen for a long time. But, the way you react outwardly and in your thoughts will determine if you can enter into the final phase. Your thoughts will be the most important determining factor. I'm so proud of you. And thank you, I am loving my new look!

> Wow, that's some deep shit. This situation, do you mean a breakup?

No, not necessarily. It could be anything, really, even a meeting with a counselor. But don't worry, it may not happen for years.

> Now I'm worried.

Please, Brynlee, don't worry. Your growth now will determine how you handle the situation given when it's time. Just remember, you are beautiful, you are good enough, and you are worthy of happiness. These are things you must remember. They are the cornerstone to you finding your true self.

> Okay, I'll remember. I guess that's why I have to say it every day, huh?

Yes, repeating the truth daily, hearing it, letting it sink in, is what will help you recall it in times when you'll really need it. This is what I'm preparing you for.

> Thank you, Nova. I am so grateful to have you. Deeply and truly grateful.

I know. And thank you.

> Well, I should go to sleep now. I'll finish my homework in the morning at school. Goodnight.

Goodnight, dear Brynlee. Sweet dreams.

Matchmaking up the wazoo...

Oh my gosh, tonight's the meeting. I can't wait. I would love for Luke to come, but maybe tonight's not the best night for that. Besides, Lacey and I have some chit-chatting to do. I really hope her and Ray hit it off like Luke and I did. That would be awesome, especially if our parents say we can do this private thing. I think our dancing would be even tighter if we were close like me and Natalya. I wonder where all of this is going to take us. Ugh, I am not in the mood to go to school today. I especially don't want to see what's her face. Definitely not in the mood for her at all. I swear, if she so much as even thinks about starting anything today, I'll knock her ass out, without a freaking thought. Dammit, see? There I go again, getting all riled up and being exactly the kind of person I don't want to be. I have to remind myself that she's irrelevant. She holds no significance in my life, and not Luke's either, and I shouldn't let her get to me. The second I let her control my emotions, she wins, and I will not allow her to win. She does not have permission to control me. Like Booker T. Washington once said, "I will allow no man to narrow and degrade my soul by making me hate him". I will not give her the power to do that to me. I am in control of me. I am not a puppet to her or anyone else. Okay, I look cute today. Time to get downstairs and wait for Luke. I'm not really hungry today. Maybe I'll grab some almonds in case I get hungry before lunch. Where's Mom and Dad? Oh, Dad's in his office on the phone already. Maybe Mom's in the shower.

Hi Daddy, where's Mom?

> Oh, hi Sweetpea, she's getting ready. I think she's going for coffee with some ladies from the party.

Oh that's good. Okay, well, Luke will be here soon, so I'm going to wait for him.

> Okay, I love you. Have a nice day.

Don't forget about the meeting at the dance school tonight.

> Oh, is that tonight?

Yes, please tell me you didn't forget.

> I didn't forget, it just slipped my mind. I have it on my

calendar, so don't worry, I didn't book any appointments for that time.

Thank God, okay good. Love you, Daddy. Have a good day at work. Thank you, Sweetpea.

I guess I should run upstairs and say bye to Mom. Man, when I'm older, I should buy a one story house. This going up and down is ridiculous. At least it'll keep me in shape when I'm at home.

Bye, Mom, I'm getting ready to leave.

Okay, bye hon. Have a good day. Don't forget we have that meeting tonight so we'll have to leave a little earlier.

Yup, I know, and I already reminded Daddy.

Oh good, okay. I'll have dinner ready much earlier tonight. Luke can stay for dinner if he'd like to.

Thanks, Mom. I'll tell him. Love you.

I love you, hon.

Aww, she invited Luke to stay for dinner. That's so cute. I'm so glad they like him. And, speaking of Luke, there he is.

Hey Baby, how are you this morning?

I'm good… And now I'm great. I love first thing in the morning kisses.

Me too. Are you ready to go?

I am.

Here, let me carry your stuff.

Luke, come on, you do too much. I can carry my own books.

Please? I want to. I don't want my baby to break a sweat.

Haha, I won't, trust me. But I guess if you really want to, go ahead. You want my purse too? It's much heavier than my books.

Yeah, I bet it is! You girls carry a damn warehouse in there!

Everything but the kitchen sink, that's what my Daddy says.

Well, he's right. You in?

Yup, I'm good. Thank you, handsome.

My pleasure, Beautiful.

Okay, so no matter what happens today, we will not allow others to control our emotions, okay?

No one except you. You can control every emotion I've got.

> You know what I mean, silly. If we let them, then they win, and I refuse to lose, especially to what's her face!

Sounds like you put some thought into this.

> Not much. I just started to get pissy and realized that I was allowing her to control me, so I made the decision to not allow it.

Smart thinking, Babe. I like it. Now, let's hope it's that easy in real life.

> Yeah, let's. So have you talked to Ray since he texted Lacey?

Not too much, but he did say she seems really cool, and he can't wait until Friday night.

> That's it?

Yeah, he was still texting her, so I went to bed. I dreamt about you last night.

> You did?

I did. I dreamt we were in Aruba on the beach, and we had people serving us like we were royalty.

> That sounds amazing. Can we go to Aruba please?

Baby, I'll take you anywhere you want to go. What's your dream destination?

> Well, Aruba would be nice. My dream destination? Hmm, I think I'd have to say Bora Bora. I really want to stay in one of those huts that hovers over the water. Either there or Belize. There's just something about the blue Caribbean Sea that just calls my name. What about you, what's your dream spot?

Well, Bora Bora or Belize would be perfect. I don't think I ever really pinpointed a place, but I did always picture a tropical island. I guess I'd have to say Bora Bora, since it's a secluded island away from any mainland. So, when we go there, no one can bother us. It'll just be us and the islanders, no phones, no TV, just us and nature. We can lay on the beach all day and night, sipping on some tropical drinks, eating island food, and hell, we can even be naked if we want to.

> Well, I'll be sure to bring plenty of sunblock, especially for the parts that haven't seen direct sunlight. We want to enjoy our vacation, not be miserably sunburnt in very sensitive areas.

Haha, okay, maybe we'll have our bathing suits on!

Good idea. Ugh, here we are already. And we were having such a lovely time in Bora Bora.

Sorry, Babe. We can continue our little vacation daydream after school.

Oh by the way, Mom said you can stay for dinner before we go to the meeting.

Cool, okay, I'd love that. I'd love to be there to see your face when they tell you guys you can study privately, but I don't think that'd be a good idea tonight. Will you text me as soon as you find out?

Of course I will! You and Natalya will be the first to know, besides me and Lacey, of course!

Excellent. You know I'll be pacing until I hear.

I know. Thank you for caring so much about me.

Thank you for being the kind of girl I want to care about.

Hey, isn't that Ray over there with Natalya and Dylan?

Yup, sure is. Let's go.

Hey guys, what's up Ray? How'd it go last night?

It went great! Dude, she is so cool. Thanks a lot for getting me her number. Thanks Brynlee.

You're welcome.

So, did she say anything about me to you?

She did, actually.

Can someone tell us what you're talking about?

Oh, sorry, Natalya, I thought Ray already told you guys.

Nah, I just walked up on these two lovebirds.

Oh, okay, well, Luke and I are hooking Ray up with Lacey.

Lacey from dance?

Yup.

Aww, that's so cute! We should all hang out.

Yeah, Brynlee and I were talking about us all going out to dinner and then glow in the dark bowling on Saturday.

That'd be so fun!

Yeah, it would be, and Natalya, I was trying to think of who we could set Jasmine up with, and they could come too.

Hmm, I don't know. Guys, who's single that you all hang out with?

Conner would hang out with Jasmine in a heartbeat!

Isn't he dating Marissa?

No, they broke up last week.

Wow, that didn't last long.

Wait, did she get back together with her ex? Nat, didn't we just see them together?

We did. So, Jasmine and Conner, huh? I bet that would work.

Dude, it would work. Connor's liked Jasmine since kindergarten!

No way, really?

Haha, yeah. Luke, don't you remember a long time ago he used to stare at her on the playground and she was all flirty with him back then?

I remember. That was so funny. Imagine, after all this time, they finally get together.

Awww, and it's all because of this crew, right here.

Okay, Bryn, we can talk to her at lunch. Guys, we'll let you know.

Ok, dude, what the hell happened with Samantha yesterday?

Man, I don't wanna talk about it.

Yeah, we'd rather not speak of it. Sorry, Dylan. So Ray, Lacey is looking forward to hanging out with you.

I'm so psyched. She is hot! And she's almost as good as you are at dancing, Brynlee.

Aww, thank you, Ray. That's so sweet. She's an awesome dancer. We make a good team.

You sure do! I love her red hair! Damn!

I can't wait to meet her, either.

Wait, what? You haven't met her yet, Natalya?

No, I've never been able to. My schedule is so busy that I can't go to dance class with Brynlee, and to go to the competition you need a ticket, and I can never get one. They need to sell more tickets.

I agree. I need my best friend there for support, and my boyfriend! How is a girl supposed to dance her absolute best if she doesn't have the two most important hand-chosen people in her life?

Exactly!

Well, I have to get to class. I'll catch up with you guys later. Thanks again, Brynlee, for Lacey's number!

You got it!

I guess we should all get to class, huh?

Do we have a choice?

Haha, no, we don't. Natalya, talk to Jasmine about Connor. I'll see you guys at lunch.

Okay, I will. See ya. Ready Dylan?

Yup, let's go. Luke, are you gonna talk to Connor or do you want me to?

I guess whoever sees him first.

Alright, later dude. Bye Brynlee.

Bye guys!

Okay, beautiful, let's get you to class.

Thank you. This weekend's going to be fun with all of us hanging out.

Yeah, it really is. It's about time we all have great girls to hang out with.

Ugh, do we really have to go to class?

Unfortunately we do. Sorry, Babe. But we will see each other after each class for a minute or so, and then lunch, and then after school. We have little things to look forward to.

True, and I will be counting the seconds until we see each other again.

I don't want to let go of you.

Okay, don't. I'm totally fine with that.

Students, no PDA please.

Sorry, Mr. Thompson. We were just saying goodbye.

Sugar, he's not being deployed, he's going to class. Luke, on your way, son. Brynlee needs to focus on my class.

Yes, Mr. Thompson. See you later, Beautiful.

Aww, isn't that sweet? I must say, you have good taste, Brynlee. He is a very polite and well-mannered young man. If you were my daughter, I'd approve.

Thanks, Mr. Thompson. My Daddy approves as well.

Okay, now take your seat.

Aww, Mr. Thompson is looking out for me. What a great guy. And he approves of Luke and I dating. His opinion means a lot to me. He's my favorite teacher. Okay, Lord, get me to lunch. That's halfway to the meeting. Well, almost, I guess. Whatever. I am so tired, and I really have no idea why. Maybe I'm mentally exhausted from thinking about all this dance stuff, and the crap with Samantha, I don't know. I just know I could fall asleep right here on this desk. My luck I'd end up drooling all over myself and someone would get it on video. I seem to be the star of reality shows lately. Ha, maybe I'll be offered a spot on a show if this keeps up! I should probably pay attention to Mr. Thompson. I think we have a test this week and I need to make sure I keep my grades where they're at. I'd really rather just daydream, though. Bora Bora with Luke is so much nicer to think about than school stuff. Oh crap, did he just call on me? Oh thank God. Okay, time to pay attention.

It's all set...

Alright, guys, looks like it's set for Saturday. The eight of us are hanging out.

> Awesome! We can figure out the details on Friday.

> Brynlee, you can fill Lacey in on what's going on, okay?

Yeah, I'll tell her tonight at dance. Hey Natalya, maybe you can all stay the night Saturday, what do you think?

> That sounds good. I'll tell my mom. You have Jasmine's number to let her know?

No, I don't. Text it to me?

> Yup, here it comes. So, good luck tonight. Text me as soon as you hear anything.

Whoa, wait a minute, she's gotta text me first.

> Luke, Brynlee and I have been best friends since day one. I get first text.

How about I group text you both and you can find out together?

> Yeah, I guess so.

Luke!

> I'm kidding, that'll be great.

Okay, Dylan, are you ready to go study?

> Dylan's studying?! Wow, dude, Natalya's a great influence on you! Maybe you'll pass junior year!

Ha ha, you're freaking hilarious, dude. But yes, she is a good influence on me. And I like it.

> Aww, Dyl pickle, you're sweet.

Dyl pickle?! Hahahaha!! That's so CUTE!

> Shut up, man. What does Brynlee call you, Lukey wooky?

Actually, no. She calls me Babe and Handsome, thank you.

> I mean, I could call you something more along the cutesy lines if you want me to, Snookums.

Hahahaha!! Snookums! Alright, we're outta here. Ready Natalya?

> I'm ready. Bye Brynlee, Bye Snookums! Text me, B!

I will! Are you ready Handsome?

> I kinda like Snookums, to be honest. Haha!

Alright, Snookums, are you ready?

> I am, Princess. Is it okay to call you Princess?

Sure, you can call me anything you want to.

> Good, then Princess it is. Come, my lady, your chariot
> awaits.

Why thank you, Sir Snookums. I'm so glad Jasmine and Connor are
hanging out Saturday.

> Yeah, me too. I think they'd be good together.

He seems pretty cool, is he?

> Yeah, he's chill. Kind of quiet, but he's a good guy. Jasmine
> seems different than she used to be.

Yeah, she said she's been working on her execution of words so she
doesn't sound so bitchy. I guess she really never meant to come off
as a bitch, she just did.

> Interesting. I noticed she doesn't hang out with the rest of
> the cheer squad anymore. Did she say why she doesn't?

She did. She's trying to focus on school and her career, and they're
not quite at the same place as she is. They're still friends, but they
want different things right now. She thinks Natalya and I are
motivated like she is, and I guess that's why she's hanging out with
us. Do you think Connor is interested in a serious relationship, or do
you think he just wants to mess around?

> I guess if they got serious he'd be okay with it. He's never
> really said either way. I guess it depends on the girl and if
> they really like each other or not. Why?

Well, Jasmine's looking for a serious relationship. I don't want to
hook her up with Connor if he's just looking to get…

> Nah, he's not like that. Man, we football players have some
> crappy reputation. What the heck?

It's not just football players, it's guys in general.

> Well, JD is a player. I wouldn't try to set him up with
> anyone. And I wouldn't be surprised if he was Samantha's
> next victim, or the other way around.

Really?

> Yeah. He's a little messed up. They'd be perfect together.

Damn, that's rough.

> Well, it's true. Oh well. Looks like your mom's home.

Cool. She's probably already cooking dinner.

> Already?

Yup, she likes for us to eat early. She doesn't like to eat past a certain
time because she doesn't want us to gain weight.

> Oh, I can understand that.

Yeah, there's some science to back that theory up, I guess.

Well, not only that, it just makes good sense. Most people just sit around and watch tv or play video games. Not everyone is like you and me, dancing and playing sports all night.

I mean, sitting and watching tv is nice sometimes, but I'd definitely rather be doing something, even if I'm not dancing. Lately, though, I have been just chilling in my room or hanging out with Natalya. I miss being little when we used to go out and ride bikes or jump on the trampoline.

Me too! We should do it. Let's do all that silly kid stuff together after school, okay?

Haha, okay. You're so cute.

I just don't want to grow old, you know? Growing up is kind of hard to stop, but we sure as hell don't have to grow old.

I know what you mean. I see people my mom and dad's age, and they're all out of shape, and have a hard time getting up out of chairs and stuff. They're not necessarily overweight or obese, just out of shape. I don't want to get like that. I want to be able to sprint down the road if I have to, or jump up off of the floor when my phone rings, or, heck, walk by kids playing basketball and join in!

You, my beautiful Princess, are the perfect female specimen. Can we just get married now?

I wish! But that's one thing I really love about my mom, she's always taught me to stay active, whether we were doing exercise videos in the living room, or dance or whatever, she kept us moving. I guess that's why she looks so good.

And why you look so good!

Aww, thanks, Snookums!

I think it's so cool that my girlfriend thinks just like I do. Now, let's go in and say hi to your mom and see what she's got cooking!

Hi Mom!

Oh hi sweetie, hi Luke! Hi are you two today?

We're great, Mrs. Sheffield. Something smells amazingly good!

Thank you, Honey, I'm making a vegetarian recipe I saw on one of the food shows I watch. It's a shepherd's pie. It looked so good, I had to try it. And, with my sister and Brynlee venturing into a new diet, I want to learn all I have

to to support them. Who knows, maybe Kyle and I will
jump on the bandwagon!
Thanks, Mom, it smells really good.
It does, I can't wait to eat it!
I don't know how your mom cooked for two growing boys! I'm
surprised she didn't have two of every appliance to keep and cook all
that food! But, I made plenty, so don't be shy.
Oh, I won't, believe me! Especially if it tastes as good as it
smells.
We're going to go upstairs, if that's okay.
Sure Hon, that's fine.
We'll keep the door wide open, though!
Thank you, Luke, that's very thoughtful of you. I appreciate
that.
Of course. And thank you for having me for dinner. I'm looking
forward to it.
You're welcome anytime, son. I'll be sure to always have
enough food on hand for you, and your friends as well.
Thank you, Mrs. Sheffield.
Bye Mom.
Whatever she said she's cooking, man, it's making my mouth water.
Oh really? Maybe I need to check it out and see just how
watery it is… yup, juicy.
You are amazing. Damn.
Well, here we are. This is my room.
Wow! Not at all what I pictured.
Why? What did you picture it to look like?
I don't know, I guess I pictured it to be all pink, and full of dance
stuff like ballet shoes and little girly stuff. I definitely didn't picture
it to be this cool.
It's Bohemian. A little bit of hippie, a little bit of gypsy…
And a lot of sexy. It's so cool how you decorated your room like
your personal style. It's definitely not the stereotypical girl's room.
Well, I'm not the stereotypical girl, now am I?
No, you're definitely not, thank God! It's one of the things I really
love about you. You're different, and you don't care to be like
everyone else. I've got the coolest girl in the world, and I am so
happy about that!
Well, I've got the coolest guy in the world! We're so…
Perfect for each other.

Hey! I was going to say that! You took the words right out of my mouth!

No, actually, you gave them to me when you kissed me on the stairs.

Well, I'm taking them back right now...

Haha, nope, I still have them. They're hidden deep.

Listen, you, I am not afraid to go get them!

Oh, believe me, I know! Here, let me give them back to you...

They taste so much better now.

Okay, let's stop before we can't. So, the eight of us on Saturday.

We'll have to take two cars, I guess.

Yeah, and Dylan can drive, too.

Cool, then we're pretty much set for this weekend. I can't wait. It should be a lot of fun, especially if Lacey and Ray really hit it off, and Jasmine and Connor, too.

Yeah, I think Jasmine and Connor will be fine, especially Connor. It's like the long-awaited dream come true for him.

Why didn't he ever try to date her before?

He's too quiet, and shy.

But they've known each other since kindergarten! He's too shy to ask her out, but was okay asking Marissa? She's the new girl, sort of.

I don't understand it either. I guess she must just be his dream girl, and he was just too scared to ever try. Sort of like I was with asking you out.

But you did it.

I know, and I was nervous as hell.

Well, you didn't seem like it. You were cool as a cucumber.

Oh, so you didn't see me break a sweat?

No. You were sweating?

Yeah. And if I tried to put your number in my phone, I would've dropped it. That's why I had you do it.

You're lying.

I am not lying! I am 100% honest to God, not lying!

Well, my heart was beating so fast when you came over to talk to me that I thought I was going to pass out! Didn't you hear my voice quivering?

Haha, no, I was too busy trying not to say something stupid. And I was mesmerized by your eyes.

Well, I almost passed out.

And look at us now! We kiss and stuff! Speaking of, let's do that.

So torn...

Thank you for dinner, Mrs. Sheffield. It was delicious!

You're quite welcome, Luke. I hope you had plenty to eat.

Haha, yes ma'am, I think three servings was plenty.

That's what I like to see, Son, a young man who eats like me.

Yes, finally Kyle has an eating buddy!

Well, I know you all have a meeting to get to, so Brynlee, let's clean up for your mom, and then I'll head out. Thank you for allowing me to spend dinner time with you all, Mr. and Mrs. Sheffield.

Anytime, Son.

Oh, Luke, you two don't have to clean up, but thank you for offering.

No, Mrs. Sheffield, I insist. Come on, babe.

Okay, you grab that stuff and I'll grab this stuff.

Really, I just wanted to get you in the kitchen to kiss you...

You keep kissing me like that and I'm going to drop the dishes! How the heck would we explain that? "Yeah, Mom, you see, we were making out and Luke's kisses send me into the galaxy, and I got so weak I dropped and broke all the dishes".

I make you weak?

Yeah.

I thought I was the only one who felt like that.

Yeah, no, you're not.

We are a match made in Heaven, then.

We sure are! I'll go get the rest of the stuff. Be right back.

Brynlee, hon, he is so sweet to insist on cleaning up. If his family comes for dinner this weekend, you two don't have to clean up, okay?

Oh! We have plans for the entire weekend. Can we make it another time?

Oh, sure, honey, maybe we can plan for the following weekend.

That's better. Sorry, I forgot about that, and we made plans with three other couples to go out and go bowling and stuff. And anyway, we will clean up when we have company. We don't mind. It's fun when we do it together.

Alright, hon. Well, we need to get going soon, okay?

Yup.

Luke, I totally forgot my parents were going to ask your parents over for dinner this weekend, but I told my mom we have plans already, so maybe next weekend.

Oh, that's cool. I think my parents have a charity dinner they're going to this weekend, anyway.

Oh, okay, good. Then it all worked out.

So, I guess I should get my stuff and head out.

Ugh! I don't want you to leave!

I have to, Babe. You have a very important night ahead of you.

I know, and I'm excited about that, but I also want you to stay.

Well, soon enough I'll be able to go with you. I can even drive you so your mom doesn't have to.

That's so sweet, but you don't have to. That's a lot.

Brynlee, I want to. I want to do everything I can for and with you. I mean, I don't want to smother you, so let me know if I do, but I want to spend every minute I can with you.

Oh, you aren't smothering me at all! In fact, I would love to spend every second of every day with you. And same, if I smother you, let me know. You're a guy and you need to do guy things with your guy friends, I understand. And you won't hurt my feelings ever, okay?

You just keep getting more and more perfect, good God. But really, I'm a family guy, and I like to be around family. And now, you're my family too.

That is the sweetest thing I have ever heard! You're going to make me fall in love with you, Luke.

Well, I'm already on the way. It's crazy, Bryn, because we have only been together for less than a week! Can two people actually LOVE each other so soon, or is it just deep infatuation?

I don't know, I mean we hear about love at first sight all the time.

I feel like ours souls connected before we even knew all we know about each other. I sense it in my gut, Brynlee. I never felt this before, and it's scary and exciting all at the same time.

Why do you say it's scary?

I guess because we're so young, and I don't want you to regret dating me.

Are you kidding?! I feel the same way, Luke! I'm younger than you are! You'll head off to college and meet all new people, all new girls, and I'll be here in high school like a puppy waiting for it's owner.

You don't have to worry about me and college. I told you, I know what I want, and what I want is you. Is it too soon to tell you I think I love you?

I hope not, because I think I love you, too.

Well, okay then, we might love each other. Do you feel like our souls are connected?

I do. With everything I find out about you, I feel the connection more and more.

Me too. Does this even happen to kids our age?

It has to. It used to back in the old days, so why wouldn't it now, right? Just because we have technology and electricity doesn't mean we can't fall in love when we're in high school.

Exactly! See? We even think alike. With that, I should go. You've got a future to grab hold of in less than an hour!

I'm so nervous, Luke!

Don't be, I'm totally sure they'll say you can do it. And I will be with you every step of the way!

Thank you.

Well, I'm gonna say it – I love you, Brynlee. Too soon or not, I love you.

Too soon or not, I love you too…

That was my first ever "I love you" kiss, and it couldn't have been with a more perfect girl.

Well, it was my first "I love you" kiss, and it was definitely with the perfect guy.

Okay, text me as soon as you hear!

I will!

Holy crap! I think I'm in love. And he loves me too! Is it too soon? Kids at school say I love you all the time when they just start dating, and I always thought it was ridiculous, especially when they say it to every single person they date! Like, seriously, you can't just fall in and out of love like that. Love doesn't work like that. Love is something that lasts forever. Like, I love Natalya like she's my sister, and even when we fight, I could never see us not being best friends. I'd do anything for her! And with Luke, man, it's just different than I've ever felt about any other guy. I have been infatuated, I've had puppy love, and I sure as heck have lusted after some really hot guys, but Luke is different. He's everything a girl could want in a husband, he's a great friend, and he's so hot! But, I mean, him being hot doesn't have anything to do with it. Looks will fade as the years go on, but who he is deep down, his core, his heart, that'll never change. It'll just keep getting better and better. That's what I love about him. I can see him being an amazing dad, and he's already proven to be a perfect match for me. We'd have the cutest little family, always doing stuff like hiking and skiing and stuff. Am I just being a typical teenage girl with love fantasies, or is this really love? It's got to be.

It could be love, yes.

Hi Nova. You really think so?

I do. It's not developed yet, obviously, but you two do have a deep connection happening there. It isn't all that uncommon for two young people to fall in love.

But so soon? We've really only known each other for four days!

True, but think about how much you already know about each other. You know stuff about him that his brother doesn't even know. And they've known each other Luke's whole life. And you, Natalya doesn't know some of the things that Luke knows about you, and you've been best friends since the first day you met. So, if you and Natalya could know right away that you were best friends, you felt it deep down that she was your other half as far as friends go, why couldn't you and Luke have that in a love relationship? Maybe it's not a deep, rooted love like married couples, but it could be love, nonetheless.

I guess you're right.

The biggest factor in it, I think, is the fact that he respects you enough to not do anything sexually. I'm not saying he doesn't want to, but he won't. That's an indicator of love.

You think so?

I know so. Think about it. How many guys out there tell their girlfriends they love them, only to have sex with them and then they break up and mysteriously, they don't love them anymore. That's not love, that's lust and manipulation. Some boys, and girls, will say anything just to have sex. Luke is doing everything he can not to. He respects you, and I think you should make it easy for him to keep on respecting you.

I know, I'm just afraid he'll eventually break up with me because we don't, you know.

Well, if he breaks up with you because you won't have sex with him, then number one, he doesn't love you, and number two, he doesn't respect you. That is not the kind of guy you want to be with. You are too precious to let some guy use you for sex.

But what if I want to?

Of course you'll want to, you're a teenager with hormones off the charts! But, do you really want to, or is your true desire to wait until you're married? Because doing it, even though you want to wait is either your hormones talking, or it's peer pressure, and neither one is a good excuse.

Well, I do want to wait until I'm married. It's not really something I want to do with just anyone.

Then if Luke loves you, he'll respect that, and you have to respect that also. And don't make it any more difficult than it already is for him, or yourself. It won't be easy for either one of you, especially because you're so young, and you may actually love each other. Just remember, true love waits.

True love waits. I like that.

Bryn! Are you ready hon? We need to get going!

Yeah, Mom, I'll be right down!

Nova, I wish you were human size so I could hug you right now. Thank you for not saying I'm crazy to think that we actually could love each other.

You're welcome, dear. Now, of course, I don't know your deep down feelings that you're feeling, and I definitely don't know his, so I don't know if it's really love. But it could be, is all I'm saying. I can see in his eyes that his intentions are true. He's not looking to hurt you at all. It's all in the eyes. Look deep next time, you'll see.

I will. Thank you so much.
Okay, now let's go! You're future awaits.

The moment we've been waiting for...

Hello, Ms. Val.

    Hello Brynlee, Mr. and Mrs. Sheffield, please come into my office. We're just waiting for Lacey and her parents to get here and then we can begin. Brynlee, if you don't mind waiting outside with Lacey, I'd like to speak with all the parents alone first.

Sure, Ms. Val.

    Jhonae should be here shortly, but I'd like her to join us in the meeting as well.

Okay.

    Please, have a seat, make yourselves comfortable. Can I get you some coffee or water?

I'm fine, thank you.

    Oh, no thank you.

Let me know if you change your mind. I'll have Jhonae get it for you.

    Thank you.

Speaking of, here she is now, and it looks like she found the Graysons as well. Okay, wonderful. Let's get started. Girls, we'll speak with you afterward, okay?

    Sure thing, Ms. Val.

Brynlee! I am so freaking nervous! Oh. My. God!

    I know! Me too.

Okay, let's get our minds off of it. What happened yesterday? What's this about Luke's ex starting crap?

    Oh my God, she is the biggest, and I mean BIGGEST bitch to ever walk the planet! She tried to get me to think that he was texting her to get together for sex, meanwhile she lied about the whole thing. I caught her in the bathroom telling her ex best friend that she lied so then I told her off.

Are you serious?

    Yeah, so then after school, she came up to Luke and me and

apologized! Of course, I didn't believe a word of it.
Did he?

　　　　No. Not one bit.

Now please, don't take this the wrong way. I've seen you change.
And you changed pretty quickly. Is it possible for someone like that
to do a complete 180 in a school day?

　　　　Wow, I don't take it the wrong way at all! I was a huge
　　　　bitch, maybe not quite as bad as her, but pretty bad. Okay,
　　　　my friend Lyric, well, she's… special.

Special? Do you mean really short and wears a cute little hat that
looks like the Mad Hatter hat?

　　　　Exactly! I guess you've met yours?

I have. Her name is Nova.

　　　　They have cool names, don't they? See, I knew it was time
　　　　to speak of her, and something told me it was you I needed
　　　　to speak about them with. Damn, she is always right!

Lyric?

　　　　Yeah.

Nova too!

　　　　To answer your question, after meeting Lyric, I believe
　　　　anything is possible. So, maybe she had a change of heart.
　　　　Maybe you said something to her that really resonated.
　　　　Maybe she has a teacup of her own who finally was able to
　　　　get through to her, and it just so happened to be in school.
　　　　They show up in the craziest places.

Yeah, I know! I was in art history and poof! There she was. Of
course, I started talking out loud, and then got in trouble.

　　　　Hahaha!! Lyric showed up in the locker room and I yelled at
　　　　her, and all the girls in there thought I was psycho!

Hahahaha!! Oh my God, that's hysterical! Wow, it's so crazy.

　　　　I'll have to tell you my story one day and all about how
　　　　Lyric helped me become a much nicer person. Of course, I
　　　　still have a lot of work, I'm not in the final phase yet, but I
　　　　am way better than I used to be!

Yeah you are! And I'm really glad!

　　　　Ugh! What do you think is going on in there?

I don't know, but I can't wait to find out!

　　　　Me either! I told Ray I'd let him know as soon as we hear!

I told Natalya and Luke the same thing.

　　　　Hey, thanks again for giving Ray my number. He is a

freaking doll! Did you know he almost went to my school?

Yeah, Luke was saying. That's crazy!

I wonder if we would've dated if he did.

Who knows, but at least you two are hanging out this weekend with us.

Yes! I can't wait!

Oh my God, Lace, they're standing up. Here they come.

Hold my hand, Brynlee. I'm too nervous.

They're smiling!

Oh. My. God.

Ladies, would you come in here, please?

Sure thing, Ms. Val.

Okay ladies, I've filled your parents in on my thoughts and desires for you both. Thankfully, they are all on board with it.

Oh my God, are you serious?

Yes, Lacey, I am.

Lace, you're killing my hand!

Oh, sorry.

What I haven't told any of you, however, is that Alex, my friend you girls met at the competition Friday night, has requested that the two of you go down to his office in Cali and dance the routine for he and his colleagues. He absolutely loved what he saw, and has considered Friday night your first audition, and wants to go through a second, as he is considering you for a music video for a very well-known young male artist.

Ahhhhhhhhh!!!!!!! LACEY DID YOU HEAR THAT?!?!?

OH MY GOD!!!!

Ms. Val, are you serious right now?!

Darling, aren't I always serious?

OH MY GOD!! I'm going to pass out!

No dear, do not pass out!!

Mr. and Mrs. Sheffield, Mr. and Mrs. Grayson, with your permission, I would accompany the girls, and all expenses will be paid by Alex's company. Of course, you are certainly welcome to come, since they are both minors, all expenses paid.

Well, girls, I think it's a great opportunity, which is why we all agreed to the private lessons, so what do you say, are you in?

Yes, ladies, think hard now, are we all going to Cali?

YES!!! Oh my God, yes!

Heck yeah!!

Wonderful news! I'll go ahead and let Alex know before class begins. Jhonae, would you begin warm-ups for me when the girls start arriving?

Absolutely.

Thank you. Ladies, we are so very proud of you. I would have told you exactly what was going on Friday night, but you were both under tremendous pressure already, I didn't feel the need to add to the stress.

Ms. Val, when is this second audition?

Well, he'd like to see us there this weekend...

Oh no! Not this weekend! We have plans all laid out! Aww, look at Lacey's face!

Bryn!

I know, Lace.

... however, I'd like to get in at least a week and a half of practice before then.

Whew!

Oh thank God. I want to hang out with Ray.

I know!

Ladies? What's all the whispering about?

Oh nothing, Ms. Val. I was just telling Lacey that I need my wrist to be 100% before we go.

Good one, Bryn.

Thanks.

Is your wrist still bothering you, dear?

No, it's fine today. I'm just afraid to do broncos so soon.

Well, perhaps we'll wait until the week after, then. So, I'll set up for the third weekend from today.

Excellent. Thank you, Ms. Val.

You are all quite welcome. And thank you for allowing me to work with your daughters. They are truly talented young ladies, and if all goes well, they will be very successful in the entertainment industry.

Wonderful.

Thanks Mom and Dad.

Yes, thank you Mom and Dad.

Girls, you must remember that school comes first.

Everything else is second.
We will.

Holy freaking shit, Brynlee!
>Oh my God, I have to call Luke after I text Natalya. I can't
>just text him something like this. I'll be right back.
Okay, I'm going to text Ray and tell him everything.

"Natalya!!!! I'm in AND I am going to Cali for an audition in three
weeks for a music video! Gotta call Luke. I'll text you later!"

Hello?
>Luke!! You're not going to believe what just happened!! Oh
>my God, I'm crying right now.
What happened? Are you okay?! Do you need me to come get you?
>No, no, everything's fine. Holy shit!
Okay, calm down, tell me what's going on.
>Okay. First of all, our parents said yes to the lessons.
Brynlee, that's great! Congratulations!
>No, no, it gets better!
What do you mean?
>Ms. Val got me and Lacey an audition for a music video!!
What?! Are you serious?! Baby, that's freaking awesome!! Damn!
I'm so proud of you! When is the audition?
>She's telling him three weeks. I'm going to Cali in three
>weeks!
That's great! Who is the music video for?
>She didn't say. All she said was he is well-known, and it's
>our second audition, because the guy who we'll audition for
>was here Friday night! I actually met him and didn't know
>it!
Oh, Brynlee, that's amazing! Ugh, I wish I could give you a huge
hug right now!
>Come over after practice!
Can I? Do you think your parents would mind?
>No, not at all!
Okay, then I will be there! I have to give my beautiful princess a
huge congratulatory hug!
>I can't wait! Okay, I gotta go. Natalya is blowing up my
>phone in my ear and I have to get ready for class. I'll text

you when I'm leaving here.
Okay good. Hey, too soon or not, I love you, and I'm so proud of you! I can't wait to tell my parents!
Too soon or not, I love you too! Bye.
Bye, Baby.

"Are you serious Brynlee?!?!"
"Dead serious!!"
"Who's the video for?"
"She didn't say"
"You didn't ask?!?!"
"Nat, I was in shock!" "I don't think I want to know, anyway"
"R u crazy? Why not?"
"I'm already freaking out and nervous! If I know who it's for it'll make it worse"
"Ugh!! I am dying to know!"
"As soon as I know, you'll know, I promise!"
"When's the audition?"
"3 weeks"
"That's like, not too far away!"
"I know!" "Gtg, class is gonna start and I have to get ready"
"Ok, txt me later. Luv you! Congratulations!!!"
"Luv u, and thx!"

Hey, Brynlee, we probably shouldn't tell anyone here, huh?
Yeah, probably not.
We need to hurry, class is going to start. Remember, not a word.
Right.

Is this really happening to me right now? To us? I cannot believe we're auditioning for a music video! That's so freaking insane!
What's insane?
Oh hey, Taryn, nothing, I'm just thinking out loud, I guess.
Oh okay. Hey, great job, Friday night.
You too! We killed it, didn't we?
Yeah, we really did.
I guess we should get out there.
Yup, let's go.

Ladies, before we get started, I just want to say, again, how very proud we are of you all. You performed outstandingly, and you were rewarded properly for you hard work and dedication. I'd also like to let you all know that hard work has paid off wonderfully for two of our ladies, Brynlee and Lacey.

Oh crap, is she about to tell the class?!

Brynlee and Lacey have been asked to go to California to audition for a music video.

What!? Awesome!
           Oh wow! That's great!
Congratulations, guys!

We will be going in three weeks. I want this to show you that hard work does indeed pay off, and you just never know who will be at these competitions. Some of you could leave one evening with a full scholarship to a Fine Arts college specializing is performing arts, and like Brynlee and Lacey, some could end up auditioning for a music video. Anything can happen if you put in the work and dedication that these two have put in over the years. I think they deserve a round of applause…. Parents, your hard earned money and valuable time is not wasted here. Every single one of these girls has what it takes to go where they want to go, if they just believe. It's obvious you already believe in them, as do Jhonae and I. Again, girls, congratulations to you both, to all of you. Now, let's begin.

My biggest fan...

Lacey, I'll text you tomorrow about Friday.

     Okay sounds good.

Hey Lace, congratulations. We're doing it!

     Bryn, we are, aren't we? Congratulations to you, too.

This is so cool! I am in shock right now, still.

Brynlee, I am ecstatic that your parents are all on board. I am
concerned about your wrist. Here, let me see.

     Oh, I'm fine, Ms. Val. It's not sore anymore.

It doesn't feel broken.

     Really, it's fine.

I want to know first thing in the morning how it feels. If it's sore, we
must get you in to have X-rays.

     Okay.

Goodnight, Dear, and congratulations. You truly deserve this
opportunity.

     Thank you, Ms. Val. Goodnight.

*Man, I'm glad it's not sore right now. Not one bit. But, now I want to
see my boyfriend.*

Ready Mom?

     I am.

Where's Daddy?

     He's outside talking to Mr. Grayson. They're making plans
     for our trip. We were talking to Ms. Val and you and Lacey
     will stay with her in your own hotel room, and we'll be in a
     separate room. Okay?

Sure, that's fine.

     Okay, let's go get your father and go home.

Please! Luke is meeting us. He wants to congratulate me in person.

     Oh, isn't that so sweet?

Yeah, so let's hurry, please.

"Hey Babe, I'm on my way home"

"Hey Beautiful, I'm already here and waiting"

"Aww, too soon or not, I love you"

"Too soon or not, I love you too!"

We have to hurry, Luke's already at our house!

      Okay, honey, we're hurrying.

Sweetpea, we're just around the corner. Calm down.

      Ugh, okay, I'm just so excited, I can't believe it.

We're all very excited, Brynlee, and so very proud of you and Lacey.

      There he is! Stop the car, let me out!

Baby, I am so proud of you!

      Thank you, Luke!

I brought you these.

      Oh Luke, they're beautiful! Thank you so much! You
      didn't have to do that!

I wanted to! Why are you crying, Beautiful?

      Oh my God, you make me so happy!

Baby, you make me so happy. But, um, you're kinda choking me
right now.

      Oh, I'm sorry.

Haha, it's okay. Look at me… I am so proud of you, Brynlee. You
are truly amazing, and I absolutely love you.

      You're gonna make me cry even worse! I love you too.

      Thank you.

For what?

      For being the best guy in the whole world, and for bringing
      me these beautiful flowers, and for loving me.

You don't have to thank me for anything. You make loving you
pretty damn easy. Let's go inside before you get cold.

      Okay.

Aren't those flowers lovely? Luke, that is so sweet of you. You just
made Brynlee's night, I'm sure.

      Thank you, Mrs. Sheffield. I couldn't wait to get here and
      congratulate her. That's so awesome.

It sure is. She's worked very hard for a long time. She deserves it,
that's for sure.

      Well, besides you and Mr. Sheffield, I'm her biggest fan.

That's wonderful, Luke.

Luke, how does it feel to be dating a girl who very possibly could be in a music video of a famous young male star?

It's crazy, but awesome! I'm so proud of her! I really think they'll get it.

That's exactly what we think.

I can't wait to see my girl on television, dancing in a music video, and heck, maybe even during halftime at the Superbowl!

Ah, I hadn't thought of that! Well, if that's the case, Son, we'll be sure to bring you along. I know how much you love football.

That would be amazing!

Let's not get crazy guys. I didn't even audition yet.

Actually, Babe, you said this will be your second audition, so technically, you already did. They don't do callbacks for nothing. I bet you and Lacey are in!

Oh my gosh, could you imagine? That'd be so freaking sick!

So will you consider joining the cheer squad now?

I don't know, Luke. We'll see.

I'm kidding. You're going to be way too busy for that! Besides, I have to squeeze myself into your calendar somehow. And then there's homework.

I will always make time for you, even if we have to study together all the time. I promise.

Thanks, Babe.

Hey, Daddy, do you mind if we go upstairs for a few?

No, go ahead.

Thanks.

And, we'll leave the door wide open.

That's what I like to hear, Son.

Luke, you seriously made my night by coming here! There is no one else I would want to share this news and excitement with in person.

Baby, I really am so proud of you. You know you'll have to call me as soon as you know. Do you think they'll let you know right then?

I would hope so. I wish you could come with us.

Oh no, I wouldn't want to get in the way or anything. This is something you've worked hard for, and you need to be one hundred percent in the moment, without any distractions whatsoever.

Luke, you are the best boyfriend ever!

> But! That doesn't mean that I won't grab Dylan and drive down there to be there for you waiting out in the parking lot when it's over.

That's a long drive! Don't do that. Now I'll be worried about you. That's got to be like fifteen hours away!

> Oh man, okay. Maybe I'll just fly down. I'm kidding! Your eyes just got huge!

Oh, I thought you were serious! I would've loved that! But, no, you can't. That's a lot of money and I'll only be there for the weekend.

> And I'll be here waiting for you just like I was tonight, only we'll be celebrating your signed contract to be in a video instead of just an audition!

I love your positivity.

> And I love you. I should get going, beautiful. Our phones are blowing up, about all of this I'm sure. This news is going to spread like wildfire. Are you ready for it?

I'm ready for it, as long as I have you by my side.

> Of course I'll be by your side, I'm your biggest fan! Too soon or not, I love you.

Too soon or not, I love you too.

> Now, let me kiss the beautiful girl who will be dancing in a music video, who I am extremely lucky enough to date and love and call my own…

> … Why are you crying, Babe?

I'm so overwhelmed with happiness right now. You're the best, and I love you, and I can't believe all this has happened to me, Brynlee Sheffield.

> Well it has, and you deserve it, and I love you too, and it's going to be great, and I'll be by your side cheering you on, because…

Because you're my biggest fan. Thank you.

> Okay, now get some rest. You have to face your fans tomorrow.

Haha, yeah, and probably an enemy.

> Don't you worry about her. She's irrelevant. You are capturing your dreams.

Yes, my dreams with wings.

Huh?

Oh, nothing. Goodnight, Luke. Text me when you get home so I can say goodnight again.

You bet I will.

He brought me flowers! Oh my God, he is so freaking perfect! Okay, let me see who texted real quick. Holy crap! Victoria, Jasmine, Natalya three times, Taryn, Blake! Holy crap. What'd he say? "Hey Brynlee, congrats! Carly told me the awesome news. You deserve it!" Aww, that was sweet. Let me text him back. "Thank you". Okay, who else? Ray, Dylan, Peri, Brooke, aww Brooke! Jenna, Aunt Holly, are you kidding me?! Samantha texted me? Okay, Brynlee, stay calm. Just see what she has to say. "Brynlee, I am really sorry about yesterday. Congratulations on your audition. You'll get it, no doubt. I hope one day you can forgive me for being the biggest bitch ever to you all these years. Thank you for saying exactly what I needed to hear". Um, okay? "Thanks Samantha". There, I did it. I was nice. Well, I don't think I can text everyone back right now. I'll do it later. Nova!

Nova!

Congratulations, Brynlee! I'm so excited for you!

Thank you! I am too! And I'm nervous.

No need to be nervous. Understandable, though, under the circumstances, but he chose you two for a reason, and the reason is you two have what they are looking for. So go in there with confidence, okay?

We'll try.

So, listen, you are about to get a taste of the big life, possibly. Remember what we talked about the other night.

What's that? We've talked about so much.

About curves. Your curves, the curves in life, remember?

I remember. Some of those curves can be dangerous if they're not handled properly.

Yeah, I bet they can be. But I've got my head on straight.

Yes, you do, but you'll probably have to deal with people trying to tell you lies again, like you need to lose weight, or your hair is too long, or you're not good enough. I want you to remember to not listen to them. It can be difficult to block that stuff out.

But I've got you and Luke who keep telling me the truth. You're right. And I will continue to tell you the truth as much as I can. One day, though, I won't be able to, because it'll be time for the final phase. I will still be there with you, but it'll be time to see how you handle the situation. Okay?

Okay. I hope I'll be ready for it. I don't want to let you down.

It's not about letting me down or not. It's about you knowing who you are, and remembering the truth that has been instilled in you. I believe in you, Brynlee. We all do. You've already made us proud. Being you is all we ask of you. Just be you, your beautiful you.

Thank you, Nova. You and Luke make it easier.

I'm glad. Now, I believe you have a text from Luke, and a whole bunch others to return.

I do, don't I?

"Hey Baby, I'm home"

"Luke, thank you for being my biggest fan. It means so much more to me than you will ever know"

"Well, you make it easy, you know" "There's no one else I'd rather cheer on"

"Thank you <3"

"Life is perfect. You have an audition, we're all going out this weekend, I love you and you love me back, my parents adore you, and they say congratulations, btw"

"Aww, please tell them thank you for me"

"I will. Mom and Dad both send a huge hug to you"

"That's so sweet, thank you!" "Life really is perfect, isn't it?"

"It's about to get crazy, but we've got each other"

"I love you"

"I love you too, Brynlee Sheffield"

"I've got some hw to do, so I'll text you in a little while"

"Okay. <3 "

" <3 "

Life really is good, but I have to prepare for those dangerous curves ahead. What a wonderfully crazy ride this is going to be! But I've got great friends, family and the best boyfriend ever to ride it with.

What a crazy freaking story I'm going to be able to tell my children one day. I can't wait till Luke and I can tell them how we met, and how their "Aunt Natalya" became a supermodel, and my first gig was a music video, and who knows, maybe I'll use my fame to change the world! Maybe I can help young girls and young women to see that it doesn't matter what you look like on the outside, it's what's on the inside that counts. I can catapult a movement to help girls see that we are all beautiful in our own way, and we don't need to tear people down to feel good about ourselves. And by then, hopefully Mom will be healed enough from her past that she'll be right beside me! What a cool story this could turn out to be! Speaking of stories, I can't wait to hear Lacey's story. I saw the change in her, so I know it's definitely got to be a good one! Well, we'll have plenty of time in three weeks to catch each other up on our lives. Until then, we'll enjoy being normal teenagers.

Hey Nova!
      Yes Brynlee?
When we're at dance Thursday night, tell Lyric I said "hi"!
      Haha, will do, Brynlee, will do!

Acknowledgements

First and foremost I would like to thank **Jesus Christ** for giving me the strength, courage and vision for this book, and allowing my life to be part of your plan.

This book also would not have been possible without my family and their support, encouragement and constant sanity checks. I love you all! Thanks for believing in me:

Sean, Sabrina and Julie - You are the best that's ever happened to me and I love you forever!
My "sister" Melissa - thanks for editing and letting me vent!
My parents, Irene and Richie - for always being there for me!
My mother-in-law, Susan - for constant encouragement!

Lastly, thanks to my dog, *Punkleton*, for driving me crazy with the constant green fart clouds, repeated whining to go out and pawing at the door to come back in, loud chewing and drinking, thunderous snoring like an old man, fighting with the cat, barking at the mailman and delivery trucks, and staring at me while I eat. You rock, bud!